A DAY OF FIRE
A Novel of Pompeii

by

Stephanie Dray
Ben Kane
E. Knight
Sophie Perinot
Kate Quinn
Vicky Alvear Shecter

With an introduction by
Michelle Moran

A Day of Fire

Cover Design and Interior format by The Killion Group
http://thekilliongroupinc.com

Roman Eagle logo by Erebus-Art.com.

ISBN-10: 0-9903245-7-5
ISBN-13: 978-0-9903245-7-7

TABLE OF CONTENTS

INTRODUCTION

Michelle Moran

I doubt anyone has ever visited Pompeii and not been transformed. To visit this site where two thousand inhabitants lost their lives during the volcanic eruption of Mount Vesuvius is to step back in time to a city which was almost perfectly preserved by the falling volcanic ash. You can walk the streets of this ancient Roman city today and imagine the horror of burning pumice raining from the sky. Thousands of people had been left behind, but even as they tried to flee, lethal gas and burning ash killed them slowly, filling their lungs, hardening their internal organs. As the ash-fall continued, their bodies stiffened, and all across the city of Pompeii, human statues were created, frozen in time. In 1863, archaeologists discovered a method of preserving these bodies with haunting results. There is the woman in the Villa of Mysteries who clawed her way over the falling rocks, only to finally die at the top. The heavily pregnant woman adorned in gold jewelry discovered with her loved ones, huddled together in their house. And the doomed families in the Garden of Fugitives, where mothers were found clutching their children and a single man tried to rise from the ash in a futile effort to shield the rest.

In *A Day of Fire*, six of the most talented authors I've read have resurrected these lives and many others, along with a once-thriving city where fighting, sex, and gambling was the norm. It is a novel written in six parts, each by a different author, and each comprising a complete tale unto itself. Yet because the plots are woven together, a fascinating story emerges in the end of a city where spirituality and profanity, squalor and immense profit, existed side by side in the gladiatorial arenas, temples, brothels, and inns.

It is easy to elevate the Romans. After all, they left behind impressive contributions to literature, philosophy, architecture, and science. But Pompeii, in its unbelievably preserved state, tells the real story. In these ruins we find not only the great and lofty accomplishments of Roman civilization, but the remnants of a society so steeped in sexploitation that there is no way for any responsible historical author to turn away from it, and these authors certainly have not done so.

Like all historical novels, readers should know that minor changes to the historical record were made. For the sake of accessibility, the authors have adopted English words and conventions over the Latin. For example, while the Romans did not use weeks to measure time, the authors do. Moreover, since timelines for the eruption of Mount Vesuvius vary slightly from expert to expert, the authors have adopted the one set out by scholar Mary Beard in *Pompeii: The Living City* with several minor modifications and one major one: namely that they decided to adopt more recent scholarship suggesting that the eruption took place in the autumn of 79 rather than the long-assumed August.

A Day of Fire is one of the most entertaining reads I've come across in historical fiction. In the hands of these wonderfully diverse authors, we glimpse what life must have been like during those last, fatal hours in Pompeii, and it's not just horrifying, it's fascinating.

PART ONE

THE SON

Vicky Alvear Shecter

"The depth of darkness to which you can descend and still live is an exact measure of the height to which you can aspire to reach."
—Pliny the Elder

Pompeii
In the first year of the rule of Emperor Titus Flavius Caesar Vespasianus
Augustus

I discreetly tightened my loincloth as I approached Pompeii's Sarno Gate. The mere sight of the chipped arch funneling us into the city — the knowledge that I was that much closer to *her* — made my body respond in a most embarrassing way. I did not need my tented tunic announcing to the world my business in Pompeii. Thank Priapus for the pressure of the cloth.

The line into the city inched along like a bloated leech. I shook my head to clear the image from my mind. My uncle's insistence on regular bleedings drove me to distraction. "Balancing your humors will help clear the spots on your face," he'd said. "And it will help you grow. Some boys don't finish growing until they are in their twenties," he added with undisguised hope.

I resisted scratching the spot on my back where the last of the little suckers had been removed after the physician bled me, and I suppressed a shudder at the memory of that glistening, slimy body swollen with my own blood. So far, my uncle's "plan" to help me grow bigger had failed miserably. The former general, the great naturalist, the admiral of Emperor Titus' navy, was a big, ox-like man. As was my father, everyone always told me, though I never knew him. It was almost as if my uncle took it as a personal affront that I did not take after him or my father but am built like my mother — his own tiny sister, Plinia — instead. As if I were pleased by this cruel trick of the gods.

Reeking rivermen and sweat-stained traders from Salernum pressed in all around me. I would have to scrub well at Julius' house before going to see my girl.

Of course, just as I was almost through the arch, some old farmer got the wheel of his onion cart stuck in a rut, forcing the rest of us to stop. I should have known. Pompeii was such a busy port town; there were always delays. Like my lover, the city teased me continually. And as always when there were delays, I wondered if I should've come in through the Herculaneum Gate or even the Marine Gate. But I reminded myself that I was less likely to run into people who might recognize me on this end of town. I needed to stay anonymous. Even to her.

When I finally emerged into the dirty, bustling inner streets, I began counting as I always did. Just three hundred and thirty one steps until I got to touch Prima again.

At step seventy-five, the crowd in front of me parted and I almost slammed into a pile of bricks stacked up in front of a large house. Only at the last moment did I avoid a collision, staggering onto the road and barely missing a man walking a donkey so laden with jugs, it looked swaddled in a clinking, clay blanket. A couple of barefoot urchins laughed at my inelegant arm waving as I fought for balance. Did those little street rats put the bricks there on purpose to steal from me?

I wouldn't put it past them. Pompeii was a city of grabbers and opportunists, which was part of its charm. Unless what someone grabbed was yours. I swatted at my coin purse beneath my tunic belt and grunted with relief to find it still securely attached. Out of the corner of my eye, I saw a couple of workmen trundle to the pile of bricks and reach for them with mud-caked hands.

It wasn't the kids after all. Still, on principle, I scowled fiercely at the ragged creatures, which only made them giggle more. The little boy's stick arms clutched his belly as he laughed.

In truth, I often felt not much older than that dirt-smeared boy. I'd had my manhood ceremony during the Liber Festival just that spring and had been certain everything would be different as soon as I donned the *toga virilis*. Certain that I would finally *become* the man the law said I was. But nothing had changed. Every loud, wheezing breath my uncle took in my presence seemed to vibrate with disappointment. A disappointment reinforced in public when he did not formally adopt me at the ceremony as my mother and I thought he would.

At step two-hundred-and-forty-five, I stopped at Julius' house, the House of Polybius, the current *praetor* of Pompeii. There was something magical about passing through his home's brightly-painted blue door. When it closed behind me, all the chaos of the street melted into memory.

A steward led me into a sun-drenched atrium surrounded by walls frescoed in vivid reds, yellows, and blacks. One day, I would have a lovely home like this, I told myself, maybe even on this block in this very city.

"Caecilius!" shouted Julius when he saw me. "What a surprise!"

I snorted. *Surprise* indeed. He'd likely been pacing all afternoon waiting for my arrival. "I'd like to get cleaned up before we set off," I said.

He punched me on the arm and muttered, "You're the only fool I know who washes *before* seeing a whore."

"Shut it, you *cacator*," I hissed. He knew I hated it when he called Prima a whore. But at least he was smart enough to keep his voice down, lest word of my entanglement somehow reached my uncle. On principle, I threw an elbow, but he was too quick for me, managing to avoid it with graceful athleticism that left me looking like a goose tripping over my own flat, webbed feet.

"Julius, be nice!" a young, female voice called. Julilla, his sister, emerged from the columned shadows. Her large pregnant belly emerged into view first. With her small hands supporting it from below, she gave the impression she was presenting me with a giant *trigon* ball wrapped in fine aqua linen.

She kissed me on each cheek as I breathed in her lovely scent of lotus oil.

"You look magnificent," I murmured, as heat flooded my cheeks. Julilla's green eyes and dark glossy hair always made me think of the sleek black cat that held court in the Temple of Isis. Amazingly, even in her advanced pregnancy, she still moved like water dancing in the sun. Her husband was a very lucky man. Would I ever be so lucky?

"Are you well?" I continued, remembering that she and her husband lived in Rome now. They must have come to Pompeii so she could have the baby in her childhood home. It made sense. The calming scents and sounds of the ocean were never far.

"Yes, yes!" she said. "Though I am more than ready to meet my son." She said the latter with the kind of emphasis that indicated she believed that if she said it enough times, it would be true. She turned to her brother. "I suppose you two are setting out for the forum?"

Julius' eyes flicked toward mine then he smiled down at Julilla. "Yes, to catch some lectures," he said, vaguely. "Then a *symposium* where we will drink and argue all night and then start all over again in the morning."

She laughed prettily. "By the gods, I'm glad Titus is too busy climbing the *cursus honorum* to engage in such trifles. Have fun, boys," she said turning and ambling toward the inner courtyard.

"Get going," Julius said, giving me a playful shove toward a shaded corner of the atrium where a servant had set up a small cleaning station for me. Fragrant mint leaves floated on the surface of a bronze water bowl surrounded by several small vials of fragrant oils. Pompeii's strangely hot autumn and increasing tremors had resulted in a water shortage in the city, but clearly not in Julius' home, thanks to his father's wealth. As I well knew from my uncle, power came with privileges. I dipped my hands into the water and began to scrub, "Hurry up!" Julius called. "I want to get out of here already."

Jupiter's balls, I did too, friend.

On the narrow street outside his house, I slicked my short wet hair forward, wishing I had Julius' shining curls, but Uncle always insisted I sport a short military haircut. After all, *it was good enough for him!* Unfortunately, the close-cropped hair only seemed to draw attention to my skinny neck.

"So, my unclaimed friend," Julius said suddenly as we maneuvered down the street, "when shall we reconvene to align our stories?" he asked.

I gritted my teeth. Julius knew I hated being called "unclaimed." He *knew* that the fact that my uncle had not formally adopted me at my ceremony was like an open wound. Yet he continued teasing me about it—ever since I'd shamefully admitted to him my hurt and dismay at my uncle's lack of public affirmation.

"Oh, stop looking like a toothless old woman sucking on a lemon," Julius said, elbowing me. "You must learn to laugh and joke about the things that sting. It takes away their power!"

"So you say," I muttered.

He sighed. "You are much too serious, Gaius Caecilius."

After confirming when we would gather again, Julius turned on the street leading to the fancier, more expensive brothels on the Vesuvian end of town. "Have fun with your little *lupa*," he called loudly to the amusement of passers-by.

My face flamed. "You too, you *asinus*," I shot back, but he hadn't heard me. My voice didn't carry like his.

WHEN my eyes adjusted to the darkness of the low-ceilinged *caupona*, I caught sight of my Prima pouring wine from a chipped clay jug. My heart pounded in my ears. She looked up at me with her black eyes and grinned. Something in the center of my chest melted like a piece of honeycomb left out in the sun. Her owner emerged out of the shadows with his hand out. Without so much as a word, I placed a pile of coins into it. He knew the arrangement. I got Prima for the whole night in one of the inn's rooms—not one of the curtained cubicles on the street she had to use with other

19

customers—and I paid handsomely for it.

Prima grinned wider and jerked her head toward our usual upstairs room. I raced up the dark wooden stairway while she spoke with the old *asinus* who owned her.

Once inside the small room, I said a quick prayer to Venus at the tiny altar to the gods built into a small niche. And I paced. Back and forth, back and forth. Still, she did not come. I strained to hear her light steps on the wooden stairs.

Did she do this to me on purpose? She claimed she didn't, that she had to ensure all the tavern and inn customers were taken care of and that somebody else—usually her chesty blonde sister—covered for her before she could join me, but I wasn't so sure.

Finally, *finally*, I heard Prima's soft step on the stairs and jumped up. She'd barely sidled inside before I had her up against the door, my nose buried in her neck, breathing in her smoky-sweet scent. Gods, I loved the feel of her skinny little body writhing against mine. She was so tiny she even made me feel big.

"*Eheu!*" she laughed, putting her hands on my chest. "Let me at least take a breath and say hello."

Already panting, I let her push me away, smiling back at her.

"You have been away from me for too long," she pouted. "I thought you had found someone else, and I've been walking around broken-hearted!"

"Never," I said, reaching for her again. Even through my blinding hunger for her I registered her words and a thrill of pleasure surged through me. Did she ... did she feel about me the way I felt about her?

She skirted past me, smiling that adorable, slightly gap-toothed smile that always sent shivers down my back and up again through the center of my belly.

"I am glad to hear this," she said. "I missed my young bull! You've kept me waiting for you much too long."

She missed me. *Gods*, she had missed me! "I missed you, too," I said, trying to keep my voice level while, at the same time, guiding her down on her bed.

"Oh no you don't," she laughed, wriggling away. "I'm in charge here." She pushed me down onto the thin, rush-filled mattress. My elbows slammed down hard on to the frame, but I didn't care.

"I have an idea," she said with a glint in her eye. "Let's get the first one out of the way quickly so that we can relax and enjoy ourselves, yes?"

She knelt between my legs and pushed my tunic over my hips. I flopped back onto the bed with a strangled groan.

"WHAT are you doing?" I croaked, waking to find her shuffling through our clothing on the floor.

"Nothing," Prima said, startled. She placed the small oil lamp — in the shape of an engorged Priapus — on the warped wooden chest and straightened. I relished the sight of her, the flickering light dancing over the angles of her lithe, naked body. She could be a sea nymph — all dark sleekness and wild beauty — emerging from Pompeii's surf to slide into my arms.

"I am ... I'm hungry," she said. "I was checking to see if you brought me anything to eat."

I sat up and rubbed my eyes. "You are always hungry."

She put a hand on her hip and gave me a crooked smile. "That is because you keep me so busy, I forget to eat."

"What hour of the night is it? Can you go downstairs and bring food up for us?"

She nodded. "*Dominus* doesn't like that, though," she said. "You know if he sees me he will try to foist me on another customer."

"I paid for the whole night and he knows it!" I stood up and went to my coin purse, which I'd hidden in my shoes. "And I will pay for the food. Bring us up some wine and sausages and whatever else you want," I said, giving her a handful of coins.

Her smile seemed so genuine and full of joy I found myself grinning back at her. In a blink, she'd thrown on her tunic and dashed out of the room.

PRIMA ate the way she made love, with complete absorption, closing her eyes and making small sounds of pleasure. I laughed. "The sausages are not *that* good."

She opened her eyes in surprise. "Maybe not to you," she said, cheeks bulging while she chewed. "But I brought up the ones *Dominus* saves for his best customers. I never eat these unless I'm with you."

"One day, I'll bring you the duck and goose sausage our cook makes. You will not believe how delicious they are!"

Her eyes lit up. "What else will you bring me?"

Anything and everything you want, I thought. "Tiny cheese tarts with sweet fig jam in the center," I said.

She groaned, smiling. "And?"

"Cheese and olive paste on fresh crusty bread."

She licked her lips and closed her eyes once again. I watched her mouth, transfixed. I moved closer, whispering into her ear, "And the fluffiest little balls of nuts and honey you've ever tasted." I covered her hungry mouth with my own.

THE bed rustled. "Don't go," I murmured to Prima.

"It is almost sunrise," she whispered. "I must clean downstairs or the master will be angry."

"Can't your sister do it?"

She chuckled. "She gets distracted too easily. If I don't go down and help her, she'll do it poorly, and the master will beat us both then."

Gods, I hated hearing her talk that way. I hated being reminded that she was the property of a man who did not appreciate the wonder of her. Or that other men paid to have her. I would buy her one day, I told myself. Make her only mine. Just as soon as I figured out how get my hands on the money I'd need. Uncle kept me on a tight leash. As it was, I was grateful he didn't dig too deeply as to where my monthly allowance went.

I must have fallen back asleep because I woke to the shaking of the bed and the sound of crockery breaking down below. The increased frequency and duration of the tremors in Pompeii were disconcerting. Everybody had a theory — that Vulcan was angry or that the giants were stirring in Tartarus. Uncle probably had multiple theories of his own based on his research of Campania.

"Did you sacrifice to Neptune yesterday?" a shrill voice floated up. The *caupona* owner's wife. "You didn't, did you? You gambled at dice instead, I know you did! You cannot continue to anger the Earth-Shaker!" she cried. Ah, so she was blaming the god of the sea and earthquakes. A man's low undertones followed.

With my hands behind my head, I stared at the low wooden ceiling. I did not want to leave the bed, awash as I was in the scent of her and sex.

My mind drifted to my pre-Prima days. When I was about fifteen, my uncle had discovered that I had neither availed myself of any of the slaves in the house nor visited the fancy brothel in Misenum. A boy didn't become a man until he entered a girl or boy, he reminded me, and I had done neither. I wanted to complain that all the slaves in the house were elderly, like him, but I dared not. The truth was, that was only an excuse. My crippling shyness left me terrified of the act. But no Roman boy or man would ever admit to such a weakness.

Uncle had his man take me to his favorite brothel in Misenum. I bore the humiliation of men drunkenly cheering me on as I walked through the main room. The bare-breasted women, seemingly drunk as well, hooted at me. It didn't help that, with my cheeks aflame, I probably looked about twelve.

When we entered the room for "special guests," I could not look the older, painted woman in the eye. Why did it have to be so public? With so many people knowing what was supposed to happen?

When I couldn't even speak my preference, the madam sent me into a room with a pretty naked girl of about fourteen. After shutting the curtain in the small room, the girl turned to me and inspected me coolly from head to toe, which chilled my blood. When I made no move, she rolled her eyes and crossed her arms. Then, without

23

saying a word, she walked naked across the room and yelled out for a boy.

But I didn't want a boy! I was just scared and overwhelmed. When the naked boy arrived, I wanted to crawl into the woodwork and disappear like a mealy worm. Now *both* were laughing at me.

"I will say you entered me for two silver *denarii*," the girl said looking at me shrewdly. But I didn't have the money, my attendant did.

She thought my silence was bargaining. "Fine," she said. "One."

I nodded. The boy looked at the girl and said, "You have to give me some or I'll tell."

"Fine," she said smiling, and I realized she hadn't expected to get even that much for her promise. She could "afford" to be generous.

She mussed her hair—making strange noises all the while—then smiled mischievously at the boy and sauntered out. "All done," she announced and stood beside my uncle's man with her palm out.

"So quickly?" the madam asked, clearly amused.

"Fast little man."

"Give her an extra *denarius*," I croaked to the slave, whose eyebrows went up so high, they nearly touched his hairline.

"A generous tipper," the madam laughed.

The fear that my secret would be divulged—that I was still a *boy*—haunted my every waking moment. How would I bear the humiliation if anyone found out? It marred my manhood ceremony during the festival of Liberia, though the heavy drinking helped. I avoided the brothels afterward in the fear that I might see that boy or girl again or worse, respond to another whore with shameful, flaccid panic.

Then I had gone to Pompeii to visit my friend Julius, who eventually insisted we spend our time at the brothels. When I refused, I lied and told him that I had a girl nearby. He laughed at me, of course.

I went in the opposite direction when Julius headed toward his favorite brothel. When I realized I had inadvertently circled back again close to his house I snuck into the neighborhood *caupona* to avoid being seen by anyone in his household. And that's when I met her.

That day, sulking on a stool at the counter, while I waited for Julius to finish manly deeds I could not perform myself, Prima brought me wine, then bread and olives, throughout the afternoon and into the night. When it got very late and very quiet, she slid onto a short stool across from me.

"You must be very wise to be so sad at your age. Most boys are happy and dim-witted."

"I am not a boy," I slurred. "I am seventeen and a man."

"I didn't say you weren't a man," she said. "All I said is that you seem different from most boys."

I shrugged.

"Has some girl broken your heart?" she asked leaning toward me.

"I don't have a girl."

"Would you like one?"

I had been staring into my empty cup but I quickly looked up at her. The movement left me slightly dizzy. Was she making fun of me?

When my eyes focused I saw that she was not laughing at me at all. She looked tired, and a little lonely. She glanced at the man measuring wine at the counter and sighed. "I may be a slave, but I like to choose for myself sometimes. And I choose you. If you'll have me."

With her, there had been no nerves, no shyness. She had chosen me. She had wanted *me*. I'd been hers ever since.

I dressed and went downstairs. Prima was pouring wine into clay beakers. "Good morning," she said, eyes dancing. Gods! I wished I could drag her back upstairs that very moment. My feelings must have been evident on my face for she mouthed the word, "tonight."

Right. For now, I would go to the baths — even though the water shortage meant only the *tepidarium* would be open. Julius would probably be there waiting for me.

"*Ai*, what's talking you so long, my skinny little slut?" a man across the room called out to her.

Prima's back went rigid. "Coming!" she called, trying to hide the disgust that flashed across her face. She scurried over with the wine cup while I tried to take in the fact that somebody dared talk to my Prima that way.

The man grinned up at her. I saw her jaw flex as if she were gritting her teeth. A deep, dark hatred of this man uncoiled in my chest. He turned to look at me.

"I do not know you," the man said, draining his cup. "And I know everyone in Pompeii." He stood. To my dismay, he towered over me. Worse, he was handsome, with blond hair, a straight nose, and the muscular body of a man who exercises in the *palaestra* regularly. I gave him a sullen look, hating that his size and athleticism left me with familiar feelings of self-disgust.

"I am the new *aedile* in Pompeii, Cuspius Pansa," he said. "I offer greetings. And you are?"

"Caecilius," I muttered, for the first time becoming aware of the crowd of companions waiting for him nearby.

"Where are you from, Caecilius?" he said, cocking his head slightly, ignoring the great rudeness I'd shown him in not providing my full name. The thick, gold cuff around his wrist glowed in the stream of sunlight from the open door. It was vulgar, just like he was.

"Are you visiting from Herculaneum or perhaps Nuceria?"

He was fishing. Did he know my uncle? "Nuceria," I blurted.

"Ah, now we are getting somewhere." He gave me an oily smile, as if he knew I was lying. "In what *regio* do you live? And what do you think about your gladiatorial champion defeating ours in the arena? An outrage to Pompeii but you must be pleased. What was his name again...?"

The air in the *caupona* felt thick. I cleared my throat. "Excuse me. I am late for meeting a friend at the baths," I said. Turning to say goodbye to Prima, I was shocked to see her wide eyes full of loathing as she stared at the blond man. She'd reached out a hand as if to stop me.

Had this man hurt her in some way? Was he going to hurt her *now?* I took a step back toward her and she shook her head almost imperceptibly. A sense of utter helplessness froze me to the spot. I wanted to protect her, but how?

Go, she mouthed, as if she were trying to protect *me.* I looked at the slimy magistrate. He was watching me carefully. Too carefully. She was right. I needed to go, but I hated myself for doing it. I turned and walked out into the bright light of a busy Pompeian morning.

Half-blinded, I walked fast, trying not to imagine that disgusting man touching Prima. But of course, that was all I *could* imagine. Did she prefer him to me? Because of his size? His handsomeness? No. No. She was *disgusted* by him. That was clear.

All the way to the forum baths, I had the sense that someone was following me, yet whenever I looked around, nobody seemed to be paying any attention to me. The streets were bustling with people on the way to and from the *Macellum.* The tall blond man would've been easy to spot, I knew. And hadn't he said he had just won the aedileship? No magistrate would be able to follow someone like me even if he wanted to. Countless people would stop to talk to him, either asking for favors or complaining about something. Still, I could not shake the sense that someone had eyes on my back.

In the forum district, several gladiators loitered outside the entrance of the abandoned theater, which served as a surplus barracks. It seemed like a strange place to house gladiators, but Pompeii had its own rules. One scarred fighter watched me as I passed.

What in Prosperina's tight ass do you want? I thought at the grizzled fighter. But of course, I didn't say a word.

The man seemed to read my expression. He uncrossed his arms and yelled in my direction. "Hey, you, boy! You better bet on Pugnax at the upcoming fights, or I'll *eat* you!" the gladiator shouted at me. His mock scowl quickly turned into a grin when several men called out, "*Io,* Pugnax!"

I *hated* the man for his size. Gods, one forearm was as big as my thigh! Knowing that men like that slimy *aedile,* or even that monster

27

gladiator, could use Prima — could *hurt* her — any time they wanted left me roiling with a furious, impotent rage.

I was not a child, I reminded myself. I was a man. And I had to *do* something. Something that would save her and keep her safe. Something that would make her mine. The solution was clear. I had to find some way to turn the fantasy that one day I'd be able to purchase her into reality.

The idea was so thrilling, it burned away the sense of helplessness the way a hot plunge melts away muscle tightness. I would do it. Sure, my uncle wouldn't be happy, but the household could always use an extra hand, couldn't it? Or, even better, maybe I could arrange it so that Uncle would never even have to know about Prima. I could keep her here in Pompeii — in a little *insula* room facing the ocean. I could almost picture white drapes billowing with salty sea breezes cooling the sweat off our intertwined bodies.

But how much did a slave like Prima cost? I stepped into the next tavern I saw. After chatting up the owner and ordering his best wine, I asked him how much that pretty slave in the corner cost.

"For an hour or for the night?" the man asked.

I shook my head. "No. My apologies for not being clear. I want to know … if a man came in here and wanted to buy that girl from you, how much would you charge him?"

The man looked me up and down, then solemnly gave me a figure.

"Thank you," I said and marched out.

"Wait," the man called. "Make me an offer!"

The sum he'd named was more money than I had. Certainly too much money to ask for outright from my uncle. I would have to figure out some way to get the money on my own.

But how? How would I get the money?

I passed the baths without stopping to look for Julius. He always had extra money. How did he get it? Did his rich father give it to him? Having no father of my own, I would have to find a different way. Walking past a group of men in an alley throwing bones reminded me that Julius also gambled. Of course he did. But Fortuna had never smiled at me when I gambled, not even in Pompeii. Besides, I saved all my coins so I could pay for my nights with Prima.

Without realizing it, I had walked onto the street of leatherworkers and booksellers. The smell of tanning leather and the calls of booksellers woke me out of my trance. A man in a threadbare tunic held up a scroll like a *pilum* as if he was about to spear a customer with it.

"I have here in my hands, the original work of our beloved admiral!" he brayed and I almost laughed out loud. What a liar. My uncle kept very tight control over who got original drafts of his works. Still, the tactic drew a crowd. "Impress your friends with this treasure! Also, I have all of Pliny's *Natural Histories*. Written by his own hand! No scribes! No educated person's library in all of Campania should be without the whole set!"

For a moment I wondered if the man knew who I was, whether that's why he had begun hawking my uncle's writings. But he wasn't looking in my direction. He faced, instead, a knot of men dressed in fine linen tunics and golden armbands.

Instantly, I recognized them as the peculiar product of Pompeii: former slaves who had made their fortunes investing in the city after the devastating earthquakes the year of my birth. Most of the families of nobility left the city, never to return, leaving beautiful homes to be purchased by freedmen and tradesmen like fullers, bakers, and *garum* makers. They had my grudging admiration for the way they had filled in the cracks of what was missing in the city, much like Prima filled in the cracks of what was missing in me. It was men like these, after all, who likely discovered Pompeii's strange mud that hardened like stone underwater and made their riches selling it as concrete for aqueducts, piers, and bridges across the entire empire.

But were these same men really so eager for respectability that they would allow themselves to be swindled with forgeries of my uncle's work? Glittering with gold and shining with oiled curls, the men surrounded the bookseller. "Written by his own hand, you say?" one of the men asked. "How can you prove such a thing?"

The man carefully unrolled a corner. "That's Admiral Pliny's seal, right there!" The gaggle of men clucked and nodded with appreciation.

Meanwhile, I could barely contain my laughter. Writers of scholarly tomes didn't put their seal on the papyrus or parchment like letters. What fools!

"How much do you charge for this?" one of the bejeweled men asked.

When the seller answered, I nearly choked. "A bargain for such impressive works for your growing libraries," the man added.

I stopped cold under the awning nearby. The men were *considering* paying that much for an obviously fake scroll? By the gods! Just thinking about all the original works crammed into Uncle's library made me gasp. What if—

"Order or move on!" a sweating lady waving a ladle said.

I blinked. The woman nodded at the *dolia* sunk into the masonry counter, which reeked of badly mulled wine. She waved her hand like a showman over the other earthenware containers in her *thermopolium,* one with fish cakes swimming in *garum* and another with stewed octopus tentacles. "Just caught this morning," she said, pointing to the octopus. "So fresh you can almost see them twitching," she added grinning, showing brown teeth.

She was clearly proud of her offerings. But then everyone in Pompeii seemed to take great pleasure in even its most rustic charms.

"No, thank you," I said stepping away.

"Finally," a man muttered behind me. He quickly placed an order for the octopus, along with some olives and figs.

I walked blindly after that, considering what I'd overheard. Former slaves desperate to appear cultured would pay outrageous sums for the original works of my uncle, whose desk overflowed with manuscripts that he'd begun then set aside as another thought or observation caught his fancy.

The gods had given me the answer to how I could get the money I needed to purchase Prima. I turned and headed for the Sarno gate— and the stable—burying two small coins under a pile of flowers on a niche altar to the god of crossroads in gratitude for giving me the solution to my problem. Julius would probably not even notice that I was skipping the baths and although I hated missing a night with Prima, it would be worth it in the end. I'd have her forever soon enough.

I arrived back in Misenum — at my uncle's villa — deep in the dark of night as I'd hoped. To my horseman's dismay, I told him to prepare fresh mounts and wait for me on the road. Uncle's cliff-side villa, which overlooked the beach and a naval garrison, stood out like a pearl on black silk. The pinpoints of light in the night sky glowed over the dark water with such beauty, I felt as if the gods themselves were smiling down on me. Venus surely was!

For the first time, I saw the villa where I spent most of my youth with fresh eyes — imagining what Prima would think when she saw the multiple tiers of bright white walls carved into cliff rock, the glittering red roof tiles as they caught the sun, the exquisite statues of the Muses in our gardens. She would be enchanted.

But she wasn't going to see this villa, I reminded myself. She would always be waiting for me in Pompeii.

As I came closer, the silence of the place took me aback. The villa was usually bustling with noise and activity, but this total stillness seemed unearthly. Usually, the murmuring of the sea or a call from the garrison nightguard below floated up through the dark. But not tonight. The silence was almost oppressive.

Nobody expected me for another couple of days and everyone was asleep, I reminded myself. After lighting a small lamp, I crept through the house toward my uncle's *tablinum*.

The chest where he kept his money was shoved under a low table. Locked, as I'd expected.

Quietly, so quietly, I opened every drawer in Uncle's favorite ebony desk, a gift from Emperor Vespasian. No key anywhere. It had been worth a try. However, his desk overflowed with scrolls, as did his pigeon-holed shelves.

I'd once heard his steward tell him he should lock up his scrolls,

31

for they were worth their weight in gold. Uncle should've listened. I found a nearly completed draft of his latest work on the history of the Roman navy. No doubt, some grasping fool would pay a great deal to be able to say he was the first in Pompeii to own it. I was slipping the scroll into my travel pack when I accidentally bumped the desk. Something flashed in the light of the small lamp. My uncle's signet ring, unearthed from a pile of papyrus. I shoved the gold and carnelian ring into the bag before I could change my mind. That ring alone would pay not just for Prima, but for months of rent on a small room near the sea.

I headed back outside, certain that not a single soul knew I'd been back. Or what I'd taken.

TWELVE hours and two exhausted horses later, I was back in Pompeii. I went straight to Julius Polybius' house. I needed to find buyers for what I'd taken so I could make my bid for Prima. Surely he would know people who could help me turn what I had into gold and silver.

I was not entirely without guilt or shame for what I had done. But I told myself that I'd find some way to make up for what I'd taken. I'd study harder, do more translations for my uncle, perhaps. I'd find some way to make it up to him, I was sure.

Unfortunately, Julius was still sick from drinking the night before. I would have to wait until the third or fourth hour of the morning for him, but I was too restless to wait patiently. So I set out to Prima's tavern with my bag of stolen goods firmly under my arm.

She pouted prettily when she saw me and my heart jumped. "Why did you not come to me last night?" she asked. "You said you would."

"I had to go home—help a friend," I said. "Believe me I'll make it up to you."

"Good. Because I like my nights with you much better than with the drunk locals."

A small ball of pleasure warmed my belly. "I am glad to hear it," I said. Still, imagining drunks pawing at her in the disgusting outside cubicles—or that smarmy, blond *aedile* insulting her—made my stomach twist. Very soon she would never have to be with those kinds of men ever again.

Her dark eyes sparkled and her pink tongue peeked between the small gap between her teeth. "You're up to something," she said, cocking her head slightly.

I nodded, grinning.

"Let me get some wine and then you'll tell me all about it."

I didn't want wine, but we both had seen her owner step into the serving room. As long as I was spending coin, he wouldn't care how long we talked. "Get extra," I called out. "I am buying a cup for you too!"

Her eyebrows shot up as she grinned. She put the cups before us and slid onto a stool next me. "Tell me," she whispered in my ear, and I had to close my eyes for a moment so instant was my lust. "What are you up to?"

"I have a way for us to be together—a way for you to never have to be with men like that horrible *aedile*," I whispered.

She started back as if I'd burned her. "What?"

"I am planning to purchase you," I said, still whispering. I didn't want her owner to overhear and start working out how much he would charge for her. If I caught him by surprise, I could probably get her cheaper. "This very day, if possible."

She blinked under a furrowed brow. "I don't understand."

"I am going to *buy* you from him," I said. "And then we can be together all the time."

Her eyes grew wide, but not with pleasure. A pang of worry stirred in my belly. "Listen," I said quickly. "Don't say anything to your master yet. I don't want him to know until I can present him with the money."

She shook her head. "I'm not for sale."

I smiled reassuringly. "You will be when he sees what I am prepared to pay."

"No, you don't understand," she said, leaning into me. Her face

33

was flushed. "I can't … you can't just buy me."

"Why not?" I asked. "I could give you more than you have here and you would never have to deal with drunken idiots again."

"And this sudden plan is because you do not want to share me," she said, crossing her arms.

"No. I mean, yes. But it's not just that." Why was she being difficult about this? I thought she would throw her arms around my neck at the news. "Look, once you are mine I can free you if that is what is worrying you — as … as long as you agree to be my concubine."

"I am registered as a *prostitute*," she hissed. "I'll always be an *infamis*."

Gods was that true? But that wouldn't matter, right? Unless Uncle found out. But he rarely came to Pompeii. The chances were few that he'd find out about a former prostitute I kept. "We can get around that," I said, swallowing hard. "And if I buy you, you will have an easier life. It will be just you and me!"

The silence grew between us. Again, not what I expected. Maybe I had sounded too business-like? "I love you, Prima. And you're right. I don't want to share you. Is that so awful?"

She shook her head again, looking down at her hands.

"You … you do care for me, yes?" I stammered. "You just said you like your nights with me! Even if you don't love me, I know you care for me. And you will learn to love me when you see the kind of life I can give you."

"As your *personal* slut."

Gods that sounded awful. "No, but … well, isn't that better than being a … a—"

"Tavern whore."

I looked away. "I just don't want to see you used and abused by men like that man the other morning."

"Pansa," she said, making a disgusted face.

"Yes."

She sighed irritably. "Let me ask you something, Caecilius. How old are you?"

"Seventeen."

"And how many times have you been *in love*?"

I frowned, not liking the way she said the last two words. "Just once. With you."

"And you think that will last longer than say, oh, I don't know, until the Ides?"

"Yes!" I said loudly. Too loudly. Her owner looked over at us, frowning.

"Let me tell you something, little boy."

Little boy?

"You will fall in love a million times over before the year is out—"

"That's not true." I'd never seen her look so angry and bitter. Where had my Prima gone?

"It *is* true. And what will I do in six months when you tire of me and you have fallen in love with another whore?"

"That will never—"

"Or when you fall in love with a sweet little virgin you want to marry? I'll tell you what'll happen. You'll toss me out the back door like old fish."

"No," I said, shaking my head.

"Yes," she said, leaning forward. She looked angry. "And what about my sister?"

"What about her?"

"I am Capella's protector," she nearly growled. "I cannot be separated from her. She needs me!"

I looked down at my pack. My heart sunk. Her sister's creamy blonde prettiness would fetch a very high price. It was highly unlikely that I could afford both of them and still keep Prima in a place by the sea. "I might need some time to get more money—"

"You don't seem to understand," she interrupted and her eyes looked hard and mean. "I do not love you. I never will. What you 'love' is what I do for you upstairs. For money. It's an illusion."

Heat spread over my head and chest. "But ... but you chose me. Remember? The first time, you said ... I thought ... that maybe you—"

35

"The younger ones are easier because they finish faster," she said in a hard tone. "And you paid extra for the whole night. I'd be a fool if I didn't take advantage of that. But you're a bigger fool for thinking I'd feel anything for you. Your coin bag, though—now that *is* something I loved. But not you."

I actually curved over my wine cup, as if she had physically struck me in the chest.

She blew air out through her cheeks and stared up at the ceiling. "Venus' tit, if I'd realized how stupid you really are, I would've taken you for much, much more, boy. You need—"

"Stop calling me a boy!" I shouted.

The place went quiet.

"Pay for the wine and go, Caecilius."

The stool clattered behind me as I scrambled up. I slammed some coins on the table and clutched the bag of what I'd taken from my uncle hard against my stomach.

Prima stood wearily. "Come back when you grow a pair. I'll take your money then, same as any other."

I don't know how I got outside, or when I remembered to start breathing. The road under me began to vibrate and a bread cart across the way almost toppled over. Dizzy and nauseated, I fought to keep my balance. It took me a moment to realize that it was not just my world falling apart around me but another tremor shaking the earth.

But this one felt stronger. More dangerous. I put my hand on the wall outside the tavern almost hoping it would fall on me. When the vibrating stopped, someone started laughing too loudly across the street. A chicken squawked in outrage—wings outstretched as it ran desperately to get away from two barefoot children. People jostled me as they resumed their treks to and fro. I began putting one foot in front of the other, not caring or noticing where I went.

I let the crowd sweep me around unfamiliar streets. A man carrying a squealing piglet pushed me into a wall outside a large house as he swept by. My eye caught a word scratched onto the side of the door: *Prima*. I blinked and forced myself to read all of it.

Secundus says hello to his Prima, wherever she is. I ask, my mistress, that you love me.

She doesn't love anyone, I thought. And I was not the only fool for her. Still, the gods had led me to focus on her name. Clearly, they laughed at me most of all.

I found myself walking in circles around the basilica in the forum. I should go home, I told myself. I should replace what I took before my uncle notices. But that meant walking through Prima's end of town and that I could not do. Not yet. Besides, the horses would not be rested enough.

What a fool I was! What an idiot. The worst kind of stupid. She called me a boy. She cared nothing for me. How could I have misjudged her so completely? The humiliation washed over me in waves.

Three men suddenly stepped in front of me as I neared the unoccupied end being renovated. "The *aedile* would like a word with you," the stocky one in the center said.

"I'm not talking to anyone right now," I said, turning to walk around them.

"Oh, but you are," one of the men said, grabbing me by the upper arm. That snapped me out of my miserable trance.

"Take your hands off me!" I tried to pull my arm away but he held on tight.

They dragged me to an abandoned alcove. Scaffolding climbed halfway up the brick wall, though no one was working on it. Pompeii was like a little child with blocks: it began projects in one corner, then got distracted and started something else streets away.

The *aedile* who'd insulted Prima stepped out of the shadows. He gave me a brilliant smile. "How nice to see you again, Gaius Caecilius Secundus," he said.

Gods, the man knew my full name. What else did he know?

"What do you want?"

"Come, let us go into the shade and talk privately," he urged, as if we were old friends. One look at his thugs and I knew I had no choice. I followed.

"I wonder if your uncle knows what you've been doing in Pompeii," he said mildly.

"It's no business of yours," I said.

"Oh, but it is. *Everything* that happens in Pompeii is my business." He pointed to the bag I still gripped tightly under my arm. "Like what you have there. I think you should hand it over to me."

I blinked. "What? No!"

Pansa smiled and shook his head as if he were dealing with a recalcitrant child. And like a child, I wanted to spit in his face.

"Oh what a thrill it will be to inform the great Admiral Pliny that his nephew and likely heir is stealing from him," he said with a smarmy smile. "The favors he will owe me! That *is* why you ran home in the night and came back with that package, yes?"

I said nothing.

He stared at me for a moment then laughed. "Ha! I had you followed but could only guess what you were doing. Your silence tells me I guessed right. Now give me what you took from your uncle's villa and I won't tell him that you tried to buy a common tavern whore from a seedy *caupona* in Pompeii."

"I don't know what you're talking about."

He sighed. "You have yet to master your expressions, my boy. There is no point in lying. Prima told me everything. The skinny little slut even laughed while betraying you."

My heart thundered in my ears.

He held out his hand for the bag.

Still, I did not move.

Pansa cocked an eyebrow. "You can do this the easy way or the hard way."

That this backwoods politician thought that he was good enough to even *approach* my uncle, made me want to spit at him again. "You are a prick and an asshole and I hope Prima shits in your mouth the next time you go near her," I blustered out. "And you aren't taking anything of mine."

His lips quirked in amusement. "Well, I see you've made your choice." He signaled to his men and sauntered away.

"*Aedile!*" someone called when he stepped into the sunshine. "There you are! I have something to discuss with you ..." Pansa smiled widely and directed the petitioner away from us and into the flow of people.

Meanwhile, two of his men approached me while a third kept watch. "This is going to be too easy," one joked.

"Fuck you," I growled.

The burly man laughed. "The puppy barks," he said. "Hand it over."

The first punch came before I could reply, quickly followed by a second and a third. When I hit the ground one of the men grabbed the bag but I clung to it desperately, even as the other kicked me in the ribs. I couldn't let them have my uncle's writings or his ring. I just couldn't!

Then a kick near my eye slammed my head against the stone floor. When I came to, the bag — and the men — were gone.

I didn't know how long I had lain there, but the sun hadn't moved much, so not long. It took some time to sit up and even longer to stand. When I finally did, the ground swayed and bucked underneath me but I knew it wasn't another tremor. It was my own weak and injured body failing me. I closed my eyes until the feeling passed. Checking under my tunic belt, I noticed that my coin bag was gone too. The thugs took everything.

As I shuffled out of the shadows a woman squeaked at my sudden appearance. "Drunk idiot," she murmured as she scuttled by.

People gave me a wide berth. A small crowd had gathered in the Forum. I spotted Pansa's blond head towering over a group of adoring clients. He bent his head to speak to someone I could not see. I headed toward him, not caring about the sounds of disgust people made when I pushed past them.

Pansa laughed loudly. A thick, ridiculous fake laugh. "Yes, Senator. You are right. A very astute observation about Pompeii's endless construction."

Senator? I peered between the shoulders of some of the crowd and saw my uncle's friend with the iron-colored hair and crooked shoulder—Senator Norbanus from Rome. What was he doing in Pompeii?

If the senator's expression of hooded disdain was any indicator, he saw right through Pansa. The *aedile's* hands were empty though. He had nothing to incriminate him; he was the sort who would leave that to underlings. So I looked around for my things and spotted one of the *aedile's* men holding my bag as if it had always belonged to him.

"Senator," I called, pushing my way into the inner circle. "How good it is to see you!"

Norbanus stared at me a moment, then his graying brows rose. "Young Caecilius, is that you?"

I smiled broadly which must have made me look even more gruesome—my teeth felt coated with something thick and metallic. "Indeed," I said loudly, knowing what a sight I was.

"What in the name of all the gods happened to you, young man? Are you all right?"

"I've been robbed and beaten in your city, *Aedile*," I said, turning to Pansa. The crowd gathering around us murmured and made clucking noises of disapproval.

"A young man of quality beaten in the streets," the senator said, and turned to Pansa with deceptive mildness. "The citizens of Pompeii who voted you into office, *Aedile*, deserve better control over your domain from you."

Pansa's face flushed with anger.

"But where is your attendant?" Norbanus turned back to me. "A man of quality should not walk quarters like these unprotected."

"I left him with my horses while I visited Julius Polybius," I said.

When I swayed slightly, the senator took my arm, which made me wince a little. "You say your things were stolen?"

Pansa's thug looked like he was about to run but the *aedile* put a warning hand on his man's shoulder. "Oh! Yes," Pansa said, pretending to be surprised. "My esteemed friend found this abandoned bag and reported it to me," he said. "I was going to post a notice to help find the owner."

"Well, it's mine," I said, grabbing it. The thug's beefy arm tightened over the bag for just a moment but he let go as Pansa glared at him. "Oh, and look! This man has possession of my coin purse as well," I said with mock surprise. "I'll take that, too." I put out my scraped and bloodied hand.

Pansa's jaw worked as he gave his man a quick nod. The man reluctantly returned my money. The senator's cool gaze made it clear he knew exactly what had happened.

"Our *aedile* is an honest man and has returned lost goods," one of his followers cried. "The gods have chosen well in bringing our new magistrate to office."

There were murmurs of confusion, as well as some sporadic clapping as Pansa's entourage quickly spread the "story" that the *aedile* had recovered and returned stolen goods to a distinguished visitor.

The senator gave Pansa one last icy stare. Pansa bowed in response—managing to minutely quirk his head in such a way as to *hint* at disrespect—and took his leave without another word.

Senator Norbanus led me to his waiting litter. "Come, my boy," he said. "There is a fine villa outside the Herculaneum gate, and I know the merchant slightly. He will not grudge lending his physician to look at you."

"I'm fine," I said, clutching my bag—as well as my coin purse—with both hands but I followed him into the litter anyway. Relief washed over me when I sat, followed by dizziness. And oblivion.

I awoke to a stranger applying a leech to my cheekbone. "What are you doing?" I cried, trying to swat the man away and sit up.

The man put a hand on my chest. "Lay still," he said. "I am the physician in the house of Lepidus. The leech will take care of the worst of the swelling and bruising. Otherwise, the eye will close up."

Gods, where was I? And who was Lepidus? Was he a friend of my uncle's? The opulence of the gardens and courtyard indicated he likely was. Gods, did that mean that Uncle knew I was here?

The day's events flooded back to me. I sat up. "My things! Where are my things?" I cried.

"The senator has them. They are safe. Your deep sleep has concerned us all, young man."

"It's only because I stayed up all night traveling," I mumbled distractedly.

"I shall tell the senator that you are awake—just as soon as Master Mottled here," he said, tapping the blood sucking creature on my face, "has had his fill."

He *named* his leeches? Gods. Maybe this was all just a strange dream. But my physical aches told me it was real. So did the memory of Prima's harsh words, which cut more deeply. I closed my eyes in misery.

I awoke to find the senator sitting beside me. He handed me a cup of honeyed wine, which I drank down in nearly one gulp.

"Now," he fixed me with that keen gaze, "do you wish to tell me what this was all about?"

I groaned. "No. Not in the least."

"I thought as much." He did not look surprised. "I did not identify you to your hosts, merely told them you were a friend's son who was set upon. I suspect that the fewer who know about your 'adventure' in Pompeii, the better. Am I correct?"

I sighed. "Yes."

He eyed me a moment more, long fingers tapping. "I also suspect that it might be best for you to head back to Misenum right away."

I rubbed my face gingerly and moved my jaw side to side, saying nothing. How could I go home again? Uncle would certainly disown me once he found out what I'd done. I needed to disappear. Maybe I could still sell his things and escape to an outlying province. That way, I'd never have to face my uncle's expression of disappointment again. But then what? Gods, what was I going to do?

"You know, your uncle is concerned about you."

"He is?"

The senator nodded. "When I stopped at your villa on the way here, we had a long discussion. You had already left to visit the house of Julius Polybius."

For whatever reason, the thought that my uncle spoke with his friend about me made my throat go tight.

Then the senator said, "I told him the problem was likely a girl."

"A girl? No. A whore." A wave of shame and disgust washed over me as Prima's words came back to me. What a fool I'd been! I put my head in my hands. "Will I always feel this stupid and weak?" I muttered.

The senator leaned toward me. "Here's a secret that few men will admit out loud. On the inside, most of us feel small, stupid, and weak no matter what our size or how old we are. You become a man when you realize none of that matters. Only what we *do* matters. A man of Rome will do his duty even when he feels broken inside."

I shook my head. "Men like you ... like my uncle. I cannot imagine that you ever feel anything but strong and powerful."

He laughed. "Look at me! I'm a cripple of forty-three who looks sixty, feels a hundred, and stands shorter than you by half a head. I rarely feel strong and powerful. Actually," he mused, "I'm not sure I *ever* have ... but you would not know that, would you?"

"No." I had barely noticed his crooked shoulder or his modest height. What one noticed when meeting Senator Norbanus was his voice with its quiet ring of authority, and his gaze that could make even a man like Pansa squirm.

"A man's measure is not taken by his feelings, young Caecilius." The senator's tone was gentle. "He is measured by how he faces the world, and carries out his civic and family duties. Do you see?"

I shrugged in misery.

"Consider that long-armed reptile *aedile*, Pansa, for instance. He lies, cheats, and steals in what I imagine is a bottomless desire for power and influence. But men like him are never satisfied. They grow worse—even more corrupt over time—because the more they fight to acquire the trappings of power and confidence, the more it eludes them."

Silence. I did not want to talk about Pansa. But the senator clearly expected a response.

"I did not know you were a Stoic," I said, trying to be flippant.

He shrugged. "'Virtue is rewarded with happiness,'" he said, quoting Epictetus.

I couldn't imagine ever being happy again. The senator must have read my expression, for he added, "Do your duty by your uncle. It may not bring happiness, but it will bring a measure of peace."

I left soon after, assuring the senator that I was headed straight back to Misenum, but I wasn't sure I would ever go home again.

AT the Sarno stables, my uncle's man yelped in shock when he saw my face. "*Dominus*, what has happened? I knew I should've accompanied you! A man of your station should not walk the streets alone. The master will flog me for this!"

"No, he will not," I said wearily. "I gave you a direct order to stay with the horses. You cannot be punished for obeying me."

The older man, skin darkened and leathered from a life spent outside with horses, did not seem so sure. He twisted his hands with worry.

"And I am giving you another order," I added. "You are to leave my horse here and ride back to Misenum right away. Without me."

He gasped. "No, no, *Dominus*. That is impossible. I cannot allow that."

"I am not going back to Misenum. And you have Uncle's other horses to tend to."

"But ... but the horses need more rest." He stared at the bag I continued to clutch tightly against my side. "And what do I tell your uncle?"

"Tell him I threatened you with crucifixion if you didn't obey."

"But young *dominus*, you did not ..."

"I am sparing you the rod, Eponus. Now do as I say."

He did, while I sat in a pungent corner of the stables near my horse and considered my options. Where could I go where I wouldn't be found? How would I actually live after the money from selling Uncle's goods ran out? I could escape to the provinces and try to earn money as a tutor to some barbarian's child in some distant outpost, but just about every legate in every province would know my uncle. They'd be on the watch for me.

I was trapped.

The senator's words — "Virtue is sufficient for happiness" — came back to me and I snorted derisively. No, senator, it is most definitely *not* sufficient for happiness. I'd never be happy, no matter how virtuous I'd try to become. All I had to do was remember the cold look in Prima's eyes when she called me "little boy" for the pit of humiliation and despair to open up and swallow me again. It did not seem possible that there would ever be a time where it wouldn't. Besides, what did virtue mean in this situation?

That I returned what I took and told my uncle the truth? The very idea made my insides turn to water. But running and hiding from him felt worse. It felt childish. And I wanted so much to stop feeling like a little boy. Wearily, I stood up and began preparing my horse for the journey. Home was the better of two miserable options. At least I could try to face Uncle like a man.

EVEN walking my horse battered my injured body in new ways. My ribs ached, my head pounded, and my stomach roiled. It was slow going.

I arrived late the next morning to a house in chaos. Servants rushed to and fro. Some of the women were crying.

"What is happening?" I asked one of the kitchen women when I entered the courtyard.

"Someone stole from *Dominus*! And we are all being forced to line up for interrogation," she cried. "But none of us stole anything. Please, young master, let me go to talk to my children outside and warn them."

I released her with a nod and went toward my mother's chambers.

"Gaius!" she yelped when she saw me. "By Jupiter, what has happened to you?"

"Nothing of importance," I said. "Mother, you must call off the interrogation of the household slaves immediately—"

"But your uncle is beside himself. He was so agitated I insisted he take a sunbath and a cold plunge—"

"Listen to me. You must tell him to call it off. I have ... found his things. And as soon as I get cleaned up I will bring them to him."

She looked at me quizzically. "But how ..."

"Mother, it is a long, convoluted story which I will discuss only with him. Please do as I say."

After a quick plunge in the baths, I knew I could delay no longer. I grabbed the things I had taken from him and walked slowly up the outdoor terrace stairs. If Uncle disowned me, this could be my last time. I paused, taking a deep breath, which only made my ribs twinge with pain. Gods, I didn't want to do this. But I was no longer a child, right?

In the corner of every marble step stood a painted pot overflowing with pink and white flowers. The sun glittered off the calm waters of the bay, shining like precious gems—here turquoise, there sapphire, and dark lapis lazuli out into the gulf. Sea breezes rustled the potted palms clustered in the corner of the terrace. I wondered if condemned men facing execution experienced this kind of almost painful visual clarity of the beauty around them. Again, a part of me screamed to run, to get away, to hide from what I'd done. But still, I climbed, one heavy foot after another.

I found my uncle dozing in the shade of an inner room facing the sea. His chin rested on his chest, nestled within the folds of his neck, a partially unrolled scroll on his lap. I stared down at him, surprised to see him looking so vulnerable, so ... so *soft* in sleep. Ocean breezes had ruffled his gray hair into a boyish mess and his thick fingers were smudged with ink. It was easy to imagine him as a young child with dirt-caked hands in that moment. But then I remembered that he was already leading armed attacks in Germania as an officer at twenty-three. Only six years older than I was. It seemed inconceivable to me that I would ever command that kind of respect.

With a sigh, I dragged a heavy chair over the tiled floor, knowing that the sound would wake him in a way that we could both pretend he hadn't been sleeping.

"Gaius!" he said, his bloodshot eyes flying open as he raised his head. "Plinia tells me you found my things! I don't understand how that is possible but surely the gods were smiling down upon such a strange coincidence — "

"Uncle," I interrupted, sitting heavily. "I did not 'find' your missing scroll and signet ring." I pointed to the things I'd placed on a small round table between us. "I took them."

He stared at me slack jawed. "I don't understand. But you left for Pompeii days ago. I used my signet ring the day after you left!"

I nodded. "I snuck home in the night."

He blinked several times. "But … but *why*? Why would you do such a thing?"

Taking a deep breath, I began the whole story. "In Pompeii, there is … there *was*, a girl."

As I finished, Uncle squinted out to sea, his brow furrowed into deep, dark ruts. Only the occasional squawk of a sea gull broke the heavy silence.

Despite his expression, I was relieved the worst was over. I had spoken the truth. I had admitted to my terrible acts of theft and cowardice. A strange sense of calm descended over me. Was this momentary relief and lightness the "virtue" the senator meant?

"You do understand we were rounding up the slaves to begin the interrogations," Uncle said, sounding tired.

The full realization of what he meant hit me hard. By law, every one of our slaves would've been tortured in the process of investigating the thefts. Whoever broke under the torture and admitted to the theft — even if they were lying just to make the pain stop — would then be whipped and possibly crucified. I tried to imagine Uncle's secretary or Mother's hairdresser being tortured and my stomach clenched in disgust. And all for Prima, who had pretended to care for me but had only barely tolerated me for my

47

coin. Again, shame clogged my throat. How, *how* could I have been so stupid?

"I am more sorry than I can say, Uncle," I finally managed. "I will accept whatever punishment you deem appropriate for my foolishness."

Uncle snorted and shook his head as if there were no punishment strong enough. I couldn't blame him, really — I deserved his disdain. If I were exiled or disowned, I would just have to learn to handle it. Perhaps such a hardship would finally harden me into a man.

"I believe," Uncle said with one of his breathy, wheezing sighs. "That the memory of the slave-girl's cruelty — which I can tell you, you will *never* forget — is probably punishment enough."

I blinked. "But ..."

"Gaius, every man has at least one Prima in his life. Usually the first. She is aptly named."

Swallowing hard, I cleared my throat. "You aren't going to — I mean, I thought you would — "

"Tell you that I had never shamed myself for an unworthy girl?"

"Well, yes," I said in confusion. "I cannot imagine you with a girl like Prima."

"Then you lack imagination. Over my long life, I have had several. The worst, however, was a girl in Germania." He shook his head again, this time with a sad smile.

"What happened?" I prompted.

"It was during our campaigns there," he began. "The legions hired a great many local weavers to make heavier tunics for us before the snows came on. Gods, Sigihild — that was her name — was a beauty. Buxom redhead with a smattering of freckles across her nose and a sway in her hips that always left me weak in the knees."

"What happened?"

"I professed my undying love to her. She married a local villager. The butcher, I think." He smirked. "But not before taking every ounce of salt and coin I possessed — which I eagerly turned over to spend time in her bed. I would have stolen for her too if it had ever occurred to me to do so. She knew what she was doing, though. She was a smart girl."

"And I couldn't have been more foolish," I said. To my horror, a sob nearly broke free my throat but I swallowed it back. Just barely.

Uncle watched me very carefully.

He nodded. "Good. A true Roman never lets his emotions take possession of his dignity. You are doing better than I ever did."

I raised my eyebrows.

He laughed ruefully. "I sobbed like a baby when I learned of my German girl's marriage. And in front of my men too," he added with a shudder. He gave me a sidelong look. "Close your mouth, Gaius. A gull may try to build a nest in there if you're not careful."

Snapping my teeth shut, I continued staring at him, incredulous.

He shook his head, smiling at a memory I'd have thought unbearable for a man of his *gravitas*. "As a result of my less than impressive response, I was sent to the swamplands to build canals during the Chauci campaigns. I had to win back my dignity somehow. And I was twenty-three, not seventeen, so I should have known better."

For the life of me I could not picture my giant, strapping uncle sobbing over a girl. And in uniform no less. *In front of other men!* I stared dumbly out to sea for a long time.

"So what is your plan for taking care of the situation?" Uncle asked.

I stared blankly at him.

"What will you do to ensure that you do not fall into this trap again?"

Groaning, I rubbed the uninjured side of my face. What could I do? Already I'd had to fight the temptation to throw myself at Prima's feet and beg her to forget my foolishness and bring me back to her bed. Yet I couldn't humiliate myself like that again and hope to ever hold my head up.

"Well," I began, clearing my throat, "I can begin by trying to … by staying away from Prim—from Pompeii," I said, clearing my throat. I had come to love the city nearly as much as the girl I went to visit there—Pompeii and Prima would forever be intertwined in my mind. I couldn't risk the danger of going near either of them again. "Probably for a long time."

He nodded. "Good. Only a man who understands his weakness can master it."

"And I plan on taking on some translation work to pay you back for the loss —"

"I lost nothing," he cried, pointing to the scroll and ring I'd set on the small round table between us.

"I have lost your trust," I said, hoping the quaver I felt in my throat did not spill out into my voice. "And I must earn it back."

"You already have," he said. "It took balls of bronze to march up here and tell me the truth. A boy is not capable of such a thing. Only a man is."

The shock of his words was swept away by the alarmed voices floating up from the lower terraces. My mother came scrambling up the steps. "Brother!" she called. "Have you seen what the mountain is doing?"

"The mountain?"

I helped him up and we walked to the edge of the terrace where we stared agog at a strange vision from across the bay.

"What mountain is that?" Mother asked. "And why is it spewing dirt?"

"I cannot tell," Uncle said. "What in Vulcan's world could have caused such a cloud?"

A thick, whirling, billowing column of ash and dirt climbed eerily and silently into the sky. Several *stades* high, the gray-brown cloud began spreading out as if it had grown tired. "It looks like an umbrella pine," I said.

"Extraordinary," Uncle mused in that curious way of his. Then he sent the order to prepare a boat for us to take a closer look at the strange phenomena across the bay.

"Do you think it is like the fire mountain in Sicily?" I asked as we continued staring.

He shook his head. "Impossible! And Aetna actually has fire when it erupts," he said. "I've seen it. Here, there is no fire, no lava. Only clouds, as if the fire is deep inside the mountain."

"Fascinating," I mumbled.

"Indeed!" agreed Uncle, his eyes shining. "It is hard to tell from here, but it looks like Vesuvius is responsible. Pompeii and Stabiae will lie beneath that cloud."

My mother turned to her brother with a worried expression. "Are you two going to explore the edges of the cloud? Or will you go all the way to Pompeii?"

Staring into that strange dark cloud, I tried to imagine what Prima must be feeling. Gods, she must be terrified. I saw myself running through the panicked city until I found her. How she would throw her arms around my neck in relief and beg my forgiveness for her cruelty. How she would say she lov—

"Gaius," my uncle called, and I jumped. "Are you joining me on this journey? The winds will probably take us straight into Pompeii."

Why was he asking? Normally he would just order me to accompany him and I would do so without question or complaint. And then I understood. He was testing me. Hadn't I *just* promised to stay away from Pompeii and Prima?

I raised my chin and looked at my uncle in the eye. "I am keeping my word and staying here," I said. At the look of confusion on my mother's face, I added, "To finish my studies." Even I could hear how weak that sounded, but my mother did not say anything.

"Good man," my uncle said, smiling proudly at me. "A Roman always keeps his word."

When an ash-coated messenger came barreling up the cliff and into the house bearing a message from a dear friend of Uncle's begging to be rescued near Pompeii, the investigative excursion turned into a naval rescue mission. The fleet was put on high alert. All of Misenum, it seemed, came to the docks to bid farewell to the heroes of the day, led by my uncle.

Just as he was about to board, my mother grabbed his hand. "Brother, perhaps you shouldn't go. I have a terrible feeling ..."

"Plinia," he said gently. "Do not worry. The mountain will burn itself out. But we really must help those people who are either trapped or panicking. It's my job to keep unrest to a minimum in the region and I intend to do so."

"But what if—"

He flashed a look in my direction. "Gaius is the man of the house while I am on duty, Plinia. He will take care of you and the property."

She stood on tiptoe and kissed her brother's cheek. "May Fortuna keep you and Neptune watch over you," she whispered and turned away to begin the long trek back up the path to our villa.

"Admiral, if we are to leave, we must do so now!" an officer said.

"Yes, yes," he replied. "Let us go."

I wanted to say something to him, to thank him, but for what, I didn't know. My mind reeled, trying to find a way to undo my promise—just this time. He needed my help, didn't he? I shouldn't let him cross the bay to Pompeii alone! A pang—a sense of impending doom—squeezed my gut.

As if he could feel me struggling, he turned to me. "Your job is to stay here and take care of things in my name," he said with finality.

I nodded.

Just as his first officer led him toward the boarding dock, he turned back to me and called out, "Goodbye, son."

It was only later, looking out to sea and watching Uncle's *trireme* disappear into the strange black cloud hovering over Pompeii, that I became aware of the significance of his words. He had called me "son." He had claimed me.

I never saw him again. But in his will, dated to my manhood ceremony months before, he'd named me his heir, formally adopting me upon his death. He had believed in me all along. I prayed I could live up to the greatest gift of all—his name.

I was known, from then on, as Gaius Plinius Caecilius Secundus.

Pliny. The younger one.

PART TWO

THE HEIRESS

Sophie Perinot

"The world was not being merely shaken but turned topsy-turvy."
— Pliny the Younger

AEMILIA

Three days earlier...

THREE days. Three days until my life is over.

Reaching out, I snap a branch off the nearest myrtle. It is still damp with morning dew. A few fading, star-shaped blooms cling to it. Casting it down, I grind it beneath my sandal. Glancing about to make certain I am unobserved, I take the doll from the pouch at my girdle. She is not the finest of my childhood playthings. Not one of my carefully carved, jointed dolls. But she is my favorite, made by Mother from scraps of linen and clothed in a dress of blue silk left from one of my own. I give her a little kiss, then push her beneath the bush. Another treasure spared from the flames.

I am a creature of fire, born in the back of a wagon as my parents fled Rome during the great conflagration in the reign of Emperor Nero. I've been told the harrowing story a thousand times. Told too that my extraordinary delivery is the reason my hair is red as flame. Well, fire may have birthed me and marked me, but it won't have the mementos of my girlhood. I do not care that it is Roman tradition for a girl to burn such things on the morning of her wedding. I will make no offering to Venus because, were it up to me, I would not be a bride—at least not the bride of Gnaeus Helvius Sabinus! I push the doll further out of sight, then straighten to see my father emerging from his private wine cellar. Blinking in the bright autumn sunlight, he secures the door behind himself, extinguishes his lamp, and then smiles at me. An only child, I am the center of his world. I turn my back as if I have not seen him and head briskly for the atrium. Mistake. I can hear the earnest voice of Gnaeus Helvius Sabinus resonating from the *tablinum*. My intended is asking for Father. Good. Let Father deal with him. Father always smiles to see Sabinus, whereas I find nothing pleasing in the face or figure of the middle-aged man who will soon be my husband.

I have known all my life that Father would select my groom — that is what fathers do. What I did not anticipate, could not imagine, was how wretched fulfilling a daughter's obligation would make me feel. Perhaps it is as Mother always says. Perhaps I was shown a faulty amount of indulgence as I grew — presented with five fabrics by my doting father where only one was needed to make a gown — until I believed I would be offered choice where I would not. Or perhaps it is the fact that Sabinus is an old man, and I have met a younger one I like better. Whatever the reason, I cried the day I was told of my betrothal. I remember Mother, looking perplexed, as she often does when dealing with me, and saying, "He is a fine, honorable man from an old Sabine family. What more can you want?"

What more? Everything more. While what my mother said was entirely true, there is nothing extraordinary about Sabinus. He is the sort of man who does not stand out — neither tall nor short, fat nor thin, ugly nor handsome. His voice is always moderate, his mode of address always correct. Only his interests make him noticeable, and *not* in a good way. Sabinus is highly educated, yet he professes no interest in art or philosophy. Instead, he is fascinated by the workings of machines, by details of construction and hydraulic engineering better left to workmen, and by the geology of the area surrounding Pompeii.

By rocks. Yes, rocks.

I have no intention of getting trapped into another painful conversation with him — doubtless about earth tremors because, since the latest shaking started some weeks ago, that is the only subject he seems capable of discussing.

Turning with alacrity, I move through the *oecus* with its graceful paintings of fluted columns and lush garlands, toward the man who is everything Sabinus is not. I must lift a sheet of coarse fabric and walk beneath a scaffold to enter the dining room. My breath quickens at the smell of the paint. Letting the drape fall, I hear my name. The flesh on my arms, on my whole body, begins to prickle. Looking into the scaffolding, my eyes find Faustus — long, lean, his fingers holding a brush, his eyes locked on me. I take a step forward.

"Stop there! The light has caught you." His voice is excited and exciting. "I wish I could paint you as you look at this moment. Paint you as Erato. Lower your chin."

I comply. Beneath my gown I can feel my nipples growing hard under his gaze. "Would you make me beautiful?"

"Of course."

He sets aside his brush and climbs down, his movements fluid, the muscles of his arms taut and those in his legs plainly visible under the short tunic he wears while he works. He moves around me as I have seen lions move during games at the amphitheater, in a slow circle, his eyes hungry. I am certain mine are as well. Faustus is the one good thing that the expensive and frantic preparations for my nuptials have brought — hired and set to work restoring our villa's ancient and much admired frescos before I even knew the reasons for these efforts. But the same ceremony that drew him to our villa will separate me from him forever.

Drawing close behind me, he whispers, "You want me to touch you."

Of course I do. But I focus on a larger dream. One that is dangerous and that, until this moment, I have left unspoken. "I want you to marry me."

I hear his breath catch. More than a catch, he gasps. Good, I have impressed him with my boldness. "How I wish I could." He stammers slightly. "Yes, that is what I want," the natural confidence returns to his voice, "to be your husband."

"My father would support your career." Why not, I think, Father certainly has the money for such patronage. But I know the thought is nonsense. Even if there were no Sabinus, no betrothal, my father would never consider a penniless tradesman as a suitor.

Faustus' breath on the back of my neck is warm. "Oh Gods," he groans. "No more touching up the work of others. Only my own, better, work, immortalizing you for the ages. If only it could be so."

My eyes travel over the figures on the room's rich, red walls — all movement, color and mystery. I've been told the painted figures engage in sacred and mysterious rituals, designed to turn a girl into a woman, a virgin into a wife. Small wonder then that I see my own face among them. I am the bride sitting, wistfully touching her hair and gazing into the distance as an attendant beautifies her. But I do *not* see my groom. Instead, I see my artist, Faustus, my personal Eros — though he is far, far more handsome than the winged figure depicted in the final panel of the mural.

"Come tonight," he begs.

Two nights ago I crept from my *cubiculum* as my ancient nurse lay snoring. Came here, to the *triclinium,* in darkness, for a stolen kiss. I wonder, on my wedding day as I sit beside Sabinus on a banqueting couch in my *flammeum*, my girdle tied into the knot of Hercules, will my eyes seek the corner where, beneath the scaffolding, I let Faustus' lips touch mine for the first time?

The drapery in the doorway from the portico twitches. Faustus jumps back as if my hair were not just flame-colored, but fire itself.

Sabinus sticks his head in. "Aemilia Lepida, I thought I might find you here." Is it the light, or do his cheeks color? His blush makes me nervous. Whatever my attachment to my artist, I have been chary. I may be angry at my father, but I have no desire to shame him or to dishonor my family. "I have finished with your father," Sabinus continues. "Come walk with me in the *viridarium*. Your mother has given permission."

He holds back the drop cloth. There is nothing for it, I must go. Once we are in the portico he offers an arm, which I ignore. I am careful not to look directly at him as he walks beside me. His unnerving way of locking his eyes on mine whenever he can catch them gives me the feeling he can see the things I am careful not to say.

My mother's ornamental garden is her pride and joy: all carefully sculpted shrubs, tinkling fountains, and exquisite marble sculptures. As we enter, I notice that she sits at the far end, near the freshly painted statue of Livia that will shortly be moved to the newly created shrine to her. I should have known—Sabinus is overly nice on such points; he would prefer to be chaperoned, even so few days before we are wed. *Your worry for my reputation is wasted, Sabinus. Both because you are too staid to lay a hand on me, and because Faustus already has.* I shiver at the thought of how close Faustus stood just moments ago, but Sabinus does not notice for he is waving to Mother. She smiles in return. Then he turns and walks me toward a bench beside the long shallow pool. I sit. He looks down at me intently.

"I have been thinking about our future—"

So have I, if dreading counts as thinking.

"—I mean to be a good husband to you, Aemilia Lepida. I have watched you grow up. I understand the care and esteem you have been accorded by your father, and I mean to proceed in the same vein."

He speaks true. Sabinus visited this house before I lived here, before I was born. My father bought the villa after it was damaged in Emperor Nero's quake—bargaining the price down to nearly nothing. He intended it to be a place to spend summers by the glittering sea away from the repressive heat of Rome, and a place to indulge in the viniculture that is, appropriately for a wine merchant, his dearest hobby. Sabinus, father's old school friend, was already living in Pompeii and supervised work restoring the villa when Father could not be here. And when my parents fled to Pompeii as fire swept Rome, my nurse told me that Sabinus waited beside her at the entrance to help them down from the wagon.

"When you were a little girl, I thought you fond of me." The eyes, which have changed from brown to startling gold in this light, press still further into me. "But I know you do not favor me now."

Here is a level of bluntness I do not expect from the mild-mannered Sabinus. I can feel the heat rising in my cheeks. Of course I had no ill thoughts of him those many years — I had no apprehension anyone thought of him for my husband. He was just a family friend who listened to the fanciful stories I liked to make up, and laughed in the right places. Someone who took me to the market if Mother had one of her headaches or my nurse was too tired, and marveled at my facility for doing figures in my head the way Father does. Someone who called me Vesta, jokingly, because of my hair. But Vesta is not merely the goddess of the sacred fire; she is goddess of hearth, home, and family. It ought to have been a clue. I feel a sudden surge of anger at myself for missing it. Also a burst of irritation at Father. If Sabinus was to be my husband, why could I not have been told long ago? Given time to accustom myself to the idea? *Would that have mattered once you met Faustus?*

"I will be patient and hope — Did you see that?"

I am left not knowing what he hopes — not that I particularly care — as Sabinus moves past me, his eyes on the pool. I turn, curious. He stands at the water's edge, his head tilted to one side. "Yes!" Turning back, he appeals to me. "Do you see the ripples on the surface? Another tremor! Too faint for us to feel perhaps, but the water apprehends what we do not."

I stare hard at what little water is left in the pool thanks to an exceptionally hot summer that has left the city short of water. I do see small ridges. "Perhaps something fell into it from above."

"No, such a disturbance would create circular ripples emanating from the place where the falling thing broke the surface." He illustrates by tracing the rings on his left palm with the index finger of his right hand.

I can hear my father as we dined last evening: "Sabinus, you become obsessed with your earthquake prognostications! You have not heard one word I have said about the new press I am installing in my *calcatorium*." And hear my mother's furious whisper when I snickered: "Aemilia, a proper Roman wife does not laugh at her husband, only with him." Looking at Sabinus, now squatting at the pool's edge, I think: *not my husband yet.* But I think something else as well. However little I fancy him as a groom, Sabinus is by any measure an intelligent man and he is right about the pattern of the ripples.

The earth begins to shake, hard enough that I cling to the edge of the bench and Sabinus puts a hand on the ground to steady himself. Across the *viridarium*, a bust falls from a niche and Mother gives a little scream. "Go to her," Sabinus urges. "I must go to the forum. My conscience will not be easy until I try Gaius Cuspius Pansa again. If those who love me well like your father do not heed me, I have little chance with the *aedile* who dislikes me deeply. But I must try."

SABINUS

"WITH all due respect, Pansa—" Sabinus tried to keep his voice low, for while Pansa had agreed to withdraw with him to a spot between two of the new travertine columns along the east side, one was never truly alone at the forum. The handsome *aedile* rolled his eyes behind lashes that seemed unfairly noticeable for a man of such fair complexion.

" —Sabinus, you never show me the respect I am due." Pansa gave an amused smile. "What *would* your grandmother think of such behavior?"

Fine, Sabinus thought, *trot out the election graffiti, again.* Whichever of his supporters had painted, "Vote for Sabinus, his grandmother works hard for his election" on a wall really hadn't done him any favors. *I am quite certain my grandmother sees you as I do: all corruption and guile wrapped in a pleasing appearance.* He didn't say it, but gods he wanted to.

"This is not about our personal history, Pansa—"

"Everything is." Another smile.

If he was interrupted one more time, Sabinus wasn't sure his temper — much as others considered it one of his finest qualities — would hold.

"Aedile" — it cost Sabinus something to use the official form of address, and the slight bow he gave to accompany it cost him more still — "the signs, as I have told you before, are significant: wells and springs drying up outside the city despite the summer rainfall, dead fish in the Sarno, the increasing frequency and severity of tremors. Surely you felt the strong tremor a short while ago."

"We've had tremors before. They are part of living in Pompeii and mean nothing. Nor are these the first to bring down scaffolds or walls since Nero's quake."

"Your family, like mine, was here then," Sabinus replied, grasping on to the reference. "You lived through the devastation. Gods, Pansa, we are still rebuilding seventeen years later." *Longer than my bride-to-be has been alive.* Where did that thought come from? This was not a time to think of women or weddings, but to be honest, Aemilia was never far from his thoughts lately. He could see her in his mind's eye: bent over her mother, comforting that lady as he left the Lepidus villa to come in search of Pansa, her red hair, caught in the sunlight, making her lovely skin even more translucent.

"Yes." Pansa's voice shattered the vision, and he no longer sounded amused. "And one of the things you demand is that I order any scaffolding adjacent to primary roads be taken down. A major inconvenience to many. An order sure to delay work and make me unpopular. Yet you say this isn't personal?" Pansa straightened his shoulders, showing off his height. Rubbing it in. "Forget your grandmother, Sabinus — *you* are an old woman! If I were to order evacuations every time a few pieces of crockery were shaken off the shelves in this city, Pompeii would be destroyed in no time. Not by tremors, but by fear. I cannot allow that. The Cuspii Pansae cannot allow that."

"I am not asking for evacuations. I am asking you to lay plans for them should they become necessary."

"And I," Pansa stepped right up to Sabinus, thrusting a well-manicured finger into his chest, "am asking why I should do anything for you when you go behind my back? When you send letters of a hysterical nature, implying I am not doing my job?"

So he knew about the letter to Admiral Pliny. So soon. Sabinus had not expected his correspondence to go unreported. Pansa had spies in the same abundance that he had money. But Sabinus had believed it would take longer for his appeal to the august Admiral to be discovered.

He drew another measured breath. "Because, I am telling you that something enormous is coming. And because, Pansa, you have a duty to the city and to its inhabitants — a duty that encompasses more than presiding over public festivals."

A step back. A smile re-fixed in place. Damn but Pansa was composed. "I like festivals. I like entertainments of all sorts. People cheer me. Has anyone ever cheered you, Sabinus?" Without waiting for an answer — "No, I thought not."

Sabinus' head was beginning to throb, possibly from clenching his jaw muscles.

"We have gladiatorial games coming up in a few days. The money has already been spent to host them. I am not going to start a panic that might thin the crowds. It is in the public interest that the games go forward. After all, they may appease the gods and stop the tremors that so worry you."

"Have a bet on a gladiator, do you?" Pansa did not care about appeasing the gods, just about adding to his purse. Sabinus was not a betting man himself, but that was a wager he would have taken.

"The scaffolding will stay in place, the games will go on. I will have a lovely afternoon watching men bravely fight and then I will come to your wedding and admire your bride."

Sabinus' head wasn't just throbbing now; he could actually hear his blood in his ears. He was fairly certain he was turning red as well.

"I'll give you this, Sabinus, you secured a nubile young thing. Her father's fortune would be reason enough to marry her, but you get good looks, too. I ought to be more worried about the former because you will be better funded next time you run against me. But let's just say that whenever I see your Aemilia in the theater or marketplace, it's not the richness of her dress that draws my eye."

"I will take my leave," Sabinus had to choke the words out. The thought of Pansa casting lustful looks at Aemilia made his throat close.

As Sabinus turned to go, Pansa added, his tone light, "If you want me to act on your suggestions, engineer, I suggest you come back with less talk and more coin. I am not an unreasonable man."

Sabinus ignored the insult, and considered bribing the *aedile* for a moment—but to pay a dishonorable man was to throw money away. So he kept walking, out of the forum and into the street. There he paused, breathing heavily. The unseasonably warm autumn air did little to relieve the pounding in his head. He needed something to draw the blood elsewhere and take his mind off his various troubles and worries. He knew just the thing. He turned his step in the direction of his favorite *caupona*. The wine was good and the spicy sausages better, but more importantly there was a woman there who would wipe his mind blank. Not the skinny, swarthy whore with the sharp tongue who belonged to the place, but her rosy, well-rounded sister, Capella, who was always both friendly and obliging.

IT was not until she got off her knees to rinse out her mouth that Sabinus felt a twinge of guilt—for thinking of Aemilia while Capella had him between her lips.

"Will you take a glass with me?" he asked with a certain contrition.

Capella paused in the process of tidying her glorious golden mane, and looked at him curiously. They were not in one of the little street-side cubicles where she ordinarily plied her trade, but rather above the *caupona*; Sabinus didn't mind paying for the added privacy. Capella smiled at him. "Until my master notices—he doesn't like me to linger too long with one customer."

When they'd settled at a table in a dark corner, far from the open front of the place and thus less likely to be seen by anyone who knew Sabinus well, Capella spoke again. "I think something is bothering you, and I believe I know what it is."

Could she know? Could she be concerned about the tremors too?

"A man of your age and stature shouldn't be nervous about marrying," she continued, offering a smile. "Marriage is a blessed thing, a gift from the goddess, and I think you will enjoy having a wife to cook for you. Besides, any woman would be lucky to have you. Is she pretty, your betrothed?"

"She is pretty." *And she does not need to cook for me*, he thought. Someone will do that for her. Someone will dress her, do her hair, carry her purchases in the marketplace, and refill her lamps — all unimaginable luxuries to the girl who sat across from him. He lowered his voice. "Maybe too pretty for me. Or better say, maybe I am not pretty enough for her. I suspect she is infatuated with a youth nearer her own age."

"Does he return her affection?"

"What youth would not?" Sabinus cut himself off before his bitterness ran away with him. Why was he telling her this — something he had not said out loud to any other? Telling his secret insecurities to a tavern maid? Perhaps it was her kindness. He perceived that quality in Capella whenever they met.

"Beauty is a great attractor for the young," Capella conceded. "But as she grows in wisdom, your wife will come to value other virtues. Does a little infatuation bother you so much?"

"Of course." Again his own candor surprised him. "I saw them together this morning. He was standing so close to her, and her eyes … Let's just say they never regard me in such a manner."

Capella gave a musical laugh. "Do you know how few Roman husbands care how their wives' eyes regard them? You have a secret streak of romance in that practical soul, Sabinus! For that reason alone, your bride is lucky to have you."

Romantic? He had never thought himself so. Watching Aemilia grow up, knowing long before she did that Lepidus intended her for him, Sabinus had thought of himself as tending his future property. But perhaps he had been falling in love. This was a painful and slightly embarrassing thought. He shuffled his feet beneath the table and cleared his throat. "I am not romantic. I am a man more interested in engineering than poetry."

"And you wish to engineer a happy marriage, don't you? If I may be so bold, I recommend you worry less about the arrows of Cupid. Your wife-to-be is surely a high-born girl. There is nothing, therefore, to fear in terms of her virtue."

"Isn't there? What if he has kissed her?" Sabinus had no solid evidence of such a thing, but he'd seen it in his mind's eye for weeks. "What if Cupid's arrow has struck her, and when she sees me she thinks of him?" This came dangerously close to what he'd been doing himself a short time before — imagining Aemilia while reveling in Capella.

The rosy girl leaned forward and took the very unusual liberty of pressing a small kiss at the corner of his mouth. "So what if he has kissed her?" she asked, as if to remind him that he had done more, much more, than kiss her before they came down to share a drink. With her blue eyes sparkling merrily, Capella added, "And if she sees you and thinks of love and desire, is that not to your benefit? It is a trick I have used many times myself ..."

It ought to have enraged him, this coupling of Aemilia's name and Capella's work. But, surprisingly, it failed to raise his ire. Still, he felt foolish. Capella was right about one thing, even if her reasons were not his own. As a man, he ought not to worry so much what his betrothed, or his wife for that matter, was thinking. He shrugged and hoped the gesture was convincing. "Whatever her attraction to the boy, she will be mine in a matter of days. And perhaps you are right, perhaps it does not matter what is in her head so long as I am the one in her bed."

"I suppose I won't see you here so much then?" Capella asked, as if she might genuinely regret it. "Because if she is yours, then you are also hers, or at least that is what we worshippers of Isis believe."

Isis? A cult for women. He had no desire to be rude, particularly as Isis worshippers had supported him in the election, but he was still feeling less the man than he would have liked. "I am no woman's property. So you will most assuredly see me." He had the sense that his tone lacked conviction. He'd never been a particularly good liar.

And Capella was not fooled for a moment. With an indulgent look, she asked, "Then why are we sharing a farewell cup of wine?"

Before he could answer or feign another unconcerned shrug, his eyes were drawn to the wine in his cup—little ripples disturbed its surface. A tremor! He noticed that Capella's eyes were on the cup as well. "You see it," he said with wonder.

She startled, glancing up at him with wide eyes. "And you see it, too? The vision in the cup. Of the fire and darkness?"

"Vision? No. I see waves as upon the sea, only smaller. Results of tremors too slight to be felt by the body. Smaller by far than those that have been scaring horses and breaking bits of statuary these last weeks. I fear they presage an earthquake of such force, such power, that Nero's quake will be forgotten in its shadow." He paused. He was relieved that someone other than himself paid attention to the intensifying tremors and associated them with destruction. But he did not like the idea of a prophetic vision. "Tell me what you see," he said, leaning across the table.

Drawing her brows together, the girl lost some of her color. She bit her lip, as if wary to tell him more, but his prediction plainly frightened her. "I see waves, too—but of a different kind. It started for me in the Temple of Isis. The pilgrims who bring the Nile water were pouring it into the cisterns, and when I looked upon the water I saw a black sky denser and darker than any night. This sky transformed into black swelling rain that fell until it became a river, and the river in turn was washed away by a dark sea of violent power. By this I foresee a flood, coming to wash our spirits clean of flesh and blood. And an ethereal blaze, bigger and brighter than the fire that burns in any lighthouse, which will guide us to salvation."

Sabinus felt cold. Everything the girl saw could result from an earthquake: waves rushing in from the bay, high enough to sweep away men and buildings, fires raging as buildings fell and lamps with them. So much fire that thick smoke might block the sun, adding to the horror of the destruction. It was as if Capella had seen his fears in that temple cistern. He knew enough of those who followed Isis to know they ascribed great power to the waters of the Nile. For a moment he was in the main atrium of the Lepidus villa, standing beneath the painted views of the Nile that adorned its walls. Could the blue, so calm in paint, really have the power to give visions? If so, surely it would not extend them to a mere tavern maid?

He shook his head to clear it. Everyone knew the Isis temples allowed the imaginations of slaves and women to run wild. He needed to be sensible. If destruction was coming, it could surely — by proper planning — be minimized. The idea of it being redemptive, an idea that shone in Capella's eyes, was nonsense. Another excuse for inaction.

"Do not worry." He allowed his hand to rest for just a moment on hers. "The city's officials may be slow to listen to me, but they are reasonable men. Should disaster come, they will do their duties. And I, I will keep an eye out for you while doing mine."

"I am not worried," Capella said, reaching down to her ankle and fingering one of the small charms that hung there. All the charms were the same. Sabinus thought each looked like an inverted drop of water from which a long straight bar extended downward, crossed by a shorter horizontal one. The color had returned to the girl's cheeks. "I need never worry," she touched the token again, "for Isis is my guide and salvation."

He rolled his eyes, but he hoped that she did not notice.

"WELL, my treasure, a buyer has come to relieve me of that infernal animal." Father plants a kiss on the top of my head as I sit weaving. Although I cut him dead this morning, I cannot resist looking up and smiling. "Will you come to the stables with me while I transact my business? You might even find occasion to hide a little something while we are there." He winks. The stool before Mother's loom is empty. She is lying down with a headache, doubtless the lingering result of her overexcitement in the garden this morning. "But perhaps not this." The hand that was behind Father emerges, and his fingers open to reveal an exquisite agate ring with shades of orange and russet rippling through it. "It reminded me of your hair."

Looking at the jewel and at my immaculately and expensively dressed father, anyone might think he was a patrician from an ancient and preferred family rather than the grandson of a freedman. Then again, he always tells me that the state of his coffers gives his lineage away. *"Remember, my girl, some of the greatest wealth in Rome belongs to those who've had the nerve and industry to earn it."*

"I will come." I take the ring, then kiss his hand. He beams.

"Hurry. We would not be rude and keep her waiting."

Her?

A slender form in a dress of brilliant scarlet stands before the stall, attended by a slave. She has hair so blonde it is nearly white. She leans on the gate, eyes devouring the stallion inside, who tosses his head and paws the ground.

"Lady," father bows, "it is an honor. This is my daughter, Lucia Aemilia Lepida." The woman glances at me, but only for a moment before her eyes return to the horse.

"Diana of the Cornelii." She reaches up to seize the stallion's tossing nose. I notice that her palm is as callused as a groom's although the name of the Cornelii is old and noble. I would be chastised roundly should I allow my hands to become so. "How did a wine merchant come to own a racing stallion?"

"A combination of desperation and bad luck, Lady. I had a debtor who could not pay me other than by relinquishing this brute. He is too high-strung to be of any use to me for business or pleasure. Never advance credit to a chariot faction director, Lady, even if the vast quantity of wine he orders is for his wedding."

She gives a swift nod like a man. "Let's see him move."

The grooms lead the horse up and down in the dusty yard outside. Muscle bunches under his red hide like silk, and Diana of the Cornelii smiles broadly. "I like a chestnut," she says to no one in particular, as she watches the motion of the flashing legs. A lock of hair escapes its combs. The name Diana suits her. She is a huntress, lovely and unkempt. Did she travel all this long way from Rome alone? If so, how did she manage such a thing?

The grooms bring the stallion to a halt, and she bends to run her hands over a foreleg. No ring on her left hand, I notice. I rotate the plain betrothal ring Sabinus placed on my finger, a ring I secretly take off at night. She must be at least a decade older than me. How has she escaped being some man's property, just as this horse may shortly be hers? I envy her freedom.

"He's a bit heavy, but he might anchor a team on the inside." She peels the horse's lips back to examine his teeth. He does his best to bite her, but she merely swats him on the nose. "What are you asking for him, Lucius Aemilius Lepidus?"

My father cannot be beaten at haggling when it comes to his business. He drives a hard price for an amphora of wine, and does it with a smile. But on this occasion, he is bested. I listen in astonishment as the woman in the red dress pushes him to half his asking price. To see a Lady of high birth conducting her own business! It is unbelievable.

"You have the better of me, Lady," Father says ruefully, but he does not look unhappy. Doubtless he is just pleased to have the stallion off his hands and no longer terrifying our grooms.

I would have the better of you, Father. Or if not precisely the better of him, better than I am offered now. My father raised me in his shadow. So much so that Mother chided him many times for treating me like the son he never had. Father hears and even seeks my opinions on everyday things, yet I was not asked for one on the man I will marry. And everything my father has built will pass over me to that man. Sabinus will someday possess the grapes ripening outside and the murals being made splendid again on the villa walls as certainly has he will possess me. The unfairness of that causes my eyes to prick.

"I leave for Rome in three days," the stallion's new mistress says. "May I collect him then?"

"Can I persuade you, gracious Lady, to wait one day more? We are in chaos here as my daughter marries on the very day you name."

"Congratulations." Her eyes rest on me, faintly pitying. But perhaps I only see pity because I feel it for myself. I wish the lady and I were friends, as close perhaps as I am to my friend Julilla, for then I could ask her advice. Not how to be a model Roman wife — I get enough lectures on that from Julilla and Mother — but on how to avoid being Sabinus' wife, good, bad, or indifferent. "I won't interrupt your wedding, Lucia Aemilia Lepida. I'll come for the horse the day after."

"Excellent." Father offers another of his winning smiles. "Lady, will you come in and take some refreshment?"

"Thank you, but I have messages to send to Rome." She gives the stallion's neck a final rub as the grooms lead him back toward his stall. "I should tell the Reds faction director he has his next champion."

"Well then, if you will excuse me, I have tradesmen and petitioners waiting, and artists who need pushing if we would not hold a wedding shrouded by drop cloths." He bows, then shifts his glance to me. "Aemilia, you might check on your mother, but before you do, I believe you have business in the stables." He gives me a knowing smile. As he turns away, Lady Diana looks at me curiously.

"What business do you have here? Do you ride?"

By way of answer, I draw my small crescent moon pendant — the virgin's symbol — from my pouch and hold it up. The wood is rubbed

73

smooth as stone from all the hours I have fingered it without even being aware I did so. How Mother scolded me for that fidget. "I do not ride, Lady. I hide."

She understands at once. "You don't wish to burn it before your wedding."

Perhaps because she is a stranger, and strangely unlike any woman I have ever met, I have the courage to confess the truth. "I do not wish to be a bride so I will not do as a bride should do."

She tugs a silver chain out from the red drape of her gown, and I see a crescent moon like mine but made from silver and worn just as smooth. So she fidgets, too. "I didn't wish to trade this for a red veil, either."

"I would be well content if the only thing red I wear upon my head is my hair. How did you avoid being wed?"

"I knew how to manage my father. He's far too absent-minded to plan dinner, much less my future – and I took full advantage." She smiles. "The law gives our lives to our fathers to manage, but not all fathers take the trouble. My father stays wrapped in his own affairs, so I am free to breed horses and manage myself."

"I know how to distinguish grapes with nearly the same skill as my own father," I say proudly. "But I will never be a wine merchant, and the vineyard that stands outside this villa will one day belong to Gnaeus Helvius Sabinus, not to me. I fear, Lady, that I have not your knack for managing fathers."

"Gnaeus Helvius Sabinus might prove easier to manage than your father. He may be glad of a wife who knows her grapes."

Here is a thought. If I must have Sabinus, perhaps I can hold sway with him. For a moment my hopes rise. But they quickly sink again. If Sabinus looked at me as Faustus does, perhaps. I believe I could get Faustus to do anything for me. But I see no hungry lion in Sabinus. I turn my eyes to the little wooden moon in my hand and stroke it lovingly.

"So you intend to hide it here in the stables?" she says.

"Yes, though I will miss it sorely."

She unloops the chain from her neck and drops her little silver moon into my hand. "Silver doesn't burn. Keep this one."

I look into her eyes, my own dimmed with tears. "Thank you Lady. And perhaps you could keep this for me?" I hold out my little wooden charm. "I know it would be safer with you than hidden in a stall."

"What's safe? I may get kicked in the head by my new horse. Your bridegroom might run off with a tavern maid. Maybe the gods will spare you marriage after all. They did me." She closes her callused fingers around my charm. "But I'll keep it for you. Though Diana herself knows I haven't needed a virgin's symbol for years."

My jaw drops. She laughs and gives a kiss to each of my cheeks. "Until we meet again."

I mean to meet Faustus after dark while the household slumbers. Such an encounter is perilous. Being found with Faustus alone would mean both our ruins. So I must be as careful as possible. I dare not creep out until my nurse is insensible. But she cannot seem to settle into a deep sleep. She moans and groans, tosses and turns, and keeps calling out my name, putting my nerves on edge—so much so that I light a lamp, as if I were a child. At some point, I hear footsteps outside my door, and swear I hear a low voice say my name, once, twice, three times. I know it is Faustus, and the silence that follows tells me he has gone to his rest and there will be no precious time alone. No kisses. No hands exploring the curves of my body through my tunic. I drift to sleep weeping in frustration.

And I have a horrible dream. A dream of being kissed—by Sabinus! Just over Sabinus' shoulder I can see Faustus, his face contorted in revulsion and anger.

I wake shaking and reaching for Lady Diana's moon at my throat because I cannot draw breath. That is when I recognize it is not I, but the room, that shakes. My lamp lies on the floor broken. A rivulet of burning oil runs across the mosaic tiles like a river of fire, causing a good deal of smoke. Frantically I spring from my bed snatching a cover to smother the flames. I hear a ping as the betrothal ring I'd tucked beneath my pillow falls to the floor and rolls. I pay no mind, eager to address the fire, but another tremor sends me sprawling. Again I cannot breathe and clutch my throat. My nurse sits up, her eyes wild, and screams. An instant later a figure dashes into my room—a male figure. He beats at the flames with the coverlet I dropped as I fell, and stamps them too. *Faustus! Not gone to bed. Waiting in the peristyle beyond, hoping against hope that I might still come to him.*

Another man runs into the room. This one with a lamp in hand. It is my father. Here is a catastrophe greater than fire. What will he think to see Faustus here? I must explain, and quickly. But Father holds up his lamp before I can marshal my words, and his face registers surprise. "Sabinus?"

I am struck dumb.

"It is not what you think," my betrothed says quickly. "I was sitting in the garden, looking at the stars when I heard screaming."

"The stars, eh?" The corners of father's eyes crinkle merrily. "Yes, that will do. Fortunate thing we have a wedding in three days."

My father's intimation and the affable way in which he makes it summons heat to my cheeks. I must look away from his amused face, although I know I have done nothing wrong.

Sabinus glances in my direction, registering my mortification. To his credit, he looks equally aghast. And in that moment the warmth I feel shifts from embarrassment to gratitude.

"Lepidus, I am in earnest." Sabinus appeals to my nurse. "You were here with your mistress, you can vouchsafe she was alone."

My poor old slave, doubtless addled to be awakened in such a manner and still terrified, looks between the two men. "I was here. And all the gods help us there was a fire."

"Fire," Sabinus echoes the word. "A river of it no less." Running a hand through his hair, he seems to have forgotten the rest of us. "No, it cannot be." He looks utterly, utterly miserable.

I find my voice. "It is just a broken lamp." I feel an urge to comfort him, perhaps because he defended my honor. "I left it burning when I fell asleep. I am sorry. It was careless of me."

My nurse squats down and begins to gather the broken shards. For an instant, Sabinus stoops beside her, then rising he says, "Why will no one listen?" His voice is distraught. "Why will no one see? Well, not *no one*, but no one in a position to do anything useful."

"Sabinus, my friend" — Father lays a hand on my betrothed's shoulder — "next time we drink, I mean to send you home a few cups short of what we had tonight. You are not a funny drunk."

Sabinus draws himself up, squaring his shoulders. "Lepidus, I am not drunk and there is nothing humorous in this situation. You think I would defile your daughter — "

Father holds up a hand. "Pish! Enough. I believe you — "

" — and worse still you think I am out of my wits for obsessing over the increasing tremors."

Father looks sheepish.

"Please, Lepidus, I am begging you. Take your wife, your daughter, your servants and slaves and leave Pompeii. Do it tomorrow. If you will not do it because you believe me, then do it because you care for me and want to give me peace." Sabinus takes the lamp from father's hand, and holds it close to his own face. "Look at me, Lepidus." With his face heavily shadowed, the poor man looks like a specter. "Look at the circles beneath my eyes. I can no longer sleep."

Father's eyes reflect genuine concern. And something more — love. Yes, that is it, for I have seen the same in his eyes when he looks at me. He truly loves his friend. "Sabinus, you are not well. It is the stress. The lost election, the coming wedding, this constant shaking of the earth, all combine to prey upon you. You will stay here tonight as my guest. You will have a bath, I will mix a draught for you and then, as if you were Aemilia awakened from childish sleep by a nightmare, I will sit beside you until you slumber."

Sabinus' shoulders fall.

My father sighs. "And as soon as the wedding is over, I swear to you we will all of us go to Nuceria to pay a visit to my brother and his family. The next day if you like."

Sabinus nods. "Just four days," he whispers. "Surely the gods will grant us so long."

As Sabinus lets Father lead him from my room, I realize the whisper—Sabinus' lowered voice—is the same that said my name. Sabinus not Faustus was in the *peristyle* outside my door. Why?

IN the morning, I cannot find my betrothal ring. Ordering my nurse to search every corner of my chamber and then search it again, I go to looking for Sabinus to ask him why he was outside my door.

The slaves seem surprised that I seek him, and their shocked looks make me uncomfortable. If I have made my distaste for Sabinus obvious, then I have embarrassed him. Whatever I think of him as a prospective husband, he does not deserve that. Nor do my parents deserve the gossip that might arise from my exhibition of such a lack of breeding. Thank heavens I thought to hide my ringless left hand as I made my inquiries. Making up my mind to be kinder to Father, I stop in the kitchen for figs before going to his *tablinum* as I do every few days to check his accounts and spare his eyes the strain. He has circles under those weak eyes where he sits at his desk, surrounded by dozens of untidy tablets and scrolls.

"Herculaneum figs!" he says, accepting my offering with a smile. "Perhaps our Pompeii figs are more renowned, but I still say these are sweeter." He seems equally pleased when I ask about Sabinus. "He and I were awake for many hours after we left you, but that did not stop him from departing early to inspect the latest sections of lead pipes laid in that water project that is his concern. Nor have I been neglectful of my duties. I made the rounds this morning, telling all the workmen that what cannot be completed by the waning of the light will have to wait until after your wedding. The scaffolding must come down. The slaves must have a day to scrub and decorate the villa, just as your mother tells me she must have a day to scrub and decorate you." He pops a fig into his mouth then licks his fingers.

"Will the workmen go?" The distress in my voice is obvious.

Father looks at me oddly.

"I mean … if they are returning to complete the work, it makes no sense to send them away." I pray I have covered my unthinking comment, that Father will not be left wondering why I should care if a collection of craftsmen depart.

"Ah, my Aemilia, always so shrewd! You are right to be concerned about releasing them." An approving nod as another fig disappears. "Gods know, I had a hard time securing the best of them to begin with. I have given them money to drink to your health and told them not to get so drunk that they cannot resume their work two days after your nuptials."

"We both know which instruction they will most likely follow, and which they will ignore," I say.

Father laughs. "Are you recovered from your scare last evening?" His face takes on a look of pride. "But then you did not seem scared, even with your nurse wailing and Sabinus despairing. Poor man …"

But, whatever pity I felt for Sabinus last evening and whatever resolutions I formed this morning not to disdain him publicly, I am uninterested in him at this moment. Faustus will be leaving as night falls. When he returns, I will no longer live here.

"It will take more than a little fire to scare me." I tilt my chin up. "I am fire's daughter, isn't that what you always tell me?"

"Fire's and mine." He holds out a hand to me and when I give him my right—being careful to keep my left behind me—he squeezes it. "I am proud of you. No man has a daughter like mine. As I love you, I tell you that no woman will have a husband like yours."

I turn my face away.

"I know," again he squeezes, "I know you cannot understand my choice right now. But you must trust that seven-and-thirty knows more of life than fifteen does. Must trust that, as I have always made certain that your mother and you have the best of everything, I have chosen as I have to secure a future for you that will see you well treated all the days of your life."

I think of Lady Diana with her confident swagger. I can feel her silver charm lying cool against my breast as I take a deep breath and turn to meet my father's eyes. "Father, I trust you, but can you not also trust me? Sabinus is a fine man, but I have a better one already. I have you. Can I not remain unmarried?" *This is not the time to bring up an alternate groom.* "Who will check your figures if I go?"

Father's eyes are warm. He brings my hand up and presses it to his lips. "So that is what this is about. It is natural for a girl to be apprehensive about leaving her home. The crying and struggling a bride must do by tradition when her husband takes her away have roots in feelings that are, in the best cases, noble and true. Know this, Aemilia: you will always, always have me. Sabinus' house is not far inside the Herculaneum Gate. You will be here nearly every day, or Mother and I will be with you." He gives me a teasing smile. "Unless you and Sabinus do not intend to invite us to dine."

"But—"

"No more, Aemilia." Father shakes his head. "I am too tired." Releasing my hand, he stands. "I am going to walk among my vines. Will you come?"

Ordinarily, it is an activity I love—strolling with my father in the brilliant autumn sun—but I shake my head no. Watching him go, I think, *Oh, Lady Diana, I certainly do not have your knack for managing fathers.* I feel a tear tracking down my cheek and wipe it away fiercely. No doubt I will cry when I see Faustus, but I would not spoil the beauty he praises by going in search of him with a red nose and puffy eyes.

He is sitting on the black and white tiles of the *triclinium* floor, carefully laying out his brushes on the cloth in which he will roll them. I am about to speak but he shakes his head to warn me. Two slaves are taking down the last of the scaffolding.

"You do not work today?" The thought that he is leaving earlier than he must stings.

"I am at a good stopping point, Lady." He says the last word rather more loudly than the rest, to make certain the slaves hear it. "And I would not start a figure I cannot finish properly. Half-restored is worse than not restored at all."

More slaves arrive and begin loading their arms with the dismantled scaffolding. "Where do you store those?" he asks.

"We have been instructed to put them in one of the outbuildings."

"Make sure they do not get damp," Faustus admonishes. "I do not wish my delicate work made more difficult by being forced to stand on warped boards."

As the last of the ladened slaves disappears, Faustus rises and, tucking his roll of brushes beneath one arm, makes the complaint: "I thought to see you last evening."

"I wanted to come."

"A slave girl told me Gnaeus Helvius Sabinus was found in your room last night."

"What slave girl?"

"Oh, I don't know her name." He gestures dismissively, but colors.

"Sabinus was a guest here last evening and came to help my father put out a fire in my chamber." It is not the precise truth, but that would be too complicated to explain. Besides I am vexed at his accusation and at the idea that gossip about me makes the rounds of the slaves' quarters.

He moves close and puts a hand on my waist—making me uncomfortable, for anyone walking in might see. "I was insanely jealous when I heard the rumor." His eyes burn and the hand tightens. "Come, come with me for a moment. I know a place."

"I cannot be seen walking through the villa with—"

"With what? A lowly painter? Is that how you think of me?"

"No! Without a chaperone and in the company of any man so wholly unrelated to me. I must think of my reputation."

"More than you think of me." He scowls. "I was desperate to see you last night. I could not sleep. Will you meet me? It is our last chance."

"Where?"

"Your father's little cellar."

"It is locked."

"There is a key in the niche beside the small oven in the kitchen. It is hidden beneath an amphora. You could get it."

How does he know this? He leans forward stealing a quick kiss, and my curiosity fades as my heart begins to race. "All right."

My feet have wings. By the time I reach the stairs in the small garden, I am out of breath, as if I have run much further. Opening the door, I duck inside and light a lamp in an arched niche on the wall. Wines are my father's passion and these are the best he holds. The space is more crowded than when I saw it last, doubtless because the wine for my wedding waits here. I notice something on the ground, a band of cloth such as one of the kitchen girls might wear around her head. Perhaps it was lost when someone was sent for wine — though it seems an odd task for a female slave. The door behind me eases open and someone slips in. I know it is Faustus even before I feel him pressing against me, feel his mouth where my neck meets my shoulder. His hand slips around and takes hold of my breast through my tunic.

I lean back against him, momentarily overwhelmed by the sensation.

He whispers in my ear, "Did you let Sabinus touch you like this last night?"

I jerk away and turn to face him. "I told you, he merely came to my rescue. Nothing else."

"I can't help it. I am so jealous. I long to be your husband, but he will have you. In two short days, you will be in his arms."

"Do not speak of it." My dream of the night before comes back to me.

Faustus pulls me into an embrace and kisses me. As our lips part he whispers, "He will have you, but let me have you first. I know a way—"

"We can't."

"He won't know, your husband. No one will. There are places I can enter—"

For the second time I pull free of him. "I am not a whore, Publius Crustius Faustus!"

"But you say you love me. And I love you. I burn for you. I am in agony. If you love me, you will offer some relief." His voice is pleading, his eyes too. "This is the last time we may meet in private before you are wed. I will not be in the house tonight. Like the rest of the workers, I will lodge in the city." He takes a step forward. I do not retreat and he kisses my throat. When his lips move up to mine, I kiss him back. I think, or rather hope, he has forgotten his ugly suggestion, then he murmurs, "I will be gentle. I will not hurt you."

Another man who is not listening to me! I shove him with both hands—hard. "Get out!"

A beseeching look. It wrings my heart. I am on the verge of repenting my harsh order to go. Then he shrugs. The nonchalance of the gesture makes my anger return and stills my tongue. Another moment of silence and he is gone. I need to compose myself. Moving toward the niche to extinguish the lamp, my steps unsteady, I remember that I have a hair comb in my pouch. I will hide it while I am here. As I reach out to place it between two large *amphorae*, my fingers trembling, my eyes catch a bit of writing on the wall, low and almost hidden. It is a strange place for words to be painted. Lifting the lamp I lower it until I can read clearly:

Here I have penetrated a girl's open buttocks; but it was vulgar of me to write these verses.

Suddenly the scrap of cloth on the ground makes sense, as does Faustus' knowing where the key to this place was kept. My cheeks burn. What he would have done to me had I let him, Faustus did to a slave girl on this very spot! Bile rises in my throat. I feel sick. How could I have allowed myself to believe he loved me? And if he does love me, how could he bear to shame me so? I blow out the lamps as quickly as I can so that I will not have to see the words—they are his strokes, in the very paint he uses to restore my father's frescos— content to feel my way back to the door, though I stub my toes and scrape an ankle in the dark. Better such little injuries that the greater one the horrible words inflict.

I climb the few steps to the garden and find myself face to face with Sabinus. He blanches at the sight of me. Oh gods, has he been here long enough to see Faustus emerge? If Sabinus tells my father, and they go below will they think the graffiti Faustus left refers to *me*? If they do I will be disgraced in the most horrible manner. *Would all of my Father's love save me from a beating, from being turned out, or even worse if he believed I permitted Faustus the use of my body?*

"Aemilia Lepida, I came to see how you are." Sabinus' tongue trips over the words, reinforcing my sense he saw Faustus.

Exposed, frightened, embarrassed. But I must say none of these. "I am fine, Sabinus," I manage to get the words out. I take a deep breath. "Thank you for asking. And thank you for coming to my aid yesterday." I ply him with civility, hoping to assuage him if he has the power to compromise me.

He smiles. I cannot remember the last time I saw him smile. "I will always come to your aid. Such is my duty and my pleasure. I will protect you from harm as best I can. You have my word." He says the last very solemnly.

Relief floods me. He will not tell Father. Whatever he saw. Whatever he thinks. I am so thankful, so very thankful, that I offer my hand. He hesitates, then takes it in his own quite gently. He fumbles in his pouch.

"I believe you lost this last evening."

My betrothal ring! Sabinus spares me not only possible ruin, but this embarrassment as well. For if its absence were not noticed before, it should certainly be remarked upon at our wedding and even my considerable imagination might not be up to the task of devising an explanation for its loss.

"I do not like to see you without it, Aemilia Lepida." He slips it back onto my hand.

"I believe, Sabinus, you should call me Aemilia. I will be your wife in two days." It is the first time I have acknowledged as much out loud in front of him. The eagerness my pronouncement sparks in his eyes reminds me of a very young child being praised by its mother. In that brief, unguarded moment he seems a good deal younger than my father, and a good deal less the always-in-control man with a penchant for mechanical things. "Do you think you can manage that?" I ask, teasingly.

"Yes, Aemilia, I believe that I can."

SABINUS

SEEING his ring on the ground among the oil and broken pottery on her chamber floor the previous night had twisted his heart. Seeing the handsome painter emerge from the cellar just before his Aemilia moments ago had nearly broken it. Sabinus would confront the boy and warn him off.

But halfway to the servants' quarters, he reconsidered. Such a confrontation would be undignified. It might start gossip. More than this, Sabinus recalled what Capella had said—Aemilia was a wellborn girl and well raised. If she was infatuated, it surely went no further … and if it went further, what good could come of dwelling on that or shaming her? He was not willing to lose his friendship of many years with Lepidus. Nor did he desire to call off his wedding.

Gods be damned! Capella was right, he *was* a starry-eyed fool. His heart did belong to a fifteen-year-old girl with a lithe figure and red hair that curled about her pale forehead when the weather was humid. He'd had a hard time letting go of her hand when they parted in the small garden. And to own the truth—at least to himself—he'd had absolutely no interest in the stars when he'd gone to sit in that same garden last evening. He had just wanted to be near her. He pulled the small doll in blue silk from his pouch. Sabinus had found it last night as he'd sat on the ground, head on his knees, against a myrtle—hoping its scent would soothe him.

Just three days, he told himself, gazing down at the toy. In two, Aemilia would be his wife, and in three, they would be trundling toward Nuceria, safe. Safe from both the temptation of the boy artist and the massive quake that he felt in his bones was imminent. Let Pansa and the other officials deal with what came to Pompeii. He had made up his mind: he, his bride, the whole of her family, and his grandmother would avail themselves of the hospitality of Lepidus' younger brother until word of the new quake arrived. Doubtless everyone from Pansa to Admiral Pliny would be sorry they hadn't listened to him. But he would be sorry, too. So sorry. *Will you be sorry you left them*, he wondered. So many died in Nero's quake. How many might die in Pompeii if he was right about another quake, this one cataclysmic?

Sabinus tucked the doll away. Pondering the death of many reminded him of his own mortality. There was something he wished to tell Lepidus, something he had meant to tell him last night.

Sabinus found his friend in the *torcularium*, admiring the windlass mechanism on his new press. "Ah, Sabinus, though you are not the most discerning wine drinker, the lover of machines in you must admire the efficiency of this." Lepidus slapped his friend on the back, and Sabinus found himself grinning despite his general melancholia.

"Stand aside, old man, and let me have a look." The jest was not new — Sabinus had begun to rib his friend the moment the betrothal ring had slipped onto Aemilia's finger — but Lepidus still enjoyed it.

"I will demand more respect from you when you are my son."

"It is a strange thing," Sabinus replied, "but you will be both my father and — until your daughter and I have one of our own — my son of sorts."

Lepidus' brows rose. "Here's a riddle."

"Not at all. I have been meaning to tell you this for weeks, but have been distracted" — he didn't need to say by what, not to poor, longsuffering Lepidus — "in preparation for my wedding, I have made a testament. Should I die, I have left my grandmother enough to make certain of her comfort and have bequeathed the balance of my property to you."

Lepidus rocked back on his heels and regarded Sabinus disbelievingly. "If I did not know you better, I would think this another jest. Come, man, look around you. I would not boast and draw the wrath of the gods, but I do not need your money."

"If I die, I still wish to do my duty by your daughter. I wish to provide for her. Besides, who else should I leave my things to? Thanks to Nero's quake and a certain regrettable run of bad luck in my family line, I am *paterfamilias* — and a *paterfamilias*, sadly, without an heir. You are my oldest friend."

"One more poke at my age, Sabinus, I warn you!" Lepidus feigned a glower. Then his face softened. "I am touched. We will drink to it —"

At that moment one of Sabinus' slaves entered. "Master," he said apologetically, "a deputation of shepherds arrived at the house, come all the way from the slopes outside Herculaneum looking for you."

"For me?"

"Well, for the man who talks to everyone of the increasing tremors."

"Ah, Sabinus, it seems you have made a name for yourself with your madness." Lepidus smiled indulgently.

"They were most insistent, so I brought them here," the slave continued.

"Your petitioners, my atrium. A fitting union considering we are on the cusp of being family. Come, Sabinus, aren't you curious?"

Sabinus was curious, but as they made their way to the atrium, a different sensation overwhelmed him — dread. Shepherds were not men of leisure. If they had left their flocks in the care of others to journey so far in search of a man whose name they did not know, if they had shown the necessary tenacity upon arriving in Pompeii to track him down, there could be nothing good in it.

There were three, tanned and wizened, perhaps with age, perhaps with weather. The man in the center spoke. "Are you the one? The man who collects information on the aquifers and the wells at the farms and vineyards? The man who tries to convince others that the recent shaking of the earth presages something ill?"

"I am. Gnaeus Helvius Sabinus, at your service."

87

Quite unaccountably to Sabinus' mind, the man bowed, and as he straightened Sabinus saw it. Around his neck, the shepherd wore a symbol Sabinus wouldn't have recognized save for seeing it on Capella. It was exactly like the charm she wore at her ankle. Like her, this man must be a follower of Isis. "The ground where we graze our flocks lives." The shepherd said it simply, as if it were an ordinary thing. "It growls like an animal and sometimes claps like thunder when the sky is clear. It coughs up wisps of smoke."

Smoke. It put Sabinus in mind of last night, of the smoke in Aemilia's room, of how she clutched her neck. How the acrid vapors made it difficult for him to breathe as he began to beat out the flames. *Fire, Capella, fire. But what is the dark river and what the sea? When will they come?*

Nonsense, Sabinus thought. *Get hold of yourself, man.*

"Why come to me?"

"Who else will listen? We tried others first: men in Herculaneum, patricians who own villas, overseers of farms between there and here. They would not heed us. And somewhere along our journey we began to hear of a man who, like us, begged others to attend to such observations."

"If you heard that, you must also have heard that no one pays me any more mind than they have paid you."

The shepherd looked pained. Clearly, Sabinus thought, he has heard other people ridicule me, but he does not wish to offend. He felt a flash of irritation, but it would be wrong to take out his frustration on this tired, well-meaning delegation. "I will put what you have told me in my notes. Your observations will be part of the record I am keeping."

This appeared to satisfy, for all three men nodded as if he had made some sage pronouncement and, after pressing his hand, they left.

Sabinus himself was not satisfied. He longed not merely to record but to understand the phenomenon the shepherds reported. But their disturbing observations of Vesuvius were incomprehensible. *Fool*, he thought, *if only you were a brighter man.* He wondered what other heretofore unknown occurrences such events might portend. Was the mountain somehow the source for all that was currently unnatural in nature?

Sabinus looked at Lepidus. "Why not tomorrow?" he asked.

"Because I've spent a fortune on this wedding and because I had thought you eager to be a groom. Are you sure this is about earthquakes and not nerves?"

"I will marry Aemilia today."

"And what about the wedding guests? I am known for the liberality of my hospitality. What will be thought of me if I uninvite everyone? Or do you propose we sneak off under cover of dark and allow the guests to find this place empty and shuttered when they arrive two evenings from now?"

Sabinus had not thought about the guests, dozens of them, from all the most important families in the city. And that realization sobered him. *Truly, this has become a mania with me. I must master myself and my thoughts before I am made an irredeemable fool.*

AEMILIA

"WAKE up, sleepyhead! When you are a married woman you will not be able to lie in so late, I assure you." My friend Julilla laughs lightly as she pulls the covers from me. She is hugely swollen with child and seems to think this fact makes her even more of an expert on a wife's role. I am about to say something to that purpose but realize that Mother, who stands just behind my friend, is unlikely to appreciate such a comment. She urges me to mimic my friend's behavior nearly as often as she encourages me to emulate former Empress Livia, deified and held up to Roman girls everywhere as the personification of ideal womanhood.

A whole day to make me ready—Father warned me yesterday. I normally love beauty rituals, but today they will remind me of tomorrow's inevitable wedding. And for the first time a slave's tweezers will pluck the hair from more than my eyebrows. They will remove the hair that has guarded the entrance to my virginity since I became a woman. Thanks to a private conversation with Julilla, I have an idea this process will prove painful. I wince at the thought.

It turns out the pain I anticipated was nothing compared to the exquisite agony of the actual experience—possibly the first time my fertile imagination has proved insufficient. How grateful I am for the plunge into the cold pool! As we move to the *tepidarium*, I find myself walking very carefully.

"You think you are sore down there now," Julilla says with a knowing look. "After tomorrow night when Sabinus claims you ..."

I expect Mother to shush her. Never mind the graffiti I've read over the years on Pompeii's walls, or the gossip of slaves I've overheard, Mother generally permits no discussion of acts of intimacy in my presence. But this time, as the slaves begin to oil and scrape me, Mother gives Julilla a look of encouragement.

"You know how blessed I feel to be expecting, Aemilia, but if you choose not to undertake motherhood too early there are things you can do to defer it." Julilla strokes an absent hand over her belly. I know full well how important the babe inside is to my friend. She lost her first, miscarried dead, and was devastated.

Mother nods. I feel uncomfortable. Not so much because of the allusion to that which must precede motherhood—over the past weeks as my attraction to Faustus awakened my body, I have found myself eager to explore such acts—but because I do not wish to think of Sabinus in that way. Do not want to imagine him naked. Do not wish to wonder, as I find myself doing, if he looks like the phallic door knockers, symbols of prosperity, scattered liberally throughout Pompeii.

"You can buy little packets of elephant dung imported from the east in the marketplace, if you know the right stalls." Julilla bites her lip. "You place such a pessary inside yourself before your husband comes to you."

"Or," Mother chimes in, "many women have excellent luck by squatting and sneezing after their husbands are finished."

"And a man does not have to ..." Julilla glances at Mother, her face coloring. "There are other places he can put himself."

One of the slaves working on me titters. I do not know where to look. All I can think of is the graffiti in my father's cellar — of Faustus putting his organ into the slave girl from behind, and worse still of his suggesting such a thing to me! Thank the gods I cannot imagine Sabinus proposing such an act. He is far too reserved. A serious man. I find myself glad of that.

"But remember," Mother says, "though you may permit such things, you must show disgust in them. You are a wealthy, well brought up girl — not some whore willing to take a man into her mouth for the price of a bit of bread. So struggle and make every appearance of being repulsed."

It will not be an appearance.

"And," Julilla adds, "make him buy you something pretty afterward."

"I certainly will," I say. "Even forgetting his own fortune, given my dowry, Sabinus can well afford to buy me many, many pretty things." The thought of a new gown or piece of jewelry distracts me nicely from the uncomfortable feelings that Julilla's and Mother's earlier words conjured.

"I would be worried your husband will spoil you," Mother says, "but it is too late for that. Your father already has. What do you think — now that you are done being scraped you shall bathe in asses' milk just as Empress Poppaea did." She gestures to a nearby tub.

Asses' milk! It is an exquisitely expensive treatment for the skin. I clasp my mother's hand in delight.

She pats my shoulder. "Don't thank me. Thank your father. He insisted. And he ordered enough for me to have a soak as well. Doubtless he is trying to appease me. Exasperating man! As if weeks of wedding preparations have not left me worn out, yesterday he told me we go to your uncle's the morning after your ceremony."

"What?" Julilla gives Mother a sympathetic look.

"Yes." She helps me step into the tub. "When I asked him why, he said it was just his whim. Well, he may well have a whim but it is I who must supervise the packing—this afternoon when I could be better doing other things. I warned him it will be his fault if I arrive in Nuceria and collapse."

I know Sabinus is to blame for these sudden plans, not Father. But I slide down into the milk until it is up to my chin without coming to Father's defense. Sabinus guards my honor; the least I can do in return is not draw Mother's ire upon him.

"Thank heavens my husband is not capricious. I could hardly travel now should such a whim strike him."

"I have precious little cause to justly complain about Lepidus, but when he gets an idea in his head," Mother shakes her own head, "he will not let go of it."

This is a trait he appears to share with Sabinus, I think, reflecting on my betrothed's current obsession with earthquakes and his insistence we leave the city.

"That, daughter, is where you get your stubbornness," Mother continues. "And more's the pity, for what is merely vexatious in a man is entirely inappropriate in a woman." She smiles in spite of herself, and I use my toes to splash milk upon both her and Julilla.

"My father is much the same way, and my mother grateful I take after her." Julilla reaches a hand into my bath and splashes me back.

AT bedtime, Father comes to tuck me in. He has not done so since I was a little girl. He pulls the covers up to my chin, and generally fusses. My nurse is much the same, hovering about as Father takes a seat.

"When you wake, it will be your wedding day."

I do not need the reminder. I feel hollow, as if something is ending and nothing will ever be right again.

"Is there anything you wish me to take away with me?" He tugs my ear—the gesture another vestige of my childhood.

I shake my head.

"What will your mother say when you have nothing to burn at the altar?"

"Oh, I've kept a few things. That ghastly wooden snake bangle my aunt gave me for Saturnalia one year. A set of combs I never liked ..."

"Clever girl!" When father says this, it is a compliment as it is not from so many others. "Your mother will know of course. Don't look so skeptical, Aemilia. She is clever, too. You do not give her enough credit. She has only learned to wrap her requests in soft looks. Her cleverness is stealthy where yours is brazen. You will learn to shade the lamp—we all do as we age."

I wonder if he means all, *or* all women?

"In the meantime, be glad that Sabinus knows you so well. He will not expect reticence and obedience." Father laughs and pulls my ear again. "Though he is entitled to both. Try and remember that, Aemilia." Rising to go, he leans down to kiss my forehead.

I don't know if he notices the tears welling in my eyes, but my nurse certainly does. "I can remember when you were so small that this bed seemed to swallow you up," she says when we are alone. "Shall I sing you to sleep as I did then?"

"You did not sleep well last night," I remark, trying to distract her from my distress by bringing up her own.

"It's Nuceria." She wrings her hands. "I do not like to go. But your dear mother says I must."

"There is much to see there, for it is larger than Pompeii. Just think of all the things we will discover in the market."

"Pompeii is just the right size, Lady." She shakes her head, dismissively. "What we do not have in our market is not worth seeing."

"Well then, you can rest in the sun while I go shopping. My uncle's farm is large, his house bright, and my aunt, despite her appalling taste in snake bangles, is very sweet."

This only seems to increase her agitation. "I have never been to a farm, and I hope I am not so old that I need to rest in the middle of the day."

She *is* old, very. Now that I think of it, I am not sure how old. She came to my father with the villa because its former owner thought her too aged to be worth taking where he went next. And that was before I was born. "When was the last time you left Pompeii?" I ask.

"I have never left it. Not really. I was born within its walls and I traveled quite far enough when I came to live here, outside the gates."

The cause of her restlessness last night and her current anxiety becomes clear. I do not like to go against Mother, but the nurse is my slave, not hers. Father told me that she was part of what I might take away with me when I married. "If you will only calm down, you need not go any further, ever." I reach out and stroke her withered arm, soothingly. "I will make arrangements for you to go instead to my new home—within the city proper. Now sing me to sleep. We could both use a good night's rest. Tomorrow is a big day."

I wake in the middle of the night thinking of two men—the one who behaved honorably yesterday and the one who did not. Admittedly, the longer I stare into the dark the more I think of the latter. What Faustus demanded was insulting and wrong, but his request was driven by his mad love for me. Have I not wanted things that were wrong in the grips of the same love? Of course I have. I have sneaked from this chamber to taste his kisses. And I have dreamed of more than kisses. Faustus is a man, and thus more subject to the urges of the flesh and more accustomed to having them satisfied. My cheeks burn at the thought of him taking the slave girl, yet might he not have done so to help him resist his urges to dishonor me? Roman men have sex with slaves, though ordinarily their own slaves, as is their right. That cannot mean none of them love their wives. Oh, if I could see Faustus again. He would surely apologize for his intemperate behavior, but I would as well. Not for refusing him sex but for being so abrupt and sending him away in such anger. I do not wish to become a wife with this bitterness between us. I wish to part from Faustus with kisses and soft words so that I can cling to those in the dark of the night when I must lie in another bed.

SABINUS

THE shaking of the bed awakened him. Sabinus lay, waiting for it to stop, fearful that if he tried to rise he would only stumble into something. But it did not stop—it got stronger. Sabinus' teeth chattered in his head as if he were freezing. His bed scuttled sideways despite his weight. He could hear things falling across the house. A slave in the next room cursed. And then he heard something more—a grating, grinding noise, and a series of larger crashes. At the corner of the shuttered window nearest the bed, a crack appeared, proceeding down the wall until it met the floor. He watched in fascination as it opened until he could see into his garden. Then, and only then, did the earth stand still and the screaming begin. Not just his slaves, and some of them were certainly screaming, but individuals in the house next door and in the street. Scrambling to his feet, Sabinus snatched up his fine tunic and pulled it on. Too impatient to bother with all the folding that putting on his wedding toga would require, he merely grabbed his belt and pouch, taking a moment to pluck Aemilia's doll from his bed and stuff it in inside. Without quite knowing why, he also added the keys meant for his bride on their wedding day. He was fastening his sandals when he looked up to find his grandmother on the threshold in her night things.

"My boy, the tiles on the roof above my chamber have gone clattering down onto the street, and one of the columns in the atrium leans oddly."

"Get dressed."

She nodded. He'd always been told he got his calm, measured nature from his grandmother and here, he thought as he watched her turn and glide away, was the proof.

Sabinus charged out into the street. The couple who kept the nearby bakery were outside already—he running frantically up and down and she screaming—for their bakery was on fire. Sabinus could hear horses in the stables across the street whinnying in terror.

Perhaps at the smell of smoke, but he rather thought it was because part of the stable roof had collapsed and some number of animals were trapped beneath. He hoped his own was not among them. He planned to be on it, the sooner the better. Heading past the outdoor shrine, Sabinus stooped to help an elderly man lying beside it. The poor man had struck his head in falling and was bleeding. He grasped the front of Sabinus' tunic leaving two dirty marks.

Never mind, Sabinus thought, looking at the mix of blood and grime as he handed the man off to the surgeon who lived a few houses away. His wedding tunic was spoiled but there would be no wedding today. Whatever he had promised Lepidus, or whatever he had to promise, Sabinus would see them all on the road within the hour. He and Aemilia could be married in Nuceria. Doubtless his betrothed would be delighted by the postponement—and he wouldn't care if she was, as long as she was safe. So long as Lepidus and all his family were safe.

Inside the stables, the damage was considerable. Grooms struggled to lift a fallen timber from an injured beast, its eyes wide in pain and fear. No one paid any attention to Sabinus. Thank Equestrian Neptune, his horse was unharmed. Still, the animal was wild, kicking and snorting—sensing the fear of his brethren. Sabinus lowered his voice and spoke soft nothings, biting back his impatience. To show anything but calm to the horse would only make matters worse. At last he was able to get a bridle over the animal's head and a saddle onto his back. This moment of triumph was short-lived. As Sabinus led the animal across the street, he realized he could hardly put his grandmother on horseback with him. Once they arrived at the Lepidus villa, there would be wagons and mules, but to get there would require her litter. The slaves needed to carry it were, if anything, more skittish than his horse. Additional calm talk was required. Nor could he show impatience with his grandmother. Disrespect would not see them out the Herculaneum Gate any more quickly.

By the time they reached the gate, it was clear they were not the only inhabitants for whom the last tremor was the final straw. A collection of people—families on foot, merchants in wagons, men he recognized from the forum, and the retinues that surrounded them—moved through the gate's three channels in a steady stream and onto the two roads branching off beyond.

"Gnaeus Helvius Sabinus!" an acquaintance hailed him. "I fear we will not be at your wedding. That last bit of shaking took down the wall I had buttressed only last week. We are headed to Herculaneum to wait out the repairs with my wife's brother. We will call upon you when we return."

A short time later, Sabinus recognized another figure, one he had hoped never to see again. The artist Publius Crustius Faustus was on foot, his sandy hair tousled as if he had just rolled out of whatever bed he'd slept in last night. *Was he also headed to the villa to make certain Aemilia was all right?* The proprietary nature of such an action nearly made Sabinus reconsider his decision not to speak to the boy. But whereas a warning yesterday might have occasioned undesirable notice, confronting the youth today would slow Sabinus' journey. So he merely urged the slaves to move more quickly and Faustus was soon passed.

The quarter mile to the villa had never, Sabinus was sure, taken longer to travel. More than once he found himself cursing under his breath and speculating that the eight slaves he'd rounded up must have been the slowest among those he owned. Looking back at the city, he was surprised how normal it appeared. Only a few plumes of smoke—rising from his *regio*—suggested anything at all had happened this morning. As they at last drew near Amelia's family home, Sabinus was happy to see it looked entirely ordinary as well.

Lepidus came out to greet them, his eyes full of curiosity. But, to his credit, he held his tongue until Sabinus' grandmother had alighted and been shown inside. "A bit early for a social call."

"Surely you felt that last tremor."

"Yes, as I did the ones before it."

Sabinus raised his eyebrows.

"All right, it was different. More sustained. What of it?"

"The wall of my bedroom cracked open, Lepidus. I lost a column in my atrium."

"Take my daughter home to a different bedroom this evening and have the damage seen to while we are all in Nuceria." As he finished speaking, Aemilia herself padded out, barefoot, hair undone.

"Father, there is a large fissure in the pavement of the veranda and Mother's statue of Livia has gone over. I fear the Empress has lost some fingers." Then, as if noticing him for the first time, "Sabinus?"

"It is worse in the city. Buildings on fire, roofs fallen in." Sabinus was exaggerating of course, though not lying, he told himself—the stable roof had definitely fallen. "It is time to go, Lepidus." Sabinus had promised himself he would not be wounded by Aemilia's look of relief, but it hurt nonetheless.

"I will dress and pack," she said. Sabinus was glad for her abrupt retreat when, a moment later, Faustus appeared.

"Boy," Lepidus said, "have you forgotten there is no work here today?"

"*Dominus*, the inn where I lodged shook something horrible and a bit of the roof fell onto my bed—"

Bless the boy, Sabinus thought. *I hate the very sight of him but his testimony helps me.*

"—The innkeeper turned all of us on the second floor out, and I have not sufficient money to pay for a place on the first. I thought perhaps ..."

"You may return to my servant's quarters."

Sabinus barely waited for the youth to disappear. "You see, Lepidus. This earthquake did significant damage, but nothing compared to what the next will do. I've read the accounts of Nero's quake. You know that I have. Every one of them. Then as now, smaller tremors provided warning—warning unheeded—growing closer and stronger."

"Surely we can wait until tomorrow."

"Things are crowded at the Herculaneum Gate already." Another half-truth. "By tomorrow the roads will be overrun and travel will be more unpleasant than if we go now. My grandmother is frail; I do not wish her to endure more hardship than necessary."

"Your grandmother is as hale as I am, Sabinus. But the fact you are willing to lie about that ..." Lepidus shook his head. "If your concern is such that it begins to make you less fastidious about truth then I know you to be, it is an unkindness to make you suffer longer. We will go."

"Now?"

"As soon as furnishings can be packed."

Furnishings. Sabinus plowed on. "I remember the first time you told me the story of your escape from the great fire in Rome, Lepidus. You told me that, knowing that nothing you owned was as important as the life of your wife and your unborn child, you could not be bothered to clear your household. This is another moment for such action. Whatever you have here — leave it."

"For looters?"

"For looters, for the ground to swallow up, or, if I am proved a nervous fool, for you to come back to. In the latter case, you can have a good laugh at my expense." Clasping his friend's arm, Sabinus looked directly into his eyes. "You are a man blessed, Lepidus. Not by your great wealth, but by the finest of wives and the most exceptional of daughters. Take them from this place before death comes to claim them."

Lepidus pulled him into an embrace. Stopping a slave passing beneath the portico, he said, "Spread the word, we leave as quickly as mules can be put in traces and horses saddled."

AEMILIA

I gaze at myself in the mirror with unutterable satisfaction, waving away the slave who comes forward to do my hair. "Pack," I tell her. No parting with a spear for nuptial good luck, no elaborate coiffure, no wedding! In the corner the slave joins my nurse in pulling things from my cupboard as I swiftly plait my hair into a single, simple braid. For a second time, Sabinus enters my bedchamber. He stops for a moment, staring down at the portion of my floor where three nights ago he beat out the flames from my lamp. A strange look crosses his face.

"It is time to go, Aemilia."

"I am not ready and my packing has just begun."

"Come." He says it with a tone of command and holds out a hand.

I can hear my father as he sat with me last night, reminding me that I owe Sabinus obedience. But not yet. "I have told you I am not ready."

In two strides he reaches me. In a single swift and unexpected motion he picks me up. I struggle slightly, more surprised than anything by his presumption. And in reaction to my struggling, Sabinus throws me unceremoniously over his shoulder. "You were born in fire, Aemilia, but by all the gods I will not let you die in it." The words come out half spoken, half growled. The last thing I see as he carries me off is the shocked faces of the serving women with their hands full of my clothing. "Leave it," Sabinus instructs them. "Get outside."

"Put me down," I demand.

"No. Not until I put you in a wagon." And tromping outside, he does just that—heedless of the stares of those we pass and even of the shocked expression on my mother's face as he deposits me next to her.

Mother takes my hands with fear in her eyes. I am not afraid, just angry—furious to be handled so. Sabinus looks at me as he helps his grandmother into the wagon. I avert my eyes. All around, members of the household swarm into other conveyances. "Here they are," Father says, arriving with Mother's favorite slave carrying Mother's jewel box.

My nurse! Springing from the wagon, I nearly knock over a servant with the strong box from the *tablinum*.

"Aemilia!" There is warning in Father's voice.

"I am not leaving without my nurse." This is not a moment's pique. She is *family*.

He nods. "Hurry."

I find her sitting in the atrium. A sole still figure as those other few slaves still in the house run about so as not to be left behind.

Looking up at me she pleads, "You said I did not have to go to Nuceria."

"It is different now. Everyone is going. Sabinus says we are in danger."

"He said that before, and you did not believe him."

I do not entirely believe him now.

"My bones are old, too old to be jolted in a wagon. Leaving Pompeii will kill me. Let me stay. Let me wait for you to come home."

Looking down, I see tears in her eyes. I have no desire to distress my nurse and no real reason to impose my will on her even if that is my right. As a lifelong resident of Pompeii she knows to get out into the open during serious tremors. If an earthquake comes, I cannot be certain it will injure her, but from the way that she said leaving Pompeii would kill her, I feel certain it will.

I stoop and embrace her. "Stay then."

She embraces me back. "I will be here when you return to help you down from the wagon just as I helped your mother, with you in her arms, fifteen years ago."

Tears blur my eyes as I walk back through the *peristyle*. Nearing my bedroom I hear a voice I recognize and did not think to hear again inside these walls. *Faustus, my darling love, you have come for me!* I approach the door to my chamber, heart thudding in my throat. All my anger at Faustus drained from me last night, and now the love returns full force to fill the void, fed by the fact he seeks me as everyone else rushes to secure a seat in one of the wagons.

"I love you." The voice is low and stops me at the threshold. He must see me. My eyes search for him. Dear gods, what they find! He is on my bed — *my* bed — with one of my slaves, pushing her tunic up impatiently. It is so high that I can see the curly dark hair of her most

101

private place. I flatten myself against the door frame, unable to move or look away.

"No," the girl arrests his hand. "We mustn't. I am supposed to be in the wagon with *Domina* by now."

"We will be quick, I promise." He kisses her ear.

She gives a little giggle, then a sigh and releases his hand. "If we are caught, I will be beaten."

"How can you worry about such a thing at a time like this? I tell you the city is in ruins. I was lucky to get out. Who knows when the shaking will begin again or if we will escape with our lives when it does?" He runs his hand along her cheek and she bites his thumb. "If I must die," his tone is as urgent and ardent as any he ever used with me, "let it be in your arms."

He ought to want to die in my arms.

In a swift movement he raises his own tunic and for an instant I see it. Then he is inside my slave. She arches her back and her hands curl in the covers at her side — *my* covers. "Say it," she demands.

"I love you," he replies.

The words crush my heart and free my feet. I run through the vestibule and out to the wagon, tears streaming down my cheeks. Sabinus, beside the wagon, reaches out to hand me in.

He must think I cry at leaving my nurse and my home. "You will see her again," he says gently, "and this place."

But I do not know that I care to see it again. And I swear I will never set foot in my chamber again. It has been despoiled by the acts of a man I loved and who swore he loved me. The moment I am settled, Father nods to the driver and we begin to move, leaving behind a few carts that are still being loaded. As Sabinus brings his horse alongside where I sit, there is a great deal of pain in his expression. Why, I can't help wondering, should *he* be unhappy when he is getting what he wants?

WE ought to have been in Nuceria already. We should have arrived at my uncle's by late morning. Looking up, I judge that the sun has nearly climbed to its apex. Mother frets because we brought nothing to shade ourselves from it. "We will be as brown as *plebs*," she complains.

I have other things to trouble my mind.

"I will say this, Sabinus," Father draws his horse alongside that of his friend, attracting my attention, "you are most definitely not the only citizen of Pompeii who felt unsafe in the city this morning."

That is why we are still on the road, crawling. Mother is not the only one frustrated. The mules themselves complain—hawing, snorting, tossing their heads as if to ask why they cannot go faster. But the road is clogged with people and worse still with their things. Poorly packed household goods litter the way, and must be moved from the path or skirted.

Looking at the flat fields to our left, Father declares, "We must have a break. Let us pull off the road and take some refreshment."

Sabinus nods.

I clamber down, eager to stretch my legs. Despite the haste of our departure, it appears the kitchen slaves had the presence of mind to pack some food. As they begin to lay it out I am startled—the items are delicacies and must, therefore, have been intended for my wedding. But of course, the cooks would have been up since before dawn preparing for the evening's feast. This association with my nuptials makes me look for Sabinus. He has walked off some distance to a little rise and is staring back in the direction from which we came. I have halved the distance between us when a most unexpected figure steps into my path.

Faustus—dusty from the road and with a brow glazed by sweat, but still looking like Apollo with his fair hair tousled, doubtless from his exertions in my bed. How can he be so very wicked inside and so very handsome? He must have been quick indeed with the slave girl if he managed to catch a wagon, because I was not long with my nurse.

I turn my face from him.

"Lady," he says awkwardly. "I fear I have fallen out of your favor and have only myself to blame. Driven by my great love for you, I was too hasty in the cellar. But I am repentant."

It is the apology I longed for last evening. The apology I would have accepted with joy in my heart. But now it is meaningless—just more smooth words from a man who, it appears, will say whatever is most likely to get him what he wants at any given moment.

"Publius Crustius Faustus," I use his full name intentionally to put distance between us, unnerved at the same time by the realization that I need distance. "This is not the appropriate time or place for us to sort what passed between us."

He offers me a crooked smile. "You were not always so fastidious about what was appropriate and what was not."

The playful tone used to charm me, but it no longer has that power. I remember the explicit words in my father's cellar and the slave girl on my bed. How many women has he had while protesting his love for me—I shudder to imagine. I force myself to look him full in the face so that I will not seem cowed by him. "Is that the smile you used to seduce a slave girl in my father's cellar?" His eyes widen. But he has not heard the worst I have to say. "Which one is she?" My voice rises. "The same one whose legs you parted on my bed this morning?"

Faustus jerks as if I slapped him, but he recovers quickly. "She is nothing, Lady, nothing." He is so glib. I wish that I could slap him but that would draw unwanted attention. "She was merely a bit of fun. All men take slave girls." It is the same thing I told myself alone in the dark last night—the same thing that nearly convinced me to pardon him. How differently I feel now. I am so angry I cannot speak, and he seems to interpret my silence as encouragement. For rather than retreating he lowers his voice and says, "You are different. I wanted to marry you. I still do."

"But you know you cannot, and you always knew as much," I spit the words at him. "So it was safe for you to say so—whether or not it was true. Perhaps you are merely smart enough to realize that the same words cannot be used on the daughter of a good family as are used on her property."

"No! I swear it. Please, Amelia, I may have acted badly and forfeited your affection, but can we not be friends?"

"No. You have lost my friendship and, more important to you. I suspect, my future patronage. My husband Sabinus will want me painted." Speaking the words Sabinus and husband together feels remarkably satisfying at this moment. "I am beautiful and worth immortalizing—you said it yourself. Sabinus will spare no expense and you can be *sure* that is a commission you will never get." Gods, the look on his face is more gratifying than if I had slapped him.

My eye travels past Faustus to where my betrothed stands. His eyes are on me. Without another word I brush past the artist, hoping that my cheeks are not too red from castigating him, and proceed toward Sabinus. He watches me come—those gold-flecked eyes unreadable. When I am close he turns away, back toward the city we left.

"Surely you cannot see Pompeii from here?" I say, seeking to draw his attention.

"No, but I know where it lies by its relation to Vesuvius." He points. "It should be just there."

"What are you thinking?" I truly wish to know, how strange.

He turns to me. "That I would make you happy if I could."

The words are not soft, not words of love. Nor are they regretful. They are plain, and matter-of-fact. Their lack of artifice is refreshing after Faustus' smooth phrases. I notice he holds something in his hand, worries it. Can it be my little doll? Yes, it is, though I do not know how he came by it. I look away from it so as not to embarrass him and for the blink of an eye I wonder if, perhaps, Sabinus might make a good husband after all. Wonder if he might, in and of himself, bring me happiness. The blink of an eye is all that I have.

I am thrown to the ground, as I was by the tremor on the night of the fire. Thrown to a ground that is shaking wildly. And Sabinus is there with me, also knocked from his feet. He crawls toward me, and pulls me into his arms. Terrified, I clutch the front of his tunic. And still the ground shakes, as if Atlas were walking nearby, staggering under the weight of the sky. I watch with fascination and horror as fellow travelers on the nearby road fall from their mounts; as the line of umbrella pines undulates as if pushed and then released by an unseen hand; as my little doll and a scattering of rocks near us scuttle across the earth like large beetles.

"It has begun," Sabinus says into my hair — though I have the sense he speaks to himself and not to me.

The shaking seems to last forever. When the stillness comes, it feels even more still. I know that makes no sense but it is so. Scrambling up, Sabinus pulls me to my feet. He does not notice that I bring my doll with me. His eyes fly to the horizon.

"What are you looking for?"

"Smoke."

I tuck the doll into my pouch and glance across to where the wagons stand. Mother rocks with her arms about herself, wailing. Sabinus' grandmother has a hand on Mother's shoulder. One of the mules is down, and making a horrible noise. Slaves are howling. But from this distance, all the activity feels like a play acted for us in Pompeii's small theater. Father strides toward us.

"You were right, Sabinus! Right!" he exclaims. "Are you all right?"

I nod my head dumbly, aware that my hand remains in Sabinus'.

"Yes," he says, looking at Father for the first time.

If Sabinus is all right, why is his voice anguished?

"But they are not." He points back toward Vesuvius, toward Pompeii. Serpents of black smoke curl into the blue sky. "Just like after Nero's quake, the city burns."

Father puts a hand on Sabinus' shoulder, "And thanks to you, my friend, we are not there to see it or to suffer from it. Come man, you have saved us. Surely that is an achievement worth a smile. A smile and a wedding. Even with so many fellow travelers, we must be in Nuceria long before dark. You can still be married tonight."

This no longer seems like a fearful pronouncement.

As if finally aware that he holds it, Sabinus lets go of my hand. He looks from Father to me. I let his eyes hold mine without being uncomfortable. It is he who looks away, back to the west. He swallows visibly. "Another day. I must go back."

"What?" Father's voice brims with disbelief.

"Lepidus, I must go back. It is not enough to be right. I thought it would be, thought that this morning when I came to your villa to beg you to flee. I believed that getting you, my good friend, and your family out of Pluto's grasp was all that mattered." I shudder at the mention of Pluto's name, and Sabinus looks at me again. "And it *does* matter. It matters the most. Please believe that. But I have another duty—"

"To whom?"

"To Pompeii itself. To the people there who, I fear, will be failed by men like Pansa."

"They elected Pansa, not you." Father shakes his head and throws up his hands.

"But I can still serve them."

Father stares at Sabinus and then he nods.

This time it is my turn to throw up my hands. For if Father understands, I do not.

"Gnaeus Helvius Sabinus," I say, "it is too dangerous! What if the next tremor brings a wall down on your head? Or you are trampled trying to get back into a city that everyone else rushes to leave?"

I do not mean it to be funny, but Sabinus smiles.

"To be felt this far from the city, that last tremor was enormous. It was not a warning, it was the quake. Surely then the worst is over. There will be no heroics for me, Aemilia, only the dirty job of helping to clean up: the examination of walls, the assessing of water systems and streets—all tasks fitted to a man who loves architecture, mathematics, and engineering."

I believe Sabinus is wrong. Perhaps not about the worst being over—that is something he would know better than I—but about himself. Standing, shoulders squared, his golden-brown eyes focused and resolute, he has the bearing of a hero. Or at least of a very good man determined to fulfill the demands of his conscience. Sabinus' determination cannot make him younger or more handsome, but it does make him more appealing. More appealing than the striking but insubstantial artist I wasted months being infatuated with. More appealing than I ever thought to find him.

SABINUS

HE took his leave of his grandmother first. As she provided him with a list of friends to check on, Sabinus' eyes strayed west. Columns of smoke hung over where Pompeii must stand. *How much was still standing?* Mentally he added names to his grandmother's list. He had promised Capella he would keep an eye out for her. And he would — even if he had to go the temple of Isis to find her. And he would check on Aemilia's friend Julilla and Aemilia's nurse. His bride was worried about both. *She was worried about me too*, he thought. *About my safety. Worried that a wall will fall on my head.* The thought made him warm inside — not a wall falling, but that Amelia cared whether or not it did.

And yet, he had seen her with Faustus just a short while before the earthquake. Seen them talking and observed the flush in her cheeks. An idea came to him. Why not? He meant to come back and claim her; meant to exasperate her into throwing up her hands again in that captivating manner. He meant to take her in his arms for purposes other than throwing her over his shoulder and carrying her out of a house or holding her safe while the world shook around them. But if he didn't come back ...

I would make you happy if I could, he had told her. Was it a lie? He hoped not. He would prove to himself that it wasn't.

Lepidus approached with a bundle, Aemilia at his side. "I've had the slaves pack some provisions," his friend said. "If you find the city in ruins, you will be glad not to need to forage for food. Come to us at my brother's as soon as you can."

"I will. I swear it. And I would ask an oath from you in return."

His friend looked at him searchingly.

"You know the terms of my will. If I do not return, I ask you to promise that all I have bequeathed to you will become Aemilia's dowry—and that she be permitted to choose her husband herself." It was not until he finished speaking that Sabinus had the courage to look at his intended. Her eyes were wide—nearly as wide as they had been when the earth was shaking.

"You have my oath," Lepidus said, "pray gods it will prove unnecessary." Sabinus clasped his friend's arm and turned toward his horse. He had only gone a few steps when he felt a gentle touch from behind. Aemilia was there, her eyes now wet instead of wide. She said nothing, only rose on the balls of her feet and bestowed a swift, soft kiss upon his lips. Still silent, she watched him climb into his saddle. He drew the keys to the doors of his home from his pouch, the ones he would have given her this evening when she arrived there as his wife for the first time. He thanked the gods for whatever impulse had driven him to snatch them up. "These are yours," he said, bending down and handing them to her. "A symbol of my promise."

"Your promise to find us in Nuceria," she said, staring at him, hard.

"Of both my promises then."

"And this is yours." Reaching up, she presented him with the little doll. "To let you know I will be waiting for you. And that when you come back, I will not hide her, but will gladly burn her on the morning of our wedding."

Her pledge felt pregnant with a promise of good things to come. It gave him an urge to reconsider his course of action—a strong urge. But he knew his hesitation was pure selfishness and that if he stayed with her now, he would never feel worthy of her. Without embarrassment, he pressed her doll to his lips before tucking it into his pouch. Then he smiled. *A starry-eyed, romantic fool, indeed.* And clicking his tongue, he put his animal in motion.

"I will pray to Vulcan for your safety," she called after him. "And watch over you myself until you are out of sight." As he began to thread his way through the throng on the road he looked over his shoulder. She was watching, just as she had said she would be. Sabinus could have sworn he felt her eyes upon him long after her figure was lost to his backward glances.

AEMILIA

I did not choose to be born in fire. No one chooses the manner of their birth, I suppose, and women have precious little choice about anything after they draw that first breath. Fifteen years ago, the Fates decreed I be born a girl, slippery and willful, as my family fled Rome in fire and blood.

Being reborn is a different matter. As I felt my city quake from a distance today, and watched tendrils of smoke rise from her, I elected to be reborn a woman. Reborn not in the act of putting on a wedding veil, or consigning my childhood treasures to the flames, but by choice—a choice given me by the grace of a man's understanding, and by the actions I will take hereafter in response to his act of faith.

As my eyes strain to follow his shrinking figure, I pray that the gods will keep him safe. Pray that he may enter a city on fire and come back to me. For now that I understand myself and have more sway over my future than most, male or female, can even imagine, I find that I would rather have him than the power to choose any other.

PART THREE

THE SOLDIER

Ben Kane

"A black and dreadful cloud bursting out in gusts of igneous serpentine vapor."
—Pliny the Younger

Hours earlier…

LUCIUS Satrius Rufus woke, over-hot, and with a pounding head. Wiping his sweaty face on the pillow — uncaring, because it could get no dirtier — he wondered if it *had* been the heat that had roused him, as it had every day for the previous he-didn't-know-how-long. A strong tremor beneath him, shaking the bed, rattling the chains of the oil lamp, told him otherwise. *That* was what had woken him. He lay back, feeling two more movements before the world returned to normal. Rufus shut his eyes and tried to go back to sleep. It was a pointless exercise — his mind had turned over his many problems. Rolling his tongue around a mouth that felt as foul as it tasted, he sat up. The bedclothes he'd been sprawled on were stained with sweat; the air in the small, dark chamber, fuggy.

It's hot enough to be midday, or thereabouts, he thought. *I didn't drink enough to sleep that long, did I?* Outside, the world was quiet, and he calmed. If it were midday, the street noise would be audible. Palming his eyes and willing away the thick feeling in his brain, he stood.

A twinge from his bladder made him glance at the pot beside his bed. It was nearly full, the product of his efforts overnight. He hesitated. Mustius, his servant, would grumble if it were overflowing. He sighed. Better to hold on, and go outside. That might make Mustius happy. Happier, he thought. Mustius was never really happy. Nor was *he* ever, if it came to it.

When he'd been in the legions, thought Rufus ruefully, all he had ever dreamed of was getting out. These days, he mostly did the reverse, wishing to be transported somehow back in time, to a younger, fitter, debt-free version of himself, when his hair was red rather than gray. As a soldier, the only important things had been doing his duty and occasionally risking his life for the Empire. Now he had notables such as Gaius Cuspius Pansa and Lucius Caecilius Jucundus breathing down his neck the whole time. Pansa wasn't the worst, he had to admit. Pansa loved gladiators, and he had some respect for a man who'd served in the army; he knew too that Rufus was good for his rent money, even if it was a month or two late. That ugly bastard Jucundus, though, he was a different matter ...

Shoving his main debtor from his mind, Rufus pulled back the fabric partition of his chamber, letting in the bright sunlight that bathed the other room. Morning hadn't passed. Tinges of red yet colored the patches of sky that were visible through the small, barred windows, but dawn had come and gone. Ordinary noise carried in from the street—a creaking cart going by, and two old men debating whether the tremors were of real concern: one maintained they were—had the northwest quarter of the town not been damaged earlier?—while the other rubbished the notion.

Despite the powerful earth movements, Mustius was still asleep: lying on the couch in his customary position, mouth open, snoring. As ever, his maimed arm rested on his chest, with his good one lying protectively over it. Rufus' mouth turned down. It was sad to see a good soldier brought so low.

Some said Rufus was a fool to have a free man rather than a slave as a servant, but Mustius had saved Rufus' life when he'd taken that wound to his arm five years before. Discharged from the legion early because of the injury, Mustius hadn't been entitled to a single coin of the payment that "full-timers" received. Until Rufus had come upon him begging in the forum upon his own return to Pompeii two winters since, he had been destitute.

If Rufus admitted it, his slave girl had been better at maintaining the apartment, but he'd had to sell her some time before, to raise money for his creditors. He had been left with Mustius, whose cooking was awful, and whose arm limited his ability to wash clothes and to clean. Mustius did his best, however, and he never asked for money, knowing Rufus had none. That was all a man could ask for. They endured life together, as they had on campaign in the old days, in Germania.

If he was to piss outside, he might as well save Mustius the bother of emptying the pot. Rufus crept back and retrieved it. With a last look at his servant, he slid back the bolt on the front door, which opened directly into his living room.

No atrium and grand tablinum *for me*, he thought with a trace of bitterness. Every time he was summoned to see Pansa, whose massive house formed the "spine" and entire back of the block of buildings in which Rufus' apartment was situated, he was reminded of his lowly position in life. Pansa's atrium alone had six chambers leading off it. Six. The open space within the atrium was several times larger than Rufus' two rooms. And as for the rest of the dwelling?

Stop it, he told himself. *You are the son of a former slave. You did well to end your career in the legions as a* tesserarius. *Pansa is a nobleman and a member of one of Pompeii's most powerful families. Having a problem with him is like fighting the existence of the sun in the sky. He's all right — and better than Jucundus anyway.*

As he emerged onto the street, one of his neighbors, a supercilious perfume maker, appeared at his own door. "Did you feel the tremors?" he asked, waiving his usual snobbery. "Aye," muttered Rufus. "They've stopped. Gods willing, they'll stay that way." *At least until the day's games are over*, he prayed.

The perfume maker nodded, but still seemed worried. He was distracted by the pot under Rufus' arm then, however, and gave a disapproving sniff.

Rufus shot him a resentful look. "Not all of us can afford a place with an inside lavatory. I'm entitled to throw this wherever I choose." Feeling the man's eyes on his back, however, he abandoned his plan of pouring out the pot's contents a few steps from his door. One of the gossiping graybeards—a resident of the apartment two doors away, and a regular culprit in the emptying of night soil outside—gave him a knowing wink, which Rufus returned.

His step soon lightened. He was up and about now; he might as well make for the forum bathhouse, which lay across the street. After tipping the urine into a sewer, he could avail himself of the bath's facilities. Yet as Rufus neared the side street's intersection with the larger thoroughfare upon which the building's front lay, he began to feel self-conscious, even a little worried. Given his recent run of luck, Jucundus would be taking an early morning stroll as he heaved into sight, hair standing on end, pot of piss under his arm, still in the drink-spattered tunic he'd worn to the tavern the night before.

To Rufus' relief, there was no sign of Jucundus among the passersby, a collection of slaves running errands, travelers heading for the Herculaneum Gate and tradesmen walking to work. Shopkeepers whose premises had shed roof tiles thanks to the tremors were sweeping up the broken pieces of baked clay. A family led by a grim-faced father passed by in a mule cart, the children protesting that they did not want to leave, and the wife telling them to watch their tongues.

Fools panic easily, thought Rufus. *Things aren't going to get any worse. They can't, not with the fight that's on today.*

No one gave him a second glance as he crossed toward the bathhouse. By pure chance, a wagon loaded with bricks happened to pass in front of him as a pair of heavy-set men came into sight. He recognized one of them because of his bandy-legged gait. The pair was also walking from the east, where Jucundus' house lay. They were two of Jucundus' thugs, for sure. His heart beat out an unhappy rhythm as he sneaked alongside the far side of the wagon, slowing his pace to that of the ox drawing it.

After twenty paces, he chanced a look over his shoulder. The two men had strolled by, oblivious to his presence. *Were they on other duties, or were they looking for him?* he wondered nervously. The answer came almost at once. Reaching the corner of Pansa's building, the thugs turned down the side street, toward Rufus' door and the sleeping Mustius. Feeling guilty, he resisted the urge to sprint back and confront them. His reasoning was sound. Pugnax, his one gladiator, was fighting in the amphitheater later on. How would it look if he came to collect his winnings with a black eye, a bloodied nose, and perhaps even a broken arm? The high and mighty of Pompeii had to see him as someone worthy of backing, the next time Pugnax fought. If he stayed away, only Mustius would get roughed up. Rufus hoped he would understand. He would make it up to Mustius — give him some of his winnings, maybe.

Cutting down the next alley to the right, Rufus strode to the bath's main entrance, which lay on a street parallel to the one on which he lived. The smell of frying sausages reached his nose from one of the shops alongside the bath's doorway, making his belly rumble. A surreptitious check in the purse on his belt revealed a handful of copper and bronze coins. Vespasian's unsmiling face regarded him from one of three silver *denarii* that also lay within. Trying to ignore his hunger, Rufus tied the drawstring tight and patted the worn leather bag. His father would have food when he visited later. He had enough cash to get into the baths, but why waste money on that if he didn't have to? *Fortuna, be kind to me this morning*, he prayed.

His prayer was answered. There was no one that he recognized in the already busy exercise area, and the crop-haired slave he wanted to see was on duty at the entrance to the men's baths.

The slave nodded as Rufus approached his desk. "Vulcan was busy with his hammer this morning, eh? Let's hope he's done for now."

"Gods keep him quiet until this evening anyway," replied Rufus with heart.

"Got any decent tips for the fights today?"

"Pugnax is sure to win."

The slave's eyebrows lowered. "Ha! You say that because he's *your* gladiator. The fool lost the last two contests you told me to back him in. That cost me twenty *denarii* — each time!"

119

What I could do with your forty denarii, thought Rufus wearily. His first choice would be to place it on Pugnax, of course, but then there was the chariot driver that Mustius had been talking about. Apparently, almost no one knew that his sponsor had just bought him a new team of horses from Hispania. In consequence, the odds on him for the race two days hence at Nuceria were still five to one. I'd make two hundred *denarii*, Rufus decided. Added to the money he'd make later, he could have had a sum that would have shut up Jucundus for a couple of weeks.

"So what's changed?" demanded the slave.

How Rufus wished that he were still in the army. A slave would not dare to address an officer in that manner. *An almost-broke civilian with a drink and gambling problem was a different matter, however*, he thought bitterly.

He pulled a smile that was more a grimace. "His form's changed, believe me. Most of the bet makers won't have it" — he pretended not to hear the slave's muttered "I can see why" — "but he's sure to win this afternoon. You can find ten to one odds on him, maybe even thirteen."

The slave's tongue flickered across his lips. "Thirteen to one, you say?"

"My servant got that yesterday, near the amphitheater. He put a tidy sum on for me," Rufus lied. Would that I'd had more than eight *denarii* to place, he thought.

"Maybe I'll do as you say." The slave nodded, as if to convince himself. "You're wanting a bath, I take it?"

"Yes."

"Anything else? Massage? A woman?"

"A bath will be all."

"Two *asses*."

Rufus smiled. "After the tip I've just given you, you can't expect me to pay, surely?"

"I should have known this was coming." The slave jerked a thumb at the doorway to the baths. "Get inside, before my manager sees you."

"My thanks." At that moment, Rufus would have loved to have emptied his pot over the slave's head. It would have got him nowhere, however. Breathing deeply to control his anger, he walked off. A soak in the cold pool of the *frigidarium* would put the world to rights — he hoped. It was hard not to feel bitter, however. By now, his life should have been easy, content. After the army, he'd had his cash payment for completing his service, and his house had already been purchased. Why then had he started gambling? Why had he frittered away almost everything that he owned?

The truth of it was that Rufus had been bored. Half a lifetime spent in military service had ensured his few interests were hunting, drinking wine, gambling, and consorting with whores. Maybe he should have found himself a wife, as his father had recommended. His doubt didn't last for more than a few heartbeats. Every married man that he knew spent his time complaining about his wife's constant nagging, about how she wouldn't lie with him as often as he wished, about her never-ending demands for more "household goods." Having children might be ultimately rewarding, but the price one had to pay for them was too high. It was better that he remained a bachelor.

After he bathed, he would call on his father Satrius, a retired imperial secretary. A different worry reared its head. His father had been ailing for some time. The heat wave wasn't helping his condition, which the surgeon maintained had to do with poor circulation, or a weak heart, or both. The medications prescribed by the surgeon were expensive and didn't seem to do much, but, Rufus thought, at least his father's pension meant that they could be bought. There was little that he could do other than to visit regularly and to make offerings to Aesculapius for his father's recovery as often as he could afford it.

If it weren't so hot, I'd try to persuade him to come to the games today, he mused. Seeing Pugnax win would do him good. It'd show him that I'm capable of doing something right.

Fresh doubt gnawed at Rufus. Would Pugnax really triumph? His aging gladiator had been lucky to be reprieved the second time he'd lost, two months before. If he were defeated yet again, Rufus wouldn't just have debts on his hands, he'd have a dead gladiator. The compensation he might receive would be paltry.

Pugnax will do it, he thought fiercely. He has to, or I will have nothing to pay Jucundus' thugs with. And *that* would eventually result in more than a beating.

The appeal of the *frigidarium* lessened a little.

Rufus consoled himself with a vision of Pugnax winning. When that happened, bookings and down payments for other fights would come flooding in. It was ironic that he should feel grateful for the earth tremors like the ones this morning. The earth had been stirring all month. Because of them, more contests were being held than was usual for the time of year. The tremors had unsettled Rufus too, but unlike the easily terrified citizens he'd seen leaving this morning, he didn't need to be placated by the staging of games and gladiatorial fights. He grinned. If this was the response of the rich and powerful when there was even a hint of unrest, who was he to argue?

RUFUS bypassed the forum on his way south. This early, Jucundus wasn't likely to be in the town's largest public space, where so much business was conducted, but various employees of his would be. It was easier to avoid trouble than to extract oneself from it. Thus Rufus' eyes scanned the street ahead as he walked; every so often, he glanced over his shoulder. Pompeii was small enough that it was a constant battle to elude his debtors. At least he only had two major ones, Pansa and Jucundus. The others — and there were a host, from tavern owners to butchers and bakers, and a fuller who had recently made him a fine tunic — weren't owed enough to want to hunt him down. Yet. Guilt tugged at him. *I'll pay them all soon,* he thought. *When Pugnax wins.*

Rufus felt more remorse as he passed the street that led to his father's house. He had decided to postpone his visit while in the baths. *There'll be time to call in before the fights began,* he told himself. It was more important that he saw Pugnax first and filled his head with ideas of victory. Rufus was sure that Pugnax's streak of ill-fortune was in part due to the self-doubt that plagued him.

The man thought about things too much. His father's saying came to mind: "Don't worry about a task that's before you, no matter how hard it seems. Get on and do it. Then it's done. If it proves impossible, you've tried your best." The maxim didn't quite apply to Pugnax, Rufus decided ruefully. If his best weren't enough later on, he'd be dragged out of the Gate of Death while the crowd bayed for more blood. But that wasn't to say that Pugnax shouldn't do his utmost. *That* was the way to win.

The main gladiator barracks was situated in the portico of a large, disused theater that was situated close to the Stabian Gate, in the south wall. It had been moved there from a spot by the amphitheater after the major earthquake seventeen years before, when so many of Pompeii's buildings had been damaged. The change in location suited Rufus; the barracks were a much shorter walk from his apartment than from the amphitheater, which lay in the far southeastern corner of the town. In this heat, the less time spent outside, the better.

A hundred paces from the theater, his lips twisted upward. The bellows of the *lanista* were already audible. If he were ordering about the gladiators this early, Pugnax wouldn't have had time to feel worried. The guards at the gate, two scarred army veterans whom Rufus knew, grinned and saluted when they saw him. "*Tesserarius*," said the more senior.

"There's no need for that, brothers," Rufus replied in a half-hearted way, but the little reminder of his former status lifted his spirits, as always. "The *lanista* is in fine fettle this morning. I could almost hear him at the forum baths."

"He's in a bad mood. The heat kept him awake half the night, he says."

"Like all of us. But what can we do?" added the second guard with a shrug.

"Aye, but just when he was falling back to sleep, the tremors woke him again."

Rufus felt a twinge of concern. "There's been nothing about the games being canceled, has there?"

The senior guard shook his head. "It takes more than that to put off a man like Pansa."

"Have you seen Pugnax?" Rufus watched the men's faces carefully.

The senior guard chuckled. "Oh, yes. He went for a run before dawn. Said he'd had a dream that the gods would favor him if he did. Did the whole bloody perimeter of the walls, in his armor, and ended up at the temple to Mars, where he offered a sacrifice. He came back with a huge grin plastered all over his face. Murranus is a dead man, he said."

"Excellent." Previously, Pugnax had been a little worried about facing Murranus, a *murmillo* and fellow "Neronian" who'd been bought not long before from the imperial gladiator school at Capua. Rufus felt himself smile. Today was going to be a *good* day. Pugnax *was* going to win. "I hope you'll be betting on him?"

The guards exchanged a look. "We might do, sir, yes."

Rufus didn't care if they believed that Pugnax's run of bad luck was over or not. He did. "Let me in, will you?"

"Of course, sir." The senior guard stepped away from the archway that formed the barracks' entrance.

The hobs on the soles of Rufus' sandals clashed off the plain mosaic floor in the short passageway, reminding him of the immense noise as his legion had marched along imperial roads. In summer, the dust had been unbearable, but the sound of thousands of feet hitting the ground in unison had always filled him with pride. Even now, he loved to see soldiers on the move.

Beyond the passage was a square open area, filled with training gladiators, and surrounded on all sides by a colonnaded walkway. The *lanista's* apartment and the bedrooms of the best fighters were situated above, on the second floor. As Rufus had expected, the *lanista* was standing on the wooden balcony outside his quarters, where he could best oversee his men. Apart from his well-cut tunic, the short-haired man looked no different than many of his fighters.

His muscles rippled under nut-brown skin that was welted with cicatrices, and under his lowered brows, his eyes were hawk-keen. He took in the visitor at once. "Rufus. You're here early." He didn't sound pleased.

Rufus kept his face serene. "It's an important day. I wanted to see Pugnax."

"A man who's on his last chance. Murranus will gut him, or I'm no judge. Then I'll no longer have to feed the greedy bastard. He eats more porridge than any two other fighters," said the *lanista* with a scowl. He pointed to a far corner of the training area. "He's over there."

"My thanks." Rufus strode off down the walkway, glad that he'd remained calm. It was unusual for a private citizen to have a gladiator here, among a *lanista's* troop, but the legal agreement he'd made with the trainer still stood. It was odd, but he had Pansa to thank for it—another reason to be grateful to his second largest creditor. A year ago almost to the day, Pansa had been sufficiently impressed with Pugnax—a fighter whom Rufus had just purchased—to lean on the *lanista* to let Pugnax live and train among his men.

"He'll be a fine addition to your lot. Neronians of his quality always bring in the crowds," Pansa had said. Rufus had been overjoyed, but Pugnax's instruction in Capua had made little difference to his subsequent career. That would all change today, thought Rufus determinedly. Pompeii would see what Pugnax the Neronian was capable of.

"Take it easy, Murranus!"

The name halted Rufus in his steps. He searched for Murranus amid the nearest gladiators. There was only one *murmillo*, recognizable because of his fish-crested helmet.

Murranus was sparring against a *thraex*, a Thracian. Both men bore wooden swords, but they were in the full armor they'd wear in the arena. As well as his helmet, Murranus had a large, rectangular shield. A single greave covered his leading, left leg, and protective padding encased his right arm. His opponent wore the griffon-crested helmet so characteristic of the *thraex*; he also had thick fabric and metal padding on his right arm. Because his curved shield was quite small, the *thraex's* greaves were very tall, reaching up to mid-thigh.

It was clear that Murranus was the more skilled fighter. Clashing his shield off that of the *thraex*, he drove him back several steps, battering his sword off the other's helmet in a flurry of blows.

"Murranus!" shouted the *lanista* even as the *thraex's* knees buckled. "This is a training session, remember! Save your efforts for the arena."

"*Lanista.*" Murranus raised his sword in salute before watching with evident pleasure as his opponent rose groggily to his feet.

Rufus hurried off along the walkway before Murranus saw him. His confidence in Pugnax was a little weaker than it had been, but he wasn't going let that show. "Pugnax!" he called. "I hear you've been up for hours. Would you care for a cup of wine, to grease the joints?"

PUGNAX was taking this fight with deadly seriousness, thought Rufus proudly. He'd had the innkeeper dilute his wine to a far greater extent than the normal ratio of one to four. "I have to stay sharp," he said, his brown eyes dancing. "There'll be time to get drunk tonight."

"There will. And the night after, and the night after that." Rufus regarded his gladiator with pride. Pugnax was probably ten years younger than him—so, about thirty-something, which was old for a fighter. Fortunately, he didn't look it. There wasn't a gray hair to be seen in his thick black thatch, and his broad, pleasant face was unmarred by wrinkles. If it weren't for his crooked nose, he'd have been handsome. Like most fighters, he was heavily built. The layer of fat that covered his well-developed physique was a form of protection against injury, allowing him to take flesh wounds that didn't damage the muscles underneath.

"Did you see Murranus training?"

Nonplussed by the direct question, Rufus floundered for an answer. "Err, yes."

"He's looking good, eh?"

"I suppose." It felt wrong to say something positive about Pugnax's opponent.

"There's nothing wrong with speaking the truth, master. He's been out in the yard from dawn until dusk for weeks now."

"He seemed sharp," admitted Rufus, wondering what Pugnax was playing at.

"I'm glad. It wouldn't look good if I defeated him too easily. Everyone likes a close contest." Pugnax bared his teeth. "He won't see tomorrow's dawn, though, I swear it."

"That's the spirit!" Rufus clapped him on the arm.

In unison, they clinked their clay cups together. "To victory," said Rufus. *And to Jucundus giving me a little more time once I've given him my winnings*, he added silently.

"To victory," echoed Pugnax.

They both drank deep.

"How long does a man have to wait to get by?" cried a voice outside.

"Calm down, graybeard," growled someone in reply.

"I've been following you for an eternity now. You're stopping at every damn inn."

"Course I am. Lucius Caecilius Jucundus supplies all the taverns in this quarter with their wine, and today is delivery day. If you've got a problem with that, me and my mate would be happy to discuss it further. If you prefer, you could take it up with Jucundus directly."

Like most, the *caupona* they were in was open-fronted. Rufus peered out onto the street. A wagon drawn by two donkeys had pulled up right outside. Its load was an enormous leather bag; the wine within was dispensed at the back, from a long metal tube with a tap at one end. Two farm workers, both solid as tree trunks, were in charge. It wasn't clear which one had intimidated the old man with a small cart behind, but both looked capable. The short cudgels in their hands were further proof of their willingness to use force.

The innkeeper had seen what was going on. A pair of slave girls were sent outside, one small and dark, the other buxom and blonde, each managing to carry a pair of medium-sized *amphorae* over their shoulders. The old man watched with poorly concealed resentment as Jucundus' men set about filling the vessels with the speed of ill snails. There were at least two other vehicles that were being delayed, but no one dared challenge the deliverymen.

"I wonder if there's *anyone* in Pompeii who likes Jucundus?" muttered Rufus angrily.

"D'you owe him money, master?" Pugnax's stare was appraising.

Rufus tried to conceal his surprise, not that Pugnax was aware of his debts—he mentioned them often enough as a reason for Pugnax to win—but because he'd never named names. A sigh escaped him. It was logical to guess that Jucundus—one of the town's most prominent moneylenders—might be one of his creditors. "Yes. A lot. If you lose, well—" He stopped himself. If that happened, Pugnax wouldn't be around to care. "Never mind."

"I'll win, master. The priest at the temple of Mars said so. You'll have some money at least to give that leech Jucundus." Pugnax leaned in close. "You know the fuller's workshop around the corner?"

"Yes," replied Rufus, confused. "Why?"

"Meet me there in a few moments, when the mayhem has died down." Pugnax winked, and with that, he was gone.

Intrigued, Rufus watched as Pugnax sauntered to the far side of the street. Jucundus' men paid him no heed; he looked like any other pedestrian. Whistling tunelessly, Pugnax made a show of reading the election notices that had been painted on the wall right on the corner. Many enjoined citizens to vote for a certain Julius Polybius—but the responding graffiti advised in no uncertain terms that Polybius was corrupt, a degenerate, or both. Now and again, as anyone might, he glanced at the wagon and what lay behind it.

What in Hades is he planning? Rufus wondered. Intuition told him that it was something to do with the wine, and that it wouldn't be good. It was playing with fire to do anything that would piss off a man as powerful as Jucundus, but in that instant, Rufus didn't care. His rage at Jucundus, impotent for so long, bubbled at the back of his throat, and so he observed in silence, and waited to see what Pugnax would do.

At length, Pugnax moved on from the notices to the coppersmith's. There he began to peruse the wares on display, picking up a bracelet here, and a pot there. He studied the wagon again.

Rufus felt a pang of worry. What if they noticed him? The sound of children's voices, high-pitched with excitement, drew his attention away from Pugnax. A schoolmaster, complete with a dozen pupils in tow, came into view. A bearded, stern-looking man with a writing slate in one hand and a switch in the other, he was scolding his charges for talking, for not listening to what he was saying, for not walking fast enough.

Pugnax made his move at the same time as the boys crowded past the wagon, blocking the path of a woman carrying a basket of freshly woven wool. With bated breath, Rufus watched Pugnax disappear from sight behind the vehicle. The woman was complaining to the tutor about his students' behavior. While apologizing, he tried to grab the ear of the boy nearest him. His target ducked back out of the way, stepped backward off the pavement and collided with one of the donkeys that was tethered to the wagon. In reply, it kicked him. The boy screamed, and all eyes turned in his direction.

Rufus longed to go outside for a better view, but he dared not, in case someone remembered later that he'd been there, had anything to do with whatever Pugnax was at. He poured some more wine, and took a swallow. "What food have you got?" he asked the buxom blonde, who was quite attractive. Rufus forgot his rumbling stomach for several heartbeats. If—when—Pugnax won, he could always come back here for a screw.

"Bread. Cheese. Olives. Fried fish. If you're really hungry, I can cook you up some stew." The slave's gaze slid to the commotion outside.

Rufus decided against eating. Whatever food his father had would cost him nothing. "Hmmm. Let me think on it."

"Shout when you've decided," said the slave girl, mopping her brow, and wandering to the edge of the pavement.

A moment or two passed. Then, despite the plethora of noises from the street, Rufus' ears picked out the sound of liquid spilling to the ground. Lots of it. There were no fountains nearby to overflow, and in his gut he knew it wasn't a chamber pot being emptied from above.

"Jupiter's hairy ass crack — who's done that?" roared a voice — it had to be one of the deliverymen.

"What?" cried his companion.

"Are you blind, you fool? Look!" screeched the first man. "Someone's cut a fucking great hole in the leather!"

"Wine!" shouted another man. "There's wine pouring out all over the street, citizens. Grab a jug, a beaker, a pot, anything! Free wine!"

Rufus had to look at the floor so no one would see his broad smile. Pugnax was responsible. No doubt he'd done it low down, too, so the entire contents of the bag would be lost.

"Free wine! Free wine!"

A crowd descended with the speed of seagulls on a piece of rotting meat. The opportunists had containers of every kind. One man had a chamber pot; Rufus even spied an attractive patrician woman with white-blonde hair, who, when she saw him eyeing her up, gave him a most unexpected wink. The mob jostled and pushed to get a place near the streams of ruby red wine. Those with nothing to collect the liquid cupped their hands and drank as much as they could before others shoved them out of the way. Helpless before the mob, Jucundus' men stood by and glowered. Rufus could hear them arguing about who the culprit might have been, and what would happen to them as a result.

This was why he loved Pompeians, thought Rufus. They were so resilient. Show them some free wine, and they forgot all of their worries, even the unexplained earth tremors. Biting the inside of his cheek to hold in his mirth, he sauntered outside. Mounting the raised doorstep of a house, he scanned the street beyond the wagon. There was no sign of Pugnax, which explained the deliverymen's confusion. It had been utter genius to act when he had, Rufus thought. It was a shame that Jucundus would never know that it had been his man who was responsible, although to be truthful, he didn't need the trouble that would surely follow such a revelation. *Better to enjoy it in secret,* he concluded, ambling around the corner in search of the fuller's.

Pugnax wasn't there, but he arrived from the opposite direction before Rufus had much chance to examine the various wool tunics on sale within. Red-faced and sweating, he snorted with delight when Rufus greeted him. That set Rufus off. They both dissolved into uncontrollable laughter. The slave who was attending the shop's front counter looked on uncomprehendingly.

Rufus regained control first. "Gods, but I haven't enjoyed a joke as much in an age," he said, wiping away tears of amusement. "My thanks, Pugnax. I needed that."

Pugnax gave him the same wink as he had before. "My pleasure, master. It was worth the risk, eh?"

"Damn it, yes!" Glancing at the sun, Rufus grew serious. "It's time to visit my father. I want to see him before going to the arena."

"Shall I accompany you?"

"Today's your day," said Rufus with a smile. "What's best for Pugnax the Neronian?"

"I'll walk with you, master."

Rufus inclined his head in grave acknowledgement, as he might at Saturnalia, when slaves became the masters for one night. "As you wish."

"THANK all the gods for the awning, and Pansa, who paid for it," said Satrius, using a square of linen to pat the moisture from his forehead and the bags under his cheeks. He pointed upward, at the massive strips of cloth that were suspended on long poles over much of the arena. "It would be worse than Hades in here if it weren't for those."

"Aye," replied Rufus, studying the mottled color of his father's complexion sidelong, and trying not to worry. On a good day, Satrius looked like an older version of himself. In these good seats that Rufus had managed to secure, he resembled a freshly expired corpse. It was no surprise. The best seating was low down in the amphitheater, near the arena. Even with the awnings, it was warmer than the *caldarium* in any of the city's baths. *Was that why the place was half empty?* he wondered. Or was it because more people than he'd realized had left town, scared by the shaking of the earth? Either way, Rufus hoped the decreased attendance wouldn't sway Pansa toward calling the games off.

"Maybe it wasn't such a good idea for you to come out."

"Rubbish, my boy. I want to see this contest. This is going to be your day, and Pugnax's. I'd never forgive myself if I missed it. Besides, the fight will take place soon. We can leave the moment it's over."

Rufus half smiled, but wished that he'd held off visiting his father until later. He should have anticipated that Satrius would insist on attending. It would have been better to check on Mustius, but Rufus had been put off doing that by the heavy who still lingered close to his door. He offered up a prayer to Aesculapius, the god of medicine. *Watch over my father, I ask you, Great One. Do not take him from me yet, please.*

A piteous cry was instantly followed by a roar from the crowd, and their attention was drawn back to the circle of sand. As part of the day's entertainment, Pansa had paid for a score of African antelope, five lions, and one rhinoceros — the famed "Ethiopian bull" — to be hunted down in the arena. Rufus had been busy when the antelope were herded into the open to meet the *venatores*, the men who would end the antelopes' lives. He had seen them from a slit window in the network of tunnels that ran beneath the seating, but his priority had been to get Pugnax a good spot in one of the alcoves by the doors that opened onto the sands. In the time it had taken him to do that, greasing the palm of a guard with his last *denarii*, most of the antelope had been slain. The few survivors hadn't lasted much longer. Desultory applause had met their demise, but a real cheer of enthusiasm had risen when the first lion had been released.

When all the cats had been killed, three *venatores* lay dead in the golden circle. Their blood soaked into the sand, turning areas of it crimson. Several of the hunters had been badly injured. Loops of gut hung from one's belly, while jagged stumps of bone jutted from another's arm. One man had been bitten on the shoulder and had claw marks down both legs, but the worst of all was the *venator* who'd had a lion rip off half of his face. These unfortunates thrashed about, calling for their mothers, for help, for an end to their suffering. But instead of being allowed to leave, or having a surgeon sent in to tend them, the rhinoceros was goaded into the arena.

"No one deserves to die like that," pronounced his father through pursed lips as the massive beast gored the first man it found, before tossing him into the air and trampling him as he fell. "Not even criminals. Kill them quickly and be done."

"Aye." Before his time in the legions, Rufus would have watched dispassionately. Now he looked away in distaste. There had been so many casualties because the *venatores* were not professional beast hunters, but convicted prisoners. *Even Pansa's purse wasn't bottomless*, thought Rufus.

He scanned the dignitaries' boxes, but Pansa hadn't arrived yet. With a little luck, he would have taken his seat by the time Pugnax came out. If Pansa saw Pugnax win, he'd be more likely to agree to him fighting in another of his contests. And if the ground kept shaking as it had this morning, that would surely be held soon. On the back of a victory, the payment would far exceed today's meager hundred *denarii*.

Be patient, Rufus told himself. *Put together with my winnings from the betmaker, I'll have over two hundred denarii. That will appease Jucundus. I won't gamble a single coin of what's left, by everything I hold sacred. What's left will keep me and Mustius in food and fuel until the next purse comes in.*

For all his good intentions, Rufus knew how tempting it would be to place a bet on some of the fights that came later in the day. He was a good judge of the local fighters. He could double his two hundred *denarii*, perhaps even triple or quadruple it. What would Jucundus say if he produced such an amount? *Don't even think about it. You'll lose every last* denarius, said a little voice in his head, one Rufus knew all too well. It was his moral side, and he was used to tramping over it in his hobnailed sandals. With an effort, he stopped himself short of doing so again. He would seek out Jucundus the instant that he'd collected his winnings. Once the money had been handed over, the temptation would be gone, because he'd have virtually nothing to spend.

"How did a maggot lowlife like you get a good seat like this, eh?"

Rufus would have fallen as he was yanked backward but for the hand gripping the back of his tunic. Twisting his head to try and see his assailant, he managed to scramble his legs off his bench and onto the flooring behind. His heart sank as he recognized the bandy-legged man he'd spotted earlier. "I have friends in high places," he began.

"Shut it," growled Bandy Legs, twisting his fist further into Rufus' tunic. "I'm not interested."

"What is the meaning of this outrage?' demanded Satrius, his face purpling. "Release my son at once!"

"This sewer rat is *your* offspring? I should have guessed. There is some resemblance, I suppose, although *you* look ready to cross the Styx."

"How dare you?" Rising, Satrius tottered forward, but Rufus waved him back.

He longed to wheel on Bandy Legs, punching and gouging, but there was no point in making a scene. Despite his military training, he wasn't in the best physical shape. Bandy Legs might best him. In addition, the people around them were watching, and listening to every word. If his reputation weren't to sink deeper into the mud, he had to play along.

"Stop, Father. This is Jucundus' man. I'm sure that his master just wants a word with me."

"Yes, that's all." Bandy Legs' snicker suggested that far more might be on offer.

"I'll be back soon," said Rufus with a confident smile. "Why don't you put a few coins on Pugnax while you can? The betmakers won't be accepting wagers for much longer."

"That's good advice," Bandy Legs agreed. "You might as well waste some of your money now, old man, because you won't be around to enjoy it for much longer."

"Leave my father out of it, you dog," Rufus snarled.

To his surprise, Bandy Legs subsided. "That way." He shoved Rufus toward the passage leading to the outside of the amphitheater. With an apologetic glance at his father, Rufus obeyed. The faces of the nobles he passed were either knowing or disapproving, or both. He saw no sympathy.

To Rufus' relief, there was no one waiting with a knife in the gloom of the tunnel. *Relax*, he told himself. *If Jucundus wanted me dead, he wouldn't order it in so public a place.*

Even so, he flinched away from Bandy Legs' next hefty push. Yet again, he wished that he were still in the legions, and about to fight a battle, with his men around him. But those days were gone, and it was his own fault that he was in this sorry situation. Seeing Jucundus' familiar shape at the end of the tunnel, along with several other figures, Rufus' stomach lurched.

For all his wealth, Jucundus hadn't been blessed with looks or stature — unlike Pansa, who'd been blessed with the looks of a god. Although it was well covered by his fine toga, Jucundus' gut exaggerated his lack of height. A long nose wasn't the worst feature in the world, but his was broad too, dominating his face. The large wart on his left cheek drew everyone's eyes. Like many middle-aged men with a receding hairline, he combed his thinning locks forward, fooling no one but himself with his appearance. Today his hair lay in neat, oiled lines on his sweating forehead. To cap it all, Jucundus' ears stuck out at right angles to his head.

*Truly, you should be called "Urceus," * thought Rufus. *You might have a slave to hold an umbrella over your head, but you still look like a damn jug. An ugly one at that.*

Out loud, he said, "Greetings, Jucundus. It's always a pleasure."

"Always the silver-tongued one, aren't you?' Jucundus sneered. He gestured.

Before Rufus could react, Bandy Legs had struck him with a heavy object—a cudgel, perhaps—in the side of his right knee. With a roar of agony, he collapsed. Jucundus watched impassively. He let Bandy Legs kick Rufus a number of times in the belly before waving him off.

Coughing and sucking air into his empty lungs, Rufus managed to sit up. "Was that really necessary?"

"I'd say so," snapped Jucundus. "You missed out on a beating this morning. Where were you?"

"Where was I when?" Rufus immediately regretted his cheek. It took a longer moment for him to catch his breath after Bandy Legs had kicked him again.

"Two of my boys called to your rooms just after dawn. They found only your crippled servant."

"Ah, *then.* My servant—is he badly injured?"

An amused snort. "I'm told he'll live. Where were you?"

Poor Mustius, thought Rufus. Somehow he stilled his hate for Jucundus. "I had gone to the baths. I was woken early, you see, by the tremors. From the bathhouse, I went to check on Pugnax. My fighter."

"I know who Pugnax is." Scorn dripped from Jucundus' voice. "It's a shame that I didn't make you sell him before today. Whatever measly sum he raised would have meant a little more money for me."

"Pugnax will triumph," said Rufus robustly. "And when he does, I'll have two hundred *denarii* to give you. That's only the start. He'll win his next fight, and the one after that."

"Ha! The *lanista* tells me that Murranus is in the best form of his career. I'll take his word over yours. By sundown, you'll be without a gladiator. Then you'll have nothing to give me but whatever paltry things you haven't gambled away. I'll see you evicted too."

Dread filled Rufus at the prospect of Pugnax dying. As to Jucundus' second threat … "Evicted?"

"Once your debts have been proved to the town court, I can't see Pansa wanting a tenant like you. You'll be on the street within days."

Rufus clenched his jaw. "And the money I owe you?"

"You'll pay that back by coming to work for me."

"I see." Looking at Bandy Legs, he could imagine the type of toil that would be expected of him. "Where will I sleep? How will I eat?"

"You'll have a roof over your head, never fear, and food in your belly. All costs will be deducted from your pay, of course, as in the legions."

Rufus could imagine the hovel he'd be expected to sleep in, the slop he would be fed with Jucundus' other low-paid workers. It wouldn't come cheap, though. There would be precious little left each week to give Jucundus. He was to become a slave in everything but name. His shame battled with real anger. There had to be a way out of this.

"Well?"

Jucundus' question rammed home the brutal truth that he had no choice. "Very well. I accept."

"I knew you'd see sense." Jucundus' smile was toothy, like one of the large eels found deep under the sea. He turned to go.

Rufus rallied the last of his hope. "And if Pugnax should win? Will you accept two hundred *denarii* as a payment until I can arrange his next fight?"

"Pugnax is going to lose!"

"You're probably right—but if he doesn't? I swear on my life, and that of my ailing father, that I will pay you back every last *denarius*, starting today. Just give me a little time."

Jucundus regarded him down his long nose, as he might a speck of shit on his toga. After a moment, he shrugged. "You've caught me in a good mood. So be it. Pay me two hundred *denarii* today, and my men will leave you be for a week. If you haven't paid me the same sum by that time, court proceedings will begin. You'll also wind up with a broken nose and cracked ribs, rather than your servant."

"Thank you," muttered Rufus, relieved, and sorrowful for Mustius at the same time.

Trumpets rang out from within the amphitheater, silencing the crowd. A herald began to speak, sparking off a few cheers.

"The gladiators will be parading soon. That's always worth a look." Without another word, Jucundus strolled off down the tunnel, his entourage in tow.

Rufus glared after him. *You're an evil bastard*, he thought. *May Pluto take you soon.* It was tempting to think of drawing a blade across Jucundus' throat, but Rufus had had to slay too many men during his army career. Nearly all had been in the heat of battle, but there had been times when prisoners taken were too much trouble to keep alive. Cold-blooded murder was no longer his way. He wondered about asking Pugnax to kill Jucundus, but even that was not to his taste. A man needed to sort out his own problems, and as honestly as he could.

Even if that meant working for Jucundus for the foreseeable future.

That isn't going to happen, Rufus thought fiercely. *Pugnax will beat Murranus!*

So he hoped with all his heart.

RUFUS' father didn't believe a word of his muttered explanation about Jucundus wanting assurance about Pugnax's chances, before placing a large bet on him. Satrius could not interrogate Rufus further, however. After a fanfare of trumpets, a pair of gladiators emerged onto the circle of sand to rapturous applause. The clash pitted a classic pairing of a *retiarius*, a net fighter, against a *secutor*, or pursuer. The two men were relatively inexperienced—hence their appearance in the first contest of the day—but their arrival was greeted with unbridled approval from the audience.

There were still fewer people than would have been normal by this stage of a games, thought Rufus. Few things were more attractive to the average citizen than fights at the arena. Animal hunts were enjoyable for some, but nothing brought the crowds flocking in the way two men engaged in mortal combat did. The shedding of gladiators' blood, even if they no longer fought during funeral rites as they once had, was sacred. And everyone loved blood. They loved it even more if the shedding of it was laid on for them free, by the notaries of their town, and if they could gamble upon the outcome of the fights. They seemed to love it even more today, perhaps because they believed it would placate the gods, and put a stop to the earth tremors.

Under normal circumstances, Rufus also enjoyed gladiatorial contests. He didn't like it when men died because of the crowd's whim, though. So when the *retiarius* lost, and the spectators didn't think he had fought well enough, he was one of the few who waved his hand in the air and shouted "*Mitte!* Let him go!" Waving his square of linen, Satrius weakly echoed his call, but the vast majority of the audience felt differently. A forest of thumbs jabbed at throats, and thousands of voices roared, "*Iugula!* Kill him!" The thick, hot air reverberated with the blood lust, the desire for someone to die. Pansa, who had arrived in time for the clash, was in no mood to go against the spectators' wishes. Almost at once, he gave the signal, stabbing his own right thumb toward his Adam's apple. It seemed he felt the shedding of blood appropriate today, too.

Poor bastard, thought Rufus, but like everyone else, his eyes were locked on the pair of gladiators.

Wounded or not, the *retiarius* was ready to do his duty. Already kneeling, he lifted his chin and gazed straight at the burning sun. Stepping in close, the *secutor* raised his sword high, checked with Pansa one last time that he was doing the right thing—and brought down his blade in a blur of motion. It entered the *retiarius'* flesh exactly where it should, in the hollow at the top of his breastbone. In it went, slicing apart the skin, the subcutaneous layer and the deeper tissues: blood vessels, lungs, and more. The *retiarius* jerked to and fro on the sharp iron. A bubbling, choking sound left his purpling lips, and he died.

The *secutor* tugged free his blade. Jets of blood spouted into the air as it came free, showering him from the waist down, and decorating the sand with lines of crimson. The slack-limbed *retiarius* toppled sideways and landed with a soft thump.

The crowd's satisfied *ahhhhh* morphed into a roar of "*Habet! Hoc habet!* He's got it!" as the *secutor* raised his bloody sword high.

The *summa rudis*, or referee, waved his stick and a team of slaves trotted out with lengths of chains, and hooks. Few noticed the *retiarius* being dragged away or the "demon" Charon striking him on the head with his hammer, to claim his soul for Pluto. Instead all eyes were on the *secutor*, who was being awarded a palm wreath and a cash prize, and on Pansa, who was standing to receive public acknowledgement of his generosity.

"Your man's on next, isn't he?" whispered Satrius.

"Yes," Rufus replied, his stomach knotting with tension. He wanted to run down to the tunnel and pour some last encouraging words in Pugnax's ear, but it wouldn't be permitted. He had to sit tight, and trust in the gods. Trust in his man and his ability. He closed his eyes and prayed some more.

"There he is!" hissed Satrius, nudging him. "He's looking good, I have to say."

Rufus watched with pride as Pugnax swaggered out of the tunnel, lifting his shield and sword above his head, as if the crowd's applause was entirely for his benefit. Murranus, a couple of steps behind, did the same, yet he didn't receive the same response. Pugnax had already drawn most of the attention. Quickly, he spun in a circle, drawing loud laughter and a reprimand from the *summa rudis*.

"PUG-NAX!" roared Rufus, eager to keep the audience on his man's side if possible. "PUG-NAX!"

To his delight, the call was taken up at once. "PUG-NAX! PUG-NAX! PUG-NAX!"

Murranus' fans, who were plentiful, did their best to compete, but the initiative had been lost. For a few moments, the amphitheater echoed to the sound of "PUG-NAX!" Pugnax turned slowly, motioning with his arms, working the spectators for all he was worth.

Murranus did the same. More and more people began to shout their support for him. "MUR-RAN-US!"

The shrieking of reed pipes blown by musicians standing under Pansa's box ended the clamor. An expectant hush fell as both fighters walked to stand in the center of the circle. Perhaps ten steps separated them.

This was it, thought Rufus, licking dry lips.

Pansa nodded, and the *summa rudis* gestured with his stick.

Murranus didn't hesitate. With an animal roar, he charged at Pugnax.

"Gods, he wasn't ready for that," observed Satrius.

There's no need to point it out, thought Rufus irritably, hoping that this elementary mistake wouldn't prove to be Pugnax's last. To his relief, Pugnax braced himself so that Murranus' shoulder charge didn't send him flying. Parrying a powerful sword thrust, he launched a counterattack, reaching around Murranus' shield with his curved blade. There was a yelp of pain, and Murranus took several steps backward. The audience behind him roared in appreciation.

"First blood to the *thraex*!" Rufus heard the *summa rudis* shout, and his heart sang.

As the two fighters circled one another, each looking for a chance to strike, he saw the wound on Murranus' back. It was over the shoulder blade, and was bleeding profusely.

"It's not deep," said his father.

"That's all right. Murranus' shield is as heavy as a legionary's *scutum*. It'll already be agonizing."

Sure enough, Murranus' left arm had begun to drop. That didn't mean he was beaten, however. With another fierce cry, he launched himself at Pugnax. Throwing his body weight behind his shield, he drove back Pugnax much as he had earlier with the *thraex* in the school. In danger of taking a bad wound, Pugnax retreated at speed.

Shit, thought Rufus. *The crowd won't like that*. But before his worries could coalesce, Pugnax raised his sword and shield high and did a twirl. He had none of the grace of a dancer, indeed, he looked ridiculous. It seemed he was aware of it, because even as Murranus chased after him, Pugnax spun around again.

Laughter broke out to Rufus' left, and then to his right. Men pointed. Some shouted encouragement at Pugnax. Others poured abuse on Murranus, whose supporters were doing the same to Pugnax. But the shouts of "Coward!" and "Fight him!" were drowned out by the roars of amusement.

Rufus grinned. "He's trying to tire out Murranus," he whispered to his father.

"He'd best not flit about for long, or the crowd will turn again."

It was as if Pugnax had heard Satrius' words. Lowering his arms, he faced Murranus, who spat something derisory. The noise in the arena drowned out what he said; Pugnax's reply was also inaudible, but it sent Murranus running forward at him. The two traded blows for a time. Sunlight flashed off their blades and their helmets. The sand, which had been so well raked, was thrown and dragged up by their bare feet. Their shields banged off each other with dull thwacks. Murranus knew well the advantage of his shield. He was able to deflect Pugnax's every blow. The tactic wouldn't win Murranus the battle, Rufus decided. He wouldn't be able to keep it up for long. All Pugnax had to do was not to take a wound, and not to run away too much. Sooner or later, Murranus would weaken enough for Pugnax to injure the bastard again. When that happened, it'd all be over.

Yet Murranus was no fool. Grunting with pain, he raised his shield high. Before Pugnax could react, he brought its rim down on the top edge of Pugnax's, whose arm was driven down by the weight. At once Murranus thrust his blade at Pugnax's unguarded breastbone. Gasps rose from the crowd, and Rufus felt sick.

In utter desperation, Pugnax twisted sideways. Instead of running him through, Murranus' sword sliced a long cut across his chest. Pugnax reeled back in agony, blood pouring down his belly. Murranus was after him like a lion on an injured antelope. Somehow Pugnax held up his shield, resisted Murranus' first strike and then his second. Shuffling his feet, he backed away as fast as he could.

The audience bayed their bloodlust. Men rose to their feet, and were shouting at Murranus to finish the job, to kill Pugnax. *They're so damn fickle*, thought Rufus furiously. *Don't listen to them, Pugnax. Stay strong. Murranus has spent his energy in that attack.*

Sure enough, Murranus wasn't able to pursue Pugnax for long. He halted after only a few steps, and placed his shield on the ground, so that he could rest his left arm and shoulder. His chest heaved in and out. Boos and catcalls rained down on him, but they were also being thrown at Pugnax, who was taking the opportunity to rest too.

Rufus found that he was biting a thumbnail to the quick. Pluto only knew how the contest would go from here, but it didn't look good for Pugnax. His wound wasn't deep, but it was long. Runnels of blood coated his whole front, and had turned his off-white undergarment crimson. The strap that helped to hold the padding in place on his right arm had been partly severed, allowing the layered linen and leather to sag down and expose his biceps. If he didn't finish the *murmillo* with his next attempt, he might never win.

That was, Rufus thought grimly, *if Pugnax even had the strength to fight on.*

Beneath him, Rufus felt his seat shift. For a heartbeat, he didn't appreciate what was happening, but then he saw the cloth awning overhead shaking. His heart pounded. "Stay where you are!" he hissed at his father, whose complexion had gone even grayer.

Wails of terror rose as those around realized what was going on. "Vulcan is angry with us!" cried a man. "The fighters aren't good enough!" shouted another.

Pandemonium reigned in the moments that followed. The dominant sounds were those of roof tiles falling from buildings, people yelling and crying, or calling on the gods to spare them. The ground shook. Incredibly, the entire structure of the amphitheater trembled, like a terrified child about to receive a beating. A number of the statues that stood on the lip of the enclosure—including the one of Pansa—swayed and fell into the arena, landing with heavy thuds on the sand. An awning tore in two with a loud ripping noise, closely followed by another. A terrible screech of stone off stone, came from within the tunnel. There was a loud crash, as something immense struck the ground. Several men who had been about to enter the passage retreated, screaming that part of the roof had fallen in.

Just like that, the tremor stopped.

Rufus studied his father's face. "Are you all right?"

Satrius nodded slowly. He looked very old. "What should we do?"

"Stay put. The amphitheater is well built. It should withstand any further tremors," said Rufus, hoping he was right.

"Very well. We'd risk our lives trying to get out anyway," said Satrius, indicating the next tunnel over, which scores of men were fighting to enter.

"Aye." Rufus eyed Pugnax. He had not won, but at least he wouldn't die. Understandably, neither gladiator had restarted the contest. Now it would be called off, leaving Pugnax to fight another day. Rufus had no idea how he would persuade Jucundus not to ask the court for Pugnax to be sold, but it was better that he had a live fighter to worry about rather than a dead one.

He hadn't reckoned on Pansa.

The trumpets began to blare. They went on for long enough to the panicked audience to stop screaming, and to pause in their headlong flight.

"Citizens of Pompeii!" yelled Pansa as the notes died away. His very figure—tall, golden, confident—demanded attention. "There's no need to leave! The earth has stopped moving. We are safe here. I ask you to take your seats again, for the contest has not ended! Afterward, there are more fights on the agenda, with gladiators of far greater skill. Before that, in the interval, there will be wine and bread for all. For all! Provided at my expense, naturally."

Pansa was taking a real gamble, thought Rufus. Most times that the earth shook, there were a number of tremors before things returned to normal. Yet, as his heart beat out ten and then twenty beats, the ground and the amphitheater did not move again.

With nervous laughs, the audience began to sit down. "It's rude to turn down free wine," cried a graybeard off to Rufus' left. "And bread!" added his companion, a man with a bad squint. More jokes were cracked, about how the statues wanted to join in the fight, about who'd been first to get up and run, about someone who'd wet himself.

On Pansa's orders, the reed pipes sounded once more. With jangling nerves, Rufus studied Pugnax. The bleeding appeared to have stopped, but he was moving with painful slowness. Happily, Murranus didn't seem in much better shape, carrying his shield at least a hand span lower than was wise. They closed in and began to spar, each trying to find a weakness in the other. Neither managed to land a decent blow, and the crowd began to rumble unhappily.

Rufus glanced at Pansa. *Let him end the contest,* he prayed. *They're both injured, and there could be further tremors.*

But Pansa wanted blood. "Get on with it, you yellow-livered cowards, or I'll have you both taken out and crucified!" he shouted. "The gods must be pacified!"

Murranus moved first, somehow finding the energy to charge at Pugnax. Rufus' heart raced as Murranus tried the classic one-two legionary tactic, punching with his shield and following that with a sword thrust. But Pugnax anticipated the move, jinking to the left so that Murranus' lunges met only air. Unable to use his *sica* because of his body position, Pugnax brought his small shield down on Murranus' helmet with a loud metallic clang. Murranus' knees buckled, and the audience roared with approval.

The move must have caused Pugnax considerable pain, because he staggered a little as he moved away, and fresh blood ran from the open-lipped wound on his chest. Rufus clenched his fists. Then, to his surprise, Pugnax closed with Murranus again. The *murmillo* was moving slowly, as if he had drunk too much wine. Within a few heartbeats, he'd taken a thrust to the top of his left arm, forcing him to drop his shield on the sand. With a grunt of triumph, Pugnax advanced, *sica* slicing the air. Murranus retreated from his shield, and Rufus exulted. There would be only one outcome now.

Soon, he would collect his winnings. Jucundus would be appeased. Once the surgeon had stitched Pugnax up, he'd just need time to heal. Within six weeks or so, he'd be ready to fight again. *With Pugnax a winner once more,* Rufus thought, *his creditors would become more amenable.*

Another tremor struck, more powerful than the first. Five statues tumbled into the arena this time, and a large section of awning fell into the crowd. The timbers that held the cloth aloft were as thick as a man's arm, and several people were injured, or worse, when the timbers landed. It was too much for most. Screams of fear rose from everywhere—An old man: "Flee! We must flee!" From a child: "Mother! Where are you?" A terrified looking merchant moaned, "Forgive me, Pluto. I should not have taken your name in vain."

Ignoring Pansa's cries that they should remain where they were, the poorest spectators, who were in the upper parts of the amphitheater, fled to the exits and the stairs that led down to street level. Seeing what was happening, those lower down reacted in the same way. Some ran upward, some down, toward the tunnels that weren't blocked. A few even jumped down into the arena and demanded to be let out through the passageway used by the gladiators.

When Rufus urged his father to remain where he was, he seemed content to obey. They weren't in huge danger of dying by staying put. Their position was only just over a man's height above the sand. Even if the building collapsed, they didn't have far to fall. There was greater risk, for his father especially, in wading into the midst of a terrified mob. People had been trampled to death during the panic of the earth shocks of the previous month. *No,* thought Rufus, *we will wait and see what happens.*

Pugnax and Murranus had stopped fighting again: they both looked exhausted. This time, no one ordered them to continue. Pansa wasn't all talk, Rufus saw. His box was empty, but that was because he was among the crowd, trying to persuade them to stay. His voice was being drowned out by the general panic, however. The fight was over. Rufus mouthed a foul curse. If Pugnax hadn't actually won, he wouldn't get paid the victor's purse of two hundred *denarii*. All that he'd be due was the measly fee for Pugnax fighting. Rufus could already hear Pansa's agent saying that the whole amount wasn't payable because the contest had been inconclusive. He'd argue the point of course, but if Pansa had made up his mind, he would have to agree to it.

Rufus' spirits sank to a new low at the thought of Jucundus' response to his revised circumstances. There would be no sympathy, no mercy. He would be evicted as soon as the court could hear Jucundus' case against him. The moment that Pugnax had healed up, he would be sold to raise money for his creditors. Rufus raised his eyes to the sky. He wanted to scream at the gods, but didn't quite dare, given what was happening. He held in his rage, instead asking silently, *Why did you have to make the earth move now, Vulcan? Could you not have waited for even one hour?*

You have ruined me.

Satrius' grip on his arm drew him a little from his misery. "What is it, father?"

Satrius placed his hand on the stone seating between them. "Feel it. Another tremor."

Rufus didn't need to obey. He could feel the vibration in his buttocks, far stronger than the two previous movements. His stomach did a neat flip, but he managed a reassuring smile. "Don't worry. Nothing will happen to us."

A wave of hot air such as Rufus had never felt, even in the *caldarium*, hit him in the face. It was so strong that he was rocked backward and almost fell. He threw out an arm and just managed to prevent his father knocking his head on the stone of the seat behind. Clouds of sand lashed everyone in the audience. In the arena, the blast sent Pugnax and Murranus sprawling to the ground.

BOOOOOOOOMMMMMMMMM!

BOOOOOOOOMMMMMMMMM!

The double sound was louder than anything Rufus had ever heard. It ripped the air apart, drowned out everything else, even the speech of those right beside him. It felt as if they were all inside a

147

giant drum that had just been struck an almighty blow by a god. Rufus' guts turned to liquid, sweat ran down his face in rivulets. Open-mouthed, more scared than he had been in his life, he turned to his father. Satrius looked equally petrified.

RUMBLE.

The noise was like that made during a horrendous thunderstorm, but thousands of times louder. The fact that there wasn't a cloud in the sky made it infinitely more terrifying.

Rufus' money worries vanished. "*What* was that?"

Satrius' eyes were dark pools of fear. "I don't know. Perhaps the world is ending."

The rumbling died away, and was replaced by shouting and screaming. The struggle to leave the amphitheater became even fiercer. At the top, a man who was pulling at those with their backs to him was given a shove backward. The man tripped and fell, tumbling down the staircase in an untidy tangle of limbs. At the last, his head struck the stone with a sickening crack. He twitched once and lay still.

Rufus paid him no heed. His gaze was locked on a toga-clad man above, someone he recognized, who had stopped trying to push his way to the exit. Instead he was pointing to the northwest, his face twisted with pure fear. "Vesuvius! Gods above, look at Vesuvius!" he yelled over and over.

"Don't move! I'm going to take a look." Leaving his goggle-eyed father behind, Rufus sprinted up the steps. By the time he'd neared the press of people, their desire to flee had been subsumed by the need to witness whatever was happening to the mountain. Everyone's gaze was locked on Vesuvius.

Nothing could have prepared Rufus for what he saw. An enormous brown column protruded from Vesuvius' peak, pushing so high into the sky that it seemed bound for the stars. The muddy colored pillar was soaring upward with incredible speed, and broadening as it rose. Around him, men were screaming that a giant, such as the one that lived under Mount Etna, had broken free of his chains. Rufus had no idea whether that was true, but when the column began to flatten out into a cloud-like shape, it occurred to him that the hot wind in his face was coming straight from the mountain. Whatever was in the column—and no one needed to tell him that it would be bad—would be heading their way.

Fast.

It was time to leave Pompeii.

He pounded down the steps toward his father. There had been occasions—all battles—during Rufus' time in the army when he had felt an urgent need to flee. He never had, because his duty had been to stand with his men and fight, and if necessary, to die. Today, yet again, he could not do as he wished. Although every instinct was telling him to run to the nearest gate and head south, he had his father to look out for. He couldn't leave Mustius any more than he could Pugnax. Servant or slave, injured or no, they were loyal. The sky above darkened a fraction, and Rufus felt an overwhelming urge to piss. He shoved the feeling away ruthlessly. *I might be a drunk, and have a gambling problem, but I look after my own,* he thought. *I always have, and always will.*

Whatever the price.

"I have to rest."

The constant rumbling thunder meant that Rufus only heard because Satrius' mouth was close to his left ear. He had been half-carrying his father. Without answering, he guided them to the nearest open doorway, that of a house, walking with care so that he didn't trip on the irregular layer of rocks and pebbles that coated the ground. Some time had passed since the three—Rufus, Satrius, and Pugnax—had left the amphitheater and already the paving stones underfoot were growing hard to discern. The rain of stones hadn't stopped; if anything, it was growing heavier. There were constant cries from those on the street as they were hit.

Rufus felt a stinging blow on his right elbow and spat an oath of his own. He had lost count of the number of times rocks had connected with his flesh. He could take the pain, and so could

Pugnax, who was trudging along behind them, but his father, who was also being struck, was a different matter. With every step, he seemed to grow weaker. Taking even more of Satrius' weight, Rufus covered the last few paces at speed and pulled them in through the doorway.

Too late, he saw the shape of the crouching dog on the mosaic beneath his feet, and read the words, "CAVE CANEM." There was a ferocious growl. Out of the corner of his eye, Rufus saw a large, black shape lunging forward. Instinctively, he tried to put himself between the guard dog and his father, but his reaction was far too slow.

TCCCHHHINKKK!

Relief bathed Rufus. The chain that tethered the beast had dragged it to a halt a few paces short of their position. With bared teeth, it lunged at them repeatedly, to no avail.

"Friendly thing, isn't it?" said his father. "Maybe it doesn't like our hats."

"I'm not surprised," replied Rufus, grinning. All three had tied seat cushions from the amphitheater on their heads as protection from the lethal rain of stones. They were also coated in ash from head to toe. "We look like circus fools, eh?"

"Better these cushions than to suffer a staved-in skull," his father observed.

No one argued. They had seen more than one person lying on the street, killed as neatly as they might have been by a slinger's lead bullet on the battlefield.

Rufus gave silent thanks to Aesculapius. His father might be too weak to walk unaided, but he still had a sense of humor. There was hope for him yet.

"Let's hope its chain is well secured to the wall." Pugnax raised his sword, which was stained with Murranus' blood. "I could always use this on the brute."

"Leave it be. It will calm down eventually, and the owners could be within," said Rufus. "Besides, we won't be here for long. Just keep an eye on it."

After helping his father to sit with his back against the wall, Rufus peered out onto the street. Fresh fear clawed at him. In the few moments that they'd been inside, it had grown even darker. It couldn't be more than an hour past midday, but it felt as if night were drawing near. There was no sign of the barrage of stones ceasing. They clattered down on the roof tiles of the houses, raising an awful racket. Sprays of water rose from a fountain opposite as it filled little by little with rocks.

The throngs of people passing the doorway were all heading the opposite way to Rufus and his companions. South. Everyone who wasn't desperate, criminal, or insane was going south. Away from Vesuvius. For the twentieth time, he cursed his apartment's position in the city, that they had covered barely ten blocks. Yet again, he considered abandoning Mustius to his fate. Like as not, he had fled already.

You're risking your life, and that of your father and slave, on a wild goose chase, he thought. *Maybe so*, his moral side bit back, *but what if Mustius is unconscious, thanks to the beating that should have been yours?*

That possibility drove the doubt from his mind. Yet it was clear that with his father in tow, it would take too long to reach Mustius. While Vesuvius was this angry, the city was no place to be. He beckoned to Pugnax, who padded over, cat-soft on his feet. Satrius, whose eyes were closed, didn't even notice. "How's your wound?" Rufus whispered, studying Pugnax's chest. There didn't appear to be any fresh bleeding.

Pugnax grimaced. "I'll live. Why do you ask, master?"

"My father's not fit to make it to my apartment, never mind all the way back to the Nucerian Gate. Even the Marine Gate would be too far for him. But if he rests here with you while I fetch Mustius, he should be able to manage it when we return. I want you to look after him."

"You pulled me out of the arena when you didn't have to, master," said Pugnax, his eyes warm. "I'll guard him with my life."

Although Pugnax was his slave and had to obey him, Rufus felt a rush of gratitude. "My thanks. If the owners of the house appear, tell them who I am and beg their pardon for taking shelter. Say that I'll be back soon." He glanced at his father, who appeared to have fallen asleep. "Explain things to him if he wakes up."

"Yes, master." Pugnax's gaze was steady. "May the gods bring you back swiftly."

"Aye." Rufus took a moment to adjust the cushion on his head. Then, before his resolve weakened, he slipped out of the door.

It was apparent within a few paces that he'd have to use the backstreets and alleyways. Every larger way was clogged with people, mules, donkeys, and carts. It was human nature to try to carry away everything one owned, Rufus supposed, but there were times when common sense took precedence over items of furniture or livestock. Again and again, he saw owners berating slaves as they carried chairs, tables, and even cupboards from houses to the street, where they were loaded onto wagons. He felt a stab of gratitude that he'd been a soldier. Even before his debts had necessitated the sale of any valuables he had owned, he'd had precious few objects worth more than a few *denarii*. If he got out of here in one piece with his father, Mustius, and Pugnax, he'd be well content.

The gloom that hung over the streets was even worse in the tiny alleys. If he were not to lose his way forever — Rufus' bowels loosened at that thought — he needed light. He cast his eyes around the nearest doorways. Someone else's ill-fortune proved to be his good. An old man lay half in, half out of the entrance to a shop. The crimson stain in the center of his tunic proved he'd been the victim of crime, not Vesuvius. A small clay lamp, the type that everyone used at night, sat on the counter close by the body. Rufus supposed that the man had set it down as he was about to leave, or as he was assaulted and his premises robbed. Hoping that he'd died fast, Rufus took the lamp and plunged into an alley that would take him northward.

His sandaled feet were soon covered in piss, shit, and worse. Even when there was a drain nearby, many of the town's poorer inhabitants found it easier to empty their chamber pots, and the waste from their kitchens, close to home. Trying not to breathe the foul odors, Rufus gave thanks that he did not have to fear the rain of stones from Vesuvius. The spaces between the two- and three-story buildings were so narrow that all but a few rocks were prevented from coming to earth. For this reason, it wasn't surprising that others had taken shelter in the alleyways. Finding a street urchin cowering in one, he urged the boy to make for one of the southern gates. The boy, wide-eyed with fear, scuttled away from him into a space so tight that Rufus couldn't follow. With a weary shrug, he left him to it.

His first major obstacle was the main street that led from the Vesuvian Gate to the Stabian. It was packed tighter than he'd ever seen it, a mass of wailing, terrified humanity. There were family groups, fathers carrying children, mothers with crying infants in their arms. Behind them, with the slaves, came the ailing grandparents or aged relations. Carts drawn by mules or oxen— once, one of each—were piled high with material possessions, or those too weak to walk. Straw mattresses gave those unfortunates more protection than those who were standing. Cries filled the air from one street to another as the relentless volleys of stones continued from above. In a new development, Rufus noted that many of the rocks were burning hot. A quick, dangerous glance upward revealed mesmerizing dots of red and orange pouring in from a sky that was as black as pitch.

Acid stung the back of his throat, and he wondered again if he should continue. *Damn you, Mustius saved your life*, he thought. Gritting his teeth, Rufus elbowed his way across the Stabian Road. When his path was blocked, he crawled under a cart. Reaching the other side, he aimed for another alleyway. From there, his luck appeared to be in once more. Crisscrossing the larger streets, he traced a path to the forum without hindrance. Normally, he would have cut across the open space to reach his apartment faster, but that wouldn't be wise today. All the same, part of Rufus had to see Vesuvius, had to see how dire things really were.

The instant he succeeded, he realized it had been a bad idea.

Through the blackness, he could see orange-red patches of burning fire—on the slopes of the mountain, he realized. His face warmed as a hot wind, coming from Vesuvius, hit his face. Hard. Something—he had no idea what—was blowing toward the town, with deadly speed.

Running carried the risk of breaking his neck. Rufus broke into a trot.

If he didn't reach Mustius soon, he'd be dead.

They all would be.

"MUSTIUS! Are you there?" Rufus began shouting when he was twenty paces from his apartment. There was no reply, even as he drew closer, and his heart sank. He'd risked his life for nothing. Noticing then that the door was ajar, his heart beat a little faster. Opening it fully, he entered, lamp in hand. To his surprise and relief, Mustius' familiar shape was on the couch. "Mustius!"

Still no answer.

Gods, don't let him be dead, Rufus asked. He dropped to his knees by the couch, felt for a pulse in Mustius' neck. It was there, fast but strong. "Mustius. Can you hear me?"

Finally, a groan. With an effort, Mustius half sat up. "R-Rufus?"

"It's me," said Rufus, grinning like an idiot. "How badly are you hurt?"

"Jucundus' men did a pretty good job, sir," came the rueful reply. "Everywhere hurts. A lot. To be honest, I've struggled to stay awake since they left. Every time I did manage to rouse myself—what in Hades is going on? The noise, the screams. And that banging on the roofs. Is it stones?"

"Vesuvius has exploded."

"Exploded?"

Rufus cut him off. "I'll tell you later. You need a lamp, and a cushion tied to the top of your head. Then we have to leave. At once. Can you walk?"

Mustius' army training kicked in. "I think so, sir." With Rufus' help, he swung his legs to the floor and stood. He grunted with pain, but gave Rufus a firm nod. "I'm all right, sir. Lead the way."

Mustius' determination gave Rufus strength. He would have given much to stay where they were, out of the rain of red hot stones, the clouds of choking ash, but his father and Pugnax were waiting for him. He gripped Mustius' shoulder, as he'd done so many times before they went into battle. "Come on."

The journey that followed was worse than the trials Rufus had endured to reach his home. All light had been extinguished from the sky. The blackness was as dense as that in a mine, but with the fearful addition of the constant rain of rocks. They now lay more than ankle deep in the streets, making the going really treacherous. More and more bodies were evident, victims of larger pieces of stone or of tiles that had fallen from roofs. One thoroughfare was partly blocked by an overturned wagon, abandoned by its owners. The braying donkey that had pulled it was trapped in the traces. If he'd had time, or a knife, Rufus would have ended its suffering, but he had neither, so he walked on by.

Close to the forum baths, a man urged them to shelter in his house. "You'll die if you stay outside!" he cried.

"Maybe," Rufus croaked as he trudged by without stopping. "But people are relying on me."

"The gods go with you," said the man, and slammed shut his door.

The sound had an awful finality to it, which Rufus tried not to think about.

IF he hadn't known Pompeii like the back of his hand, Rufus would never have found the house where his father and Pugnax were sheltering. By the time they reached it, the street was unrecognizable. The roof of one building had collapsed, and several others looked in danger of doing the same. The fountain had stopped flowing and was full of smoking stones. Many of the shops had been boarded up by their owners, but the fronts of others remained open, as if one could still purchase bread, meat, or pots and pans. People's possessions that had been snatched up and then discarded or dropped were visible everywhere. *Amphorae* of vintage wine, a silver tray, an exquisite ivory statuette of Isis. A baby's cradle, complete with bedding. Rufus' eyes were most drawn to a small strongbox, wrapped by iron bands. He was tempted for a moment to pick it up. There was no sign of its owner and for all he knew, it contained enough money to pay off his debts.

He left it where it was.

The dog began to bark again as they neared the door. Rufus heard Pugnax telling it to shut up, and his spirits lifted. They fell the instant that he entered, however. His father was stretched out neatly on the floor, obscuring most of the mosaic that warned visitors of the guard dog. His eyes were closed, and a peaceful expression lined his face.

Pugnax was sitting by his side, clasping his sword. He looked up in shock. "You came back, Master."

"Of course. I—" Rufus struggled to speak. "He's dead."

"Yes. You had only been gone for a short while when he woke up and began to complain of pains in his chest and left arm. It felt like a wrestler was crushing him, he said. His breathing grew very rapid, and he lay down and closed his eyes. He spoke your name once. A short time later, he stopped breathing. Forgive me, Master."

"You have nothing to apologize for. Even a surgeon could have done little." Sighing, Rufus knelt and placed his lips against Satrius', to release his soul. "I'm sorry that I wasn't here at the end, Father. May your passage to Elysium be swift." He longed to say more, to dwell a little with the body, but to linger was to die. Rufus fought back the tears that threatened, and caressed his father's face, as Satrius had so often done to him as a boy. "Farewell." He glanced at Pugnax. "It's really bad out there. The streets will soon be impassable. We must go."

"South, to the Nucerian Gate?" asked Mustius.

"Yes. Away from Vesuvius." Rufus had no idea if Nuceria would be safer than anywhere else, but it was better than heading north, or west.

"I'm ready, Sir," said Mustius, with the same stubborn look he'd worn going into battle.

"So am I," added Pugnax.

Rufus took heart. Wounded or not, these were two good men to have with him. "Stay close. If you fall or are hit by a stone, cry out. Gods willing, we're all going to get out of here."

They exchanged grim nods. As they reached the open door, the guard dog started barking again. Rufus glanced back at it. "I'd set the brute free, but it would take my bloody hand off in the process."

"Serves it right," said Pugnax sourly.

Leaving the dog to its fate, and trying not to think of the boy he'd met in the alley, Rufus led the way outside. *There had been one benefit to his having fought against the tide to find Mustius*, he thought. *The streets had far fewer people on them.* They made good progress as far as the Stabian road, and even there, there was less crowding than before. He even had time to help a woman who'd fallen to her feet and to restore her wailing baby to her. The press at the gate was quite bad, but fortunately, some order still prevailed. Whether it was a kind of solidarity, or just because the crowding was less severe, Rufus didn't know, but it felt good.

Before long, they had exited the walls and were making their way toward the town of Nuceria, which lay some miles to the southeast. As bad as things had been inside Pompeii, it was worse without the sheltering buildings around them. To the north, Vesuvius was just visible as a fearsome black shape, its slopes dotted with fires. The only thing to alleviate the barrage of stones was the presence of other people on the road. The instant that became evident, Rufus began guiding them up to, and around, a pair of figures in front of them, the only people in sight. In his mind, there would be nothing wrong with using others as shelter. It wasn't until he drew parallel with the two shapes — men, he saw — that he recognized Jucundus and Bandy Legs. Between them, they were lugging a heavy wooden chest.

Bastard, thought Rufus. His debts *weren't* going to vanish because of Vesuvius. A tempting thought came to mind. Perhaps it was time to make a new start. With his father dead, there was no reason to stay in the area. He could take Mustius and Pugnax somewhere else in Italy, or even to Hispania. Jucundus would never find them. He wouldn't even bother looking. Feeling a little better, Rufus made to walk past them.

Of course it was at that moment that Jucundus looked up. "Rufus? Is that you?"

Rufus cursed inside. "Jucundus," he grated. "You got out too." He ignored Bandy Legs.

"Yes, thank all the gods." Jucundus' eyes flickered over Pugnax and Mustius. "So did you, it seems. Your father?"

"He died. I think his heart gave out."

"He was a good man."

A moment of civility amidst the hatred, thought Rufus. "Aye. He was." He took a step to the south, then another.

"Wait!"

Rufus scowled, looked back. "What?"

"You and your men can help us to carry this box."

"We could, but we won't," Rufus snapped.

"I'll make it worth your while!" Jucundus had never sounded so desperate. "I'll wipe out all of your debts. Just help us get to Nuceria."

Rufus considered the proposal. It was tempting, but then he studied Mustius' and Pugnax's faces. Both of them looked ready to drop. Even unburdened, this journey was a struggle. "Sorry. I'd rather pay you back."

"I command you to assist us!" cried Jucundus.

"Fuck you, Jucundus. I'm a free citizen, not a slave. Why don't you leave your money and save yourself? That's what anyone with a brain would do."

Instead of answering, Jucundus snapped an order at Bandy Legs. Together, they lowered the chest to the ground.

The whoreson has seen sense, thought Rufus. He was taken off his guard when Bandy Legs tugged out a knife and swung at him. "Gut the useless dog!" yelled Jucundus. "Then his slaves will do as I say."

Rufus lurched backward and Bandy Legs' blade whistled past without catching him. Bandy Legs grunted with anger and advanced, knife at the ready. *The next time I won't be so lucky*, thought Rufus, fighting back fear. Unarmed, he had little chance against someone so determined. "Pugnax! Your sword!"

Rather than obey or block Bandy Leg's path, Pugnax thrust his blade deep into Bandy Legs' side. The movement made his cushion slip back off his head. A horrendous shriek split the air; Bandy Legs dropped his knife. As Pugnax ripped his sword free, Bandy Legs slumped to the ground, where he lay shrieking.

Time stood still.

Rufus gaped at Pugnax, at Bandy Legs, at Jucundus.

Jucundus' eyes bulged, and his mouth worked. At last he found his voice. "You filth!"

"Your man was going to murder me!" Rufus shouted. "My slave acted in self-defense."

Jucundus reined in his temper, even managed a smile. "Help to carry my chest, and I'll forget it, as well as your debts. You can't turn down an offer like that."

"Go to Hades, Jucundus." Rufus eyed Pugnax and Mustius. "I reckon we could be safe in Nuceria, but we need to keep moving."

Their grim nods told him all he needed to know. Rufus turned his back on Jucundus. With a little luck, he thought, the man would die here with his money.

He was again taken by surprise, however, as Jucundus ran after him and tugged at his tunic. "Help me! I beg you!"

Rufus half turned. "Jucundus, I'm not prepared to—" His words dried in his throat as he watched Pugnax lunge in and draw his sword across Jucundus' throat. Jucundus' expression went from stunned to agonized, but he could make no sound. Dark gouts of his blood spattered Rufus in the face, sprayed the ground between them. The life drained from his eyes, and he fell at Rufus' feet. Blood began to pool beneath him, and Rufus stepped away to avoid it soaking his sandals. "I owe you my life twice over, Pugnax."

"He was a sewer rat, master. So is his servant." Pugnax kicked Bandy Legs, who groaned.

Still in shock at what had happened, Rufus was glad that his main debtor was dead. With luck, his debts would go the grave with

Jucundus. All he had to do now was to survive. He threw another grateful glance at Pugnax. "If we make it, you'll have your manumission, I swear it."

"Thank you, Master." Even as a huge grin split Pugnax's face, a stone shot in from above and struck him in the side of the head. Still smiling, he dropped on top of Jucundus' corpse.

Rufus knew before his fingers had even traced the depression in Pugnax's skull that his gladiator was dead. *Go well*, Pugnax, he thought. A tear streaked its way through the ash on his face, and another. Despair threatened to overwhelm him. There was no point continuing. Everyone was to die on this day of fire.

"Come on, sir." Mustius' good hand tugged at his arm. "Don't let Pugnax have saved you for nothing."

Rufus met his servant's — his friend's — gaze.

"You and me, Sir, we've seen things as bad as this. If the damn Germans couldn't kill us, I don't see why a bloody great mountain should."

"You're right, brother," said Rufus, taking strength from Mustius' valor.

Locking arms to stabilize themselves, they turned their backs on Vesuvius.

PART FOUR

THE SENATOR

Kate Quinn

> *"And now cinders, and pumice stones fell too, blackened, scorched and cracked by fire."*
> —Pliny the Younger

SENATOR Marcus Norbanus missed it when the mountain blew up. He had been knocked unconscious by a starveling whore armed with a jug.

"Senator!"

He managed to unstick his eyelids. Blackness gave way to … more blackness? He blinked, but the darkness stayed. A moment ago it had been bright, hot afternoon. *I am dead,* he thought, and smiled. Death. A great deal easier than he had expected. He had not needed a knife at the wrist after all; no need for a hot bath and perhaps a surgeon to open the veins correctly. All he had required was a skinny girl with a jug.

"Senator!" The voice came again. Not the girl who had struck him — this woman was louder, more urgent. All at once his head began to throb and so did his knee. Not dead, then. *Disappointing,* he thought, and realized he was flat on his back in the street, paving stones digging into his shoulders. His lips were caked with something gritty.

"Oh, good. You're alive." A woman's face hovered, supplanting the whirling darkness overhead. "Can you walk? You have to walk, Marcus Norbanus, because I can't carry you."

"Lady Diana," Marcus managed to say. His vision was still blurred and his head ringing, but there was no mistaking the perpetual scarlet gown (did she ever wear anything else?), the tumble of white-blonde hair, the mischievous little face. Not looking mischievous now, however. She looked deadly serious, and that startled him. As long as he'd known Diana of the Cornelii—and he'd known her since she was a coltish little girl, when he entered into his short-lived marriage with a cousin of hers—she was serious about nothing. At least, nothing outside of horses, chariot races, or the current standing of her beloved Reds faction at the *Circus Maximus.*

"Vesuvius has exploded," Diana said succinctly, seeing his look of puzzlement. "The sky has gone dark. And Pompeii has gone mad. So I ask again, Marcus Norbanus—can you walk?"

UP to that point, the day had been going rather well, or at least as well as his days ever went of late. Marcus could not help but like Pompeii—cooler and more sea-washed in this hot autumn than sewer-stinking Rome; rougher about the edges than over-polished Baiae. A vulgar, glittering, likable little resort town where everything was for sale and everyone seemed to be enjoying themselves. He had come to Pompeii on official business after a visit to Misenum to see his friend Admiral Pliny—the only other man Marcus knew who would rather stay up all night writing and debating than sleep. In truth, that was why he'd accepted Pliny's invitation: so he could fill his endless empty nights debating Pliny's treatise on the workings of nature, even though nature did not interest Marcus in the slightest.

It had been to Marcus that Pliny confided about his favorite nephew, just a few days ago. "The lad seems distracted. Forever sneaking off to Pompeii to study with that young son of Julius Polybius, ha."

"*Praetor* Julius Polybius?" Marcus asked idly. "Good man." They had worked together on a corruption case or two.

"Yes, well, if that son of his is luring my nephew to Pompeii to *study,* I'll cook my own balls. Boys that age don't run through their allowances in a month by studying."

"A girl?" Marcus suggested. "He's the age for it."

"Eh, well, the boy goes tight as a clam when I ask him anything. Perhaps you might have better luck …"

And so Marcus had kept an eye out for the boy, once he came to Pompeii. Found him in a spot of bother just yesterday, bleeding and beaten in the forum, and asked one or two probing questions. His troubles *had* involved a girl, and *Aedile* Gaius Cuspius Pansa was somehow mixed up in it, though the boy wouldn't say how. He just sat there looking despairing, and the advice Marcus heard himself uttering had sounded trite and useless. He'd finally sent the boy back to Misenum to face his uncle, but afterward felt queerly ashamed.

The young deserve more from their elders than trite platitudes, he thought. And set off this morning to question Pansa.

The man must have guessed he was coming, because as soon as Marcus set out into Pompeii's streets, he discovered that he was being followed. A lifetime of negotiating the Senate House left you a knack for recognizing it: that tickle between the shoulder blades that meant someone was watching, either for secrets or to calculate which angle best to sink a blade. *Do you have a knife, whoever you are?* No doubt he looked like an easy target—he had made himself one, coming out alone without so much as a slave for an entourage. His pursuer stayed well back, but there was less cover than Pompeii's streets would have normally offered: a series of jolting earth tremors had split the town's northwest quarter that dawn, and those citizens who had not elected to leave town were clustered on street corners in sparse little knots, trading ill omens. Just as Marcus reached the notorious local brothel, he caught a good look at his spy: no hulking thug, but a waif-thin girl with a swarthy face and a mop of dark hair, sliding like an eel through a gaggle of anxious Isis priests.

Probably no knife, Marcus decided, and felt a twinge of disappointment.

He found a seat on a listing crate against the brothel's wall, giving a polite nod to the plucked and painted boy who flashed his bare chest from the doorway. "Two *dupondii* to fuck me up the back?" he offered, lashes fluttering. "Tightest bum in Pompeii!"

"I'm sure it is, but no thank you. What did you think of the earthquake this morning? Is it Vulcan we should be propitiating at the games this afternoon, or Neptune?"

The boy was more than willing to talk bad omens. Marcus bought a jug of sour wine and a stick of dubious-looking roast pork from a passing vendor, munching as he listened, all the while keeping an eye on his pursuer, who was now lurking at the corner of the brothel. She was eyeing the skewer of meat in his hand with a hungry gaze.

The painted boy went inside with a sweat-stained carter. ("Raise your price to at least three *sestertii*," Marcus had advised. "If you really do have the tightest bum in Pompeii, you are undercharging.") He settled back onto the rickety crate, laying his food beside him on a fold of toga. His senatorial colleagues would have clucked at him; a senator's toga was supposed to be as pristine as the position itself. *In which case, we should all wear togas dipped in blood and mud.* Perhaps a hundred years and more ago in the days of the Republic, a toga had borne more honor than it did now—but perhaps not. Perhaps the much-idolized Republic had been nothing but greedy men angling for power, too. Marcus yawned, took a swig of sour wine, and let his eyes droop in the late-morning heat, hoping his hungry little shadow would come out. He wanted to discharge his duty to his friend's nephew, and be done.

He didn't have to wait long. An almost inaudible rustle sounded, and his hand snapped out to catch a set of creeping fingers before they could claim his skewer. Senator Marcus Norbanus opened his eyes. "Now then," he said pleasantly. "Who are you, and why are you following me?"

She yanked at his grip, struggling. Marcus had never been a strong man even before his shoulder had been half destroyed during his arrest ten years ago, and the girl writhed and scratched like an alley cat. He had to double her arm up in a wrestling hold dimly remembered from his tribune days. "Name?" he said in his mildest tone.

She glared murder out of a pair of big black eyes. Her best feature.

"Tell me your name and promise not to run," he said, "and you can have my lunch and my wine both."

"Prima," she said instantly.

A slave, he estimated, but he still gave a cordial nod of his head as though she were free-born, and let her go. His bad shoulder couldn't really sustain that wrestling hold much longer, anyway. "I am Marcus Vibius Augustus Norbanus, senator of Rome."

Slave or not, she didn't seem overly impressed by his status. Well, he wasn't terribly impressive outside the title and the string of names. Just a quiet man of forty-three, not tall, with a crooked shoulder and hair that had gone entirely iron-colored after the terrible events of the Year of Four Emperors. Marcus passed over the jug and the meat. She didn't need encouragement to snatch both. But the big black eyes were still wary over the jug as she drank.

"Your master should feed you more," Marcus said as an opener. "Tell me, do you belong to Gaius Cuspius Pansa?" The *aedile* was the only man in Pompeii with reason to be annoyed with him, after all.

"Pansa pays me to do his errands," the girl admitted readily enough. "But I work at a *caupona* – the master there owns me."

"Which *caupona*?"

She tore off a bite of toughened pork in aggressive silence.

He let it go. "Why does Pansa have you following me?"

She ate the rest of her pork in quick bites. "Can I have another?" Waving the empty stick.

"Do I get my answer?"

"Be nice to a girl, Senator. I'm just trying to fatten up a bit."

Marcus beckoned the vendor again. "Why?"

She snorted, smacking her own bony backside. "Would you pay good *sestertii* to poke that? Men pay more if you're plump. My sister is plump and the men all ask for her."

"I'll take your word for it." He handed over another stick of the charred meat. "I assume Pansa heard I was in town again? After yesterday's debacle in the forum, I'm not surprised he's keeping an eye out for me."

"So he is." Her eyes were still wary.

"And I am keeping an eye out for him as well. I was informed he would be paying his usual visit to this brothel this morning, to register any new whores leasing a bed. I thought I'd wait for him and have a chat." Marcus gave an avuncular smile. "How lucky he sent you to follow me. You can deliver my warning for me."

"He wanted to see what you were up to, that's all — "

"Tell him I know what *he's* up to: taking advantage of the nephew of a dear friend of mine. I suppose it seemed like easy pickings, having an innocent boy beaten and robbed, counting on the fact he'll be too ashamed to tell his illustrious uncle. But you can tell the *aedile* he will leave that boy alone in future."

"Pansa doesn't like to be told what to do in his own city."

"He may be an important man in Pompeii, but he is still only an *aedile*. I am a senator of Rome, with a bloodline that goes back to the divine Augustus himself. If Pansa crosses me again, I will crush him like a flea." Marcus gave another smile, surprised at himself. He'd never made such a bald threat before — in the Senate it was all done with hints and veiled language. *I am tired of subtlety.* He was tired of everything.

"And Pansa could crush *me* like a flea," little Prima threw back at him. "You might do better to tell him yourself because he won't like that message coming from a skinny little slut like me."

"Is that what he calls you?"

"When he's in a good mood." A ripple of extraordinary bitterness crossed her face. "When he's in a bad one, he just clips me round the ear."

"Then find a better man for whom you can run errands."

"I can't." A cynical little laugh. "Unfortunately, he's got this skinny little slut by the hairs."

"Why?" She gave an insolent shrug, but there was vulnerability under the insolence. "What is Pansa to you?"

"My blackmailer." She tore off and swallowed an impressively large chunk of meat. When he raised a brow, she snorted. "What? You think your fancy friend's nephew is the only one Pansa extorts, or are you just surprised that a tavern wench has anything worth blackmailing?"

"Everyone has something of worth."

"Well, all I've got is my idiot sister." The wine had apparently loosened her tongue. "Capella dreams of freedom. A silly dream, but I won't let Pansa take it from her. She thinks she's going to get her freedom and start some nice life, but she can't do it if she's registered as a whore. One look at me and anyone would see what I am. But my sister? She's all pretty and rosy and soft—she shouldn't be stained with it."

So you take the stain for two, Marcus thought. Whoring and spying, all for love. What people did for their families!

What would I have done if I didn't have my son?

He already knew the answer to that.

"No one of honor would hold against a slave girl what she did in obedience to her master," he said instead, wondering why he was standing here outside a whorehouse arguing with a slave who apparently had a bottomless pit instead of a stomach.

"That shows how much a senator knows about people, even one whose bloodline goes all the way back to the Divine Augustus. People haven't *got* any honor. That's how we ended up whoring in the first place. We were sold as girls with a rule that we weren't to be used as prostitutes. Didn't make any difference to our master. I got registered on Pansa's rolls as a whore, and that's done, but if I do Pansa's errands, he leaves my sister off." Prima gulped down another bite, shaking her head. "Though I'm just as much of an idiot as Capella for indulging her little dream. No matter who's on the rolls and who's not, we'll never get free."

"Not quite." Marcus felt a flicker of interest. "The law gives freedom to those used illegally in a whore's trade. It was Emperor Vespasian's innovation; I worked with him on the finer legal details." It had been an interesting case; the kind of law he enjoyed hammering out, and he smiled at this rude little slave girl for bringing him the chance to address the law in a live setting. She was insolent, she was vulgar, and she undoubtedly deserved a good whipping for the way she addressed her superiors, but her quandary was exactly the kind of detached problem he enjoyed unpicking. "Would you happen to possess a copy of your bill of sale?" he asked politely.

She stopped chewing and stared at him as though he were speaking Greek. "Of course I don't!" she snapped, as if she thought he was trying to trick her. "People like me — we eat, we shit, we fuck, we die. And nobody cares. Laws are only for rich old men like you."

"That is where you are wrong. Laws are for every Roman, high and low." Marcus imagined the look on that smug *aedile's* face if he could deliver another blow by stealing his little spy. "If you will come with me — "

He reached for her wrist again, and that was a mistake. Her nostrils flared in anger or alarm, and her hand came around in a vicious arc, smashing the wine jug against his knee. As soon as he doubled over with a hiss of pain, the jug hammered across his ear — and then it was nothing but darkness.

AND now Vesuvius had exploded, and he'd missed it all because of that jug. "A vast and entirely unique phenomenon, whether natural or divine, and I slept through it," Marcus heard himself commenting. "Admiral Pliny will howl at me."

"Not to pry — " Diana helped Marcus sit up as people buffeted past, some carrying bundles under their arms, some pausing to stare and point at the darkened sky. "How in the name of all the gods did you get yourself knocked unconscious outside the most notorious brothel in Pompeii?"

"I was looking for a man."

"Didn't think your tastes went that way," Diana said. "My cousin Marcella will be disappointed. She was always bent on seducing you."

Marcus brushed off the flippancy, his head pounding. "Yes, well, tangling with corrupt officials leads one to strange places. Even brothels."

"Why didn't you take a good hulking slave or two with you? I never met a senator in my life who didn't travel with an entourage!"

His knee was throbbing as badly as his head. "Never mind why."

"Very well. Can you walk? Lean on me."

He managed to lurch upright with her small callused hands lifting his elbow. He hissed pain through his teeth, tipping his head back, and when he caught sight of the sky, his eyes were finally clear. It was pitch dark, and specks of ash whirled like black snow. "Dear gods," he breathed. "What is this?"

"I was in the amphitheater when it happened." Diana slid her arm under his shoulder, supporting him on the injured side. "There was a huge double boom, like Jove dropping every thunderbolt in his quiver. And then an enormous cloud rose from the mountain. By the time I managed to fight my way free of the amphitheater, the sun was gone. Very bad timing."

He blinked. "Why?"

"Because all the chaos cut off a very exciting bout. A *thraex* and a *murmillo* going at it like Hector and Achilles. I was sure the *thraex* was going to win, but—" she looked up at the black sky and shrugged.

Marcus had never been a superstitious man, looking for omens in every cloud on the horizon or feather that fell from a bird's wing. But he stared into that unnatural black sky, and shuddered. "Perhaps the gods have decided to end it all."

Diana let out an extraordinarily rude snort.

"You don't see a sign in this?" He waved a hand up at the swirling ash, the day turned night. "What else could it be?"

"No idea," she said briskly. "But if you want signs, Marcus Norbanus, think about this one. I'm stumbling my way from the amphitheater to the Herculaneum Gate, and halfway across town I fall over you. What are the odds *that's* a good sign?"

If I'd been looking for a sign of good fortune, it wouldn't be you. Of all the people to be thrown together with in a disaster, he would never have chosen Diana of the Cornelii. Not merely because she was a woman—Marcus knew women of tremendous *gravitas* and good sense, and he also knew women of lethal determination and resourcefulness. But Diana was something of a joke. All through Rome she was known as a girl whose face was eagerly gazed upon and whose conversation (unless one was a Reds follower or a lover of horseflesh) speedily avoided.

But she was slanting her brows at him in inquiry, and she *had* stopped to come to his aid, which was more than a great many panicky people in a crisis would have done, so he gave a nod of thanks and said "A good sign, indeed."

She ended up hauling him into the brothel. "Better get you out of the street and sitting down so we can look at that leg. Besides, I've always wanted to see the inside of a whorehouse ..."

"Does it live up to your expectations?" A narrow hall with five curtained nooks leading off to the side; a staircase leading upward; a door at the end wafting the stench of a latrine. Marcus did not see how any man could find himself in the mood for intimacy in such surroundings, but men of sufficient youth could find the mood more or less anywhere—he remembered that much about being young.

"It seems a little depressing." Diana swept back the curtain of the first nook. The stone ledge with its straw-stuffed pallet had a mussed blanket, but the little space was empty. She assisted him through, turning him to sit on the pallet, and Marcus grimaced as his knee sent a jolt of agony up to his hip. "Rest here and let me see what I can find in the way of help."

"Don't bother," he said, but she was already gone in a whirl of white-gold hair. So much energy, galloping through life as though it was the last lap of a race—Marcus found it a little tiring. There was a good deal of speculation among the men of Rome as to just what it would take to exhaust her in bed. So far as Marcus knew, very few had had the chance to put their theories to the test. Diana of the Cornelii belonged to the colts she bred and trained on her little villa just outside Rome—not to any particular suitor.

Footsteps ran lightly down the stairs in the hall, and she was back. "There are two whores huddled in a corner upstairs moaning in a language I've never heard. Absolutely useless — they refuse to budge from beneath their blankets. Everyone else appears to have fled."

Something occurred to Marcus. "Why don't you have slaves with you?" Diana's father was far too absent-minded to impose any suitable control on his daughter, but even he would have insisted on attendants if she went traveling.

"I had a good pair of guards, but they fled when the awning at the amphitheater collapsed. Maybe they weren't as good as all that." Diana dropped to her knees. "Let's see that leg …"

Marcus caught his breath as she straightened his knee. He didn't need to pull back the folds of his toga to know it was swollen the size of a *trigon* ball.

"Strained," Diana announced, fingers seeking out the painful points. "Not broken. A bit of strapping should see you able to walk." She looked around, and tore the curtain down from the doorway.

"Since when are you a *medicus*?"

"I train my colts to run races, Marcus. You know how many times I've been thrown out of a chariot?" She began ripping the curtain into strips. "If it can be banged, bruised, or broken, I've banged it, bruised it, or broken it."

"You are the most bizarre girl I have ever known," Marcus observed.

"Aren't you lucky you ran across me when the sky fell, then?" She went to her knees again, examining his leg. "This is going to hurt. Do you need something to bite down on?"

He looked at the little cell, empty except for the bed and an obscene wall-mural in flaking paint. "Bite down on what?"

Diana rummaged under the pallet and came up with a carved wooden phallus.

Marcus gave her a look.

"It does seem a bit big to get one's teeth around," she agreed, hefting the thing. "I don't think real ones come in this size. None I've seen, anyway…"

"I assure you," Marcus said dryly, "that I can choke back a scream without needing to insert a wooden phallus between my teeth."

She tossed the thing aside, taking hold of his knee. "Then shut your eyes and pretend I'm a proper physician."

"Likely a physician wouldn't do any more good than you." Marcus shut his eyes. "'Medicine is the art of guessing.'"

"Who said that?"

"Aulus Cornelius Celsus, ignorant child. Don't you know anything?" She was winding his knee in strips of cloth, by the feel of it. Yes; it hurt.

"I know how to drive a four-horse chariot, subdue any unruly stallion in the empire, and calculate betting odds for four factions in sixteen heats simultaneously. And I know how to strap a knee. Hold still, now—"

"Why go to so much trouble?" Marcus opened his eyes as she tied the bandage off. He knew he should be more afraid than he was, but he could not summon it. Not fear, not panic—he felt nothing but a certain mild interest. "I don't really require a working knee at the moment."

"Are you mad? We have to get out of Pompeii, and I may be nicknamed after Diana the Huntress, but I don't really see her swooping down on her moon-chariot to give us a ride to safety. If we're to get out of the city, we'll have to walk every step of the way."

"What if I don't mean to flee?"

"This isn't some ridiculous display of stoicism, is it?"

"Pliny's nephew thought I was a Stoic," Marcus mused, "but no, I cannot really subscribe to that philosophy. Its precepts demand a control over emotion that can be impractical in times of—"

"Marcus." Diana looked up at him through the fringes of her hair. "I don't know if the gods are tipping Rome into Tartarus, or if Vulcan simply stripped the top off the mountain to air out his forge, but Pompeii is no longer safe. I saw people trampling each other underfoot at the amphitheater. I saw a man's head crushed against a stone step. When I finally got free, I saw people running from their houses with arm-loads of belongings, and then thugs clubbing them to the ground for a chance to steal whatever they were carrying. By the time the sky went dark, the main thoroughfare was so well lit by buildings that had caught fire from fallen lamps, I could see my own shadow running behind me. We are getting *out*, Marcus."

"No," he said quietly.

"What?"

Until now, he had not been certain. He looked around this fetid, windowless little cell that stank of male seed and female despair; he heard pounding feet and the rising mindless note of a shriek from the streets where a city was tearing itself to pieces, and he felt ... he felt ...

Marcus Vibius Augustus Norbanus exhaled a long breath. "I intend to die."

He felt relief.

WHEN did it start, the bleak, creeping tide of hopelessness? At yet another interminable meeting in the Senate House where he listened to the spite, the pride, the petty jealousies that rippled along under all the unctuous profundity, and realized that *nothing* he worked for mattered? During yet another banquet where a woman's shrill laughter reminded him of the wife who had deserted him for a young Cornelii? Or was it the pain in his crooked shoulder stabbing him dawn after gray and meaningless dawn, the pain of an arm badly wrenched out of place when he was arrested and tossed in a cell during the Year of Four Emperors?

Maybe the hopelessness had been seeded in that cell, ten years ago. A cell no bigger than this one; smelling not of semen and sweat but of stark, brassy terror; enduring the pain in his shoulder and wondering if he was to be dragged out and torn apart by a mob—all because the current claimant to the purple felt uneasy of Marcus' illustrious family name. *If they'd left me a knife, I'd have opened my veins in that stinking straw and spared myself the next decade.* A decade of bitter senatorial back-stabbing and even more bitter boredom, knowing that no matter how many laws he helped to pass, they helped nobody—the lowborn and the luckless like young Prima with her empty stomach and eyes full of scorn would still be ground to nothing. A decade of ignoring the snickers that came when he stood at the Rostra with his crooked shoulder. And he was so often tired, because his last decade was all days as black as the afternoon had turned outside, and nights that were utterly unspeakable.

"I intend to die," he said again, and the relief was violent. How many times had he thought that, awake and sleepless in his quiet *domus* in Rome, working on another treatise whose advice would never be heard? How many times had he put down his stylus and taken up his knife instead, pressing it almost idly against the blue line of the vein in his arm?

That habit might have started in the last year. When sensible, even-handed Emperor Vespasian had died and the purple passed to his hot-headed son Titus—Titus, who was not so bad a fit for the purple, but who had no sons of his own. Titus, whose health was inexplicably failing after just a year, and who had no one to succeed him but a wild-eyed and vicious younger brother. *I would rather be dead than serve that thug Domitian if he becomes Emperor.*

Or perhaps the explanation for Marcus' idle games with his knife's edge did not lie in such a noble reason. Perhaps they began when his own son departed home to finish his education, and there was no longer anyone to smile for. No longer anyone in the house at all, except indifferent slaves who thought their master a crippled fool.

Well, there was no need for a knife now. No need to walk Pompeii unattended by guards, as he'd done these past few days, because he hoped he'd be robbed and murdered. No need for anything but patience—the patience to wait for a looter come to dash his brains out with a cudgel, or for the roof of this brothel to collapse about his ears. The patience to sit calmly and wait for death.

Marcus Vibius Augustus Norbanus had never lacked patience.

He looked at Diana, still staring up at him with those blue-green eyes of hers, and hoped she was not about to weep.

"You idiot," she said.

Perhaps he shouldn't have been surprised. She could drive a chariot and a four-horse team, after all—unseemly skills, but not ones generally mastered by hand-wringing weepers.

"You're going to die in a whorehouse?" Her voice was hard. "The blood of the divine Augustus is going to make its end on a mattress soaked with the sweat of a thousand Pompeian sailors, under such charming sentiments as—" peering momentarily at an epithet scratched into the wall—"'*Arpocras had a good fuck here with Drauca for a* denarius.' Truly?"

"Not the most illustrious of surroundings for one's final moments," Marcus admitted. "But even the blood of Augustus cannot always choose."

She stared at him a while longer, still sitting back on her heels. *A good many men in Rome would have given half of what they owned to have Diana of the Cornelii on her knees before them*, Marcus thought. Much more than a single *denarius*.

She rose, folding her arms across her breasts. "Why are you courting death?"

He shrugged. They might have been the last two people in Pompeii—the sounds of screams, of shouting, of pounding feet from outside had all faded into the background. "I am done, that is all. I weary of life, and I have nothing to fill it. Let it end. Take yourself to safety. I do not care in the slightest what happens to me."

"What about your son?" she snapped.

"I would have liked to see his manhood ceremony." It was a father's purpose and pride to help his firstborn son into his first toga. *Tell the truth*, Marcus thought harshly. *The only reason you haven't let the blood out of your veins yet is because you thought to wait until Paulinus'* toga virilis *ceremony passed. Until you'd draped the folds over his shoulder, and given him some words to ease the pain of losing his father.*

He pushed the thought away. "My son is almost grown. He is near to done with his schooling, and he speaks of becoming a tribune in the Praetorian Guard. He has cousins and relatives aplenty who would aid him in such a career, in advancing the ranks, in finding patrons and clients and even a wife when the time comes. He no longer needs me."

"Rubbish," Diana said. "Get up."

"Can you drag me out of Pompeii by force?" Marcus smiled. "I think not."

She stared at him a long, speculative moment. "You're right."

"Then—" Marcus picked up her small rein-callused hand and kissed it. "May the gods see you to safety."

"No need." She crawled onto the grubby pallet of straw beside him, sitting cross-legged like a stable boy. "Because I'm not leaving."

"What?"

"You're not just going to cause your own death, Marcus Norbanus." She gave him a dazzling smile. "You're also going to cause mine."

IT was perhaps the most frustrating quarter-hour he had ever experienced. "I have had forty-three years, and it is more than enough. You are only twenty-six. Far too young to resign yourself to death."

Diana ran her finger along another line of graffiti scrawled into the wall. "'*I fucked many girls here.*'"

"Have you thought of your father? You have never been an obedient daughter to him, and he should have put a rod across your back and forced you to a good husband a decade ago, but he will still be heart-broken to lose you."

She twisted her head almost horizontally to look at another set of scratchings. "'*Victor fucked with Attine here.*'"

"No one of the Cornelii will soil themselves with horse-breeding. If you die, your family will sell all your precious horses—"

"My father shall send them to the Reds." Diana uncurled her slender legs and stood up on the mattress, craning her neck at another bit of filth high on the wall. "'*Anyone who wants to fuck should ask Attice for sixteen* asses.' Really, just sixteen?"

"A woman who looked like you could charge a great deal more," Marcus snapped.

She batted her pale lashes at him. "You flatter me."

"You are a foolish child."

"Do you want this foolish child's death on your head?"

He tried silence after that. *She will lose her nerve,* he thought, listening to the distant noise of shouting and thumping feet, curses and screams. *She will break and bolt for safety. All I need do is out-wait her.*

She fell back on her elbows — cool as though she were reclining at a banquet. He remained silent. She smiled at him. He did not smile back. The silence stretched.

The young want to live, he thought. *It is the strongest urge they know. Nerve or not, it will drive her away in the end.*

"Did I tell you why I came to Pompeii?" Diana tilted her head, looking at Marcus down the length of the pallet. "A horse."

Naturally.

"Splendid beast; a chestnut as tall at the shoulder as my eyes. Plenty of muscle; might anchor a *quadriga* as an inside runner. A season to race him for the Reds and then I'll put him to stud." She extended her legs, crossing her feet comfortably in his lap. "I'm naming him Boreas, after my old stallion that just died. Decent lineage out of Spain, sired by Aquila who was sired by Hannibal, who in turn was sired by Bubalus, and before him Hibernus — "

No one can know more than four generations of a horse's lineage, Marcus thought in horror, but she rattled off a full fifteen generations on *both* sides of the wretched animal's bloodlines, then mentioned the mare she had just brought to foal before coming to Pompeii. "Now, she was sired by Ajax, who came from Gemmula and Nereus" — on and on in that cheerful drone, listing horse after horse as her feet flexed and unflexed in his lap; it was her only sign of restlessness — "Polynices out of Pertinax, Sagitta out of Speudosa — "

Marcus reconsidered whether or not he did, in fact, have endless patience. "Will you not leave a man to die in quiet?"

" — and then there's Pegasus who just retired from the Greens; not the most original name, but that horse really could fly — "

He squeezed the bridge of his nose. "Please."

Her eyes twinkled evilly through her fringe of hair. " — and Valens wasn't much in the way of stamina, but they crossed him with a line of chariot ponies out of Britannia and got Volucer, who won more heats for the Whites than any stallion since the Republic — "

"What will it take," Marcus interrupted, "to quiet you?"

"Come with me out of Pompeii," she said promptly.

"I will only slow your escape. Believe me, I am not being noble. You will never get to safety towing me and my wretched knee."

"It's a chance I will have to take," Diana said, "because I will not leave you behind. You are family, Marcus, however distantly. I've known you since I was a child, and I cannot — "

"I *am* family, your senior in family status as well as age, and I order you — "

"I've got a lovely little mare named Callisto, she gave me twin colts last spring so of course I had to name them Castor and Pollux — "

"You may be the most beautiful girl in Rome, but you are also the most boring!" Marcus knew he was not being polite, but really, even his calm had limits. This was enough. "Even when you are not trying to annoy me as you are now, your conversation has always quite literally sent me sprinting from the room after a quarter hour!"

"I could say the same for you, Marcus Norbanus. You may be brilliant, but whenever you drone on about grain laws or the declining birth rate, my eyes start crossing. Takes far less than a quarter hour, too." Diana's wicked sparkle faded to seriousness as she looked at him. "Please — come with me. For my safety, if no other reason. You think a lone woman will be able to make it through the streets as they are now?"

"A woman of your rank — "

"Rank means nothing in chaos. I'll be robbed, raped, and left for dead if I don't have a man with me."

Marcus refused to give way for the logic of such damp sentiment. "I am an aging senator with a limp and a bad shoulder. I will be no protection, so don't use my arm's questionable prowess as your excuse."

"You have the sharpest eyes of any man I know. You can watch my back, and I'll watch yours." She swung her feet out of his lap, rising. "Please."

He looked at her, and she made his eyes hurt. All that eager pulsing *life,* sending her bouncing on her toes, plaiting her fingers together, skirts swinging; nothing about her still or soothing. He wanted to shut his eyes; he wanted to turn to stone here in this obscenity of a room and let the walls come tumbling down. He wanted her to go away.

"I can recite a lot more horse breeding statistics," she warned. "I can recite them by the *mile.*"

He gritted his teeth.

"Or maybe I'll seduce you." She flopped back into his lap, her neat hips landing in his hands instead of her feet this time. "If we're just going to sit around waiting to die, we may as well pass the hours fucking. There's a wall-painting outside the privy that shows a man humping a woman upside down; I've never tried it that way—"

"Oh, dear gods!" He stood up, ignoring the shriek of pain from his knee and dumping her onto the squalid floor. "Let us go, by all means, if you will just close that vulgar, fact-spewing mouth!"

"GODS' wheels," Diana whispered in the door of the brothel, at the same time as Marcus said again, "Dear gods."

When they first ducked into the brothel, Pompeii had been a strange dark place clouded with flecks of whirling ash, shadows dashing everywhere, shrill screams of panic ruling the air. Now they stood in the doorway looking out over a land of ghosts. The street had whitened strangely, though black clouds still blocked the sky overhead. Something pale and frothy choked the air, blanketing the paving stones, and for a moment Marcus thought of snow.

Mountains that exploded; days that turned to night—was snow falling from a hot wind any more strange? But he felt a stinging sensation on his head, and then another, even as Diana swore and clapped a hand to the back of her neck. Stones were falling from the sky, ashy white and ashy gray. Marcus stooped to sift a handful. Rough pebbles of some lightweight stone, porous, almost weightless—but the rain of it on his bowed head still hurt. "Admiral Pliny would know what kind of stone this is," he heard himself murmuring.

"Who cares what kind of stone it is, when it's raining down on our heads!" Diana tugged at the folds of his toga, draped over arm and shoulder in the usual perfect pleats. Just because a man spent his nights wishing to die didn't mean he dressed carelessly in the morning. "Here, wind this around your head and shoulders to give some protection."

"No."

"Don't start about the sacredness of a toga and how it can't be debased for—"

"I have no illusions about the sacredness of a toga." He began unwinding the heavy folds from his shoulders, and looping them about hers. "But I refuse to guard myself from the fall of stone. If a rock from the sky strikes me down, so be it."

"Marcus!"

"That is my price." He let his voice bite. "You insisted on dragging me with you; very well. I will not have your death on my hands. But *my* death is still my own privilege. Frankly, the sooner I am hit by a stone and taken from this world, the faster you will be able to get on." He wreathed her head and shoulders till she looked like a Parthian savage, and her eyes glared at him from under the heavy chalked folds. "Do we have a bargain?"

"Yes," she clipped off.

"Good." He stretched a little, letting his bad shoulder straighten without its additional weight of expensive cloth. He felt light, steady, still curiously unafraid, and he ignored the sting of the small stones against his bare head.

"Fortuna go with you," someone whispered, and they both turned back to the door of the brothel. A hunched figure stood there with a lamp: the boy whore with the painted eyes, the one who had chattered to Marcus when he first paused under the overhanging wall. His eyes were enormous with terror, and he let out a little whimpering moan at the sight of the falling stones.

"Come with us." Diana urged, but the boy shook his head. *Two dupondii to fuck me up the back,* Marcus remembered. *Tightest bum in Pompeii!*

"Get out while you can," he said gently, but the boy's head kept going back and forth.

"Don't you see?" he whispered. "The city's dead. The gods killed it. We're all dead now."

"Not yet." Diana raked the hair out of her eyes, pale strands already patched gray with ash. "Not yet!"

The boy just offered them his lamp. The handle was a penis; the god Priapus' enormous phallus jutting up with its usual jaunty air. The kind of thing to bring luck to a brothel. Now it just looked pathetic.

Diana snatched the lamp with a muttered oath and they plunged out among the ghosts.

MARCUS wondered if the fields of asphodel would be like this; the lands where shades drifted when they had lived lives neither good enough for blessing, nor wicked enough for punishing: endless, listless, half-lit twilight. Marcus' feet sank into the piles of weightless shifting stones, his knee letting out a scream with every step. Diana had wedged her shoulder under his, taking as much of his weight as he would allow, and her small, hard arm was around his waist like a band of wire as they made their halting way down the street. Diana kept her head down in its padding of toga, braced against the hail of stones, but Marcus looked about him in numbed wonder. A man dragged an ox along by the halter, the beast heaped with lashed-down bundles, stumbling fetlock-deep in the crunching debris of stones. A mother crept along with three children in tow, two linked by the hand and another clinging to her back, whitened by the fall of ash to a quartet of ghosts. A pair of men blundered ahead with outstretched hands, falling at the same moment over a collapsed roof-beam hidden in rubble—one man rose and stumbled on, blind as an ant; the other lay where he fell and just breathed up at the sky, watching the stones that fell toward his face. A gaunt alley cat darted swift and silent with a half-crushed rat in her mouth, and Marcus' eyes somehow followed the cat past the fallen man, the lowing ox, even the mother with the desperate children. A cat had no time to wonder if the world was ending around her; she saw dead rats appear in the rubble like meals delivered from the gods, and did not think to ask more. He thought of the whore named Prima; her bottomless stomach; her cynical affection for—a sister, hadn't it been?

Did you take your sister and run like that cat with her dinner, little Prima? Or are you dying in this dead city, too?

He twisted his head over his shoulder, and saw the man who had fallen to the stones was dead, eyes staring up at the black sky and filling with pebbles. Maybe a larger rock had struck him on the head and finished the task. Or maybe he had decided this was the end, and his heart shuddered its last in terror.

Marcus could still feel no fear. Just an endless, horrified sorrow.

"Don't." From under his arm, Diana sawed the word out through gritted teeth.

"Don't what?"

"You caught your breath like a sob. Don't weep, Marcus. Don't you dare weep."

"A senator does not weep," he said automatically. But all around him a city was dying: was that not worthy of grief? No man of Rome wept; that was for women and sentimental slaves. He had drunk that in with his wet-nurse's milk, with everything else a *man of Rome* was supposed to be—all those precepts he'd declaimed so pompously to Admiral Pliny's nephew. But perhaps those precepts were wrong. Marcus had been a man of Rome all his life, doing his best to find dignity and *gravitas* in all things, and it had brought him to this place of death.

Diana's voice was weirdly calm, coming from her swathe of toga. "You know what kills charioteers when they crash?"

He looked at her. "Being dragged along through scouring sand by four maddened horses."

"Despair. There's a flicker of a moment when you act, and maybe have a chance to live—or you freeze, thinking you're going to die. The instant that flicker of despair comes in, you've lost the chance. It's out of your hands, and before you get another chance to cut yourself free, the skin will be stripping off your flesh in long curls. Like the peel off an apple."

They had reached the corner; Diana paused to scout the choked way ahead. A cart blocked their path, canted on one broken wheel, its mules flinching under the hail of stones. The blind, shuffling hordes parted around it like a stream of water.

"So," Diana resumed calmly. "Don't weep, Marcus. Weeping means despair. Despair means sinking down right here and dying. You may want to die, and maybe you will—maybe I will, too. If death comes, it'll find you willing and me fighting to the end, but it will find *both* of us moving. We won't die just waiting like that cowering he-bitch back in the brothel who couldn't shift himself out the door to come with us, or that idiot who fell over a roof beam and decided he'd had enough." She drew the knife at her belt—the dagger charioteers carried to cut themselves loose of the knotted reins in a wreck. "I am Diana of the Cornelii, Marcus Norbanus, and I refuse to die standing still. So, die later—but move now."

She slid out from under his arm, pushed the lamp into his hand, and went crunching off through the stones toward the broken cart. Marcus watched her in astonishment. *Have I ever heard her string so many words together without a single reference to a horse?* he thought. *Has anyone?*

He was, despite his numbed horror, impressed.

The driver in the stranded cart had abandoned his team and was frantically raking arm-loads of possessions off the back—a silver statuette, a bundled toga, an iron-bound box. "Get away!" he screamed at Diana, seeing the gleam of her knife in the falling ash, but she ignored him and went to the mules. A few slashes and she'd freed them of their leather traces. "*Stop!*" the driver bawled, and she leveled the dagger at him before he could come any closer.

"If you're leaving the cart to save your own fat rump, give your team the same courtesy," she said, and spat through her white teeth between his feet before turning to give the mules a slap each on the bony rump. They shambled free, and Diana came back to Marcus, re-sheathing her dagger with a competent shove. "Lamp," she said, and he raised it. She peered through the swirling ash and falling rock, and she pointed. "That way," she said. "Toward the forum." She wedged her shoulder under Marcus' arm again, and he looked down at her, still surprised by his own—well, surprise. This was *Diana*: a pretty, brainless little thing with a bizarre hobby and a father too foolish to stop her indulging it.

"What did I say about standing still, Marcus?" she asked, and her voice had the snap of a charioteer's whip. "Die later. Move now."

"Yes, my lady," he said, and took another step on his screaming knee. And another.

IF the streets of Pompeii had become the ghostlike fields of asphodel, the forum was Tartarus. The world had gone mad here; the city's pleasant open space of business and worship had become a pit of muffled cries, flickering torches, and falling rock. Shapes darted wildly from the temple of Jupiter, some muffled by cloaks and cushions against the rock-fall as Diana was, some ignoring the danger to clutch arm-loads of temple treasures—Marcus caught a glimpse of what looked like a silver ewer, an amber figurine, a sackful of coins spilling down the steps. A woman shrieked from somewhere in the colonnades: "Fabia, has anyone seen Fabia? *Fabia!*" A man howled from somewhere in the forum's heart, and the sound cut off in a gurgle.

How many men will die of falling rock? Marcus wondered. *And how many will be murdered for loot or for a ride on a cart — or simply because someone sees a chance in the chaos to settle a score?* He would have put his coin that murder would see more people dead in Pompeii today than falling stones. When the world was upended, men became desperate — desperate for escape, for loot, for something to cling to. And desperate men would do anything.

They only caught a glimpse of the forum's madness, and Diana turned them away past the massive baths and toward the north. "Last time I saw a city tear itself to pieces, I had to hack a path straight through the worst of it to get to safety," she remarked. "Fortunately, this time we can afford to miss the madness."

"What city was that?" Marcus asked, diverted.

"Rome, of course. Ten years ago, during the Year of Four Emperors when number three got torn to bits. I had to haul all my cousins straight through the Campus Martius to get them to safety, gods' wheels, but that was a *horror —* "

"Ah. I was locked up during that particular riot."

"Is that when you started thinking that life wasn't worth living?"

Marcus declined to answer. He stumbled and nearly fell as a boy pushing ahead of them tripped in the piling stones; Marcus lifted his arm from Diana's shoulder and bent to raise the boy. "Careful, the footing is treacherous —" The boy was surely no older than Paulinus; on the cusp of manhood but not yet needing a shave. *Pray the gods you live to shave your chin,* Marcus thought. The boy had dropped a bundle in his fall, and he scrabbled for it with a cry. Marcus expected to see a bag of clothes or some cherished keepsake, but it was a dog, huge-eyed with fear and swathed in a blanket. Gently he replaced the dog in the boy's arms.

"Come with us if you want to be safe," Diana said, but the boy was already darting off with a gasp of thanks, or perhaps it was fear.

"A dog," Marcus said. "For some it's a child, for some it's an amber statue and a bag of coins, for some it's a dog ..." Did anyone know what was most precious, until it was threatened and you had to grab it and run?

189

That struck him, and he looked down at Diana as she slid her shoulder under his arm again. "You're empty-handed."

"So are you." She hitched along into motion, past the baths, hauling him despite his bad leg pulling behind. She was small, but sturdy as a rock.

"I have nothing here to value," Marcus said in complete truth. "Do you?"

"I do," she said. "We're just not there yet."

"And where is *there*?"

She raised her lamp as they came to another seething cross of streets, swearing as a stone glanced off her bare wrist. "There," she pointed over the bent and swathed heads of the people stumbling through the stones. "Straight northwest, toward the Herculaneum Gate."

"Why that way?" A baby was screaming somewhere in the crush; Marcus twisted his head, but couldn't see if it was a child lost from its mother or safe in her arms. He couldn't see, and he'd never know. "Wouldn't the Marine Gate be closer?"

Diana hitched into motion, pulling them into the rush like a current. A slow current: the accumulation of stones underfoot was rising like an inexorable tide. "The person fixed on death does not get to pick the route, Marcus."

"But the Marine Gate *is* closer. If we skirted the forum and made our way past the Temple of Venus—"

"That's a senator for you," Diana complained. "Always knows a better way!"

"I help build cities for a living, girl. I know how to find my way around a map!" Marcus felt a twinge of irrational irritation. "The only direction you understand is 'off the starting line and turn left for seven laps!'"

Her teeth flashed white in her ash-grimed face. "I like you better when you're not brooding."

"We *are* going the wrong way."

"Feel free to keep complaining. This is still the way we're going."

"You will be the death of me."

"I thought that was the idea."

A shape reared before them, pushing against the current of the crowd, and Diana broke into a shout of alarm. Her dagger flashed free again, but it was a girl, swathed and bulky, and she screamed as she rebounded off Marcus.

"We mean you no harm, Lady—"

But she fell on her side into the heaped stones, letting out a gasp. Diana squatted to raise her. "Get to the gate, girl, you have to get *out*, not go back into the city!"

"Can't," the girl jerked out. Her *palla* fell back, and Marcus saw her enormous belly. *My wife was never that big, even in her last month with Paulinus.* He knelt, ignoring the wrench of agony from his strapped knee, and helped Diana raise her. "Th-thank you—" the girl gasped. Fine-boned and pretty; all her body's weight seemingly coalesced into that giant ball of belly. Her fingers linked around the arc of her stomach like a frail bracelet, and Marcus saw the flash of a betrothal ring. It proclaimed her a woman, but she looked so young he could not think she was anything but a girl.

"Where is your husband?" he asked gently.

"Home. I'm trying to reach him—I had a litter, but my bearers ran away. I was on my way to a wedding—" Looking down at herself; giving a laugh that was half sob. She was all finery: an emerald-green *stola*, gold bracelets and gold rings and gold combs in her ash-clotted hair. Wedding finery, not clothes for walking through Tartarus. "I was arriving early to fix Aemilia's veil. I'm supposed to be leading her to her husband right now, and I don't even know if she's alive—"

The girl broke off with a gasp, clutching at the huge arc of her own stomach. Her eyes flickered panic, but Diana stretched out a hand and laid it on the swell of green silk. "Just a spasm." Diana had no ring on her own finger and a slimness that said she'd never given birth in her life, but she spoke with such calm authority that the pregnant girl's eyes pooled relief, and Marcus' own apprehension checked in his throat. "You won't be birthing for another ten days at least; it hasn't dropped low enough. You could come with us to safety—"

But the girl couldn't walk above a waddle; even Marcus could see that. "She needs to get home and wait out the madness," he said briefly. "I'll take her."

Diana looked at him, and he looked at her. She gave a terse nod, all ash and grime and narrowed eyes that had never, not once since this gruesome disaster descended, filled with tears. He nodded back, and suddenly he wanted to tell her to think well of him after he was dead. If he died helping this young mother-to-be in her jeweled finery to safety, would that at least meet Diana's standard of moving, of not waiting for death like a dumb beast?

I want to die with your good opinion, you little horse-mad girl.

The pregnant girl's cry broke the long stare between them. "Sabinus! Sabinus, is that you —"

Another vague shape in the whirl of falling rock; a man with red-rimmed brown eyes, and a wailing child clutched inexpertly on one hip. The woman's husband, perhaps — she fell on him with another cry.

"I will see you home safely." The man's reddened eyes were full of horror, and he spoke with the brusque efficiency of a centurion or an engineer, but his tone was kind. In a moment that was nothing but panic and despair, it was almost bizarre. "Can you take the torch so I can carry my little friend here? Found her in a gutter." He squeezed the tiny girl as if to comfort her. "Don't worry, now we've found you, we'll keep you safe!" And then a mutter: "Dear gods, the world is mad."

"When will it stop?" the pregnant girl wanted to know as he passed her the torch, but he had only a weary shake of his head.

"We could take the child," Diana started to offer, but the little trio plunged back into Tartarus even as the man shifted the child to his shoulder. Diana looked after them for a moment, then shook her head. "I hope that girl gets under a roof. She's probably giving birth soon."

"What?"

"I've delivered more foals than I can count, and my cousins have birthed seven children between them. Believe me, I know the signs.

The stomach drops and hardens; it — " A shrug even as Diana came up under his arm again. "Her baby will likely come tonight."

"You said — "

"I lied," Diana said, and they lurched forward into the chaos. Another street, another turn — the gate must be near; the press was suddenly frantic.

"You should have a wife like that," Diana said suddenly, half shouting to be heard over the cries around them.

"What?"

"Your wife was a nagging bitch with a voice like a chisel. You should have remarried. Someone like that girl in the green, pretty and pregnant. If you had more children after Paulinus — babies; children you couldn't tell yourself were almost grown and didn't need a father — you'd never leave them orphaned. And," Diana added, "another wife would keep your house in better order. I'd feel like dying too, if I had to live in that welter of dust and rude slaves you call home."

"The world as we know it may be coming to an end," Marcus shouted, not just to be heard over the noise, "and you're debating my marital and domestic inadequacies?"

"Not to mention that your son looks far too weedy for his age. Get a wife who will keep a good cook and kitchen slaves, and feed him up properly. You've been shoving him off on my cousins to mother for the past ten years."

Marcus heard his own voice drop to a pitch of pure icy cold. "How dare you."

"Because that girl back there and the baby in her belly and the little girl found in a gutter are probably going to die, Marcus." Diana never stopped moving, never stopped shuffling through the stones, but her voice was savage, and her arm about his waist cut viciously tight. "They'll probably all die, a child whose mother left her behind and another mother whose baby probably has not a chance in a thousand of seeing sunlight — " Diana kicked ferociously through the heaps of strange, pocked stone. "Because the rocks are falling faster, if you didn't notice. It's twice as deep underfoot as when we left the brothel, and if it keeps coming like this, everyone in the city behind us is going to die. They'll die clawing to live, clawing for one last breath, because that's what people do. Except you. You can't be bothered to live. And in this surrounding?" Motioning at the frantic crowd around them, pressing mindlessly toward safety. "How dare *you*."

"I will not be judged," Marcus said tiredly. "I have conducted my life honorably and I'll conduct my death the same way. Perhaps helping someone like that girl, who I pray will see her child born safely. In sunlight."

"I pray it too," said Diana. He looked down at her and saw she was gazing ahead with fierce eyes, lashes clogged with soot, face contorted. But not a tear fell.

IT was chaos at the Herculaneum Gate. People shoving, scratching, dropping bundles they had hauled stubbornly through the disappearing streets only to abandon them at the last. Diana staggered, losing the lamp as a huge man with the musclebound arms of an oarsmen shoved her out of his way, nearly knocking her under the rush of feet. *Desperate men,* Marcus thought even as he yanked her up. He pulled her back to his chest, and they shuffled forward like a four-footed beast, his chin atop her head to protect her from the fall of stones. The constant hail seemed less bad here, but who could say with souls screaming around them like shades clawing to get out of the underworld?

It was like being born, squeezing through that gate which had two narrow arches for travelers on foot, but which had suddenly become too small for the traffic. A desperate plunge into the darkness under the arch, the blackness overwhelming without the lamp. Sudden crushing tightness on all sides as the stone walls pressed everyone together; slave and senator, man and woman alike; all reduced to a frantic mass stinking of ash and terror. And then freedom on the other side, everyone springing loose from the gate's confines and staggering for the road which split toward the coast, toward Herculaneum and Neapolis.

But does either place mean safety? Marcus thought. *Perhaps the blackness and the ash have extended there, as well.*

"Just a little further," Diana shouted over the spreading din. Someone outside the gate had dropped a lit torch; she snatched it up before it could gutter out. "Less than half a mile, and we can stop—"

"Stop for what?"

"The reason I insisted on *this* gate and not your damned Marine Gate. Which, you were right, would have been the shorter route."

"I knew it," Marcus muttered, and forced his knee into service again as they went stumbling on into the growing piles of rock.

The light from the torch was feeble and guttering, but infinitely better than the blackness of the gate when they'd lost the lamp. They staggered on, coughing, peering ahead—it was only with difficulty that Marcus recognized the gradually-looming shape as a good-sized villa. It just looked like a lump of ash, stones heaped high on the long roofs. Every door was sealed behind heaps of accumulated debris. "If you're hoping for aid, whatever family lived there is either long gone or locked in," Marcus began, but Diana was charging grimly round the villa's side to the outbuildings.

"Help me," she called, and Marcus aided her in dragging a gate open, then went to work on another set of doors. The sight of his own arms shocked him as he leaned down to paw the heaps of rock away. His flesh was red-gray, ash mixed with blood where falling rock had slashed and bruised his skin. He straightened as Diana dragged at the cleared door, and for the first time felt pain outside his knee. His neck, his shoulders, his back stung as though he had been pummeled; the muscles of his legs burned from the wading and clambering through all the sky-fallen rubble; he could feel another set of trickles on his neck that he suspected was blood from yet more cuts. *How have I not been struck on the head and killed?* he wondered, and felt a real irritation.

Diana finally managed to drag the door open, still holding her torch, and an unmistakable smell hit Marcus' nose. He sniffed again. "Manure?"

"It's what a stable usually smells like, Senator." She ducked inside. "Hold the torch and keep well back from the stalls. Horses hate fire."

He followed her just inside, lifting the torch high, and the cessation of the pebble-barrage on his back nearly made him stagger. In the suddenly-splintered darkness inside he heard a full-throated whinny and the double-thump of hooves against wood; saw a pair of fire-reflected eyes. Diana went toward the eyes and the sound, voice lowered to a sudden croon. "There you are, my love, I was afraid someone would have stolen you. Did you think I was leaving without you?"

Marcus collapsed against the wall, sinking down on a wooden trunk of some kind that probably held harness. "Please tell me we did not come all this way for a horse."

"Of course we did." From somewhere or other, Diana unearthed another lamp and brought it to Marcus to light the wick. "I bought him, so I am responsible for him. I wouldn't leave him to die any more than I'd leave you."

Marcus started to laugh. He was not at all amused, but it was laugh or throttle her. "You risked your life for a *horse*?"

She did not bother answering, just took the torch and slid it into the nearest bracket to shed more light. Marcus went on laughing, and Diana calmly unwound the filthy folds of his toga from her head and shoulders, shaking her pale hair loose. It felt like a thousand years since he'd wrapped her up at the whorehouse. She looked around the abandoned stable, and shook her head. "Just four days ago I was standing here talking to the daughter of the house. A little red-haired heiress seething resentment because she had to get married. She reminded me of me." Diana went to the water trough, making a face to find it empty. "I wonder if she still lives."

"I wonder," Marcus echoed, and his bleak laughter turned to coughing. He had the tang of ash in his mouth; his chest was so tight it might as well have been banded in iron shackles; and the fit of coughs finally turned to wheezing. He leaned his head back against the wall, wondering how much of the falling ash he had breathed in, and feeling suddenly exhausted. Now that he was sitting, he did not think he could ever get up again.

"Drink." Diana was standing in front of him, holding out the leather flask from her belt. "I can't find any water here, as short as water's been in Pompeii lately — but this is better."

Marcus lifted the skin to his lips and tasted. "Wine?"

"I've been saving it. It'll strengthen you, and we have to get moving again."

Marcus took a deep grateful swallow, feeling the iron bands about his chest ease a little. "Not a bad vintage. Wherever did you get it?"

"Accident with a wine cart this morning, oh, a thousand years or so ago. A wine-sack sprang a leak, and everyone passing helped themselves to a free cup while the carters stood there cursing us. I was on my way to the amphitheater and it was hot, so I stopped to fill up. I'm glad I did." She studied him as he drank again, her eyes flickering like blue-green sparks in an ash-smeared mask. "Good, you've got a bit more color. You don't look so much like a slave out of a salt mine. The kind that gets left to die on some windswept crag when they get too old and used-up."

"And you—" Marcus looked up, feeling a welcome strength course through his veins from the wine "—look more fetching covered in filth than any woman has a right to look."

She grinned, turning away to rummage in the back of the stables. "Drink up. We can't stop long."

"So our journey continues." Marcus held the last swallow of wine in his mouth a moment, savoring it. "You, me, the horse as a chaperon?"

"Who needs a chaperon?" Rustling and banging commenced, and Diana came back into view with a bridle tossed over one shoulder. "My reputation has long been well and truly buggered."

"What's buggered is your good sense. You risked your life to rescue a *horse*." He still wanted to throttle her for that.

"You're the one who needs the horse." Diana entered the stallion's stall, making little crooning noises and rubbing a hand down the long nose. The horse whickered nervously, but nibbled along the line of her shoulder as she rummaged for horse blankets and began folding them across its back and haunches for padding against the rock-fall outside. "You were very stoic about your leg, and really it's a wonder you got as far as this, but stoicism isn't going to get you all the way to Herculaneum on foot." Strapping the blankets down across the horse's back in a few deft movements, she came out of the stall and dropped down before him, pressing her fingers suddenly to the swelling in his knee. He drew a sharp breath of pain despite himself, and she raised her eyebrows. "You see? And this—" Her hand rose to his chest, which still sounded a faint wheeze as he breathed. "You haven't been screening your mouth like me, so you've been breathing ash for hours—that cough is only going to get worse." Her hand dropped. "You can't walk any more, Marcus. You need a ride, and I happen to have one."

"I told you I was not leaving this city."

"And I told you I would not leave you."

"So, we're back to that."

"We are."

They stared at each other; Marcus sitting stubbornly upright, no matter how much he hurt, Diana on her knees before him with no subservience at all in those narrowed eyes. The first time they had looked at each other like this, back in the whorehouse, he had thought all he had to do was wait until she lost her nerve and bolted.

He knew better now than to assume Diana of the Cornelii would ever lose her nerve.

Then find another way.

"We've come to the end of this story." Marcus felt his own heart thudding. "This is the part where you leave me behind."

Her chin jerked up. "And as I said before, I won't leave you. I need your eyes to watch my back, I—"

"Through Pompeii, perhaps. But now I will only slow you down." Marcus found a rag hanging off the end of the trunk, began wiping off his hands. "That horse will carry two, but slowly. By yourself, you will be in Herculaneum within hours. Safe. And I want you safe, Diana. I owe you that much."

She shook her head stubbornly, hair flying. "No."

"Yes." He began to wipe his face unhurriedly. "It's time for you to save yourself. So kiss a dying man goodbye and gallop off like Diana the Huntress, and I will smile and open my wrists. Because there is one thing upon which you have persuaded me, and that is that a Roman should not simply wait for death to roll over him. I'll move toward mine—" giving her a half-bow where he sat "—as I promised."

A tired, gray-haired man dying so a bright-burning young woman could live. It was at least a better reason to seek oblivion than simple despair.

Diana sat back on her heels, her gaze burning fury. "You'll open a vein, then."

"Yes," Marcus stated.

"You know how?"

"Oh, yes." All those nights in the darkness back in Rome, tracing a dagger up and down the raised lines in his wrist ... It had been hypnotic; a lulling, comforting dream. He could find his own vein even if he were blind.

"Takes a while, though, bleeding out. Who knows how long the mountain's going to give you? Try something faster." She was up and standing, dagger unsheathed in one hand. "Under the breastbone, straight and fast to the heart. That's the way to do it, Marcus Norbanus." She tossed it to the straw between his feet.

He felt his brows quirk. "How would you know such a thing?"

"Patrician women know how to die, too." She gazed at him a moment longer, then turned back to the horse. "The Year of the Four Emperors," she said, reaching for the bridle. "My cousins and I hid from a raging mob in the Temple of Vesta, with one knife between the four of us. We all knew how to commit suicide honorably, and we all knew it was a better end than being torn to pieces by rioting

199

Praetorians." She drew the bridle over the stallion's ears, fastening straps and buckles. "It didn't come to that. But we'd have done it."

Marcus gave a single nod. "Of course. I would expect no less."

"There's another reason women take their lives, and that's when they're dishonored." Diana turned back to him, reins looped over her arm and her eyes glittering. "I was dishonored that year, Marcus. I was fifteen, and I was dishonored against an alley wall. Should I have opened my veins after that?"

It took Marcus a moment to speak. He suddenly had a tide of rage and nothing at all to spend it on—her gaze utterly rejected anger and pity both.

"Well?" she challenged. "How many men in Rome would have said I should take my own life to end the shame?"

"Not I," he said quietly. "But—many."

"Well, piss on them. The man in that alley wasn't worth my shame. He didn't last long enough inside me to boil an egg, and I've been sorer after long horseback rides. I spat on the ground and walked away, and I never thought *once* about taking a knife to my wrist. I have rarely even bothered thinking about that man these past ten years. Because my life is worth more than what's between my legs." She dropped the stallion's reins over the rail and stalked toward him, two savage steps. "And your life is worth more than a habit of despair."

He rose. "Diana—"

She reached out, grabbed him by his gray ash-clotted hair and hauled his head down. She kissed as ferociously as she did anything else. Pain bloomed suddenly in his lip as she sank her teeth deep, and he swore into her mouth. She yanked away, her mouth red as a rose with his blood, and she gave a swipe of her hand across her own lips, leaving her fingers scarlet. "There." She slapped him on the chest, leaving a red mark just below the breastbone. "That's where you drive the knife in."

She stood there all over ash and rage, and he thought her splendid. *A splendid final kiss*, he thought. Even if it hurt, it was still a kiss. It had been a long time since a woman kissed him.

"You're right," he acknowledged, dabbing at his lip. "My life *is* worth more than a habit of despair. My life is worth yours."

"Marcus—"

He stooped and picked up the dagger lying in the straw between their feet. "You are correct that a blade to the heart is fastest. However, it requires a certain degree of strength, and the same unfortunate Year of Four Emperors that took your virtue also took most of the strength from my arm. Consequences of imprisonment, and a beating that never healed. So—" he slashed deep and calmly down one wrist "—the opening of a vein will have to do."

The blood leapt out as though waiting to leave the vein, pattering on the straw. Marcus felt no pain at all. It was Diana who shouted, lunging for his wrist, but he had already plunged his hand into her hair and held her at arm's length. That he *was* strong enough to do.

"I know you better than I did a few hours ago," he said, blood sliding down his arm. "You're too stubborn and too brave to leave me, even if you should. Even to save yourself. So I am removing the choice from you."

"You *ass.*" She wrenched away, lunging back toward the water trough where she'd left the unwound length of toga. She tore at the filthy purple border. "If we get you bandaged tight enough—"

"Don't make me fend you off with a blade." Marcus still held the dagger, and he hated to think of pointing it at a woman, but he feared it might be necessary.

"*I am not leaving you to die,*" Diana roared, flinging the toga down with a blistering curse and diving into the stall with the horse. "A rein, a length of leather, something to tie your arm off with—"

Marcus considered making another slash just to hurry himself along—the first wouldn't be deep enough to finish the job at all quickly—but there was a loud and very sudden creak. His eyes flashed up to see the other side of the stable doors wrenched wide, and suddenly they were not alone.

Two men stood in the straw, shaking themselves loose of cloaks and padding, swearing in loud, shaking voices. Marcus had always prided himself on being able to evaluate any Roman's status by his bearing, his face, the quality of his clothes, all before a word was spoken — a useful trick from his days of arguing legal cases — but he could determine nothing about these men. Not the color of their skins, not the fabric of their tunics, not the accents in their incoherent words. One was big and the other was bigger; they had blood on their arms and blood on their shins; they had rough voices and white around their eyes. They might have been porters or fullers; legionaries or farmers; citizens or slaves — there were no such defined differences between men anymore, not now. In Pompeii there were only the dead, the dying, and the desperate.

And there could be no doubt into which category these men fell. It came off them like the smell of a rotting corpse.

They saw him and they froze. Marcus moved first, lifting his bleeding hand very slowly. "I mean no harm." He was careful not to look in Diana's direction. She stood in the stall on the far side of the big stallion, blocked from the doorway by its tall neck, but in another instant — "There is nothing for you here," Marcus said with all the authority he had ever mustered giving a speech at the *Rostra*, but the men were already looking past him. One let out a rough cheer at the sight of the stallion.

"A horse! Gods be damned, some luck — "

"For one of us," the other scowled, and raked Marcus with his eyes. "You got any coin on you?"

"You are welcome to it." Using only his bloody hand, he loosened his belt and let the pouch drop. He still had his dagger in the other hand, concealed at his side. *You have not used a blade against another soul since your tribune days twenty years ago,* he reminded himself, *and even then it was only in drills.* But he still didn't drop the dagger. Every instinct he had was shrieking at him, shouting danger — he dared not look at the stall, the nervously snorting stallion. Diana had surely dropped down behind the stall's wall; perhaps she could slide out into the back of the stables unseen —

His knee gave a shriek of agony as the bigger of the two men crossed the stable to topple him with a casual shove. Marcus managed to fall on his side, hiding his dagger in the straw beneath him, as the giant picked up his pouch and went rifling through it.

"Ten *denarii*," he snorted. "You talk like a senator; don't you have any more than this?"

"Let it be," the other man interjected, stalking for the horse. "There'll be time to get money later. You see how many there are on the coastal road? Every rich man in Pompeii is off with his cash-box and his wife's jewels under one arm. Kill this one if you want, and let's get moving. We'll take turns on the horse—"

"I get first turn." The big man dropped a knee on Marcus' chest, unsheathing a blunt knife in a matter-of-fact yank.

"Don't kill me," Marcus blurted out, and his heart hammered in his chest. "There's no need. You have my coin, and I'm already dying—" holding up his bleeding arm. "Don't kill me."

The man considered for a moment. "Everyone's dying today," he shrugged. "And I hate patrician pricks. Always wanted to cut a purple throat like yours."

No, Marcus thought as the knife drew closer and horror expanded in his chest. *Oh, no.* Not because the thought of death didn't still croon sweet dark appeal, but because he knew what would happen if the thug's knife continued toward his throat. *Don't—*

The stallion screamed and came bursting out of its stall, sending both men spinning around. Diana was only halfway onto its back, ash-red skirts and ash-pale hair flying, but her teeth were bared as she whipped a stray length of rein across the horse's neck. It charged forward, knocking one of the men on his back into the straw, and the way before her opened as wide as a first-place finish in the Circus Maximus. She had only to kick the horse straight ahead, Marcus thought—straight out through the stable doors and she'd be gone to safety, or as much safety as this world still held.

But she didn't kick the horse ahead, and he knew she wouldn't. She brought it whirling around in another yank of rein, sending it straight at the man who half-knelt over Marcus.

The man scrambled, shielding his head. The stallion half-reared under the low roof, mane flying, and Diana leaned perilously low to slash at the huge man with the length of rein that was her only weapon. "*Bastard,*" she screamed, laying on those hunched shoulders like a whip, and the man made a grab for her arm, but missed. The horse was still whirling, all motion and flying hooves in the confined space, and Diana aimed another slash—but the man on the far side had risen, risen with a shout and re-entered the fray, and now she had men crouched and closing in on both sides.

"*Ride clear!*" Marcus shouted from the straw, but she didn't have so much as a glance for him. She was still whirling the horse, reins doubled in her fist, trying to herd the two men away from him as she laid about her with her makeshift whip, but one of the men risked a slash across the face and got close enough to make a grab. He had her by the ankle and then she was being dragged off the horse, shrieking curses.

"A horse *and* a girl," the man grinned, slapping Diana flat into the straw and holding her there by the throat. She writhed, clawing at his wrist, but he was as huge and ash-covered as one of Vulcan's giants, and she was such a little thing when you saw past the swagger and the mouth full of curses and the cool courage. *So small,* Marcus thought, dragging himself upright. His leg was utterly useless, nothing but a dead limb screaming pain, but he hardly felt it. He just saw a girl in the straw—and the same girl at fifteen, up against an alley wall gritting her teeth and spitting curses the way she was now, even as her skirts were being hauled up.

"You can have first turn on the horse if I get first turn on the girl," the bigger man was saying, turning away from Marcus toward Diana. Neither of them noticed Marcus as he struggled to his feet, and why would they? Just a useless purple-throat senator: a soft-handed, gray-haired desk-man who was swaying on his feet. Marcus didn't stop, just limped up behind the ash-covered giant and stabbed: one short blow of the dagger sliding up beneath the ribs. The man gave a curiously girlish gasp, half-turning, and Marcus twisted the blade deeper, deeper, teeth gritting so hard he feared they'd shatter, blood thundering in his own ears. The man was turning, trying to clutch at him—Marcus lifted his free hand, shoving the man's head back, and saw the blood slide down his own arm from his opened wrist. He felt suddenly giddy, and wondered if now was the moment he was going to collapse and die. *Not yet,* he thought grimly, *not yet* – and he dug his thumb into the ash giant's eye socket and heard the scream, felt the eye burst wetly even as he dug the dagger in deeper under those ribs –

They went down in a tangle, and Marcus' leg sent out a shriek of agony so much deeper than all the pain before it that his vision went white. *Not yet,* he insisted somewhere inside the agony, and felt a warm rush of blood across him and another girlish-sounding gurgle. The dagger tumbled free as the giant fell into the straw at Marcus' side.

Under the breastbone, straight and fast to the heart, he thought incongruously. *That's the way to do it.*

Then a pair of hands descended on his neck, and his breath crushed off inside his throat. "Bastard," a voice snarled, and Marcus opened swimming eyes to see the second man, shoulders blocking out the torchlight, tears cutting absurdly through the ash on his face. "You bastard, that was my *brother* –"

Oh, Marcus thought almost politely. *I'm sorry. Well, not really – your brother was a raping, looting thug and so are you –*

Then the hands tightened about his throat, and his head filled with sparks. He opened his mouth but could not even gasp. His hand thrashed after the dagger in the straw, but he couldn't find it and his head was exploding, everything was red-rimmed and fading – but he smiled. He still managed a smile. *Not too bright, are you?* he wanted to ask of the man now throttling him. *You turned your back on her.*

Diana was up from the straw as noiseless as a wraith, and she had the length of spare rein doubled between her hands. Two soundless steps and she'd whipped it about the man's throat. Then she clamped her knees around his back as though settling onto a horse, and leaned back with her full weight. She hauled on his throat as hard as she must have ever hauled a four-horse team to bring them to a halt, and Marcus could see the tendons cording all the way down her slim arms.

The killing pressure in his throat fell away. Marcus let out one enormous gasp, dragging in a lungful of air that tasted like wine, and then his hand was lunging for the dagger again. Because Diana had hauled the man up like an unruly horse, but he was three times her size and the moment he snapped back she'd go flying—

Marcus fumbled the dagger through a fistful of straw, everything moving too fast, everything but his own impossibly clumsy fingers. He brought it round in another slash but missed; the man's eyes bulged and he yanked and gurgled against the rein looped taut around his throat. He yanked, and Diana abruptly let one side go. His weight fell forward, hands peddling, and all Marcus had to do was hold the blade still.

For the second time he was crushed under foul-smelling weight. It took the man a few moments to die, gasping and choking, and Marcus just lay there, breathing shallowly and enjoying it. *The breathing,* he clarified, even if just to himself—he liked to be clear in his thoughts. It was the breathing that was so enjoyable, not the man's dying, or his weight, or his stench. The stench really was unbearable. Ash, sweat, and the kind of ingrained dirt which meant the man hadn't utilized a bathhouse in many a day. *Disgraceful,* Marcus thought. *Roman baths are available to all, even those of direst poverty. Frequent bathing is what sets a citizen of Rome apart from a rank barbarian.*

He opened his mouth to say something—he wasn't sure what; he was still trembling, and his throat was on fire, not to mention his knee—and what came out was a calm, "I think it entirely possible our assailants were not Roman citizens."

Diana stared at him. She was squatting on her heels in the straw, length of rein still dangling from one hand, and she tipped her head back and laughed. There was an edge of hysteria in that laugh, but there was real amusement too. "Gods' wheels, Marcus, is that all you can say?"

"I have never killed anyone before." He rolled the limp form off him with some difficulty, and sat up. "What is one supposed to say?"

"How should I know? No one tells these things to girls." Diana staggered upright and went for the horse, which stood sidling and blowing nervously in one corner, white showing round its eyes at the smell of blood. She crooned and cuddled it for a while until the beast's tail stopped switching, then she tied it to the wall again and came back. She settled beside Marcus, and reached out to take his wrist in her hand. The slashed wrist, which was still, he realized, dripping blood.

"I heard what you told that thug," she said. "When he was about to cut your throat. You said, 'Don't kill me.'"

Marcus shrugged.

She peered at him through her filthy fringe of hair like a mare peering through her forelock. "Does that mean you don't want to die anymore?"

It means I didn't want you to die, Marcus thought. *Because I knew you'd try to rescue me, you mad girl.*

"Don't make me kill you," Diana said, and he saw there were tears in her eyes. Not once during this unnatural night of horrors had she wept, and she was on the brink of it now. "Don't make me kill you by leaving you behind. Please."

There were a thousand arguments he could make, but the astonishment of seeing her tears held him mute.

"I know what people think of me in Rome, Marcus." Her bloodied fingers slipped through his, linked tight. "I'm a joke—mad little Diana with straw in her hair and her pennant always waving for the Reds. The women think me unnatural, and the men laugh behind my back unless they're speculating how to get me on my knees."

He felt a surge of shame that hurt more than his leg. "Diana—"

"No." She cut him off, rejecting pity again. "I don't care. I made the life I wanted, and gods know few enough women get to do that. Few men, either, for that matter. I'm mad little Diana who breeds horses and cheers the Reds, and I've faced things that would have killed half the upstanding Roman citizens I know. Today is the second time I've watched a city tear itself to bits. I saw people get out, people on the road to what is probably safety ... but I saw

207

others. People like that pregnant girl and the man with the child on his back—"

Marcus thought incongruously of the skinny whore who had smacked him with a jug and caused his entire predicament to begin with. Who knew if she was alive or dead?

"—and I wanted to save them, and I couldn't. I couldn't." Diana looked at him steadily, and that was when her eyes overflowed. "Please, Marcus. Let me save someone today besides a *horse*."

He looked at her. She cried proudly, not screwing up her face, just letting the tears snake down through the streaks of ash, her bloody fingers tight through his. He looked at her, and inevitability rose in him like a wave.

"Please," begged Diana of the Cornelii. "Let me save you."

"My dear girl …" he sighed, and heard himself trail off.

She waited, dashing a filthy hand across her eyes.

He held his wrist up. "Bandage me?"

THE horse was not at all keen on leaving the stable once it realized rocks were pelting from the sky. "Sensible animal," Marcus said, strapping his wrist closed, and Diana had to pad the beast's haunches and neck in every blanket she could find before Marcus clambered aboard and they left the enclosure. The road to Herculaneum stretched along the coast—normally, Marcus would have seen the glittering blue expanse of bay on one side, the craggy hills rising on the other into rich green stretches of farmland. It was still a black and ashy underworld; the road choked with hunched and stumbling refugees shuffling through the accumulation of rock. Pebbles still rained from the dark swirl overhead, and when Marcus turned his head back toward Pompeii—

The city was not dead yet, but it was … slowing down. No lamps, no cheery windows lit against the dark. Just the restless spark of spreading fires, and mindless spasmodic movement in the streets. *Gods help them,* Marcus thought, and could barely make out the hulking shape of Vesuvius. *When will it stop?*

The horse flinched to step out into the shifting debris of rock. "I'll have to blind-fold him," Diana shouted. "You be my eyes!" Marcus kept watch from the horse's back—not one, but two bloody knives lying openly across his knees—and he saw more than one set of speculative eyes slide away. *I helped kill two men today,* he thought, but he had no regrets. He would threaten to kill more if necessary, to keep them off Diana who led the blindfolded horse step by step into the seething chaos of the road, crooning, stroking, praising with every nervous sidling step. Her voice as she cajoled the animal forward dropped to a honeyed bedroom whisper that would have had every man in Rome trailing her with his tongue out.

I wouldn't mind hearing that kind of whisper in my ear again, Marcus reflected. His life has become a dark and arid sort of place—the habit of despair, as Diana had put it, did not really make room for female companionship. *Perhaps I should do something about that. If the gods don't decide to kill me on this road, that is.* What supreme irony that would be … He gave a passing carter a sharp glance and a warning lift of the daggers, as the man eyed the horse.

Marcus could not afterward be certain how many hours passed— only that they did, in black and shuffling watchfulness. His lungs burned from breathing ash, his eyes stung from constantly scanning the road for creeping looters, and the only constant was Diana's unbowed shoulders beside the horse's head. When Marcus first saw light he caught his breath, wondering if he was imagining it.

He was not.

"Look." He leaned down to touch Diana's shoulder; she kept shuffling onward a moment but finally looked up. She swayed back and forth in exhaustion even when still: a gray ghost in the dark. Only it was no longer quite dark. The coastal road was winding its way, slowly but surely, out of the black shadow cast by the mountain. Cries went up around them as others began to see what Marcus had. "Sunset," Marcus said, pointing at the faint rosy glow in the west. "We've walked out of night into sunset."

Her face crumpled, and for a moment he thought she was about to cry again. Instead, she just looked outraged. "We've walked out of night into more *night?*" she complained. "I've done night already. I've done night *all fucking day*."

Marcus laughed. He was starving and filthy, wheezing and light-headed, and could not remember feeling so content in a very long time. He looked at the fading red streak in the sky over the bay — the debris-choked waters were just beginning to become visible again — and he thought inconsequentially, *I shall live to see another sunset. I shall live, in fact, to see my son become a man.*

Diana swayed on her feet again. "Ride for a while," Marcus ordered in his best from-the-*Rostra* voice. "The horse is too tired to need to be coaxed along anymore." Besides, the fall of rock seemed to be diminishing, the way underfoot less rough.

Diana untied the blindfold from the horse's eyes, hesitating. "But you can't walk — "

"No. In fact, I doubt this knee is ever going to be the same again." It crunched every time he flexed it. No doubt he would be the senator with the limp as well as the crooked shoulder — at the moment, he did not care in the slightest if he was laughed at. "But you're a little thing, Diana. The horse can carry us both for a while."

She accepted Marcus' extended hand, scrambling up over the horse's withers and settling herself in front of him. He linked an arm about her waist, moving her filthy hair off her neck as it flapped in his face. "You know something," he said, kicking the horse into motion, "I'm taking your advice. I'm going to marry again."

"Mmm." She was already drowsing against his shoulder. She smelled absolutely vile, ash and blood and horse, and Marcus doubted he was any better. Rank barbarians, the pair of them.

"I'll call on your father when we return to Rome," he went on. "And the augurs. Find an auspicious date for a wedding ..."

She gave a sleepy shake of her head. "*I'm* not going to marry you, Marcus. What a terrible idea."

"Why?" He rather thought he could get used to the notion.

"What would we ever have to talk about? You think aqueducts are interesting, and you don't even follow the Reds."

"Aqueducts *are* interesting," he said mildly. "But it's true: I hate chariot racing."

"See? You think I'm a crashing bore, and you *are* a crashing bore. It's a bad fit," she yawned, and snuggled into his shoulder. "Marry some little heiress who will worship the ground you walk on and give you a dozen babies."

"Very well." On the whole, that was probably a better idea. Paulinus needed a mother, and gods knew, Diana couldn't mother anything that wasn't hoofed.

"Why did you offer, anyway?" Diana's sooty lashes didn't rise; she sounded three-quarters asleep. "Surely you don't love me."

"No." He liked her and honored her more than any woman he knew, though, and that was a far rarer thing than love. "Men have dishonored you. They have mocked you even as they desired you—you're quite right about that—and you deserve nothing but honors. I thought it appropriate to offer you mine, in all sincerity."

"Oh, don't be so noble." She gave another bone-cracking yawn. "Have me to dine whenever I come to the city for festival races. You can bore me silly about aqueducts and I'll bore you silly hashing out every lap of the race, and after dinner we'll blow out the lamps and there won't be any more talking. And *that*, Marcus Norbanus, won't be quite so boring."

Marcus laughed softly and pressed his lips against the sooty line of her shoulder. "Until I find a wife who meets your approval," he said, "you have a standing invitation."

She was fast asleep, rocking bonelessly with the motion of the horse. The red streak of sunset was gone; night had fallen all over again—but Marcus lifted his face and saw stars instead of ash. A long night ahead—Herculaneum lay not far away; he supposed they could take refuge there, but after long thought he decided to steer toward Neapolis, however many more hours of nightfall trudging that took. Why not? They had the horse, carrying them on and on with steady strength. He wanted to get as far from the blackness behind them as possible.

He could not resist one final glance back into the shadows. He looked for Pompeii, and he saw ... nothing. Nothing at all. There was no town anymore, just an expanse of darkness broken here and there by fires. And over it all the squatting shape of Vesuvius, red lightning forking within the monstrous growling column of ash.

It's over, he thought. *The worst* must *be over.* Those still alive inside those city walls surely had a chance now.

Those dead ...

He had one ragged scrap of toga left—the rest of that noble purple-edged garment had been sacrificed to pad the horse's rump, and he did not grudge it. But he drew that final purple-bordered scrap over his battered head in a sign of mourning, and said a prayer for those left behind. The abandoned children; the skinny whore; the woman who might even now be giving birth. *The ones we could not save,* he thought, and felt the same stab of grief that Diana had. *May the gods look after them. May the gods save them all.*

He knew he would always wonder, on the nights when sleep failed to come and his thoughts turned bleak. Those nights were not behind him—he had seen enough nightmares this past short day to feed a thousand years of nights as black as this one.

But this night would come to an end, and he intended they would see dawn in a bathhouse. A proper Roman bathhouse for two Romans who smelled like savages.

"First dawn," he said aloud, "then a bath." And settled Diana's head against his shoulder more firmly as he kicked the horse toward Neapolis.

PART FIVE

THE MOTHER

E. Knight

"Gross darkness came rolling over the land like a torrent ... like a room when it is shut up and the lamp put out."
—Pliny the Younger

JULILLA

MY birth pangs have started.

Slow, and not regular, but started all the same. The babe has yet to drop, but I suspect by tomorrow morning I'll have a son.

How can it be that, after how long I have dreamed of becoming a mother, of meeting the little child inside my womb, I now want him to stay put?

I reach into the pouch at my side and pull out the vial I grabbed from our kitchen: a tincture to ease the pains. But it's not the right one. I stare at the blue vial in my hand — the one that had looked clear in the dim light of the kitchen. Blue is not for pain. Blue is for something else. Blue is what our slaves used to kill the rats. I thrust the vial back into the pouch, disappointed that I have nothing to ease the pain, and no use for poison.

I lean against a smooth, marble column in the east portico gazing into our once-grand, two-story-high peristyle. The red clay tiles of the roof covering the walkway around the inner courtyard have ash slipping through their grooves, white dust sprinkling down. Where fig, cherry, and pear trees bloomed and tangy lemon trees used to scent the air. A short, five-foot ladder leans against the fig tree — figs are my favorite fruit, and in Pompeii they were the very best. One of our slaves put up the ladder just this morning in hopes of filling a basket of them for me. It's hard to breathe here. My lungs are tight, fighting against the air I try to draw in. What was once a place of tranquility is now blanketed in darkness and ash. The sky above is a reflection of a war with the gods. Is it possible that the end of the world is upon us?

I was in my litter on my way to my friend Aemilia's house when Vesuvius burst angrily into the sky. And, I too, was ready to burst, the cramps of my swollen belly coming on in my fright. Seeing the mountain as it spewed its fury higher into the heavens than I could fathom, I was stunned. Afraid for my life, I was lucky to have run into the two strangers and Aemilia's betrothed, Sabinus, who saw me safely home.

Now a cough seizes my lungs, and I hug tight to the babe in my womb.

I'm still wearing all the jewelry I put on this morning in the hope of a joyous day: gold bangles, matching necklace, and earrings. Touching the golden chains draped between my breasts, I morbidly think that I have dressed up for my death. But I shove that thought aside. *We will not die. The Pompeians are a strong people. They'll rebuild and so will I.*

A cough seizes my lungs, and I hug tight to the babe in my womb. A tiny hand clamps around mine and I stare down at my three-year-old brother, Quintus. Mother always had a weakened constitution but birthing my young brother — her seventh child — put her into a fever she was lucky to survive. Another of my brothers died not long after, leaving mother ill, not only physically, but with grief. To help her, I swept in, all but raising Quintus as my own before leaving for Rome with my husband.

I submitted to my father's and husband's desires for me to return to Pompeii for the salty air — so healthful for a woman with child — but also because I was desperate to hold Quintus again. Quintus now stares up at me, his eyes somber and filled with fear. He clutches to me for comfort. I am glad to give it to him.

"I'll keep you safe." I ruffle a hand through his hair, and he tries to smile, but his chin wobbles instead. "Here, play with the turtle."

I hand him my pet and Quintus sinks to the ground, placing the reptile in the ash-covered marble and poking at the cavern where its head has disappeared.

A kick pushes against my belly, as if to say my unborn child, too, wants protection. I press my hand to the swell, feeling a tiny foot jab against my palm. A wave of tight pain pushes at the base of my spine, and another hard kick.

My child …

Our first was whisked into eternal life before he took a breath, when he was not more than six months in my womb. His passing made this child all the more special. Father recalled us from Rome where Titus and I made our home so I could give birth in Pompeii. I spent the summer relaxing and breathing in the salted air from the Bay of Naples. Lounging in steam baths and indulging in copious amounts of warm baked bread and olives.

"Do not come yet, darling. Wait," I whisper to my belly. I do not want to give birth when the world is in chaos. In a few days' time, everything will be set right and then he can make his grand entrance. Father promises that all will be well. That we'll be protected here in our home.

But hot tears sting my eyes, burning them more than the smoky air. I feel guilty. My family refused to leave, out of fear for me not returning this morning, and once I did … it was too late to go. No one has told me that it is because of my condition that we stay behind while the rest of the city flees in panic. But I think that must be at least part of the reason.

I let out a racking cough and a soft whimper as the jarring movement makes the pain in my lower back even worse.

"Lilla, we must get you inside. Why have you not come?"

My husband, Titus, calls out from across the portico as he rushes to me from the back room, his leather shoes silenced in the carpet of ash that covers our marble floors. Father is worried that the flat roof of the front part of the house will not be able to withstand the weight of the debris falling on us, but the rooms in the back have slanted roofs to keep us safe.

Titus carries my sick brother, Albinus, into the back while the slaves prepare the two rooms for our comfort. Albinus turned twelve the week before and his illness gives him constant pain. He's had much discomfort in his tiny body since birth. The doctor said something about the fusion of his spine. He's walked with a limp his whole life, and been afflicted with illness off and on over the past twelve years — his constitution much like Mother's.

In answer to Titus, I say, "I wanted to free my turtle." I point to the ground near my feet where my pet turtle stands unmoving and Quintus still pokes at him. Tucked deep in his shell, he isn't willing to witness the destruction Vesuvius rains down on us.

Another cough makes my lungs seize and I gasp for breath, stumbling back into my husband's arms. Little Quintus lets out a yelp and grabs hold of my husband's leg. Titus smoothes a hand over my brother's head, having taken to him already. Love makes my chest swell as I gaze at my husband.

Ours was a match like no other. A political marriage, and yet we fell in love the moment we met. Titus — so tall, strong, proud, smart — and yet he allowed me to see the sweetness in him.

"Let's get to the back of the house," he says. "The walls are strongest there."

I nod, allowing him to take me back because I can no longer stand, not when I have a child wishing to push his way into a world that is unraveling. *And another child,* I think, looking to Quintus, *counting on me to keep him safe.* As we walk, I cradle my heavy stomach, praying to Bona Dea and Isis to hold the unborn babe deep inside for several days longer. At least until the mountain stops roaring. And surely it will stop soon, won't it?

"Maybe it would be safer for us to try and leave," I whisper, my voice raspy from breathing in the ash and poisoned air. "We could try."

Titus stares into my eyes, regret showing deep, and sadness creases the corners of his lips. He shakes his head. "No, Lilla, we cannot. Perhaps we could have earlier, but now the roads are rough and treacherous. We cannot traverse them with your condition." He places a protective hand on the center of my rounded belly. I was right. "Your father's house withstood the earthquake seventeen years ago. It will withstand this."

Still I say, "I do not wish to give birth here. My babe will not be able to breathe." I hold my sleeve to my lips, coughing once more.

Titus lifts me into his arms, strong enough to carry me and our unborn babe. Since the day he learned I was pregnant, he coddled me, perhaps as terrified as I was that we'd lose another baby. "You will not have to worry over that, love. As soon as the storm subsides, the air will clear. Besides, you are still weeks away from bringing our son into the world. You needn't worry."

I nod, trusting in his judgment, feeling his strength seep into me. My husband is a senior tribune and aspiring consul, climbing his way up the *cursus honorum* in Rome; he is a natural protector. He would not steer me wrong.

Pressing a kiss to my forehead, Titus stares into my eyes with emotion he dare not put into words. I want to know what he is thinking, but it frightens me.

I shake my head. He is right. I am not due to birth this child yet. Perhaps the pains I've been feeling are only brought on by my fear. Many women experience false labor. I'm sure that's all it is. "Do not worry, husband, I shall keep our child safe." A duty that as a mother is mine to uphold, just as it is his as a father.

A loud rumbling shakes the house before a crash sounds at the front vestibule.

"Get to the back of the house!" Father rushes from the entry with Mother and several of my siblings in tow. Two slaves who didn't flee rush behind them, one scooping up Quintus. The child whimpers, his lower lip quivering, but the determined set in his jaw shows he's trying for his Roman *gravitas*. My brother Julius, just a year younger than me, doesn't manage it; he looks madder than a cornered serpent.

"May the *lares* and *penates* protect us," Titus murmurs, wheeling around and rushing with me toward the back of the house, leaving my little turtle behind in the darkened peristyle that I once thought so beautiful.

I grip tight to his shoulders, pressing my forehead against his chest. The skies are already falling on our heads and now part of the house.

A surge of pain wraps its way around my abdomen, and I bite the inside of my cheek to keep from crying out at the burning ache. My fingers curl into Titus' tunic to ease the pressure. *It's false pains. Only false.* I force myself to believe it.

"In here." Father pushes open the door to the salon where our dining couches were placed during the renovations my mother arranged for the *triclinium*, where we wine and dine important guests. But the renovations aren't complete, so this little room is crowded with cushioned mattresses, pillows of silk and linen, and carved marble couches with faces of the gods etched into the legs. They were meant for our guests to lounge, eat, and drink on when they grew tired of the peace of the garden. Now they serve to give us comfort in our sanctuary.

At least it was beautiful. Shadows from our oil lamps bounce off the white-painted ceiling and panels set off with red borders and green garlands. My eye goes to my favorite panel—Apollo and Daphne in the woods—and then up to Venus under a garlanded pediment on one of the top panels. "Goddess of love and family, please protect us," I mutter and notice a side table set out with wine, figs, and bread.

Titus hesitates with his hand on the door and we all gaze out into our peristyle. How long until we can open this door again? When the house rumbles and shakes anew, Titus slowly closes the door, blocking us from the destruction.

"What has happened?" Titus asks what I cannot seem to form on my tongue.

Father looks on, stoic in his countenance, forever strong. A true Roman. "The front vestibule of the house collapsed. The same as it did in the great earthquake."

Our house has been under renovation since, slowly replacing the old architecture in several rooms, this one included. Father has been making our house stronger, more opulent, more fitting for the wealthy and prestigious family we've become. It is a shame that his vestibule has collapsed again. He'll end up spending a fortune before the house is complete, at this rate.

My father, the *praetor*, meets my gaze briefly before turning away. "We'll be safe in here."

What I read in his eyes before he turned away worries me. He isn't as confident as he would have us believe. He is not certain we'll be safe here, or anywhere.

When the mountain exploded, my family should have left. They should never have waited for me. They should have left me behind. Because of me, they are in danger. Guilt shreds my insides, and tears threaten to spill, but I push them back.

I, too, am a Roman. I will let no one see my fear, for I do not fear what the gods have in store. And I do not believe that this will be the end of us. Not yet.

My heart skips a beat and I brace for the pain that comes when my belly tightens, but it is briefer than before, enforcing my earlier reasoning that it was false pains.

Titus' jaw clenches tightly as it does when he strategizes military tactics. I touch his arm and he gazes at me, determined. "We must leave," Titus whispers, hesitant as he is to contradict my father. "I was wrong. We must at least try to flee. I will go and try to find a cart. I'll pull you to Rome myself if I have to."

"How, husband? With the front of the house collapsed there is no way out." I glance at the door closed tightly to the outside. "What if the road to Rome is filled with raining rocks? Perhaps we should stay as father has determined."

He shakes his head. Titus has never gone against my father's decisions before, and I wonder how angry Father will be when he finds out.

Titus sets me down gently on one of the soft couches and Quintus rushes over, curling himself inside my embrace. Sudden emotion catches me, and I bury my face in his soft hair, having missed him so much when I was in Rome, and he obviously missed me, too.

Titus leans closer to me, pressing a kiss to my temple. "The stairs are not blocked to the second story. I shall see if there is a way to climb down from there or see if anyone outside can help us."

I lean into the plush pillows, hugging my belly and my little brother tight. *Anyone left outside will be saving themselves, not giving their time to us*, I think. "I do not want you to get hurt. You risk too much. We'll be safe here. Why don't we play a game of dice?"

Titus kneels beside me, his hand covering mine. I stare at our fingers as he entwines them. Love tightens in my chest. I squeeze Titus' hand back, rubbing my thumb over his. "I must at least look, Lilla."

I can see the desperation in his eyes. Titus fixes things. Titus solves problems and this is just another obstacle for him to unravel. Perhaps to keep his sanity, he must look for a way out. I lean forward and press my lips hungrily to his, wanting, *needing* that closeness, the reassurance of his affection, of his very humanness. We do not normally kiss where others can see us. It is vulgar. Un-Roman. But with the world raining down on us, I do not care, and Titus does not either. He kisses me back.

"I will be safe. I want to keep you safe," he says.

I nod, unable to say, *go*, because I do not truly want him to leave.

Titus stands and looks at the painted ceiling and the panel around the door. Lounging on another couch is my mother; her breathing is rapid, and our slave fans her. My father speaks in low tones to Julius, and our elder male slave — while my fourteen-year-old sister, Little Bird, gathers the children on another couch and sings them a song.

"Charis, I need a drink of wine," I say to the slave girl, hoping the wine will calm me. I finger the *ankh* charm at my ankle, asking for the blessing of Isis and praying she ebb the pains of false labor. That she keep true labor at bay until this chaos subsides.

The *ankh* was a gift from a young woman, who jingled from the charms around her ankle at the Isis temple, where I'd gone to make an offering in honor of Aemilia's wedding a few days before. And to pray for a son.

The woman heard my prayer and gave me the *ankh* charm. She said her name was Capella, and she took it from her own anklet to make a gift of it for me. It seemed somehow wrong to take a gift from her, given that she was quite plainly no respectable woman. I could guess at her profession, given the large breasts that spilled from her too-short tunica and her overwhelming perfume. But she was, beyond all that, beautiful: golden-haired, with blue eyes that still haunt me. They were eyes that seemed to see beyond seeing, more like a priestess than a prostitute. I suppose that was the beauty of the Isis temple. Those from all walks of life could come together to worship, and in that blue-eyed woman, I found a sort of kindred spirit. She lay her hand on my belly and said that I should not worry because my son and I would be together for all eternity. And then we prayed to the Great Mother, our hands clasped, neither of us anything or anyone but daughters of Isis.

Charis hands me the cup of watered wine. I sip slowly, afraid I may retch. But the wine does its job and moments later I feel calmer, any residual pain in my back and abdomen slightly abating.

"I am going out now to look for help," Titus says, startling me from my memories.

Father whips his head in my husband's direction. "No, stay inside. Wait out the storm."

Titus gives my father a hard stare. "Better to take our chances than be buried."

Buried? Surely it isn't as bad as that. I hold my breath, and everyone within stiffens, waiting for the explosion that comes when anyone is foolish enough to challenge Father. But there is only silence. Perhaps Father hopes that Titus will find a way for us to get out, too.

At last, Father gives a curt nod. Titus' jaw loosens. A tumult of emotion sweeps through his eyes for less than a second and then he swoops in once more to kiss me. To give me hope.

"I will be right back."

POLYBIUS

I study my daughter Lilla. My oldest. My favorite, in truth. Pain etches her face. Lilla's eyes are closed and her head leans back against the pillows. One bejeweled hand splays on her swollen middle, and the other circles protectively around her brother Quintus — a child Lilla has always thought of as her own.

Images of what Lilla's own children will look like haunt me now, as I fear I will never see them in this life. I'd been certain, when the mountain began its torment of us, that we'd be safe here. But now … now I am unconvinced. Even a small bit of doubt shook my surety hours before.

The great mountain has taken my power, my pride.

For the more I recall the seemingly endless black clouds in the sky, the angry smoke rushing from Vesuvius, the more I wonder if this city will be destroyed. Even still, I cannot leave unless I chance the lives of my wife and our precious children, the life of my dutiful daughter and her unborn child. Yet, to stay, I risk them all the same.

I have to stomp on the dread that is building inside me. How can I let fear take hold in my mind? A Roman has no place for it. This is my city — what is left of it. We survived the great earthquake years before. Rebuilt. We will rebuild again. And yet, I know true fear today. I've never seen anything like this. But, this too, shall pass.

And I must set the example. I cannot simply turn my back on the city I helped to build. My father, who passed the month before, would not be proud to see me run from the post he worked so hard for me to possess. He was a slave once, and I am the son of a freedman. Now a wealthy *praetor*. Our family name has risen from the depths of obscurity and I will not turn my back on such an honor. I will show men like Pansa, that a freedman's son does not flee, either, but serves Pompeii just as bravely.

I cannot dishonor my ancestors with fear now. We'll overcome this. We are strong. And inside my house are eleven people who count on me for protection. But outside, the entire city relies on me, too, and I shall not let down my guard even when the fires of Vulcan are falling on our heads.

My son Quintus' gray eyes catch mine and he stares at me with a depth of soul unimaginable in a child his age. Can he see the fear in my eyes? Does he question whether or not I made the right decision?

If I have to save the city one child at a time, I will. Gods help me. They will remember me then. This city will re-elect me as praetor, *and in years to come I could be a provincial governor.*

I straighten my spine.

All around me, I am surrounded by those close to me: the ones I resigned to this uncertain fate. As the *paterfamilias*, I am supposed to make these decisions. To do what is right for my family — and they are to obey.

When they wanted to charge into the chaos to try and find Lilla, only I remained calm and steadfast. I sent out our strongest slaves after her and even though they disappeared, *she* came back to me, to us.

I was right then. I am right now. Within a day or two, all will be well. Even still … "I'll be back." I rush out, ignoring the calls of my wife to return. I must reach our *lararium*, where the gods of the household stand. I gaze up at the Lares, the Snake, and the Genius of my ancestors. "Protect our family from this great destruction." I swipe a hand through my hair. "A white lamb will be sacrificed in your honor every year, if you will but aid us in this. Tell me, what do you require?"

The rumble of thunder outside is my only answer. We have angered the gods somehow. "Send me a sign," I beg. "Whatever it is you require of us, we will give it!" But the only answer I have is the call of my wife.

"Gaius, please. Come inside now."

A surge of emotion wells in my chest. The gods have not answered me yet. "Two lambs!" Still nothing. Isn't it enough that we already gave them one of our own children, and my daughter, her firstborn?

"Gaius!" My wife Decima's voice is filled with fear.

I nod, finding it difficult to form words, and I whisper. "I will come with you."

I send up another prayer to the gods for Titus. But I have my doubts he will find a safe way. The two vestibules collapsed nearly on top of us as we ran when the ceiling shifted, dusting us with plaster, before shattering. The only openings to the front of the house are unstable. The openings upstairs all lead to the peristyle and kitchen courtyard, none to the outside. We were lucky to escape death. We will not be so lucky again. Especially if we are taking so many risks.

I turn to look at the woman I've been married to for nearly half my life. Beautiful still, her dark hair hangs in chaotic ringlets around her shoulders, having fallen from its pins. Though Decima's eyes are framed by tiny wrinkles, their color is still the same as it was decades ago. And I find myself staring into her eyes now as I always have, looking for the light of hope she continuously brings.

With no openings for ventilation and the courtyard filling with ashen air, how long will it take before the poisoned air leaks beneath the doorway, threatening to suffocate us all?

"Father, let me help Titus." My oldest son Julius stands beside me, his dark hair ruffled. He is the spitting image of me. And I'm afraid he will go out to help Titus and never come back.

"No," I answer, too afraid to lose him.

The boy puffs out his chest, his lips thinning in a grimace before he breathes deep and says, "I'm a man now. Let me do *something*."

My heart breaks at his words, and I clench my jaw to keep from trembling. All my life I've imagined my boy following in my footsteps, perhaps even rising beyond me. I envision him as a powerful man within Rome. And now the truth is that he may never see beyond these white-paneled walls. I cannot let him go out into the deadly hail. "Your sister's husband will be back soon."

"And sooner with my help," my son insists, his green eyes fixed on mine.

He's seventeen now. Handsome and arrogant. Feeling the house rumble around us, the distant echo of screams of terror, I wonder if he will see his eighteenth birthday. But I grit my teeth. "All right."

I walk to the door of the room, my hand still on the door handle.

"Father ..." Julius encourages. I embrace him. Pulling him tight to my chest and breathing in his scent, I feel my heart clench with fear.

"Hurry back." I slowly open the door, letting in the stench of smoke.

"What are you doing, husband? Do not let Julius out!" My wife struggles off her couch, her breathing labored. She wasn't well before the mountain exploded, and the tainted air has made her weaker.

Our boy hesitates, glancing at his mother.

I take brisk steps forward. "Lay down, love." I stroke her cheek and guide her back down on the cushions. "All will be well."

But her eyes dart behind me. "Julius!"

I turn in time to see that our boy has rushed into the blackness.

Leaving my wife's side, I hurry to the open door. "At least take a lamp, boy," I call out, but my son is already running down the portico and calling out for his brother-in-law.

I curse under my breath. "Nikon, a lamp."

Our male slave thrusts one of the oil lamps into my hands and I step out of the room.

"Father," several of my young children call out at once, fear filling their voices.

"Worry not, children. You are protected here."

My shouts for Titus and Julius do not echo but die on my lips with the sounds of debris crashing on the roof. One of the fig trees ignites, lighting up the entirety of the expanse.

I hope to catch a glimpse of their moving shadows. The faces on the wall murals mock me. A shadow moves ahead in the corridor leading to the atrium.

"Titus, is that you?"

The shadow pauses, calls out, but I cannot hear him, and then he disappears when a giant fiery stone crashes where he stood.

Jupiter, let the men of my family make it back to us alive.

"Father." The sound of Lilla's weak voice beckons me and I turn back into the room to see her face filled with worry.

Not wanting to frighten her more than she is already, I say, "Darling, child." I shut the door, set the lantern on the ground, and kneel by Lilla's side, wishing to take away her fear. She has made it so far with this child.

There was much joy when it seemed the babe would be born alive and well. Growing up in Pompeii, Lilla was liked by many and was friends with most in our elite circle, but now the future was so uncertain. Why didn't I let her stay in Rome? In Rome, where she might be out of danger. But Rome might be under siege from the gods, too. Maybe the gods are indeed destroying us all ...

"Where is my husband?" my daughter asks.

"He is coming," I lie.

But the muted sound of running footsteps in the portico alerts me that my words have no need to be false. My son and my son-in-law burst through the doors.

"We made it to the second floor, but the vestibule's collapse left a drop that is too long for our ladder. And we are uncertain of the rubble's stability," Titus says. He glances at his wife. "To jump would injure many in our family."

"I tried to climb up the rubble by the atrium. I got halfway before —"

Titus clamps onto Julius' arm. "We'll think of something else," he says.

I pull my son and son-in-law to the side of the room, away from prying ears. "Tell me."

"A man tried to help us, but flying debris caught his shoulder, knocking him down."

"Dear gods," I murmur, sending a prayer for the man.

"People are taking things and running, Father," Julius says, his voice hard and angry. "Those with ill intent are stealing."

"And fire," Titus adds. "The front part of the house is ablaze. The stones are hot to the touch."

Julius turns over his palms, showing angry red blisters already developing from where he must have grasped hold to attempt climbing out. "The women and children will never survive the fall."

Titus stands tall. "But you can make the jump. Go, Polybius. You have authority in this city as *praetor*; you can get help. I'll watch over our family. We'll be sheltered here for the time being."

I shake my head. "There is no one left to save us. Those who are strong enough have left. I will not leave my family." I will not run like a coward. I am Roman. I will stay and protect what is mine.

My son, who has been attempting with much success to remain strong, visibly cracks, his shoulders slumping, eyes glistening in the lantern light. I press a hand to his shoulder and squeeze, a silent show of my affection. "I am proud of you for attempting the climb and for your bravery."

Julius gains some control of his emotions, the muscles in his jaw flexing. "We shall attempt again when the fires have tamed. In the morning, Vesuvius will cease its attack. One of us will make the jump and go in search of a taller ladder."

If there is anything left of the city, of us.

But his words are so strong, so certain, I almost believe it myself. I have raised this boy well. He is Roman, too.

My son-in-law is more somber. He does not believe there will be a tomorrow; I can see it etched in his face. The young man has seen battle. Has witnessed death. They say a warrior knows when his end is near. Senses it.

I have never been a warrior, but I wanted to be. Perhaps that is why I chose Titus for my daughter. He brought respectability to our family, but in him I also fulfilled a dream of mine.

Titus touches the leather pouch at his waist, as if reassuring himself of its existence. Coin? A precious jewel?

The air is tighter now, feeling hot, and the smell of the city burning around us is strong. "It's a good plan. Let us rest for a while."

They nod.

Titus sits beside his panting wife, while Julius takes a spot beside his mother.

I am left to sit beside my young ones. All of the children stare up at me between fits of coughing, eyes filled with fear. "Come and let me tell you a story of Rome."

My sickly younger son Albinus leans his head against the back wall, his eyes closed as he seeks to breathe. I run my hand through his sweaty hair.

"Albinus, you're a brave boy. Do you want to choose the story?"

His eyes open, the whites red, his stare looking somewhat glazed. "Tell me of your grandfather who served Emperor Augustus."

My children love the stories of our family. We are descended of imperial slaves who served our illustrious past emperor then rose in the ranks as free men. My children are proud of this, as am I.

"Come gather here. I will tell you of the emperor who saved the life of a slave."

JULILLA

MY husband reclines behind me on the couch, his arms wrapped around me. I sink into Titus' warmth, hoping to pull some of his strength, but fearing I am too weak.

He whispers encouraging words in my ear. "We will survive this, Lilla."

His chants are meant to inspire me, to make me feel safe, and yet I feel that he says them only to enforce his need for calm upon himself. I heard the men's whispers. Fire at the front of the house. The city gone to despair, and thieves ransacking. Resentment is trying to find its way into my mind. Even if they found a ladder in the morning, how would I traverse it? And what if the world is doomed to be filled with fire forevermore?

I recall the vial in my pouch. No, not that.

The pain of childbirth has returned. It shouldn't feel this way. The pain of it fills me and it takes most of my willpower to keep it hidden — and the rest to keep from shouting my anger at the gods for choosing this moment to rain destruction down on us mere mortals.

Before now, I never had any cause to complain, unlike my friend Aemelia, who constantly laments of her place in this world and the lack of choice she has in it. My friend is a headstrong girl, questioning everything, becoming upset when her wishes are not considered. The necessity for such rebellion never occurred to me. My father and husband are good, caring men. I've trusted in them to make decisions — after all, that is their right, and my duty is to obey.

And yet ... maybe better decisions could have been made. I close my eyes against the guilt — they stayed to find me, and then they stayed in concern for my state.

I am not satisfied with the choices that have been made, and yet there is nothing I can do to change it, nor can I voice my unhappiness.

But the part of me that will not let gloom reign speaks its own measured wisdom. If I hadn't come to Pompeii, it would have been much longer before I saw young Quintus again. This precious child who I often thought of as my own. I will protect him until I draw my last breath. A child in place of the one I lost. He curls in my lap, a thumb in his mouth, his other hand wrapped in my own. I encouraged him to sit with the other children, but he prefers to be here with me as he listens to Father regale the children with tales of lives past, easing their fears.

My stomach constricts, and I stiffen enough this time that Titus whispers, "What is it?" His palm presses to my hardened belly. "Is it the baby?"

Slowly, a crossness begins to grow inside me. I have to let go of it. I cannot let it consume me. But, I am ...

Even forming the words is hard. I am angry.

"Shh ..." I refuse to let this child come now. Not if I can stop its descent into this world of destruction. I stare down at my *stola* and *palla*, both covered in soot. The silky green *stola* fringed with gold and cinched with a matching girdle. The *palla* that marks me as a respectfully married matron, as diaphanous as I dare. I donned them for my friend Aemilia's wedding. And I had my hair curled up prettily, but not so prettily as to outshine the bride.

Aemilia. What has happened to her? Where was she now?

Did she get out of Pompeii in time? Surely she and her family could have escaped. They had horses aplenty, and her father even told her they'd leave right after the wedding anyway. Their household was prepared to depart before the chaos began. Aemilia complained, but how lucky it was that her father had the forethought. I was certain they must have retreated when I was still struggling through the rubble-choked streets, grateful for Sabinus' help in seeing me home.

In recounting his story to the children, my father raises his hands in the air as he tosses imagined dinner plates to the ground, and then says loudly in his impression of Augustus, "Would you feed me to your lampreys as you would your slave? For I have now broken many dishes and your slave only one."

A million times we'd heard this story and yet our fascination did not yet wane. The story was passed down through the generations, and generations to come would tell stories of my own *paterfamilias*. Born of a freedman, Father was bred to be a politician. *Praetor*. His hopes for a higher position was only the beginning, as I knew he'd been grooming my brother Julius for greatness.

But our family's climb, our scramble to the top, seems exhausting to think about now. I yawn, tired from both the stress of the day and the dimness of the room.

"Lilla, speak to me, love," Titus murmurs. "I fear for you and the child."

"There is nothing for you to fear," I lie.

"But ..." He doesn't say anything, but I know he worries about our unborn child, has since the moment the baby quickened within my womb. He relives the moments his firstborn son died.

"Fear not," I whisper, because I cannot say aloud what I am beginning to believe. Saying those words aloud will make it real, and right now I still desperately want to believe in my father and husband. I do not want to doubt them, though a part of me is starting to believe that we are in danger, despite all they say.

I cough, and feel the baby kick, but not as strongly as before. Perhaps he will tire and cease his demand to make entrance.

"Are you hungry?" Titus asks.

I shake my head. "No, I want nothing but wine."

Titus holds my cup to my lips. "Drink." Then he hands me a fig. "Eat."

Why must he demand it of me when I've said I do not want it? My annoyance is unwarranted. He wants only to help and yet I find myself growing agitated. Perhaps, if I rest, I will feel better. Perhaps I won't feel the urge to yell my frustration.

I lean my head back against Titus' strong chest, letting the air out warily, and sucking in another shaky breath. My limbs are heavy.

He strokes my forehead, kisses my temple, and I let the anger rush away. The pain in my belly subsides and I think Isis has answered my prayers. My belief in Isis was perhaps the only disagreement between Titus and myself that I set down my foot upon. He believes Isis worship is un-Roman. He was a sworn tribune to the emperor, both our families having ties to Augustus and yet, I worshipped the goddess of Cleopatra.

But I didn't care. I told Titus he was being old-fashioned and that I would obey him in all things but this, reminding him that Cleopatra's daughter had been respected by Augustus.

Perhaps Isis will keep this baby buried deep within my womb where he can pass on securely to the afterworld when we are all dead within the rubble of my father's home. A tomb. Oh, how can I let such a horrid thought even cross my mind? We are not yet close to death!

"We will not be buried here," Titus says, as if he can hear my thoughts. "We will escape. I will get you back to Rome unharmed."

I realize I must have voiced my thoughts aloud.

Rome may be under the gods' darkness, too, for all we know. I shake my head. "We must accept Fate."

Gently my husband slides from behind me and stands, towering over me. His brow is creased with determination, his lips in a firm line. I imagine him giving this same look to legionaries before battle. "No, Lilla, we will not die here."

Facing my father, Titus once more says, "I will go and search again for a way to get out, in case I missed something the first time."

"I'm coming with you," my brother Julius insists.

"How many times must you go?" I ask, immediately contrite for voicing my fears. "And what if you don't come back?"

"*Lilla*," my mother says in a tight whisper.

My father's gaze is uncertain but he says nothing.

Titus takes my chin in his fingers and presses a kiss to my lips. "I will not fail you or my unborn son."

I want to believe him. Need to believe him. So I nod.

He gives Quintus a little tap on the nose, causing a sob to choke me. Titus will make a good father.

My own father sits beside me, his hand tugging my free one, not occupied by Quintus, into his hold. "Lilla ..." But his voice trails off for a moment, and the man I've known as a strong Roman for all of my life looks ready to break. Tears fill his eyes. "I am sorry, daughter. I've failed you. I've failed everyone."

"Father ..."

He shakes his head. "I cannot even seek your forgiveness."

"There is nothing to forgive, for you have done nothing wrong." I flick my eyes to Quintus who looks even more fearful. "Go and play with Little Bird," I coo. The children have been running back and forth in a game of tag between this room and the one connected to it, the door banging against the wall as they shove through it.

The boy runs off with a nod, eager to play. I am reminded of his innocence, of all their innocence. Of their hope in the world and the outcome of this disaster. While we all fear for our safety, they have no other concern than a moment's pleasure.

Because Mother was always ill and I was the oldest, I rarely had time to find that artless joy. I have always borne my duty with straight shoulders and absolute obedience.

"No, Lilla, I *have* done something wrong. I bade you come to Pompeii when you wished to stay in Rome where you were comfortable."

Just as he pushed me to Rome in the first place by marrying me to Titus, pushed me to leave all that was familiar, and I obeyed, because that is what daughters do. Luckily, in Rome, I attained happiness in serving my new husband. Titus' place was in Rome: the way for him to advance his career. And being at odds with the two men in my life to whom I am beholden is a complicated and uncomfortable thing. One must submit to her *paterfamilias*. And yet, if a husband were to object? That was the situation I'd been in months before when Titus insisted we move to Rome permanently.

I find myself wanting to protect my father and needing his strength to come back. If he should break, then what is left for the rest of us? "No, Father. What you wished for me was to breathe the fresh air of the bay and the mountains. To relax away from the city. To be pampered and kept healthy before the babe was due to arrive. To be near my family."

He nods, but his face is still drawn, stricken. "I gave you no choice."

I do not know how to respond, for he speaks the truth.

I had no choice, but as a dutiful daughter, a dutiful wife, I did what was expected. When he warned I'd be risking yet another of my children, my guilt forced me to beg my husband. And once I convinced Titus that my father's request was the best course, we packed and were on our way.

I only disobeyed my father once as a child. I'd wanted to play with a young girl I saw in the streets near a brothel. At the time, I had not known she was a slave—or that her future would be in prostitution. I'd sneaked away from our house and when my father found me, I received a sound lashing. What would have happened if I disobeyed as a grown woman? And besides that, where would I have gone? Who would have taken in a woman who went against her *paterfamilias* and her husband? No one of honor and respect.

My father's gaze is serious, grim. "If only there had been a sign from the gods, then I would have listened to your wish to remain in Rome."

"What?" I breathe out, shocked by his sudden change. A man once so filled with pride and certainty looks as though he regrets all the choices he ever made.

"I fear for you, Lilla. I fear for us all." His voice cracks and at that I sit up taller and hug him around his shoulders.

"Hush, Father. What are you saying? Are you giving up hope? You are the one we look to for strength. Do not abandon your strength now."

Father looks at me, nods, and swipes at his weepy eyes with the back of his sleeve. "Yes. You are right. I must remain strong." He clears his throat and then stands up, going to sit beside my mother who has curled up in a ball around Quintus, who must have sneaked away from Little Bird, and is now fast asleep in my mother's arms.

I push myself up from the couch, my feet unsteady, legs still partially numb. The pains in my belly have eased somewhat. When I feel strong enough to walk, I shuffle toward the door, intent on peeking outside to see where Titus and Julius went. The door is hard to open. I shove hard against the wood with my shoulder. When I open the door, I am dismayed to see that many layers of soot and rock have filled the portico and peristyle. I'm surprised I was able to push against it.

We are being buried alive.

The horror of that realization guts me and I find it hard to breathe.

I want to call out to Titus, but the air sucks away my breath and I cannot form the words. My lungs seize, and I cough and cough, drawing in breath, but the air must be poisonous. My lungs burn. I grip the side of the door's opening, praying for my breath to return.

Echoes of the city sound muted in the openness. There is an occasional shout of pain, of fear, but not nearly as many as before. Fading like we are, beneath the rubble. The silence between cries is deafening. Terrifying. So when they do come, they reach inside my soul and grip me tight. We are not alone in our suffering. And yet ... we are.

POLYBIUS

"FATHER," croaks my twelve-year-old boy. Though he's named for me, we call him Albinus, because he was born so pale and nearly without life. In the lamplight, I can see his skin has turned miserably gray. His lips are discolored, taking on a purple hue. He tugs at my sleeve weakly.

"My son." I scoop him up from the floor where he sits huddled with his siblings and sit with him on an empty couch. I want to comfort him, but what peace can I give him? I am becoming acutely aware that I have doomed them all. So I say nothing.

Pressing my hand to his head I feel his skin is growing cold despite the heat of this place. Albinus coughs, unable to catch his breath. His body curls in on itself as his lungs struggle to draw air. I fear his weakened state has been made all the more vulnerable.

I sit him up further, patting roughly on his bony back. "Wine!" I call out to our slaves. Charis taps Nikon, who looks as pale as my boy and lies against the wall. Charis looks at me fearfully, and for a moment I wonder if she will rebel as the other slaves did. But then she goes to get the wine.

"Albinus, breathe slow, my boy. Try to calm yourself."

But he clutches at his chest as he coughs even harder. The poor boy has not been well since he was born, so I pat him harder on the back, and urge him in whispers to breathe slow and deep, just as I have on many past occasions when his breath has been taken from him.

239

"This air ..." I murmur, not willing to finish my sentence, for the air would indeed kill him. We need water to help with his breathing. Our physician told us to dampen a rag and hold it over his mouth as he breathed. The moist air seemed to help him get his breath back. I *need* the fearful slave to get the water. "Charis, go and get water from the *impluvium*."

Water has been short in Pompeii, thanks to our hot autumn, but surely there is enough for Albinus. Charis shakes her head, fear making her eyes widen. "Master, I cannot. The ash has turned it to mud!"

"Go," I growl anyway, fear for my son's health taking away my common sense.

Charis backs slowly to the door, her fingers reaching for the handle when the door starts to shudder. Someone is tugging on it. It opens a crack and then further until Titus and Julius burst through, their skin black, and only the whites of their eyes and teeth showing.

"Step away from the door," Julius commands our slave. He and Titus push inside, their eyes darting about, haunted.

I'm afraid of what I see outside as ash falls into the room before they pull the door closed. Albinus will not get the water he desperately needs.

Titus stares at Albinus. "What has happened?"

"Another breathing attack." My voice chokes, throat tight.

Decima wakes from her slumber, unsettling Quintus, who crawls from one couch to another until he reaches Lilla's waiting arms.

My wife cries out at the sight of her son and rushes to my couch to hold Albinus' head in her lap. "Albinus, love, it will be all right."

"We need water for him," I say, hearing the desperation in my voice.

"I'll go," Julius says, but he glances at Titus and they appear to have a silent conversation.

With Albinus in his mother's care, I walk toward the pair. "Say it," I demand.

"The wall near the *impluvium* has partially collapsed, and debris now fills the well where our water was. There is no water," Titus confesses. "Ash is accumulating rapidly."

"It was up to my knees, Father," Julius says.

"I shall go then, to the cistern," I say, not willing to risk my son's life to the falling missiles any more than I already had. If I have to climb through the walls to reach our water supply, I will.

"No, let me. I've already traversed the ruins of our house." Julius puffs out his chest, his eyes pleading.

His words tear at my heart and for a moment, I feel the same loss of breath that poor Albinus suffers from. As the hours progress, I am relying more on my children than I have before. Listening to their advice. How can I not let him go? How can I deny him this chance to be the honorable man he's grown to be, when with each passing moment our situation becomes increasingly dire?

"Be safe, my son." I clasp him to me, showing him more affection today than I've given him in all the years since he was a young boy. A Roman I raised him to be, not a coddled youth. "The gods will guard over you."

"Be wary," Titus warns my eldest son. "The walls are crumbling."

Julius nods. "I will return soon."

We usher him outside amid the questioning of my other children, Lilla and Decima, who are nervous of him going again. I am, too, but I see no other way.

We close the door against the air, which is even thicker than before, and I drop to my knees and pray to all the gods that Julius will make it back to us. That he can hold his breath between ragged, poisoned draws of air.

I am joined in prayer by most of those left in the room — even the children, who take a break from their game of chase. Albinus remains on the couch; his coughing has subsided but his breathing whistles, and I feel every labored drawn breath like a knife wound to my heart. Nikon also does not rise from his inclined spot along the wall, his older face gone slack.

Our prayers are loud, and for a moment we drown out the echoes of buildings crashing down around us.

As we quiet, Lilla cries out, doubling over. She clutches her belly.

"Daughter." Decima leaps to her feet and grasps Lilla's hand while her husband carries her back to the couch.

I follow behind. "Is it the babe?" I ask. Fear makes my blood run cold. We cannot birth the baby here. Not in this. Lilla should not have to endure such pain and terror with the fires raging just beyond these walls.

"I am well," Lilla manages to speak between clenched teeth. "Simply a cramp."

But her face is contorted in pain. I realize I have not heard the whistling noise of Albinus' breath. I whirl to see him staring with glassy eyes toward to ceiling. He is still.

"Albinus," I say, but his name does not pass my lips, a groan instead.

In a leap, I am on him, knees crushing against the stone floor. I scoop him up in my arms, his lifeless body limp and heavy.

"No! No!" I cry out, forgetting my *gravitas*. Forgetting everything but grief.

But there is no grand touch of our gods. There is no miracle. There is no return of breath to my beloved son's body. He is gone from us. I press my face to his small chest, my tears running freely from my eyes, and I pray. I pray that I am in a nightmare.

"No, Gaius! No!" Decima pries Albinus from my arms, dragging his limp body against her breast. "Wake up, Albinus, wake, my boy!"

She presses her lips to his face, her hand flattened to his heart as tears stream down her face. I feel myself falling backward, my backside hitting the hard marble, and I barely move my arm to catch myself from going down completely.

"Albinus?" Lilla's soft croak is barely heard, and then her muffled cries, as Titus gathers her in his arms.

Our other children stand in a row behind us, staring at Albinus and Decima with looks on their faces that freeze me. They look resigned, as if they expected this all along. For my own children, losing their other brother some years before, perhaps they understand that death comes to those who are young. From their expressions, I fear they believe death comes to them first.

But it shouldn't. Not like this. Not holed up in a room and trying desperately to breathe.

I swallow hard, my face wet and hot.

The door flies open and Julius rushes inside. "I made it!" he calls out, holding up a small jug in his triumphant hands, but his face falls when he sees his mother clutching the still and gray body of his brother.

I watch the muscles in his jaw flex, but he says nothing. Julius sets down the jug beside the door and shuts it. He entices his younger siblings — all but Quintus, who finds comfort with Lilla — to come with him to the adjoining room, boasting about something he's found outside. But even while he keeps their attention from their grieving mother and me, he casts furtive glances back my way, and when our eyes lock, I can see the tears gathering.

I press a kiss to my wife's temple and stand.

I have failed my boy. I have failed them all.

JULILLA

I clutch to Quintus, holding him to my chest, his little arms wrapping around my swollen belly. Our mother lays Albinus upon the couch he'd occupied most of the time we'd been in this room. She takes off her soot-streaked *palla* and lays it over his silent body, bringing it just up to his neck, but her hands shake and she drops it, unable to cover his face.

I don't blame her. I wasn't able to cover my baby's face either. Instead, Titus had to step in and see to our stillborn child. Pry him from my arms.

Thinking about it brings tears to my eyes. I run my fingers through Quintus' tangles, hoping I am offering even half the comfort to him that he is to me.

"Is Albinus dead?" Quintus asks me.

"Yes," I say, my voice cracking as my gaze flicks to my brother once more.

"What will we do?"

My breath catches. My chest tightens and I force the sobs away. I cannot cry now. I have to be strong for Quintus. No one expects me to be, but I know I must. I must be strong for everyone, because I've seen Father beginning to break. And he is the strongest of us all.

"When will he wake up?" Quintus asks.

"Shh ..." How can you explain the finality of death to one so young? That we may all be doomed to Albinus' fate?

Quintus fingers the *ankh* charm I tied around my ankle with a leather thong—like any child fascinated by baubles. Staring at the charm, I can't help but wonder, what had Capella envisioned of my future? That I'd be whisked to the gods along with my child where we'd remain together forever? Or was it possible that we'd live and be together in *this* world?

"Go and play," I whisper to Quintus.

I still hold a glimmer of hope.

My mother's sobs fill the room. I push Quintus toward the other room where the children's voices carry on a song, and I go to her.

"Mother," I murmur, kneeling awkwardly at her side, the strain of the position tugging at my belly, but I ignore it.

"Oh, Lilla, he suffered so," she wails.

I nod, my throat tight with grief. "But he passed from this world with all of his family surrounding him."

A scream from Charis causes us both to turn in horror to see her kneeling over Nikon's prone body.

"Nikon!" Our slave woman looks at us, her hands covering her mouth. "He's dead!"

My heart leaps into my throat. Our deaths have begun. Two out of twelve. I retreat to my couch where Titus lounges and lean into his embrace.

"What will we do?" I ask, my voice smaller than before.

Titus doesn't answer. His throat bobs and he stares straight ahead. But finally, he speaks. "We'll play a game of dice, Lilla. Just like you wanted."

I nod. We will play. We will pretend that our lives are not near the end. We will deny that two of our own lie dead in the room.

Titus pulls a pair of dice from his purse and weighs them in his palm.

"We have to leave! My babies! They will all—" Father cuts off my mother's words with his hand over her mouth.

He whispers words in her ear that seem to soothe her and pulls her to the couch that she'd been sleeping on before. He lies beside her, stroking her hair. Calming her the way I imagined a stable master calming a wild horse.

All of us are starting to come apart at the seams.

I lean closer to my husband, needing Titus' comforting arms now more than ever. I call out to the gods in my mind, asking forgiveness for the harsh things I thought earlier about choices and my husband and father taking mine. I'd be forever obedient if only the gods would calm the storm outside and save us all.

"Do you want to roll first?" Titus asks.

I shake my head.

Charis steps briskly toward the door, her eyes darting around the room and I have the distinct feeling she is looking for a reason to escape—a way out, just as we all want. It's a feral, *must-survive* look. I've seen the look before in cornered animals. Animals that were heading to slaughter on some altar for sacrifice or a slave trapped in the amphitheater facing certain death as punishment for his crimes.

"Charis, go and check on the children," I call softly, hoping to distract her from trying to escape. There is no hope for it. No escape now.

Let the children and our remaining slave distract each other.

"How are you feeling?" Father asks me as he comes to stand beside me.

"Fine," I lie. With Albinus and Nikon dead and mother losing her sanity, he need not worry over me.

"The baby has stilled within you?"

I nod, biting down hard on the side of my cheek as my stomach tautens painfully in reminder. I am certain now the labor is real. I avoid Titus' gaze as he scrutinizes my answer. My water had not yet broken. My midwife told me that, though I was delivered of a stillborn child, this labor would be like it was my first, as I'd lost the last babe well before it was ready.

How many hours was it now since I first felt the spasms? Six? Seven? Eight? Without the light of the sun, I cannot tell the time. But I am certain that the birthing will be soon, and I am determined not to let my newborn into this world filled with smoke, ash, and the dead.

Once more, I recall the vial in my pouch. Perhaps the gods wanted me to take it.

POLYBIUS

POMPEII is lost to us. I am sure of it. The buildings are crumbling and the ash is falling at such a rate, we're likely to be buried before dawn — if dawn even comes. The air is slowly siphoned from this room and everyone grows weaker. My children play in the other room, well away from the body of their dead brother and our dead slave.

I pace. It is all I can do. I want to run out of the room to find that this is all a terrifying machination of my mind. Perhaps it is better that I go out now, so I don't have to see my family buried here. There will be no one to rescue us. We but wait for the end: I am certain of it.

If I open the door, I take the chance of letting in ash. Though what is inside is tainted, the air in the portico is even worse.

This has become our world, and I'm always the *paterfamilias*. I cannot let my family down. I will strive to do all that I can in the short time we have left together.

I glance at Lilla.

She smiles and it is one of those rare beautiful things. Tears threaten, but I hold them down. We are resigned to our fate now, and I cannot be sad for it. We must live for the moments we have left.

My wife still reclines on the couch. Her eyes are closed in slumber, and I hope she stays that way. She's already suffered too much. Anything more and I think she might rush from the room intent on ending her own life.

"Titus," my voice cracks as I turn to my son-in-law. "I need your help."

He whispers something to Lilla and hands her the dice he's holding.

"We need to move Albinus and Nikon into the storage room." Through the attached room where the children play is an antechamber and another, smaller chamber used for storage. "I do not know how long we will be in here and ..."

"There is no need to explain. I will help you."

"Tell Julius to keep the children from looking at us," I say.

Titus does as I ask, returning with a nod. I lift Albinus in my arms, and Titus carries Nikon. Through the children's play area we go. They have their eyes closed and are guessing at something Julius has asked, innocent smiles on their faces as we carry the dead through the room.

Once in the antechamber, I push open the door to the storage room. It is filled with clay pots, unused linens, and various other household items we stuck back here during the renovation. Now it will be my son and my slave's tomb. I lay Albinus on top of a crate, curling him on his side and pressing one last kiss to his forehead. Titus sets Nikon on the floor in a corner he cleared.

As we leave, both of us sober, I can't help but wonder at what point we could have departed the city and been unharmed. Was Rome even secure?

I smile at the children as we pass through the room, trying to give them the appearance of safety. Only three of my children are in here with Charis; the other two probably went back to see to their mother.

When we are only a half-dozen feet from the door, another loud thundering crack echoes, this time coming from somewhere between the two adjoining rooms. I rush to reach the door, but I am too late. The ceiling cracks, the walls shudder, and the door frame snaps. The entire thing tumbles in on itself, wood, plaster, and stone blocking me from getting to Julius, Little Bird, Quintus, and Charis.

"No!" The word tears from my chest, and all around us I hear the thunder of our roof collapsing on the floor above, sending the ceiling down in torrents around us.

It does not crush us, but we are truly trapped now. There is no way out. Vesuvius has claimed us for its own, and created a tomb of my once beautiful villa.

JULILLA

FATHER won't look at me. Mother is still unconscious. My husband holds me tight to his chest to comfort me. And my siblings stare wide-eyed at the collapsed entry. The one that blocks us. Thank the gods Charis is there with the children on the other side—it would have been much more frightening for them without an adult to soothe them.

Of all things, to have them lost to us now. I cannot bear for it to be a final separation.

Father collapses on the floor, tears streaming down his face.

But I won't have it. I won't believe it.

I settle on my knees upon the couch and bang both hands against the wall.

"Julius! Little Bird! Quintus!" I call out. "Answer me!"

There is a muffled cry on the other side of the wall. It sounds like Quintus. It claws at my heart, wrenches at my soul, and tears fall freely and in waves from my eyes. Unable to believe what has happened, I press my forehead to the wall. I feel as though Vesuvius has exploded within my own soul, pulverizing everything I hold dear, taking with it my sanity and hope. If we'd stayed in Rome ...

Swallowing past the lump in my throat, I force myself to speak, for I do not want that small child given over to my care to be frightened. And though I know he will be scared, I hope that my voice gives him some solace. "We're here, Quintus, be strong. Little Bird, can you hear me? Julius? Charis?"

"Lilla," Quintus cries—and there is no answer from the others— "It hurts!"

I am gutted. He is hurt. He is in pain. For his cries to graze my ears and be helpless to save him is unbearable. For his cries to be heard and no one else's ... have we lost them all at once?

"Lilla," Titus murmurs. "I am so sorry. This is all my fault."

I press a hand to my husband's head. "How could you think it?"

Tears spill down his cheeks as he stares at me. "I should have tried harder to find a way out."

"Shh ..." I can't blame Titus even if I want to. "This is not your fault. We can dig. We will dig."

Despite the pains in my belly I manage to stand, and I tug on Titus' hand. We both kneel before the wall and dig at the never-ending pile of rubble.

"I can see the sky," Quintus says. "I'm scared."

"Do not be scared, my darling. We are coming. We're digging to get you," I say, desperate.

"If the ceiling has collapsed," Titus says, "He cannot breathe in there. There is nothing to protect him. Vesuvius has poisoned our air."

I'd realized our air was no longer of good quality, but I'd not realized how powerfully polluted it was. "What are you saying?" I whisper.

Titus shook his head, looking toward his knees. That was answer enough.

"Quintus," Titus says, pressing his big hand, covered in soot, over mine against the wall. "Can you hear us?"

"Yes."

"Where is Julius? Little Bird? Charis?" Titus asks.

Silence.

"Quintus?" I say around a lump in my throat that chokes me.

"Julius is sleeping," Quintus says, his little voice small and scared. "So are Little Bird and Charis."

I close my eyes, unable to see any longer what has become of us. My little brother stuck on the other side of this wall, alone, afraid, and with three corpses. I know within my soul they are dead. All of us will die here.

Quintus begins coughing, the sound, breaking my heart. "Stay with me," I say.

Titus renews his digging with frenzy, and I join in, though I have to stop when a pain grips me so tight and hard around my middle it steals my breath. When the labor spasm breaks, I say, "Titus is going to dig you out." For I no longer think I can.

I am suddenly nauseated and filled with pain. I must lie down. I fear what I've been prolonging will soon come to pass. "Hold your shirt over your face."

"I'm doing it," Quintus says between coughs.

"Good boy." I sit on the couch, lean against the wall for support and watch Titus work. Ash has darkened his skin and clothes. The dust of the marble and plaster coats him in a fresh powder, making him look gray. But he gets nowhere, even when father joins him. He gives me a look of utter despair, and the strength I'd summoned earlier returns, and with it, finality.

We won't get to the other room. Not in time.

"Quintus," I say softly against the wall, "do you want to hear a story?"

"Yes." His voice is small, and he coughs hard.

I stare at Titus as I tell the story, as much to relive the happy moments of our life as to distract my brother.

"Father took me to Rome when he was there on political business, and I visited the marketplace. You've never seen a market like the one in Rome. It's filled with every kind of trinket—scarves, fabrics, sweets, and spices. Wooden figures for little boys like you to play with." I smile at Titus, who stops digging and comes to sit beside me, holding my hand.

"I saw Titus staring at me between several merchant booths. Every time I looked, he was in a different spot, closer, and I would move, as though we danced in and out of the booths. But every time he caught my eye, he smiled. Until finally, he approached me with a sugared date, and asked if he could honor me with a taste."

"I like dates," Quintus said.

"Me, too. If I could have a room filled from floor to ceiling with dates, I would. I'd climb to the very top and eat my way to the bottom."

"I would help you," my little brother said, between coughs.

"I would like that. We'll share the room." I lean my head against Titus' shoulder. "It will be our own sweet place."

"Lilla?" His voice sounds so small.

"Yes, Quintus?"

"I'm tired."

I bite my lip, knowing that it won't be much longer until Quintus succumbs to the suffocating air. "Think of the dates, sweet brother. Imagine you are climbing to the very top, that a special fat one waits just for you."

"Yes, that one is mine." There is a moment of silence. I close my eyes. "I want to lie down. I think I'll lie with Little Bird."

My response tears from my throat. "Not yet, Quintus. Hold on a little longer."

"All right," he says, but quieter now. Not as convinced.

"Now you tell me a story, Quintus," I plead. "Tell me of your favorite place."

The walls shake again and another loud crash sounds from somewhere in the villa.

"I'm too tired, Lilla. I want to sleep."

251

Father comes to stand beside me, his hand trembling as he lays it on my shoulder. "We—We have to let him go," he says.

Titus doesn't break his eye contact with me, and I see clearly that he agrees.

I want to rave at them both. I want to pound against the wall, to find a way into that room, though I already know the truth.

"Quintus. I'm here for you still," I say, scratching lightly at the wall. But he doesn't answer and fear cascades through me. "Quintus!" My voice becomes shrill.

Father shakes his head, looking from one of us to the other. "They are lost to us."

"Not yet." I rake a hand through my hair, ready to pull it out as grief consumes me.

"Oh, my darling daughter." Father closes the space between us and tries to tug me into his embrace.

"No." I pull away, standing up, and my belly tightens painfully as my labor resumes its pains.

"I care about the ones left in that room, too, Lilla. They are my children."

I lower my head in sorrow and shame. "I haven't forgotten." And then I hug my father. There is no hope now. All is lost. The gods have forsaken us.

Father pulls back, his hands on my shoulders and nods. "You were my firstborn child, Lilla, and I am so proud to call you daughter."

I reach up, wrapping my fingers around his and refusing to think about the child alone and scared, curled up beside my dead siblings and slave. I pray to any of the gods who will listen that they take him swiftly. The pain eating me up is grief or labor pangs. Perhaps it is both. I can't bear it. I'm ready for it all to end. "I am proud to call you Father."

Another pain strikes me hard in the middle and I stumble backward.

"Lilla," Father says, settling me on the couch. "You have a strong constitution, daughter. Stronger than your mother's and I think even stronger than mine."

I grit my teeth at the pain and stare up at him. "I do not think any of us should have much longer to endure it."

His silence confirms that we are not long for this life.

"I need to comfort the little ones," he finally says. "The two I have left."

I nod and glance over at Titus who kneels in defeat by the pile of rubble between our two rooms.

"Titus," I murmur, closing my eyes as another wave hits me, only this time it burns as I feel the babe inside me descend into my birth canal. I have put off his entrance long enough, somehow enduring the pains and hiding them from all. My child wants to see what is left of this world. But I cannot let him.

"Lilla." Titus faces me, his eyes resigned, and his mouth flat.

"He is coming," I whisper, sweat beading my brow. "I cannot do it, Titus. I cannot bring him into this world."

Titus shakes his head. "You must."

"No." I reach into the pouch at my side, filled with coin and something else. The vial. I am ashamed to admit the thought of using it crosses my mind before I am even certain that death will come. "I have something." I pull out the vial I never wanted to use. "A way for us to make this end all the sooner."

"No, Lilla. I forbid it!" Titus is adamant, anger creasing his brow. "Where did you get this?"

I shake my head. It is not important where I got it, only that I have it and I intend to use it. Titus grabs for the bottle, and I tighten my hold.

Our gazes lock and an internal battle between us both takes place. It is then, I feel the gush of warmth burst from my womb, pooling between my thighs and soaking the couch. My bag of waters has broken.

I shake my head, begging Titus with my gaze to let me do this.

Misery clouds us both. Pain fills my entire body, my very soul. I want a way to end it. A way to take control of my life. A way to choose. Vesuvius may have taken away my siblings, but it will not take my child. That is my choice. It will not kill me. The great mountain will not be triumphant. I shall prevail. I shall take away the one thing it seeks to destroy — us all. For I am one that will not wait. In what little time I have left, I will take charge of my fate, and that of my unborn child.

Titus grits his teeth, presses his forehead to mine. A sob escapes him, but then he says, "What say you, Lilla? Shall we share one last drink together?"

POLYBIUS

A father will die for his children. A soldier pledges his life to his emperor. He knows that with every last breath he has, every last stroke of his sword on his enemy, death will be an honor he gladly accepts. Even a lowly gladiator fights in an arena, risking his life and winning the great glory of breath when he is champion, but also gladly accepts an honorable death. Romans are fighters. We are honorable.

I am honorable. I would gladly trade my life for my wife and my children.

But I have been robbed of that choice.

I mourn the loss of four of my children. Two of my slaves. Sitting around me were future soldiers, politicians, wives of great men.

My wife. My daughter. All of them doomed to die with me.

"Decima," I murmur against my wife's ear. "Wake, Decima."

She stirs. Her eyes blinking open. "Gaius?"

"We must ..." I clear my throat, for how do you tell a woman to say goodbye to her two remaining children? She does not yet know about Julius, Little Bird, or Quintus.

Her gaze roves around the room, landing on our younger daughter and son. She closes her eyes again, and I feel her pulse kick up on my fingers where I graze her neck. She did not ask where her other children were. When her gaze centered on the collapsed door, she must have guessed. But then she responds.

"We must." Her voice is strong, determined. She sits up, her lips firm. Stronger now than I've ever seen her before.

I nod. Decima presses her lips to mine, desperately, and I cannot help but sink against her, clutching her warm body to mine. A body that once comforted. A body that grew and nurtured our many children. I want it to last forever, to keep our breaths mingled until the entire house falls on our heads and the mountain's wrath stops our hearts. But Decima pushes against me. Her eyes lock on mine and she nods.

"Children," she croons and beckons them forward.

Our young ones come to us, their eyes wide and scared. They've seen more death and misery this day than any child should. A war from the gods brought to their feet.

"Time for bed, my loves, we must rest," Decima says in a soothing voice.

The children nod and climb onto the couch, their arms wrapped around each other. Decima and I kiss them each, hug them tight and whisper a prayer. Then we turn to Lilla, a look a similar determination on her face.

"I love you, Lilla," Decima says. "I pray Isis enfolds you in her grasp."

"May the gods be with you, Mother, Father." Her voice is strained, and the veins in her neck are protruding. She is in pain. Her hands clutch her belly and her breaths come quick.

I've seen this before. She is in full labor. Decima's eyes widen as she takes in the sight of her daughter, and I know she realizes this, too.

"May the gods protect you," my wife says on a breath and kneels before our eldest daughter. "May the gods protect your child."

"*I* will protect my child," Lilla grinds out.

Titus holds tight to his wife's hand and kisses her knuckles. He glances up at me with a curt nod. "We shall see you soon, Polybius, in the Elysian Fields."

I nod, because my throat is closed tight with emotion, stealing what little breath I'm able to draw. Decima presses a kiss to her daughter's head and then pulls me toward our couch where she lies down and tugs me to join her.

"The gods await us," Decima says.

I nod. "I'll be forever at your side."

My wife closes her eyes, her fingers curling into my shirt, knuckles white. The lights flicker. Of the three lanterns we had, only one remains, and it, too, will soon die.

JULILLA

"TOGETHER."

I nod, and he bends to press his lips to my belly. While his face is turned away I scream silently to the shadowed ceiling. I cannot go on much longer. I'm being ripped in two. I feel like I'm already dying. I run my fingers through his hair as I've done many times, reliving every moment we've spent together, good, bad, and wonderful. I pant to keep the pain at bay and to keep from bearing down. We shall travel this next path together as we'd tread the last several years. Hand in hand.

Titus leans up, presses a kiss to my heart and grasps my hand in his. He touches the bottle wrapped in my grasp, its blown glass, blue and transparent.

He gazes into my eyes and I whisper a prayer I've heard many times before when death came to those close to us: *I approached the confines of death, and having trod on the threshold of Proserpine, I returned therefrom, being borne through all the elements. At midnight I saw the sun shining with its brilliant light; and I approached the presence of the Gods beneath, and the Gods of heaven, and stood near, and worshipped them.*

I pray to the gods within our home, within Pompeii, and in Rome. I whisper the words. I think them when the pain becomes too much, and then I grasp tight to the vial, uncork it, and pull it to my lips. I gaze into Titus' eyes.

He nods. "I will follow you," he says. And I believe him. For once, I am taking the lead in what path we follow.

My pain will be gone. This darkened tomb will be gone. I will be with my babies. With Titus. With my brothers and sisters and my parents.

That is enough of a certainty to me. To spend whatever the walking afterlife is in peace and happiness, surrounded by those I loved. For the pain and torment to end here and now.

"I love you," I whisper.

Before I take a sip, Titus jolts up and presses his mouth hard to mine. "I love you so much, my darling," he says. "I had wished for so much more in this life for us."

"But what we—" Pain steals my breath, my body seizes, ready to push my child into the world. I cannot allow it to happen. I squeeze my thighs tight, refusing to breathe. I won't allow my body to push this child into the world. To push him into death. Better that he die cocooned within my womb: safe, comforted.

A sob threatens, but I squeeze my eyes tightly closed afraid even that little bit of motion will propel my baby out of me. I wanted this child. Prayed for him. Made certain I was healthy. Grew him. Felt him move within me. Dreamed for him. Planned for his future, and now I was going to take that away. But what choice did I have? To be born within this tomb would only mean he'd die within an hour. There is only one choice. To save him the pain of living.

I tip the potion and drink. The liquid inside burns a path down my throat, and I choke, sputter, can barely breathe. Where it settles in my belly, burning, and I gag. I clutch at my throat, forcing myself not to vomit. I thrust the glass toward Titus. This death will be quick, and I want him to hear what I have to say. "We had a good life, Titus."

"We did, Lilla. I have no regrets." He tips the vial, draining whatever is left in it.

I have plenty of regrets. But what good does it do to dwell on them? Our fates are sealed. "We'll not look back," I gasp. The pain of the poison is not as bad as the pain of my child pushing into the birth canal.

Titus climbs onto the bed, his eyes red and bulging as he lies beside me. His hard body is warm and gives me comfort. My mouth starts to tingle, my tongue going thick and numb. I want a drink of wine desperately, feeling a thirst that will never be quenched. Titus lays his head beside me, his arm resting over my abdomen, cradling our baby. I want to wrap my arms around him, but already my hands and feet are tingling, my arms growing numb and I can't move them. I feel myself sweating. The pain of birth no longer grips me. I choke a sob. *My baby. My baby! Please forgive me. There was no other way.*

I gasp for breath, unable to draw it in. Titus moans beside me, and I feel his pain inside me. I am being flayed alive inside. But I go to my death knowing that I chose this way to leave Pompeii, this world. Knowing that I did not bring a child into this world only to have it suffer.

I no longer have control of my body.

The lamp light flickers in and out. I am dizzy. Spinning.

I am floating, numb. No longer in pain. No longer tormented, but a peace surrounds me.

I blink and blink again. I cannot see.

Darkness consumes me.

And then the darkness is gone and I am surrounded by light.

PART SIX

THE WHORE

Stephanie Dray

"There were no gods left anywhere ... the last and eternal night had come upon the world."
—Pliny the Younger

CAPELLA

DARKNESS. We are born from darkness. We perish in darkness. And then we are born again. That is the promise of Isis. It's a promise of salvation I once whispered to an empress whose death I foretold. Now I murmur that same promise to comfort the terrified boy in my arms — a man, in truth, with a downy beard upon his chin. Or at least he thought to *make* himself from a boy to a man when he parted the red curtain of the cubicle on the street outside the *caupona* where I ply my trade.

When the city began to shake again, other men fled, stopping in the *caupona* only to fill their sacks with bread or their flasks with wine for the journey. But this young man was desperate for something else, and he pressed more shiny coins into my hand than the price for me scrawled upon the tavern wall. Needing solace of the spirit, he bought solace of my body. I suppose because there is, in touch, an affirmation of life, of immortality. Which is why men pay for touch even when the earth isn't quaking beneath their feet.

When the rush to the city gates began, my master and his wife watched over the *caupona*, intent upon squeezing every copper coin from passersby. I am their property, and my body is bought and sold anew most every day, so I was told to follow the young man to the cubicle on the street where I let him grasp me roughly, hitching up his tunic only far enough to get between my thighs.

And he was inside me, rudely thrusting, when we heard the deafening roar of the mountain like a god in carnal ecstasy, releasing the hot, pent-up life force of a hero's age.

It was no god or hero who spent himself in me, though. Just a scared boy who then pinned me with his terrified weight. Together we could make no sense of the booms, the screams, the braying donkeys, the howling dogs, or the mountain's bellow. We'd disentangled from one another only long enough to peek out the curtain, but at the horrifying sight of a billowing plume spewing forth from the mountain, we had fallen back together in terror upon the stone bed where I have held so many other men. And here we are, still huddled, while darkness envelops the city, too frightened to move, not even knowing how much time has passed.

I don't know his name and, of course, he doesn't know mine. Prostitutes are called by a thousand names. *Lupae, fornices, meretrices, prostibulae* ... but we are still somehow nameless. The young man and I are strangers, even though I am covered in his cooling seed and he, with the most intimate scent of me. But it's the intimacy of our *terror* that turns us from strangers to lovers.

We cling to one another. He clings to me as to life, gibbering in his fear, and I cling to him because his flesh has somehow become as precious to me as my own. Because his flesh, tears, and need are the only things that make sense to me under a midday sun blotted out in a sky that has begun to rain ash.

I foresaw this. An onyx sky denser and darker than any ordinary night. A black swelling rain that would become a river, to be followed by a dark sea of violent power. A coming flood to wash our spirits clean of flesh and blood. And then, an ethereal blaze of fire. Like a lighthouse burning so bright that it could lead an entire city to eternal salvation.

Whatever is happening in Pompeii, I have seen it before in the pool at the Temple of Isis—a goddess of sailors and seductresses and all who fear they might lose their way.

But my sister says that visions are for priestesses, not prostitutes.

Perhaps she's right, because my faith is shaken. Instead of feeling awe and wonder for the goddess whose promises of salvation I keep repeating, I am consumed with fear. As I hear the cracks and clatter of hail falling from the sky onto terra cotta rooftops, I do not reach to touch my anklet with its jingling *ankh* charms. Nor do I yearn for my goddess. I want only the older sister who has been more of a mother to me than the woman who gave birth to us.

Prima. Surely she will find me. Even in this darkness. She will find me and protect me as she always does because she is never afraid, never cries, and never lets any man grasp her too roughly. I am determined to fly to her as soon as I can quiet the young man in my arms, who keeps murmuring of death and giants and the end of the world.

Then I hear my sister's voice pierce through the shroud of darkness. "Capella!"

Prima shrieks my name, pushing from the street into the small chamber in which I am huddled with the boy, the glow of her lantern breaking the paralyzing spell of the darkness. Prima's saffron-colored toga — worn by registered prostitutes — has somehow turned a whitish gray; a powder covers her hair and bony shoulders, but the pallor of her normally swarthy face is even paler. Her black eyes fall upon me with some mixture of relief and horror. "Capella! I have been looking everywhere in the *caupona* for you."

"What's happening?" I ask. Because Prima will know. She always looks for danger. She understands the terrible things in this world. She sees in people the evil that I prefer to be blind to.

But now, when I am desperate for her to make sense of the roaring mountain, she only answers, *"What's happening?* The sky is falling and you have some limp-pricked blubberer between your legs."

Something about the boy's tears, his youth, and the down on his chin seem to infuriate her even more. She shouts at him, "Get off my sister. Pay your money and go!"

"No, don't." I hold him tighter. I feel as if I must know his name.

But my sister digs her nails into his arms, wrenching him away.

Prima hates the men who buy us. She hates everyone. Prima is good at hate. Good at anger. And I've never seen her angrier than she is now. She beats on the young man with both fists and though I call after him in protest, he runs off, alone and nameless, into the black rain of ash.

"Why did you do that?" I demand. "He was afraid. He was just afraid!"

"Let him piss himself somewhere else," Prima says, breathless from her efforts to drive him off. "Now squat and sneeze, or do you want another misbegotten whelp?"

After three years, I am nearly numb to the reminder of the child I gave birth to. But not numb enough. Prima's question makes me wonder where my child is in all this madness. Where is the nameless little girl that *Dominus* ripped from my arms and sold away? *Home-bred slaves fetch good prices*, he said, but is my daughter here in the panicking city or did some cruel master leave her to die on a bluff over the sea years ago?

When I don't answer, nor squat, nor sneeze, Prima snaps, "Never mind. Let's get back into the *caupona* before someone thinks you've run away again."

There it is. She thought I'd run away again. That old scar of our childhood throbbing anew. That's why she's so angry. It ought to shame me, but it doesn't. Not now. Not when I see, in this destruction, the moment I have been waiting for all my life. Standing up from the bed, making myself tall, I say, "Prima, we *should* run. Everyone else is fleeing the city. No one will stop us. Not even the most fearsome *fugitivarii* can capture runaway slaves in this stampede. Let's escape together and be free. Let's go. Let's run!"

Her lower lip trembles.

Then she slaps me so hard that I fall to the shaking ground.

SHE had never struck her sister before. Not in anger. Not for any other reason. Perhaps she should have done it sooner. With a round moon face and dreamy blue eyes, Capella had a childlike sense of hopefulness about her. But if ever there were a time for Prima's sister to grow up, it was now. "Do you want them to press a hot brand into your pretty forehead this time?" Prima asked as tiny pebbles bounced from the street onto the stone floor alongside the shards of tiles that had fallen earlier in the quake. "That's what they do to runaway slaves. Or are you just so eager to run out into a hailstorm with these other fools?"

Capella held one hand to her reddening cheek as those dreamy blue eyes filled with defiant tears. "It's a hailstorm of *little rocks*. We've never seen a storm such as this. There's never *been* such a storm as this—"

Prima's hands went to her bony hips. "And there may be giants coming up from the earth to make war on the gods. Didn't you hear their trumpets? I don't want to hear about gods or your visions and madness! *Dominus* said to close the *caupona* against looters and take shelter under the stairs, so that's what we're going to do."

Prima grabbed hold of Capella's plump wrist and dragged her up off the floor and out onto the street where they braved a shower of charred, feather-light stones. They ducked under the awning of the *caupona*, retreating inside amid overturned stools, scattered wooden bowls, and an abandoned loaf of bread still warm from the oven. At this time of day the *caupona* ought to have been filled with drunk, groping patrons waiting for hot food to be ladled out of the jars set into the colorfully tiled countertop. It ought to have been filled with the sound of laughter, the scattering of dice, and big hands slapping coins down on tables. Even when night fell and Prima slid the wooden panels in place at the front of the street to lock up, the *caupona* was noisy with the arguments of drunken men in adjacent alleys. And long after the drunks found their beds, while Prima counted the earnings, she could still hear the wheels of wagons in the street … and her sister's murmured prayers to a goddess who supposedly cared about the plight of whores.

But now the *caupona* was empty as it was never empty and, except for the roar of the mountain, quiet as it was never quiet. "Where is everyone?" Prima's sister asked, with a gasp. "*Dominus* left us, didn't he? Everyone has run off. Everyone but us!"

"I'm sure the master and his wife have only gone next door to shelter with the rich neighbors," Prima said without meeting Capella's eyes, trying not to frighten her. There had been a water shortage in the city for some time, so when the jug of wine set into the counter shimmered in the glow of her lamp, it beckoned to Prima's parched throat. Since she was already sure to be whipped for doing worse than stealing wine, Prima pulled the jug to her lips and gulped at it greedily. That reminded her of the gnawing hunger in her belly, and she tore off a fragrant triangle of bread from the abandoned loaf.

"What in the name of all the gods are you doing?" Capella asked, hugging herself with those fleshy arms that were so seldom empty. "You call *me* a madwoman, but you're drinking wine and eating bread when we should be running for our lives."

"It's good bread," Prima said, grateful for the burst of fennel, parsley, and coriander on her tongue. It was a special combination of those spices that made customers look for the stamp of their master's baker on the loaf. Prima enjoyed it all the more because it helped mask the scent and taste of rotten eggs that now permeated the air. "And I'm hungry."

Prima had been born hungry. Hungrier than any other child ever born, with a hole in her center that could never be filled. So hungry that she had to be pried off the nipple for fear she would suck her mother dry of life. Or so her mother said. It was one of the few things Prima remembered about the Gallic slave woman who had given birth to her. Prima couldn't remember how her mother looked, except that she was round and rosy and fair like Capella.

Prima looked nothing like either of them.

She'd come out all dark and bony, the get of a different father. Probably a Greek, the red-haired empress once said, holding Prima's chin between thumb and forefinger. *"Unfortunate. I can't have your daughter as my cupbearer. Greeks are clever, but they're also sneaky little liars …"*

Prima poured a cup of wine for her sister and tore off a chunk of bread for her, too. "Here. Eat."

"No." Capella refused with a shake of her head. "We need to go, Prima. I know it. I know it in my soul."

Prima snorted. "Your *soul?"* She didn't believe in things she couldn't see, touch, or eat. Except maybe shades and *lemures*, those angry spirits of the dead. Because anger made more sense to her than all the spirit bodies and mysteries the Isiacs ranted about.

"Yes, I know it in my *soul,"* Capella insisted, gripping the countertop. "I've foreseen it. We're meant to be free."

Free. What use was freedom unless you were rich enough to buy it? And even then, what use unless you were a man? Prima was an *infamis*—a status not easily escaped once your name was on the roll of registered prostitutes, from which it could never be removed. Like slavery, *infamia* meant no voice, no legal status, and few protections of any kind. Better to be a disreputable but well-fed slave girl than a disreputable and starving freedwoman, Prima thought. Most of them ended up whoring themselves anyway, to survive. A master in Pompeii was good protection, and their master was no worse than any other. And yet, Capella had been prattling on about freedom her whole life.

Prima supposed she had no one to blame but herself. She had always coddled her younger sister. A pinched sweet here, a few stolen coins there, the false piety of a bowed head. Keep Capella from grieving over her child being taken from her; keep her from being registered as a whore. Anything to keep her from running away again. Anything to make Capella smile. Because Prima lived for that smile. Her own gap-toothed smile was crooked and ugly. But her sister's rosy-cheeked smile was the only truly beautiful thing in the whole crooked and ugly world.

That's why Prima had agreed to do the bidding of the *aedile*, Gaius Cuspius Pansa.

Keep my sister's name off the roll of prostitutes, Pansa, and I promise to do your bidding.

She hadn't known, when she made that promise, that it would be her doom. She was a dead woman now, even if the city didn't swallow her up in its blackness. She had done something terrible because of the handsome but loathsome *aedile*. Something that would probably see her crucified.

That is what they did to slaves who murdered senators, wasn't it? They would torture her first, she was sure. She'd seen slaves whose lips, ears, and noses were cut off before their eyes were gouged out and *then* they were nailed to a cross. Prima pushed the horrifying memory away, and said, "You'll like the bread better with some oil and olives. You've always liked that since you were a little girl. I'll open the casks in the back. Maybe we'll find half a spicy sausage left in the pan. We'll make a meal of it."

Capella shook her head violently. "I said I don't want to eat."

"Well, food is all I can give you!" Without warning, a lifetime's worth of bile rose into Prima's throat. She had been swallowing it down for her sister's sake. Swallowing and swallowing, until her belly ought to have been filled with it. But she was never full and couldn't swallow it anymore. "Eating is all there is. It's all the freedom you're ever going to have. Right here, right now, in this moment before we die."

Capella trembled. "What are you saying?"

"Do I need to say it? Are you too blind to see the truth? Of course you are. You've always been too soft for the truth. Our mother's soft and sweet baby. Empress Poppaea Sabina's favorite pet. *Such a special, mystical little girl.*" Prima mimicked. "Everyone pampers you—even that lonely engineer who pretends to befriend you. What's his name?"

"You know his name," Capella said, silent tears streaming down her cheeks. "It's Sabinus. And he's not an engineer, but he *is* my friend."

"No, he pays you to be *his* friend! He only gives you wine to wash the taste of him from your mouth so he can forget you're a whore." Why couldn't Prima stop the cruel words from tumbling from her mouth? They came out in a rush, scalding her tongue. "Where is your adoring mother now? Dead. Where is your empress now? Dead. Where is your 'friend' Sabinus? Likely dead, too. So maybe now you'll realize that your salvation cult is folly and the only thing special about you is that long ribbon of golden hair and the pillowy tits men pay to squeeze and suck. That is the truth. We eat, we shit, we fuck, and we die. That's all there is. I tell you this all the time, but maybe now you'll believe it. That's all there is for anyone, and I'm tired of pretending otherwise. This is who we are and all we're ever going to be."

CAPELLA

MY sister is afraid, I realize. Prima is *terrified*.

It has always been a joke between us that, whatever the birth order, I am the *big* sister and she is the *little* one because she is tiny, much smaller than me. But I have always relied upon her sharp elbows to make way for us in a crowd, the lash of her vicious tongue to fend off abusive men, her unsavory schemes to keep us fed. I have marveled at the way she never, *ever* cries—not even when she's being beaten.

But now I see that my sister is a hissing alley cat that I somehow mistook for a *gladiatrix*.

How have I never realized before that the source of all her anger is fear?

"You think we're going to die," I whisper. "Say it, if that's what you mean, Prima. We're going to die."

She cannot look at me. She just sits there tearing bits of bread from the loaf. She crams them into her mouth and chews, but she has clearly lost her taste for it. And when she answers, her voice is quiet and far away. "The whole world is dying and we're dying with it."

It is a horrible thing to say. But, day has become night and rocks have become rain, so maybe it's true. Strangely, I take solace in this. In the togetherness of the world ending in its entirety, if that's what is happening. I find strength in it, even. Strength enough to take my sister by her narrow shoulders and ask, "If we're dying, what does it matter if we die here or out on the streets, at least struggling for a chance?"

"Are you deaf, you stubborn cow? I'm telling you there's no chance for us and I'm tired of struggling. We've been struggling our whole lives." Prima's arm steals around my waist in something akin to a hug. "I'd rather we die with full bellies, on a soft bed, with a roof over our heads than" — Prima waves in the direction of the street — "out there."

"I'm going," I say, resolutely.

"Of course you are," she answers bitterly, letting her arm fall away. "You always run away. And look at the good it's done us."

Prima blames me — and she is right to. We were not born to squalor and infamy. No, we were born in the fabulously luxurious *insula* belonging to the family of Poppaea Sabina, a girl who rose to be empress of Rome. Our mother was that girl's slave. Long before Nero fell in love with Poppaea. Long before Poppaea convinced Nero to divorce his wife and make her his bride. Long before he killed her ...

And though I could have been no more than three years old when Poppaea Sabina became empress, I remember her well. The fiery-haired empress loved my golden ringlets and delighted in dressing me as a winged cupid to amuse her friends. The empress lived in unimaginable luxury, bathing every day in milk, but she considered herself to be a deeply religious woman.

I was with her on the day she returned to Pompeii for the *Navigium Isidis* to celebrate the opening of the sailing season. And all of Pompeii was bedecked with colorful floral garlands, the harbor crushed with crowds of sailors, all straining to see the sacrificial ship be floated into the ocean to honor the goddess Isis, who guided them home. Enraptured by the rattling sound of the *sistrums*, I drew close to the frothing waves. As I did I saw the fate of Empress Poppaea. Though I would have other visions looking into water, this was the first. And I fell to my knees in the sand in reverence for the goddess who had touched me.

My mistress, too, was moved. Seeing me on my knees in prayer, she pledged me to the temple to serve as a priestess when I was grown. It should have been enough for me. Isis had *chosen* me and I had a mistress who would surrender me to the goddess! Mine was to be a life of the spirit, of dignity, and respect.

But I knew from my visions that the empress would never live to fulfill her pledge.

So I ran.

That first time, I sought refuge with the priests, determined to serve the goddess. Prima found me in the temple and dragged me back. She took the blame and the overseer laid a scourge across her back. She did not cry; she shed not one tear. But it was a beating from which she still has scars. Fortunately, because of our youth and the mercy of the empress, we were not branded, tattooed, or maimed, but merely forced to wear wooden signs round our necks and sent to work in her nearby pottery factory. There, working until our fingers pruned with water and caked with clay, we were meant to take a lesson in how lucky we were to serve a kind mistress in a sumptuous house where our duties were few.

But I ran away again and again to the temple until our mistress sold us to the first bidder. The sale stipulated we were never to be put to work in prostitution, but Empress Poppaea washed her hands of us.

And with it, her pledge to Isis.

So it is my fault that we came of age in a tavern, selling wine and sex. I stole from my sister a life in which she might have been happy. A life in which she might never have been hungry. A life in which her name would not have been scrawled on walls with a price, her talents illustrated in obscene detail, her name not listed on the rolls as one of the registered *meretrices*.

That's why she blames me. It's why I blame myself.

"I'm sorry," I say, making Prima look at me. "I'm sorry we landed here—"

"You think that makes a difference?" she asks with a sudden snort of bitter laughter. "Feed them, fuck them, wash their clothes, clean up their piss and shit, draw their baths of milk … it doesn't matter. It's just work. And whoring is the easiest work there is. You just lay there if you're lazy. Use your mouth if you want it over quick. You think I care whether some pathetic boy tries to find love by piddling his seed on my thighs, or whether, instead, some perfumed empress uses my back for a footstool? I don't care. I don't."

But I care. It matters to me. It always has. My sister has a different way of seeing the world, so maybe she is telling the truth. But I don't think she is. "If you don't care, then why won't you forgive me?"

At this question, Prima's face screws up into a mask of anguish. Whatever words she is wrestling with are words she does not want to say, but she cannot seem to keep them caged and they hiss their way between the gap in her teeth. "Because you left me! I've always looked after you. Always. But you ran, never giving a moment's thought about what might happen to me. You left me behind. And now, after everything, you want to leave me again."

Her words take a savage bite from my heart and I bleed with guilt, because they're true. All except for the last. "No, Prima. I don't want to leave you. This time we're going together. There will be boats in the harbor. The navy will come to rescue—"

"To rescue citizens, not us."

To convince her, I say, "Sailors will do anything for even a promise of a pretty girl's body. So we're going even if I have to drag your skinny bones behind me like a bundle of sticks."

She is indignant, jutting out her stubborn chin. "As if you could."

I try a new approach. "If you don't come with me, everyone will laugh at you for a fool. You saw those people out in the street running away. What if the world *isn't* ending? What if it is only

Pompeii that is wrapped in darkness? Think how everyone who escapes will laugh that Prima was smart enough to know an easy mark in an alleyway, but not clever enough to run out the gates of the city to find a patch of sunshine."

She rears back, affronted, as I knew she would be, because my sister is fed by her contempt for others. I do not think she can bear the thought of anyone laughing at her, even in death. And she is silent so long that I am hopeful that she will give in. But then she gets up from her stool, and goes to the back room where we keep the casks of oil and olives.

So I will have to drag her, I think. I ready myself to do it, every muscle tensed with anticipation. I'll have to be quicker than I've ever been in my life, because she's fast when she wants to be. She darts like a mouse. But she does not run from me. Instead, she snaps, "Are you just going to stand there, or are you going to fill a sack with bread?"

"What?"

Her black eyes flash with impatience as she pops an olive into her mouth. "If there's a patch of sunshine out there for us somewhere, I'm not going to look for it without taking something to eat."

PRIMA

UPSTAIRS, in the room where they slept at night, Prima rummaged through their belongings, glancing longingly at the simple palette bed they shared. She wanted to curl up on it. To curl round her sister under a blanket and drift off to sleep and let whatever would come, come. But she couldn't bear to die in that bed *alone*.

So when Capella called up to her again, she threw down to her a fringed but threadbare cloak to help keep the sting of the hail from her sister's bare arms. She tossed down, too, an old, torn cushion.

Capella caught the pillow with one hand and feathers puffed out and swirled round her. "What's this for?"

275

"It's for your head, you dolt. You've already got so little sense you can't afford a falling rock knocking the rest of it out of you." As for Prima, she *knew* she'd already taken leave of her own senses. If they ran, they would have to keep on running, because if ever they did find a patch of sunlight, there was sure to be an executioner waiting for her there.

She hadn't been thinking clearly when she bashed Senator Marcus Norbanus over the head. If she'd been thinking, she would've realized there were probably witnesses. There were always witnesses near a brothel. And even the handsome *aedile*, for whom she'd performed so many unsavory acts, couldn't protect her; Gaius Cuspius Pansa would turn her over in a heartbeat. The authorities would want to make an example of her. They might even cart her to Rome to do it …

Rome. She'd never been to Rome. Not even when Poppaea Sabina became empress. Now, with Prima's luck, the only part of the eternal city she was ever likely to see was the inside of an arena just before being fed to lions.

Dying in her bed was looking better and better.

"Stop stalling!" Capella called up. "The stones are falling faster."

Prima sighed. There was nothing worth taking but a few coins she'd been hiding under the eaves. Shiny coins with the new emperor's face on them. The *aedile* had given them to her as wages for information about one of her customers: a love-struck, pimply-faced boy with an important uncle.

If he's foolish enough to trust a whore, then he deserves what he gets.

That's what Pansa had said. She'd believed him because she knew love itself *was* foolishness. An infection. A disease. Love was a delusion that made you give away your money and your body and your safety for nothing. That's why Prima didn't love anything or anyone.

Except Capella.

So she grabbed another pillow and started back down the stairs.

She lit a torch. Then she took her sister's hand and stepped out into the storm.

There was no wind, but the rumbling mountain and clatter of stones and the howling animals and screaming women made for a cacophony. "Which gate?" Prima shouted over the bark of a dog left chained at the front of a house. CAVE CANEM. *Beware of the dog*, Prima thought. Everyone had a sign like that even if they had no dog. Because dogs were stupidly loyal. They would protect that which didn't belong to them. That's what *Dominus* had wanted Prima and Capella to do. Stay behind and guard the *caupona* while they ran to safety. But their master hadn't chained them, so maybe he *deserved* to lose them.

Prima was the older sister, the wiser one, and the stronger one. She should know what to do and which way to go. But she could not think, so she demanded again, "*Which gate?*"

Capella's blue eyes were round with fright and she pulled her fringed cloak tighter around her shoulders. "I don't — I don't know."

Squinting into the blackness, Prima snapped, "Why are your visions always so vague on important details? Didn't Isis tell you where it was safe to go?"

Capella only groaned. "I don't know. I don't. But Sabinus once told me that when the earth quakes here, it does not quake in Rome. And Sabinus predicted —"

"To Hades with Sabinus!" Prima shouted.

She hated that mopey clod even more than the other men who shoved their pricks into her sister. He was a talker; one of the men who took more from Capella than just her body. One of those men who needed an illusion of love or friendship. A real man would admit to himself that paying a girl to drain his balls was no different than paying a girl to empty his piss pot. Fuck Sabinus and his predictions; Prima hoped he was dead. Dead and trampled and eaten by wild dogs. "I'm not entrusting our fate to some rich fool with deluded visions of his own."

"He doesn't have visions, he —" Capella suddenly broke off.

"What is it?"

"The Stabian Gate," Capella said, her hand tightening on Prima's as she started off in that direction, her anklet of little charms jingling as she hurried. "I am sure of it."

CAPELLA

I am sure of nothing but that I know the way to the Stabian Gate. I can find it even if our torch should go out. I can find it by hugging the walls of shops on the street in the dark, as I did once before when I was a runaway girl. The Temple of Isis is near the Stabian Gate, and I believe I can find my way there with my eyes closed and with nothing but my love for the goddess to guide me because I've done it before. As I drag my sister along, block after block, the leather soles of our sandals skating unsteadily over a layer of tiny charred stones, I trip over what appears to be an abandoned hand-cart of cabbages.

I come down hard, pillow and all, half my body off the high curb, splayed on the paving of the street, my toes digging into the ruts that wheels have made over many years. The other half of my body lands upon something soft and wet and warm.

Flesh. A whore knows human flesh.

"A dead man." I gasp, understanding in horror that the wetness now coating my hands is blood. Feeling my way up his stiffening body, I say, "His head is smashed. Someone or something smashed his skull."

My sister does not feel sorrow. Especially not for dead strangers. I expect she will haul me up and tell me to take his purse. Then she'll kick the corpse and keep going. Instead, she backs away with the torch as if to avoid bad luck in looking upon the dead. "Does he have a purple-bordered toga?"

"I don't know." I will not take it from him if he does.

My sister's fear must be driving her half-mad, because she makes a keening sound. "If he has a toga, cover him with it! Gods forgive me. Gods forgive me ... but no, it can't be him. He fell near the *lupanar*, not here."

I can make no sense of Prima's rambling. I can make no sense of anything in this moment but the promise my goddess has made to me. I am meant to be free. I am meant to be more than my body, blood, and bones. There is a part of me that will never die. I am meant to endure a thousand years and a thousand more. That is the promise of *Isis Sotera*, Isis the Savior. And in spite of my fear and doubt, her promise still burns brightly enough in my heart that I'm able get to my feet. Prima has watched out for me and protected me all my life. Now I must do the same for her.

I grab her dry and ashy hand in my blood-slick one. "We have to keep running, Prima. Follow me to the Stabian Gate."

We are not the only ones in the streets. We see dots of torchlight bobbing up and down and hear the shackles of a gang of slaves being driven out of the city by an overseer. We hear the furious neigh of a horse as it gallops by, showering us with stones as it passes. There is a pig, too, that goes snuffling and snorting by our legs. As we turn onto to the Stabian road, we're swept up with a panicked, jostling crowd. Fire glows at the end of the street.

"Torches at the gate," I tell Prima. "We're almost there."

But the gate seems farther away than can be possible. It does not help that we must stumble over those who have collapsed, groaning in pain and fear. "Stop," Prima says, slowing with every step and not only because her legs are shorter than mine. Her tiny frame is wracked with coughs, and she wheezes into the toga she'd lifted to cover her face. "I can't breathe. I can't—"

My own throat is also choked with ash. My tongue, dry and swollen. In spite of my cloak, my skin stings from the pelting debris. We need to drink. We need a respite from the stones, but where can we shelter? I feel suddenly a fool for running. Perhaps Prima was right and we should have stayed in the *caupona*. Then she wouldn't have had to suffer as she's suffering now. At least she could *breathe* there.

But every easy breath we've ever taken were breaths of lowly slaves and tavern whores.

Those breaths belonged to our master, not to us.

These breaths, no matter how labored, are *ours*.

And so I press on, pulling my sister with me, even though our torch is nearly useless against the growing dark. In daylight, we would be able to see plaques with symbols advertising the wares at each shop. Hammers for the builders. *Amphorae* for wine. A fish for pungent *garum* sauce. But now I make my way by feel—my hands scraped raw against brick, stones, and wood. Then I hear a sound sweeter to my ears than any I've heard before. Singing. The shaking of the sacred *sistrum* rattle. It's the music of mercy. And when my fingers find a glorious glowing opening in the wall, I know where I am.

We've come to the Temple of Isis, a respite in the storm. And like shipwrecked sailors, weary and drowning, we stumble up the little stairs leading to the temple courtyard. It is aglow with lamps and torches of every sort. A miraculous sight. The earthquake did not touch the temple and the doors are open!

A few of the shaven priests in their white kilts have not fled. They have not abandoned the temple or their duties. They've stayed to propitiate the goddess with song. To invoke her compassion. To burn sacrifices upon her altar. And beneath the shelter of the red-painted portico, still more priests tend bleeding refugees. Some of the wounded wade through the pool for relief though it's now filled with a slurry of stone and ash. Others stoop beneath friezes of dragons and sphinxes; they are desperate for the jugs of sacred Nile water the linen-clad priests hold to their lips.

I am struck dumb at the kindness and composure of these holy men.

So moved by it that a sob wrenches its way from my dry, sore throat.

No. I am more than moved. I am *shamed*. Shamed deeper than body, blood, and bones. Because I am a fraud. I say I am meant to be a priestess of a goddess who offers mercy, but not once since the mountain began spewing its life force out into the sky, did I offer help to anyone but my sister. I did not hold onto the boy who cried, terrified, in my arms. I let him run off alone and nameless, like the nameless infant daughter I let them pry from my arms. I did not stop to help the people who sank down onto the street, choking and coughing.

I did not even cover the face of the dead man in the road.

I am still burning with shame when we find shelter in the *ekklesiasterion*, an assembly hall for the faithful. Just inside the entryway, collapsing onto the black mosaic floor, Prima pleads for a drink, and it is given to her. I am thirsty, too, but I cannot drink the water. I am not worthy of it. Not because I have been a slave and an unclean whore, but because in my fear, I doubted the compassion of Isis.

I've been measured and found wanting.

I do not mean to say any of this aloud. I don't even realize that I *have* said it until the kindly priest holds the jug to my lips and whispers, "Drink. Nile water purifies and washes away our crimes."

And so I drink. I gulp it down.

INSIDE the *ekklesiasterion*, a merchant bickers with his wife. She thinks they should have left the city days ago, when she pleaded with him to do so. He thinks she had better shut up and that they will leave as soon as their children have rested. She chides him for his impiety in the sacred precinct but he puts no stock in Isis, to whom his wife has been praying. Their bickering is so distracting that we don't see the missile that strikes the priest.

I only hear it whistle through the sky and crash on the tiled roof just moments before he stumbles, dropping to his knees with a bloodied face. When I rush to help him, he holds up the jug of sacred Nile water and says, "Take it."

I do, only to keep the precious water from spilling to the ground. But as I stand there with the jug, a crowd of thirsty refugees reaches for me. Trembling fingers fan out before me, and some people grab at my tunica. I want to escape them just as I wanted to escape the groping hands of men in the tavern. But I do not recoil from the desperate hands that grasp my ankles, my legs, and my arms. Because in this moment, touched by these strangers, something happens. Something happens *inside* me.

Something cracks open. As if I am a seabird newly hatched from an egg, discovering its wings.

And I hold the jug to thirsty lips, helping the suffering to drink.

"What are you doing?" Prima asks.

"The work of Isis," I whisper, not knowing where the words come from. Knowing only that they are true.

The answer is there upon the murals in this place. They depict Io, a priestess who was debased by seduction, turned into a white cow, and tormented to madness, but sought mercy in Isis and lived in redemption. There, upon the wall in the flickering lamplight, I see the naked woman with bovine horns reaching out to white-robed Isis. Io found grace.

In the wake of my own debasement and torment, is grace not offered to me also?

"We need more water from the cistern," the injured priest says. But he cannot rise to fetch it and his companions have melted away to the temple.

I am the only one he looks to for help, and I whisper softly, "I'll get the water."

Unfortunately, I do not whisper it softly enough. "We have to go," Prima snaps.

"We *will*," I tell her. "But first—"

She digs her nails, sharp as talons, into my arm. "*You* said we should run. *You* said you foresaw it. *You* convinced me to leave Pompeii. I'm convinced. Let's go!"

I ignore her in favor of the priest, who is losing so much blood that it cannot be soaked up with the end of his linen garment. Doing what I can to hold the cloth against his wound, I say, "Give me the keys to the *purgatorium* and I'll get more water."

He shakes his head, clearly dizzied and torn. The Nile water is not meant to slake the thirst of the uninitiated, but the priests have given it freely. Having already made this exception, will it enrage the goddess if he grants to me access to the cistern? When he sees my anklet of *ankh* charms, it seems to decide him. He hands over the keys on an iron loop, saying, "Pray to Isis for mercy ... and before you go down the stairs, tie your shawl between your breasts in her sacred knot."

"Capella, don't be stupid," my sister hisses, trying to dash the keys from my hand. "We must go."

"Help me," I say, already unfastening my once brightly colored shawl, the fringes of which are now grayed and stained with soot. It isn't linen, a thing I hope Isis will forgive. But my fingers know the knot of the *tiet* in which all the mysteries of the goddess are held secure. And so I tie it between my breasts while my sister brims with fear and fury. "You're not a priestess," she says with a snarl. "And I'm not braving falling bricks and tiles and rocks for some strangers. If we dash from under the shelter of this roof, we do it to escape. We're almost to the gate. You said there'd be boats in the harbor. That the navy will come to our rescue. And sailors will do anything for even a promise of a pretty girl's body."

It pains me to hear her repeat these words in the holy place that has given us sanctuary. Prima is only repeating *my* words, but it seems as if I spoke them a lifetime ago. As if someone else said them.

"I'll get more water from the cistern," I promise the priest.

My sister glares at me, her black eyes burning. "If you do, you'll do it alone."

"I'll be right back," I vow to her, pulling my sister into an embrace.

At first she surrenders to it, grasping me tightly. But then her fear and fury get the best of her and she wrestles away. "I won't be here when you return," Prima warns. "I'll leave *you* this time. How will you like that? I'll leave you behind and be better off for it."

I touch her cheek and make her look at me. "The *purgatorium* isn't far. Just a few steps and I'll be back for you before you know it."

She shudders. "Come with me now or don't come at all. I don't care one way or the other. You'll only be a pretty burden like you've always been —"

"Prima —"

"You're wrong about the sailors," she raves. "Pretty means *nothing* out there in this darkness. You're going to get lost and get your skull smashed in by some falling rock. But why should I care? I hate you —"

"*Prima*," I say, with an authority in my voice I've never heard before. It silences her. She stares at me, her chest heaving, her shoulders trembling. "Prima, you're braver and more beautiful than you know. And I love you. I have loved you from my first breath; I will love you to my last. I'm not going to get lost, because you always know where to find me."

PRIMA

ONE, two, three …

Prima told herself that her sister would follow. She need only frighten Capella a little. If she pretended to abandon her, surely her sister would come to her senses. And so Prima counted her steps. Twelve steps away from the temple before she would turn around and go back for Capella.

Four, five, six …

It was more like wading, really, than walking, because the stones were now much more than ankle deep. When she looked in the direction of the mountain to see flames leaping up like lizards, she wasn't sure she would have the nerve to take six more steps without Capella.

She strained to hear if her sister was calling her. Surely, she would call out!

Seven, eight, nine …

Stubborn cow. Prima would have to go back. She'd have to give in. She'd have to go back and say that she was sorry, sorry about more than Capella could ever know. She'd have to plead with her. She'd have to beg her forgiveness. She'd have to promise anything, anything at all ...

Ten, eleven —

Prima stopped abruptly at the sight of a tall figure standing like an imposing statue of Hercules in the middle of the Stabian road. There was only one man in the city so good-looking that the ashes of Vesuvius would render him a beautiful unpainted Greek sculpture, pretty eyelashes and all. Even so, it took Prima a moment to recognize the *aedile* because she'd never seen him without his perfectly pressed toga, chalked so white it gleamed.

More importantly, she had never seen Gaius Cuspius Pansa *alone* before. As a junior magistrate, an entourage of attendants and slaves always trailed him. But more importantly, he'd been born into a wealthy and influential family; the Cuspii Pansae could count upon a small army of clients in any crisis. Which is why Prima could make no sense of finding this one alone — completely alone — the press of humanity having already passed through.

He ought to have been fleeing. Instead, he was looking back at the city in flames. Rooftops burning. Sparks lighting the dark air. Watching it, he murmured to himself, repeating the words in numb shock as if the devastating news had only just been told to him. "Pompeii is ruined ..."

She'd never known Pansa to feel a moment's sentiment for any living person. It almost made her laugh that he could feel it for a *city*. He didn't see her. He didn't seem to see anything but his wealth and power burning up before his eyes. If she had only turned back in that moment to return to Capella — if only she had not taken that twelfth step ...

Twelve.

Pansa blinked those long lashes of his. Then he blinked again, shuddering with recognition. "My skinny little slut," he said, which was what he always called her. But there was a strangeness to the way he said it now, without any of the usual contempt. And a curious emotion twisted the features of his face just before he reached for her, his hand closing around her wrist like a manacle.

She was caught. Prima's heart couldn't hammer any harder in her chest than it already was, but it leaped to her throat at the realization. She was a runaway slave and a murderer, and she'd been caught by the *aedile* who would not have mercy on her even though she had killed on one of his errands.

To her surprise, Pansa only said, "Get away from the mountain. Do not stop. Go now to get to safety."

So he didn't know what she'd done. A delicious hope was born in her breast. How many bodies had Prima stumbled over in the streets, felled by falling roof tiles or the rain of stones? Could not a Roman senator perish the same way? She might get away with it. Perhaps she and Capella really could escape the city and find a patch of sunlight. She had, after all, just been given a command by the *aedile* to do so. And as a lowly slave, who was she to disobey?

"Yes," Prima said, trying to pull free of his iron grip. "I'll get my sister and go."

Pansa didn't release her. Instead, his eyes narrowed in a most unsettling way, lit up in half-mad zeal by the distant fires. "Didn't you hear me? We have to leave Pompeii."

He shoved her forward, forcefully, with such strength she might have been flung into the air if he had not had such a tight hold on her wrist. And she protested, "My sister! Just let me get my sister."

"We go now," Pansa said, striding forward with such purposeful steps that Prima was forced into a stumbling run.

Suddenly it didn't matter to her that he was an *aedile*. That he could have her killed. It only mattered that he was carrying her off. "What are you doing?" Prima howled, trying to wrench herself away. But he was too big, too strong. "Let go of me."

Pansa did not answer or so much as look at her. Instead, his eyes fixed in the direction of the gate with a fierce determination. He dragged her toward the archway ahead, even as she beat on his arm with her fist. In the distance, she thought she heard someone call her name, and she was seized with a terror darker than the shadow of Vesuvius. Trying to make her body dead weight, she shrieked in answer, "Capella!"

Prima was too small to escape the *aedile*. After a lifetime of trying to sate her hunger, she was *still* of no weight, no substance. So when she dragged her legs and went down to the ground, Pansa simply hefted her under his arm like sack of grain and carried her out the Stabian Gate.

CAPELLA

"PRIMA!" I scream again into the now empty street.

Never did I believe she would go. Not truly. I do not even believe it now. It was only a few steps to the *purgatorium*, down the stairway and into the sacred cistern. Then back again. Now I stand by the doorway to the street with a jug full of water and a heart full of despair.

How could she go? How could I have let her? I thought she was bluffing—trying to scare me into coming with her. And now I have let Prima go off by herself into the world, frightened and alone. Just like the nameless boy who spent himself inside me when the mountain exploded. And a daughter whose name I will never know.

Please, merciful goddess. Please help me find her. "Prima!"

I listen for her voice, but I am answered only by thunder on the mountain, and by the stones falling faster and heavier, rolling from the curb into the street so that it's all level now. A flood swiftly rising to my knees.

I am bereft. Prima cannot be gone. She cannot be. I don't know how far she could have gotten, but fear I will never find her in this storm! I start to go after her anyway, though I'm nearly blinded by the ash.

But from the dark of the alleyway, a man stops me. "Help! Help me, priestess."

Priestess? In the dim light, with my shawl tied in the *tiet*, I suppose even a whore might be mistaken for a priestess. The man moves closer and the fires in the street reveal a child in the cradle of his arms. I cannot guess her age. Two or three? A cloth has been draped over the little girl's mouth to protect her from the ash, but it is caked and she's choking for breath.

"Get her inside for shelter," I say, nearly twitching with eagerness to run after Prima. "Here is water."

But he can't manage the child and the water jug on his own. I have to help him. And so we stumble back into the temple courtyard, until we are beneath the roof of the portico. Then the man lays the child down, clears the ash from her mouth and makes her drink from my jug.

That is when I realize that I know him. I know this man with the little girl.

It's my friend Sabinus — the one my sister calls *the lonely engineer.*

He, too, is surprised. "Capella? Thank the gods. As soon as I could be sure of this little one's safety, I was coming for you."

"For me?" I feel a rush of warm gratitude. Vindication, too, in having proof that he *is* my friend, no matter what Prima says. But Sabinus is a man of wealth and status; there is a city filled with people he could call friend. "Why would you come for me?"

"I once told you if the worst happened, the men of the city would do their duty. Gods help us," he lowers his eyes for a moment. "The things I have seen today ..." His voice trails off as he looks at the little girl. "I told you I would look out for you and I meant it."

My sister would doubt him. She would look for some hidden motive. But at this moment, in this dark temple courtyard, I don't hear the voice of Sabinus speaking these words, but the voice of Isis speaking through him. Words of compassion, and kindness, and goodness. And here, where priests have looked after all of us, I *believe.*

"Then help me look for my sister," I say. Before I finish the words, a stream of ash pours onto us from the battered roof over our heads where the tiles have chipped away. "Isis, have Mercy! Is it going to come down?"

In Pompeii, we know to go out into the open during earthquakes. We've been taught to beware buildings shaking apart over our heads. But none of us know what to do in a shower of missiles from the sky. If anyone does know, it would be Sabinus. So I watch him lift the lamp to look, his soulful eyes cutting a path along the colonnade, inspecting the pillars for cracks and weaknesses. "It should hold," Sabinus says, kneeling beside me over the girl. "It's the newest roof in Pompeii and Ampliatus paid a fortune for it. It was built to last."

The temple was finally rebuilt, seventeen years after Nero's quake, thanks to the patronage of a freedman, as a legacy to his goddess and to his family, and for the salvation of the city. I pray now that this temple is the salvation of the little girl who struggles for breath. Because I must go; I must leave them to find my sister. But then I am sure my eyes are playing tricks on me. Because when the little girl sips again from the jug and smiles weakly in gratitude, I see that there is a gap between her teeth.

She has Prima's crooked smile. That rarest and most precious of smiles.

"Who is she?" I ask, thunderstruck by the resemblance.

"A little friend," Sabinus replies, offering the child a smile of his own despite the circumstances. Then, lowering his voice. "I found her alone and abandoned in the streets."

Could she be my own daughter? Prima would tell me I was a fool for thinking it, even for a moment. And I *am* a fool for thinking it. It is a desperate, wishful thought; but even that tiny question in my mind changes everything. "You need to take her out of the city. Get her to the harbor. The navy — "

"The ships can't come in." Sabinus replies. "Even the fishing boats can't go out. The seas are too rough. Most of the falling stones are porous. They're floating and blocking the rescuers. In any event, your dark rain has come, Capella, and it's too dangerous to go out until the stones stop falling. My little friend cannot breathe, and if I am struck down who will take her from my arms?"

I will, I want to say. *I will take her from your arms if you are struck down.*

But I have already failed one gap-toothed girl today.

"My sister is out there," I cry. "I told her we should leave by the Stabian Gate and make for the water. Now she is out there alone and you say it's too dangerous."

"Your sister will find her way," Sabinus says, avoiding my eyes just as he did the last time we were together. He was a lovesick groom, eagerly anticipating his wedding, and there was something in his voice that told me that once he'd made love to his new wife, he would not come back to visit me again. "When your sister sees there are no ships, she'll keep going. You've said your sister is wily and strong, and this is a time for both."

He meets my gaze at last. So, these last words, at least, are not platitudes. He believes them. And I believe him. Not only because he speaks with the authority of a Roman *paterfamilias* who knows best and must be obeyed, but because my sister has always known how to survive.

Prima is simply too *hard* for the stones to smash.

Still, I say, "I have to go after her. I have to go *with* her. But there are people waiting for this water in the *ekklesiasterion*." My fingers are still wrapped tight around the handles of the jug. "Will you carry it to them?"

Before he can answer, a distraught woman in jewels shrieks from the other end of the portico. "There are men chained in the barracks! They can't get out."

Gladiators, she means. Dangerous slaves who must be chained for a reason. Or so many would say. But Sabinus does not. "I would not let a dog die chained in this," he says. "What can I use to free them? Is there anything in this temple I might wield to break a chain?"

My mind circles in a panic, trying to remember anything that might help. The only thing I can think of is the sacrificial ax on the slab near the cistern where geese are burned for Isis, and I say so.

"But you just said it was too dangerous to go out into the hail of stones!"

"I did. But you have my little friend now. If I fall, you will look after her."

He cannot mean to leave *me* with a child. To entrust a pure little girl into the arms of a prostitute. But when he dashes into the falling stone, I realize that he does mean it. Alas, I have no idea what to do as I try to balance the jug of water in one arm and the child in the other.

I have never held a child before today. Not even the one I birthed. I don't know how to comfort this little one. How to touch her. How to soothe her fears. But somehow she knows what to do, turning onto her side to press her face against my belly. Turning away from the sight of the stones piling higher, rolling over one another like the endless river in my vision.

And I fear we are *all* going to drown.

PRIMA

"LET me go!" Prima raged, raking her captor's arms, pummeling his ribs, flailing her legs. "Why won't you let me go?"

Her struggling had no effect. Though he was coughing from the ash, Pansa was too strong—able to hold her with one arm while holding up his torch with the other. The *aedile* trudged on wordlessly, stopping only when they got to the harbor, where he bellowed with pure, frustrated fury. He was charged with regulating the vessels, the water supply, the use of the streets and sewers. But he couldn't control the navy, and seeing it sail away from Pompeii, not toward it, his bellow became a bitter laugh. "They're going to *Stabiae*. Of course they are. It's wealthier than Pompeii. All that fame and public glory, and Admiral Pliny just sails where the wind blows and worries only for his rich friends."

Was it the navy's fault, though, when the harbor was clogged with debris? Regardless of who was to blame, Prima realized with horror that there would be no escape by sea. Her sister, too, would be stranded, waiting for rescuers who would never come. "Capella!" she screamed again.

"She can't hear you," Pansa said, coldly. "You *know* she can't hear you."

"I have to go back for her," Prima insisted, again tugging frantically, wondering how long Pansa could possibly maintain the strength of his grip. "She doesn't know there won't be ships. She doesn't know."

With a shrug of his massive shoulder, Pansa said, "Give her up. She is likely already dead. So leave her. Count her a loss. Move on."

Like a sausage split open by fire, Prima exploded with an angry hiss, clawing at his hideously handsome face. Trying to make him hurt. Trying to make him bleed. Trying to make him kill her. Because she would sooner die than give her sister up or count her a loss.

"You harpy!" he cursed, boxing her head until a strange ringing echoed in her ears.

But he didn't kill her and he didn't leave her for dead. Instead, Pansa hauled her up again, trudging through drifts of stone back to the road. He did not seem to tire until they came to the necropolis. There, amidst the half-buried urns and statues and plaques to the dead, he finally stopped and pulled his toga over his head in reverence. The air was hot and foul smelling, filled with sulfur and ash. Prima had been able to cover her own face with her toga, but he'd needed both his hands to hold her and the torch. He'd been gulping in breaths of bad vapors, and it seemed to finally take its toll. He gasped as if something inside him was singed and swelling shut.

But beneath the roof of a mausoleum, Pansa seemed affected by more than the burden of his exertions. He seemed … to be hovering on the edge of tears. It was unseemly for a Roman man to cry. If Pansa cried, Prima would only have more contempt for him. But what had him so upset here? These were not his ancestors, she knew. The Cuspii Pansae were far too prominent to be buried here. The tombs of his ancestors were sure to be to the north, nearer to the angry mountain. And yet, the *aedile's* reddened eyes welled. "Here sleep the fathers of Pompeii."

Prima wanted to spit on the fathers of Pompeii. She wanted to spit at the *aedile*, too. But her mouth was so dry she could not draw any spittle to her lips. "So why don't you lay down with them and die?"

His very square chin jerked up. "I should. Rather than abandon the city like so many cowards before me, I should lie down and die here with the ancestors … but I have to save you."

"Save *me*?" Prima asked with an indelicate snort. "Don't make me your excuse. Because you might as well know I can be of no use to you anymore. There aren't any pimply-faced boys on the road for me to betray. Or any senators to spy on. And if you don't let me go, I'll only slow you down."

She waited for him to strike her for her insolence, but he only said, "Nevertheless, I'm going to save you."

"You're a fool, Pansa. Don't you know I hate you? I've never done anything at your bidding that didn't make me despise you."

His grave expression crumbled, his voice thick with emotion. "And I never did anything at my father's bidding that didn't make me despise him. I did it anyway because it had to be done. We are just the same, Prima. That's why I chose you out of all the whores in Pompeii to work for me. You and I, we do what we must do."

It wasn't possible that one of the great swaggering men of the Cuspii Pansae—an elected official, a man with a statue of himself in the amphitheater—would liken himself to an enslaved tavern whore. The comparison betrayed some manner of dangerous derangement. "Are you a murderer, then?" she asked. "Because I am." Her crime didn't matter now. Not if she couldn't go back for Capella. There was no patch of sunlight in which she might ever be content without her sister. They might as well nail her to a cross. "I killed that senator just before the mountain exploded. I bashed his skull with a wine jug and he fell to the street like a sacrificial ox under the hammer."

This finally shook the *aedile* out of his strangely teary stupor. "I told you to follow him, not kill him!"

293

"You didn't tell me what to do if he caught me. And he did. He told me he could crush you like a flea."

Pansa's jaw clenched. "So you killed him to protect me?"

"No," Prima said, slumping against the wall of a tomb, so exhausted she couldn't even pretend. "I killed him because I'm a rabid dog who bites anyone who passes too near, even to offer the slightest kindness. Senator Norbanus gave me meat and he gave me wine and I attacked him anyway. That's what I do."

Pansa's eyes narrowed to slits. "How do you know he's dead?"

"Because he fell to the ground and didn't get up again."

Pansa cuffed her. "Did you stop to listen for his breath?"

"I stopped for nothing," she said, her ear ringing from the blow. "I ran. Just as I'm going to run from you when you get too tired to drag me."

"I won't get too tired."

Prima smashed her fist against his chest. "Why won't you let me go?"

His eyes still swam with unshed tears. "I don't *know*."

"Do you think you love me?"

"Shut up," he snapped.

"That's it, isn't it? A grown man should know better, but you're like those pathetic sentimental boys I steal from. I steal their purses. I steal their hearts. I steal their manhood. Do you harbor some hope that with you, it would be different?"

"I don't love you, Prima."

"Then you lust for me. Is that it, Gaius Cuspius Pansa? All this time, you've paid me to do everything but what you really wanted. Well, as long as you let me go, you can have me here, in a tomb, like one of the *bustuariae*, those filthy leprous necropolis whores who wail with grief during the day and with pleasure at night—"

"I don't want you," he said, shaking her. "I don't love you and I don't lust for you. But I'm not leaving this city alone. I'm taking you."

He was taking her. He was taking her away from the one thing that meant more to her than life. He had torn her from her sister, and she screamed, "Why, why, *why?*"

But he would only answer that he didn't know.

CAPELLA

THE priest is dying. He is bleeding out his life on the floor of the *ekklesiasterion*, which can only be reached now by climbing over the layer of stones and sliding back down into the open doorway. I go to him covered in white ash with the tiny child toddling behind me, clinging to one hand, and, like the cult statue, an *oenochoe* jug in the other. The priest looks up at me and smiles. "*Isis.*"

Then his life slips away.

I think I am the only one to notice.

When I kneel down to close his eyes, I find a sack of bread and coins. *Prima's,* I realize, and I am overcome with emotion. Did she leave it for me as a final gift? No. Prima doesn't leave food behind. She meant to come back for it—and for me. Knowing this eases the pain in my heart, but if she meant to come back, why hasn't she? She must be dead, or she would have come back! I stifle a sob of love and longing for my sister.

No. If Prima cannot survive this, no one can—she'll come back for me when she's able to. She always knows where to find me.

The merchant says, "We're going to be buried alive in here."

I look at him more closely. I've seen him in the streets before, peddling cabbages. He and his family all stare back at me, and the nameless girl's hands grip tighter on me. These people are looking to *me* to tell them what to do. But all I know is what I saw in my vision. A flood. How does one survive a flood?

"We'll get to higher ground," I decide. The beautiful temple, painted ornately in green and red, is raised on a dais over the rubble.

Last I saw it, the roof was undamaged and the glorious carved doors were open. The temple houses the cult statue; we will profane the sacred place by using the *cella* for shelter. Nevertheless, I say, "We'll go into the temple."

Pulling Sabinus' little friend to my hip and carrying the sack and the water jug, I lead the ragtag band of panic-stricken people through the stone and ash, which is bursting through windows, through doors and rooftops — through every crevice and crack. We hear the crash of collapsing buildings around us and the debris is so high we must crawl through it. We must swim. Overhead, only flashes of fire and lightning break the darkness.

It is the lightning that shows us the temple stairs, half-submerged.

We climb up them, exhausted and scraped raw, and enter the temple to find the priests gone. The only trace of them is the lingering scent of perfume and sweet-smelling smoke. Did they lose their nerve? Perhaps they have braved the journey outside to preserve the treasures of Isis. Perhaps they are hiding in their rooms or some secret chamber. Wherever they are, they have taken nearly everything but some lamps and the beautiful statue of Isis.

From her marble podium, the queen of heaven looks down on our mortal plight with a soft smile that seems to say: *You are loved.* And, in spite of everything, I *feel* loved. Differently than I have ever been loved before. Not like Prima's possessive and protective love. Nor my mother's sweet, undemanding affection.

No, Isis loves me like an immortal mother who knows that all her mortal children must die. If not in this moment, then the next. For what is a year, a decade, a lifetime, but mere moments to a goddess older than time? She loves us for what we make of our moments. And Isis loves *me* for a strength I did not know was inside me before.

So I set to work, tearing apart the linen sack Prima left behind, making bandages and masks for the people who followed me here. Sabinus hasn't returned. I worry that he is not coming back. I worry that he is dead. That even if he is not dead, he won't think to look for us here. He'll find the body of the priest in an empty room and believe that I ran away. That I abandoned him like I abandoned my empress, my sister, and my daughter—

But no. I was a different woman then; a different woman even an hour ago than I am now. Still, I am unutterably relieved when Sabinus staggers in, drenched in sweat. Before I can clasp him in relief, he throws down the ax, which is now bent and misshapen. "It's no good. I couldn't free them. Not even with the help of others there. Gladiators are trapped with stone piling up to their chests and the lady—she would not leave. One of the gladiators was her lover, but I couldn't break his chains."

Sabinus lowers his head to his hands. "I wish—I wish I were a stronger man."

Searching for words to ease his anguish, I say, "You are stronger than any other man I've known."

He glances up at me with doubt. Sabinus is a man who spends more time inspecting aqueducts than exercising in the gymnasium. So perhaps he thinks it is flattery. The sort of thing a barmaid says to sweeten the disposition of the men who put hands on her. And I *have* employed flattery before: spoken honeyed words I did not mean. Even to him. But that was before I knew he was the sort of man to look after lost little girls.

There is great strength in that. Greater than the strength of gladiators.

The merchant calls to me. "Is there more water for my children?" I go to the little ones and give them the last sips of water, fitting little masks of cloth over their faces to ease their breathing. And Sabinus stares at me when the merchant's wife says, "Thank you, priestess."

Sheepishly, I whisper to him, "They don't know me. They don't know what I am."

And he says, "I think they know exactly what you are."

PRIMA

"I'M going to kill you," Prima promised.

Alas, the *aedile* seemed far less afraid of her than of the lightning that cracked over their heads, illuminating the road to Nuceria, which, far ahead, was filled with a steady stream of wagons and refugees. Apparently fewer refugees than Pansa had hoped.

"Where are the rest?" he asked, with angry contempt. "The fools must have fled south to Stabiae. Did they think they could outrun the wind?"

Prima and her sister would have fled south. *Away from the mountain.* Without the *aedile* to guide them, they wouldn't have thought about the south-blowing wind. But the reminder of Capella, either dead in Pompeii or dying on a road to Stabiae, renewed Prima's rage. "Do you hear me, Pansa? I said I'm going to kill you."

His voice was almost amused. "And how are you going to do that?"

"I don't know yet. But you *are* getting tired," she said, taking as evidence the fact that several miles back, he had set her on her feet and merely tugged her behind him like a recalcitrant mule. Though he gave her his own toga to breathe through, she herself was beyond exhaustion. Her back ached and her legs were heavy as iron. She couldn't feel her own feet anymore. So though Pansa was supposedly the epitome of Roman manhood, she was sure he was weary, too. "You're going to want to rest, Pansa. You'll want to close your eyes. And when you do, I will make sure that you never open them again."

"Big talk for a skinny little slut. I suppose now that you've killed a senator, you have a taste for it?"

That shut her up.

She'd never killed a man before. Fish, fowl, and even a pig for the kitchen, yes. But never a man. She wouldn't have expected it to be much different, though. Never suspected it might make her feel something like regret. She hadn't meant to do it, truly. She could scarcely even explain to herself *why* she'd done it. One moment,

Senator Norbanus had been asking questions about her sister and their enslavement.

And the next, she had smashed him in an incoherent fury.

What had he said that blotted all reason from her mind? He'd told her that because she and her sister had been sold with a caveat that they never be used for prostitution, that they might now, under the law, be free. She was sure he was trying to trick her, but he'd done something worse than trick her. He'd raised in her mind the possibility that her sister had been right all those times she'd said they were meant for freedom. That the Fates had decreed it, and Capella had been *right* to run away. All their lives, Prima had blamed their misfortune upon her little sister. But what if *she* were to blame?

If Prima hadn't dragged Capella back every time she'd run away . . .

Whether he knew it or not, Senator Marcus Norbanus told Prima that she'd stolen from the only person she'd ever loved. That she'd stolen from Capella not just a few coins or a few hours, but a whole life. That was a truth that Prima couldn't bear to hear.

And so she killed that truth and the man who spoke it.

All because Prima could not bear to be alone in this world.

Perhaps the *aedile* was right to say they were the same. That made her hate him all the more.

"*Fuck*," Pansa said, stopping at the side of a body by the road.

"What?" Prima asked. "Do you know him?"

"It's that gladiator. Pugnax. He was worth a small fortune."

Pugnax was also a slave, Prima knew. But the famed gladiator was worth far more than *she*. So she could make no sense of why Pansa was dragging her along with him instead of someone—anyone—else. Didn't he have a family to worry about? "Where is your wife, I wonder?"

"Long dead, along with the babe she died trying to bring into the world," Pansa said.

"What of your father?" she asked, remembering the grizzled old patriarch who restored the amphitheater and bought the election for his son. "Did he run for the hills at the first shake under his feet?"

"He's dead, too," Pansa replied, and though his voice was flat, she felt a tremor in his hand. "Crushed beneath a fallen pillar."

Remembering his show of emotion at the necropolis, she continued to needle him. "You must be glad to be the *paterfamilias*, now. But a good son wouldn't leave his father's body behind for jackals. Isn't it your duty to bury him?" At that, Pansa stopped. His jaw tightened. Good. She'd found a sore spot. Now she aimed to strike at it again. "Instead of dragging a worthless whore, wouldn't a son with filial piety be carrying his father out of Pompeii like Aeneas carried Anchises out of Troy?"

Pansa glared as if he wanted to grind her bones down to dust. But instead of answering taunts about his father, he shouted, "Pompeii is not Troy!"

With malevolent pleasure at having found a way to hurt him, she said, "It is. Pompeii is done. The mountain is swallowing it up just like Troy was sacked and swallowed up by time. And *you* are just like pretty Prince Paris, having brought down the wrath of the gods upon your city with your scheming and corruption."

She didn't know if the destruction of Pompeii was Pansa's fault. She didn't care. It only mattered that the accusation somehow made his big sweating hand loosen its grip enough for her to escape. She took the opportunity to yank her fingers from his grasp. Then she ran—or at least she tried to run. It was more of a mad scramble over the carpet of stones back toward Pompeii. Back to her sister.

She'd always been fast and slippery, with a preternatural awareness in the dark—traits that helped her slide effortlessly through the narrow streets and alleys of the city. But Pansa was on her in an instant. The bulk of him came down on her back like a fallen beam. He knocked the wind out of her. She couldn't catch her breath. Not even when he dragged her a bit and laid her shoulders back against something rough like bark. Oh, it *was* bark. A tree. An umbrella pine bent with the weight of ash on its branches.

"Breathe," Pansa said, as if he could command such a thing.

Why did he care? She was just a slave and not even *his* slave. She wanted to keep from breathing just to spite him, but somehow sucked in an unwilling and ragged breath of stinking air.

Scowling, he asked, "Do you know what my scheming and corruption bought for Pompeii?" Prima's nostrils flared. She didn't care, but saw that he was going to tell her anyway. "After Nero's quake, other families of stature cut their losses and left behind anyone without the means to leave. But not *my* family. *My* family rebuilt Pompeii, brick by brick. We did it with scarce help from the emperor. We had to beg Nero just to make a visit. We had to stoop to allying with rich freedmen. We had to skirt the rules so things would get done. Pompeii would have *died* if it weren't for the 'scheming and corruption' of the Cuspii Pansae."

"Do you want a plaque?" Prima asked. "Oh, that's right. You *had* one with your statue in the amphitheater. It's buried in the rubble, now. So whatever you did, you did for nothing. All of it for nothing."

Her other attacks had only nibbled at the edges of his resolve, but this time, Prima seemed to have torn a chunk away. He rocked back on his heels and for a moment, she feared he might forget his Roman *gravitas*, and start sobbing. But when he lifted his face, something had changed.

He looked in command of himself again. "Seventeen years," he said. Then he repeated himself, his voice growing louder. "*Seventeen years.* That's what we did it for. My family bought Pompeii seventeen more years of life. She wanted those years and so do you. You want to know why I took you? It's because I look at you and see Pompeii! She's an obscene whore of a city, crooked as your teeth. But she's *my* city. I'm the *aedile*. I'm responsible for the streets and the buildings and the sewers and the whores. Well, the streets and the buildings and the sewers are buried now, so you're the only Pompeii left for me to save."

"I don't want to be saved."

"Yes. You. Do." He nearly spit the words in her face. "Whether it's a few years more, or a few hours more, or a few moments more, you want them. You want whatever you can get. That's who you are. I knew it the moment I offered you an opportunity to use your talents and you wrapped your greedy little fingers around my coins. You are starving for life. You suck the marrow out of it. In the end, you'll do whatever you must to survive. I don't have to drag you. I'm only doing it to spare you the pain of knowing that you can't go back. That you *won't* go back. Not even for your sister."

CAPELLA

MY back is against the wall and the nameless little gap-toothed girl clings to me as we listen to the groans of the dying city. Sabinus stands close, his hand protectively atop her precious head. At first we all jump when a heavier stone or chunk of earth smashes against the temple roof. When one breaks through, coming down on us in a shower of tile and plaster, we do our best to scatter out of the way. But eventually we stop jumping. We stop scattering. We sink down to wait. Nearly numb to the fear, there is nothing for us to do now but surrender to the mercy of the goddess.

There is a strange grace in this surrender. It makes each small pleasure immeasurably sweeter.

There is a child in my lap. A little girl who lets me stroke her dark hair and rub her back, and dream that she is my daughter. But then, they are all my children now. Each person in this temple. The girl. The merchant who cannot stop bickering with his wife and children. Even Sabinus. They're all going to die, if not in this moment, then in another. And so I resolve to love them now and help them know themselves before we die and are reborn and must start the learning all over again.

I ask the merchant about his cabbages and he tells us how to pile them up in the market, green and round with possibility, so that all the cooks will pay the best price. I ask his wife about the blend of spices in her recipe for stew. And I smile when the girl, now sitting between Sabinus and me, says the word *esurio*.

She's hungry. I know nothing about feeding a child. I have no milk in my breasts for her, nor do I know if she has been weaned. I think she must be two or three; so she should take Prima's bread. I tear off a triangle of it and feed her little bits. I hope she takes as much pleasure in it as my sister did.

Where is Prima now?

She will never forgive me, I fear. Not in this life or the one after. But I think about how she might be away from this mountain and that makes me glad. Meanwhile, Sabinus must be thinking about the gladiators, because the hand that is not stroking the child keeps squeezing the handle of the ax at his other side. He wants to go again to the barracks and try to free the chained men. But none of the others will go with him. Worse, he has been coughing ever since he returned, his airway irritated by whatever malevolent air he inhaled in his efforts.

To distract him, I ask, "How was your wedding?"

"I was to marry Aemilia tonight." He grimaces, but tries to make light of it. "I'm afraid the wedding has been canceled on account of bad weather." He draws something from the purse at his side and fingers it reflexively. I cannot see the object clearly in the dim light, but I would swear it is a small doll. "I'm sure the guests were very disappointed."

"The bride most of all," I say, with a gentle smile. "By chance, did you forget to invite the fiery god of the mountain to your nuptials?"

"*Aha,*" he says, trying to laugh. "That's what went wrong ..."

He gets up and goes to the door, coughing into his hand. "It's slowing. The fall of stones is slowing."

I listen, and it *is* quieter, like a rain shower that is weakening. But it's too dark to tell, and I say so.

Sabinus shakes his head. "I don't have my tools with me, but an hour ago I marked the height of the debris on the stairs with the haft of the ax—"

"An hour ago?" I ask, confused. Like immortal Isis, I have lost all sense of time. Without the sun, I don't know if we have been in this temple an hour or a day. "What time is it now?"

"I don't know," he admits. "But this oil lamp is marked by the half hour. So I noted where the oil stood when I returned. When it burned down another line, I checked outside. A half hour ago, I checked again. And here is the mark I just made," he says, showing me the series of marks he scraped on the stick. "The last two are much closer together. That means that either the debris is settling or … we've weathered the worst of it. Perhaps I am a fool to think so, but I am still a man of hope."

In my vision, I saw the swell of a river followed by the crashing waves of a dark and violent sea. I fear the worst is yet to come. But I do not say so, because his hope is a contagion. It leaps from Sabinus to the others, who crowd near the door holding lamps and torches to watch as the storm loses its power. The flood of rock and ash is mounded up high enough that it would have buried even a tall man, but Sabinus says, "We can go now. The debris will hold us. It's like snow on the alpine mountains. It will be unsteady beneath our feet, but we can walk on it."

I have never seen snow on the alpine mountains. But the merchant—who once served in the legions—nods his head. They want to go now. They want to run from the city. And I nearly laugh at myself for wanting to stay. All my life I have been running. And yet, now when everyone else wants to run, I want to remain still.

Yes, inside this temple, there is a stillness in me. An understanding that from the darkness, I have already been reborn.

They all look to me. Even Sabinus, whose arms and legs nearly twitch with restless energy. He wants to get back to his Aemilia, the girl he means to make his wife. Or perhaps, if he dies, he wants to die on his feet. They all do. They want to use their limbs. Push and strain and struggle with every breath.

Because that, too, is how we are born.

Only Sabinus' little friend wishes to remain, as I do. She whimpers in protest when he picks her up and settles her on his hip to go. "Ah, little one," he says, kissing her ash-covered brow, "I have something for you if you are a good girl and a brave one." The small object emerges again from his purse. It is a small doll made of scraps of linen and blue silk. He hands it to the child who hugs it to herself, delighted. "That belonged to another good girl. A brave one, too."

Sabinus and I take turns carrying the child and her prize.

It is slow going and not only because the earth is hot and shaking beneath our feet. Illuminated by the burning city, we are cautious. With every step we sink into the rubble and we must wait for it to settle enough for us to take another. We climb over fallen bricks and splintered beams of wood. Over the bodies of the dead, human and animal, in a grotesque rictus, all covered in ash.

The children who follow me walk until they fall. Then they *crawl*, until I help them up again. Their arms and legs are shaking. They are thirsty enough to lick the sweat from each other's brows. But they keep going. Sabinus is tired, too, yet he is grimly determined. I see him fall a hundred times—always careful not to land on our little charge if he has her in his arms. And always he props himself back up, straining to rise again. I think he has turned his ankle, but he will not admit it. His eyes are glassy and distant. "Are we beyond the walls, yet?" he finally asks. It's startling proof that he's disoriented, for if Sabinus does not know Pompeii then no man does. "I have promised to go to Nuceria," he murmurs, as if he were explaining himself to a servant. "Are we still in Pompeii?"

None of us know.

PRIMA

PRIMA was crying.

For the first time that she could remember, she was crying real tears. In truth, she felt herself choked with sobs. With despair. And despair *hurt*. It hurt more than anger. It hurt more than her sore muscles and aching feet ... feet that somehow kept moving, as if on their own accord, shuffling along behind the *aedile*.

He was right. He didn't have to drag her anymore. And because he was right, Prima sobbed inconsolably into her hands, "I left her. I left her ..."

"I gave you no choice," Pansa said. "That's the advantage of being a slave. You don't have choices. You don't have—"

"What would you know about what slaves have?" Prima asked, hating the way her voice no longer held its sharp edge. She sounded weak. Distraught. But he was wrong about slaves having no choices. She could've gone with Capella to get the water from the cistern. She could've stayed with her sister—and in truth, she'd never intended to leave her. If she had, she wouldn't have told such a venomous lie. She'd told her sister that she hated her. Now that lie might be the last thing she ever said to Capella.

And what had her sister said in return?

I love you. I have loved you from my first breath; I will love you to my last.

The memory drove Prima to her knees.

Prima didn't remember falling. For a moment she couldn't even make sense of the sharp edges cutting into her shins and her palms, as anguish howled through the hollow and empty place where a soul ought to be.

"Come now," the *aedile* said, softly. "Get up."

Just as her voice had lost its sharp edge, his had lost its sense of command. He was having trouble breathing, she could tell, as if something was swelling closed inside him. But extending his hand, he offered a tiny morsel of hope. "If your sister somehow survives, she'll need you alive to find her when this is all over."

"What if it's never over?" Prima asked, still staring at the ground. "What if this nightmare never ends?"

"Everything ends," Pansa said.

And so she took his hand.

They walked. Slower and slower as they came upon other travelers on the road, as if Pansa didn't want to be recognized. As if he feared people would accuse him of having failed them somehow as the *aedile*. Still, they walked on and on, until it was Pansa's knees that gave out beneath him. He crashed down like a tumbling colossus, and the torch crashed down with him, guttering out and leaving them in the dark under the starless sky.

It was the second time today that she'd seen a powerful man crumple; this time, she stopped to listen for breath. It was the smoke that got him, she thought. Pansa had been taking in big, gulping breaths to fortify his strength whereas she had breathed through the filter of a toga.

Only the gods themselves could guess how much ash he'd inhaled.

"Thirsty," he croaked, coming back to consciousness.

It startled her, though she tried not to show it. "Maybe someone on the road has water in one of those wagons. I'll get some for you."

"How?" he asked, as if he actually believed she would do it.

"I'll have to steal it ..."

"*Buy* water," Pansa said, unfastening a coin purse tied at his hip. "Get fire for the torch, too."

He put the whole heavy purse in her hand—and, when she opened it, she saw gold stamped with the faces of emperors. More coins than she had ever held in her life. Money enough to buy her freedom, she guessed.

More money than she was worth.

How foolish was Pansa to think she would use it for water and fire?

If he's foolish enough to trust a whore, then he deserves what he gets.

That's what he'd once said to her about another man—a boy, really. The one with the important uncle. Which is why she walked away from Pansa, telling herself that she didn't care if he ever got back up again. She didn't need Pansa; she just needed to follow the road to Nuceria. She told herself that she didn't care if Pansa died choking on his own thirst and his swollen tongue. He wasn't her master. He wasn't her lover. He wasn't her friend, and he certainly wasn't her sister.

He was no one to her. No one at all. Worse than no one.

She begged fire for her torch from a man who walked like a soldier. His name was Rufus. "Walk with my servant and me," he said. "It's not safe for someone as small as you, on her own."

Rufus looked like a decent sort. A veteran. She gauged him to be a simple man of simple needs. The kind of man she might be able to seduce and manipulate.

She ought to have gone with him, keeping Pansa's coin purse for herself. Instead, Prima found herself spending the coins, bargaining with other travelers for precious water.

Then, in defiance of all reason, she went back for Pansa.

He'd somehow dragged himself to the edge of the road. And he seemed almost as surprised that she'd come back as *she* was. When she'd wedged the torch between the rocks so she could cradle his head in her lap and give him sips of water, he asked, "Why?"

"I don't know," she answered.

Then she stroked his handsome cheek. She didn't know why she did that either, because there was nothing in it for her. And she couldn't guess how long she held him underneath the shelter of another umbrella pine as he slowly suffocated in her arms. There was something evil in the way a powerful man could be taken down by seemingly nothing. Was it the vapors, or had he been struck by something and she never noticed? Her fingers found no wound, no raised lump on his head, nothing to make her understand why he was stricken and she was not.

"Go," he said, shuddering with each diminishing breath. "Get safely to Nuceria."

"I will," Prima promised. But as he writhed in agony, she remembered a different promise she made to him.

I'm going to kill you. You're going to want to rest – you'll want to close your eyes – and when you do, I will make sure that you never open them again.

She wanted to keep that promise now, but not for cruelty or malice. She didn't have any more hatred left for him or anyone. It had all dried up. Evaporated. Burned away with the heat from the mountain. She only wanted to kill Pansa to end his suffering. But hadn't he said they were just alike?

Whether it's a few years more, or a few hours more, or a few moments more …

He would want them. He would want whatever he could get. And he would not want to die alone. People weren't meant to be alone. So Prima let him struggle for life in her embrace until he struggled no more. Only when she was sure he was dead, did she close his eyes, fingertips tickled by his very long lashes.

Then she bent her head to kiss him. She pressed her crooked mouth to his perfect lips while her tears wet his face. It was the first kiss she'd given a man freely in her whole life. A kiss for a dead man, and in that kiss she felt the heaviness of grief for a man she had never liked and had scarcely known. She cried for him. Not like a necropolis whore who wails with grief during the day and with pleasure at night. But like someone filled with more love than hatred.

Someone like her sister.

And when Prima finally lifted her head from weeping, she saw a miraculous light.

CAPELLA

"IS it fire?" Sabinus asks, his words slurred.

With wonder and awe at the pale, obscured haze of light in the distance, I answer, "It's dawn."

The mere hint of rising sun — even pale and obscured by ash — makes us weep. Then we laugh. We laugh with joy because we were not sure there would ever be another morning. But this one has come. Like a blazing lighthouse in a storm. And it is *glorious*.

"We're going to make it," Sabinus says, as if awakening from a nightmare.

There is not a patch of skin on any of us that is not scraped, burned, or sore, but we're alive. And the dawn rejuvenates us.

Exhilarates us. We have nothing at all but each other and the dawn to make us walk faster. But we do. The little girl in my arms hums a sweet tune to her new doll. And she twines the fingers of her empty hand in my filthy hair, as if it were liquid gold. We walk in a line, using a low wall to guide us. Once it must have been a substantial house with a lovely orchard. Now it is collapsed upon itself but for this wall.

"We're going to escape your dark flood, Capella," Sabinus says. "The mountain will not have us."

"Praise Isis!" cries the merchant's wife. "She has saved us. Isis has saved us."

After all their bickering, the merchant hugs his wife then kisses her right on the mouth.

Seeing this, I smile and Sabinus reaches for my hand.

There is, in touch, an affirmation of life, of immortality. But when our fingers clasp, I hear a different call of immortality. Of eternity. One I've been hearing all my life.

It is the roar of the ocean.

We turn together to see black waves churning violently down the mountain with a power and speed at once ungodly and breathtaking. Frothing and boiling up over the city, the darkness comes, like the spray of the sea when it smashes against rock.

It is a sight both majestic and ghastly.

There is no running from this dark sea, and not even Sabinus tries. He watches it come, his mouth slightly agape, not in terror but in something beyond that. As if fascinated by the natural power of what we are seeing.

I, too, am beyond terror, because I have seen this dark sea before. It is the promise my goddess made to me. The promise she makes to us all. We are meant to be free. We are meant to be more than body, blood, and bones. Though we are nameless, we are meant to endure a thousand years and a thousand more. There is a part of us that will never die.

I know this dark ocean will hurl us, and the remains of a whole city up to the gods; there is no escaping it. None. Which means there is nothing left but to embrace it. To the crying little girl in my arms, I whisper as if it were a day of celebration. "Here come the waves, little one. Open your arms." And just as I once stepped into the frothing waves of the sea during the *Navigium Isidis*, I walk toward the boiling tidal wave of ash.

With hot wind billowing my gown and my hair whipping high into the air around me, I hold tight to the little girl in my arms until the blast rips her from my grasp. Until the searing pain of my soul shredding away from my body makes me lose my hold on everything.

In violence we are torn away from each other, and this world into the next …

… but *becoming* is always an agony.

It all happens in an instant, but for me, it stretches into an eternity. The ocean breaks us like stones into sand. Like sand that will one day become beautiful gleaming sea glass in a thousand years or a thousand years more. We are all, all of us, every one of us in life, sailors trying to survive a rough sea. All looking for the light that will guide us home. And I can already see that bright beacon.

But first, there must be *darkness*.

We are born in darkness. We perish in darkness. And then we are born again.

EPILOGUE

WORSE than Troy, Prima thought. Not a million Greeks in a thousand wooden horses could wreak such devastation. There was a city here once, beneath her feet. Now, weeks later, just a tomb. The mountain was half gone, like a ravaged loaf of bread from the oven, still smoking at its pith. The city itself covered in a thick blanket of ash. Some of that same ash still drifted in the wind like snow.

There were no survivors.

On the day of the blast, that last deathly cloud at sunrise had rolled over the city, killing everyone and everything, leaving an unearthly quiet behind. A haunting stillness for the living to sift through and make sense of.

But Prima could make no sense of it at all.

Only the blackened rooftops of the tallest buildings gave any hint as to what might lie buried where. Prima could not begin to guess where the *caupona* had been. Nor even the Temple of Isis. People wrote on markers to help give clues. Others left only poems or tributes for the dead. Or warnings to stay away from this accursed place and the spirits who must haunt it now.

Amongst those spirits must be her sister's, though, so she would not be warned away.

Capella was dead. Prima knew this in a way that sisters know.

Just as she knew that her sister was buried beneath her feet.

You always know where to find me, Capella had said.

And so she did. Even if she did not know what this place once had been.

She'd come to make an offering on what was her sister's grave. A libation to pour, though she did not know what words she should say. She would ask forgiveness, that much she knew. Forgiveness she didn't deserve. But if anyone ever would forgive her — ever *could* forgive her — it would be Capella.

At the remembrance of her sister, her eyes blurred again with tears.

She turned to swipe them from her cheeks and, when she did, she saw a man in a toga picking through the rubble in a swirl of smoke. An older man. A senator. One of the *lemures*. An angry spirit she could not appease with offerings. A spirit that would not give forgiveness. A spirit that would want *vengeance*.

Prima crashed to her knees, babbling words to ward off evil spirits. "I'm sorry. Mercy —"

"Beg pardon? Are you well, girl?"

Her head came up at the sound of his voice. It wasn't wrathful; it was as mild as she remembered. He limped to her side and, to her astonishment, the hand that raised her by the elbow was warm and living. *Alive.* The senator was alive. She hadn't murdered him and somehow he'd escaped the destruction of Pompeii. The realization filled her with such sweet relief she gasped with the pleasure of it.

But she *had* bashed him with a jug and left him for dead. And given that he had her by the arm, she was caught. Again. Why hadn't she run before he could recognize her?

Because surely he did recognize her now. "Are you hurt?" the senator asked as she ducked her head belatedly from his gaze. But he raised her chin with one finger, and those piercing eyes flared. "Ah," he breathed. "The little guttersnipe from outside the brothel. Prima, isn't it?"

She should've lied. She should've broken free of him. He wasn't so strong—not as strong as Pansa had been. But the senator had an entourage, she could see dimly through her haze of tears—secretaries and guards and slaves in tunics finer than anything Prima had ever worn. So instead of trying to run, she said, "I didn't mean to hit you. I just wanted to get away. I wanted—"

"You did get away." The senator nodded gravely. "And in truth, I am rather extraordinarily glad to see that you got away, little Prima."

He *was* glad, she saw. It startled her: a senator in a fine toga, glad that a slave girl had survived the mountain. It startled her so much that the words tumbled out. "My sister is dead."

It was the first time Prima had spoken the words aloud.

And now that she had, she sobbed and could not seem to stop sobbing.

The senator issued some orders in a quiet voice, and someone gave Prima a stool so she could sink down and cry her eyes out. The senator crouched down next to her, waving his people away. He didn't ask her how Capella had met her end. Maybe he knew Prima couldn't bear it. He just drew a fold of his toga over his head in mourning and said something brief and beautiful.

"Who did you lose in the rubble?" she asked, assuming that must be why he was here in the smoking ruins.

"I had the good fortune not to lose anyone. Well—myself, nearly." He traced a bandage around his wrist with a small, private, bittersweet expression that did not invite Prima to ask. "The emperor ordered me to return when the ash cooled, to make assessment of the damage."

A man with the emperor's ear. "So, I'm definitely going to be crucified, then," Prima blurted. "A slave can't …" she trailed off, knowing that no matter how kind he was to her, no slave could ever strike such an important man and live to tell the tale.

"A slave can't nearly cripple a senator?" He stretched out his knee, and Prima winced to see the knob of bandages under his toga's folds. "Correct. But Prima of Pompeii is no slave, is she? She is a freedwoman now."

Prima eyed him warily, but not *too* warily. In truth, she was too heartsick to beware tricks. "How do you mean? I don't know where my master is, but even if he's dead, I'm sure he has a designated heir—"

"No one can claim among his inheritance slaves illegally used in prostitution."

So he remembered. "But I can't prove—I don't have our bill of sale."

He swept a hand out at the still-smoking expanse of ash and rock; the vents of steam like a giant's slumbering breath. "My dear girl, the evidence is buried along with the rolls upon which you were registered. Who is to naysay you? Or," he added with more authority, "*me?*"

She blinked. "You?" The chance her master or his heir might take on Senator Marcus Norbanus was exceedingly slim. "Why would you vouch for me?"

"Because Roman law says you are free," he answered. "And Roman law is for all of us. You did not believe me last time I told you that—perhaps you will believe me now."

Prima nodded. He was offering to help; it didn't matter if she understood his reasons. Only the price required. "What do you want in exchange?"

"A little trust." He rose, brushing off his snowy toga with its rich purple border. "I shall be near the ruins of Pompeii a great deal in the months to come, overseeing relief funds. As a surviving freedwoman, you would be eligible for some assistance. Will you trust my word enough to rely on it?"

Trust. It was like faith. The faith her sister had. The faith Prima never had. But now, in this moment, she wanted it. She hungered for it. So she not only believed the senator would keep his word, but found herself wishing she could give aid or comfort to other survivors. "Could I help in some way?"

"Naturally." He didn't sound surprised at the offer. Perhaps he simply expected better from her from now on. "You can start by remembering the people in this city. Their hopes and dreams. The things that mattered most to them. Too many of those lost will never have death masks or eulogies or mausoleums. So be a living monument to the nameless dead." With that, he gave her a nod, the kind of nod a citizen of Rome gave to a free woman, and disappeared into his entourage, wound in smoke.

Watching him go, Prima wasn't sure it had happened. Perhaps it had all been a vision. A message from her sister from beyond. If there *was* a beyond. Prima had said, again and again, that there was nothing but this.

We eat, we shit, we fuck, and we die. That's all there is.

But she was wrong. There was human connection. There was love of family. Love of friends. Love of enemies and even nameless strangers. Love that endured beyond life. Love beyond death. The proof of that was all around her, in the few survivors still searching the rubble of what had once seemed like a big city, but was now made quite small. Slaves, free citizens, and the high-born, all asking the same painful questions.

Have you seen him? Have you seen her? Have you seen the one I love?

I think she went to Stabiae, to Herculaneum, to Misenum, to Nuceria …

Did he leave the city before the mountain blew apart? Did she stay behind?

The stillness gave no answers … but still they asked, drawn together in grief. So unmoored from all that had once separated them that Prima and a wealthy girl might stand shoulder to shoulder.

The girl had asphodel flowers in her hand and hair as red as flame. She bent to put the white flowers on the stones for the man she said would have made her his wife. Though she was not married, the girl was draped in a dark *stola* of mourning as if she were his widow in truth. "He promised to come to Nuceria and find me," she explained, fingering a bunch of keys strung from her girdle the way

Prima's sister used to finger her *ankh* charms. "I cannot find where his house stood, and this is as close to the city as we can climb, but I think maybe he would have been somewhere near here. He would have tried to come to me — his name was Sabinus."

Then, perhaps seeing recognition in Prima's expression, the girl asked, "Did you know him?"

For Prima, the name Sabinus no longer dredged up anger or contempt. Her sister had liked the man and counted him a friend. Perhaps he *was* a friend to her in the end. Prima liked to imagine it that way.

And so she said, "I'm afraid I didn't know him at all."

"Neither did I. Or rather, I knew him all my life without appreciating him — " The girl broke off, too well-born to sob. But her voice lowered, thick with emotion. "He thought me worthy of him. I would like to be."

"I understand," Prima said, because she did.

The wealthy girl narrowed her eyes, perhaps realizing for the first time that she was confiding in a stranger. "Should I know you? Who are you?"

The wind seemed to echo her question.

Who are you?

Prima wondered how anyone could answer such a question amid the shattered remains. The world she knew had died, and a part of her with it. And yet, when she reached inside herself for an answer, her heart swelled, giving her a weight and substance she'd never had before.

"Who am I?" Prima asked, brushing tears from her eyes. "I don't know yet."

But she was hungry to find out.

Hungrier than any child ever born.

ACKNOWLEDGEMENTS

WE are indebted to our readers for their encouragement and support of this project; Michelle Moran for writing such a lovely introduction; Simon Scarrow for his kind words of praise; Margaret George for suggesting the possible connection of Nero's empress to Pompeii; Kevan Lyon for her support and encouragement; Adam Dray for his tireless but cheerful fact-checking, nitpicking and proofreading; Lea Nolan for beta-reading; our talented cover designer, Kim Killion; Giorgio for giving us logos; former fire marshal Brandon Rice for help with fire, deadly vapors, and asphyxiation; Edna Russell for consulting with us on the laws and customs surrounding prostitution in ancient Rome; Kelly Quinn for researching relevant quotes from the writings of Pliny the Younger and doing some last-minute proofreading; Ginger Emshoff for providing help with Latin and supplying us with fantastic information about graffiti. Also helpful was *Pompeii: The Living City*, by Alex Butterworth and Ray Laurence; *The Complete Pompeii* by Joanne Berry; and Mary Beard's multiple volumes of scholarship about the eruption, the town, and the population of Pompeii.

NOTES FROM THE AUTHORS

ARCHAEOLOGICAL evidence indicates that the eruption took place sometime in late September or October. Physical evidence includes the presence of autumnal fruits including pomegranates (which ripen in late September and October in Italy), as well as dried dates, prunes, and figs, typically harvested in late summer. Also, jars with fermenting wine were found, indicating that the grapes had been harvested and wine production was well underway. The most compelling evidence is the presence of a Roman coin printed after September 7 or 8 of the year 79 found in a stratification that would rule out looters or investigators dropping it there later.

Another choice we made was to present the volcano as an unprecedented event. Astounding as it may seem, the citizens of Pompeii apparently had no idea that the mountain looming over their town was a volcano. There were plenty of warning signs of an imminent volcanic eruption, and although incomplete archaeology suggests the city may have emptied, the first person account by Pliny the Younger suggests that the catastrophe caught the city and its surrounds largely unwarned. We elected to favor his eyes-on-the-ground account. Our epigraph quotes are largely lifted from his famous letters to Tacitus, though some are tweaked for easier reading.

Astute readers will notice that the locations of some buildings, such as the *caupona* where several characters work or take a drink or meal, have been shifted slightly for fictional convenience. And while all graffiti mentioned in the stories come from the walls of Pompeii, the exact locations of that scrawl may vary. The *freshness* of the election graffiti in ancient Pompeii suggested to us the names of important city officials, but did not tell us who prevailed. Because we wanted to involve historical figures rather than make them up out of whole cloth, we chose the winners and had them begin their terms of office.

And now for your individual notes...

THE SON

PLINY the Younger was not Pliny the Elder's son, but his nephew, adopted at seventeen when the elder died in year 79 during the eruption of Vesuvius. The younger Pliny provides us with the only eyewitness account of the disaster. Named Gaius Caecilius Secundus for his father, his mother Plinia was Pliny the Elder's sister. Caecilius' father died when he was young. Although posthumous adoptions were common, it was also common for Roman men who did not have male heirs to adopt during their lifetimes—which left me wondering, *why didn't Pliny the Elder adopt his young nephew while he was alive? And how might this have affected the young man?*

I was also fascinated by that fact that Pliny the Younger had the opportunity to join his uncle in the investigation of the eruption. *So why didn't he go?* At seventeen, he most likely had completed his manhood ceremony. The Roman code of manly *virtus* demanded stoic fearlessness and bravery in the face of danger. And what was his excuse for not joining his uncle? He said he had to *study*: "He offered me the opportunity of going along," Pliny the Younger wrote twenty-five years later to his friend Tacitus. "But I preferred to study—he himself [meaning Pliny the Elder] happened to have set me a writing exercise."

Really? He stayed away from the most fascinating natural phenomenon anyone had ever seen (they didn't know it was killer yet) because he had to *study?* I found the excuse flimsy. What if, I wondered, there was another deeper, possibly more embarrassing reason he declined? And what if his elderly uncle understood the reason and therefore didn't push him, as one might think he otherwise would? And what if this reason was so private, he covered it up a quarter of a century later with a lame excuse about hitting the books?

From those questions, this story was born. Historically, all we know is that Pliny the Younger did not join his uncle and that he was adopted posthumously in his uncle's will. Everything else preceding his description of events is conjecture. But as historical fiction writers like to say, "It *could've* happened this way!"

— Vicky Alvear Shecter

THE HEIRESS

THERE is more that is mysterious at the Villa of the Mysteries than the famous murals lending the ruins their name. Located just outside the Herculaneum gate, it is uncertain who owned the villa. A seal found during its excavation bears the name of a freedman from the powerful Istacidii family, and some scholars have proposed him as a possible owner. Others posit he may have been an overseer during the property's reconstruction (ongoing for years) after Nero's quake. For narrative purposes, I chose to associate the seal with such an overseer—one who does not appear in my story. Three bodies were uncovered at the villa: two women and a child. These victims may have been members of the household or, alternately, individuals seeking to escape the city who took shelter in the villa during their failed flight. I choose to imagine one in particular, a woman who clawed and scrambled to stay atop the growing pile of falling *lapilli* for hours before succumbing, as Aemilia's faithful nurse.

Since Aemilia and her family are fictional, I might have selected any setting for their story. Why the Villa of the Mysteries? Like the many tourists who flock to the site, I was drawn to the villa by its significant collection of decorative frescoes. Many of these artworks were already very old (the most famous date to the first century BCE) at the time Pompeii was lost. As a writer, I was more interested in imagining who might have dwelt among such masterpieces than in describing them (pictures are readily available for readers who want to look more closely), but any art I do depict actually exists. For example, the statue of Livia mentioned was found, missing fingers, during the villa's excavations. Of course the most compelling feature of the villa is the murals that give it its name. These are located in its rich, red *triclinium*. Often described as portraying the rights of the cult of Bacchus, for *The Heiress* I have adopted the less popular explanation of the artwork as a metaphor for a young bride's transition into marriage. Thus interpreted, the murals echo the development of my central character, Aemilia, who changes from a headstrong girl to a confident woman during the course of my story.

Finally, a note about Sabinus. Unlike Aemilia, I did not create Sabinus out of whole cloth. In *The Fires of Vesuvius*, Mary Beard identifies the candidates for the office of *aedile* in 79. Yes, Cuspius Pansa is on that list, and so is a man named Gnaeus Helvius Sabinus. Graffiti in the city suggests that candidate Sabinus was supported both by followers of the Isis cult and by his grandmother. For the purposes of our novel, the assumption was made that Sabinus ran unsuccessfully.

—Sophie Perinot

THE SOLDIER

WHO wouldn't jump at the chance to write a tale set in Pompeii at the time of the eruption of Mount Vesuvius? I owe big thanks to Kate Quinn for inviting me, and to the other authors, with whom it has been an absolute pleasure to work. Part of the appeal to me was that I could write the tale of a retired soldier, a guy who'd survived a lifetime of war. My novels are usually set during wars or rebellions, and it's a little frustrating never to be able to find out what happens to my main characters.

A few interesting details about my story: Satrius Rufus was a Pompeian home-owner, whose nameplate survives and tells us that he was a retired Imperial secretary; his son, my hero, is a fictional character. Pugnax the gladiator is mentioned in Pompeian graffiti, and Jucundus was a Pompeian banker whose name was well documented in the town.

Gladiators often fought in multiple pairs, however this was by no means universal—hence my depiction of Pugnax fighting his bout against one opponent.

It's possible that no lions/big cats fought in Pompeii's amphitheater, as the safety parapet was probably not high enough to contain them, so the portrayal of lions there was my decision.

Odd as it sounds, the giant "wine carrier" made of leather is depicted in artwork found in Pompeii.

The mosaic with the crouching black dog, and the famous warning, "CAVE CANEM," is famous throughout the world. I hope readers will forgive me using it in my story—it was too much to resist, even though the poor, savage dog didn't make it.

—Ben Kane

THE SENATOR

SENATOR Marcus Norbanus and Diana of the Cornelii have appeared in several other novels of mine, starting with *Daughters of Rome* where they struggle through the infamous Year of Four Emperors referenced in their story here. Marcus is fictional, therefore both his terms as consul and his descent from the line of Augustus are invented. Diana is also fictional, though the horse breeding business, chariot racing, and the various circus factions (including the Reds) were an obsession in ancient Rome among patrician and plebeian classes alike. The level of freedom Diana enjoys as an unmarried woman is unusual for her time, but not impossible — Roman law gave fathers the right to manage their daughters' lives (as Diana herself points out to Sophie Perinot's Aemilia), but despite the traditional image of the stern *paterfamilias*, historical records are full of indulgent or absentee fathers who did not rule their women with such an iron fist. As a result there were Roman women who seized startling freedom of movement, travel, and financial independence.

The brothel (*lupanar*) where Marcus and Diana take shelter is a real building, with some of the most notorious erotic frescoes and filthy graffiti to survive in Pompeii. The villa where Diana retrieves her horse is the Villa of Mysteries featured earlier in Sophie's story.

Marcus and Diana's appearance in this collection was a surprise to me. I had never planned for any of my old characters to cross paths in Pompeii, much less these two, but around the time this project was conceived, Marcus' polite voice and Diana's ruder one piped up in the back of my head informing me that they were present when Vesuvius erupted. The pairing of opposites has been a classic trope for a long time — think buddy-cop movies — but in Marcus and Diana I had the ultimate comic juxtaposition of brain vs. brawn, with the added twist that for once the girl was the brawn — and the rescuer instead of the rescuee. The resulting possibilities for comedy delighted me, though it's probably irreverent to say that I enjoyed finding opportunities for humor in an epic disaster like Pompeii. I don't feel too guilty, however, since my fellow collaborators explained that it was my job to give the readers a few laughs before they got their hearts ripped out by the ending. I hope I made you chuckle, whether at Marcus and Diana's bickering or at the rephrased line from Bastille's chart-topping song "Pompeii," which I couldn't resist slipping into the story. Readers interested in Marcus and Diana's future should take a look at *Mistress of Rome*, which picks up two years after the eruption of Vesuvius.

— Kate Quinn

THE MOTHER

WITHIN the house of Julius Polybius, the remains of thirteen skeletons were found — one of whom was a baby cradled in its mother's womb. The mother also clutched a bag full of coins and was decked out in jewels. Graffiti on the walls of the house asks for votes for Julius Polybius. Inside the house, a ring was found inscribed with the name Julius Phillipus, as was a mural on the wall. Given the campaigns for Polybius and that historians have named the house after him, I concluded that Polybius was descended of a freedman and was an aspiring politician — although we decided to make him a *praetor*, he could have also been a *duumviir*.

According to the DNA tests there were two older men who died in the house and were not related — we will probably never know for certain who actually died within the house walls. It is unclear whether both Polybius and Phillipus were in the house (or if Phillipus was even living) at the time of the eruption, so I left him out of my story, and instead had the second older male be a servant.

However, the DNA revealed that several *were* related subjects, which led me to the conclusion that this was a family with several slaves. During the testing, it was found that two of the skeletons suffered from minor cases of spina bifida — one a twelve-year-old boy, and the other Julilla. It was likely so minor they were not aware of it. Decima's testing revealed that she was likely ill quite often.

It is not clear how the people within the home died, but a vial was found in the hand of one of the skeletons — a male leaning against the wall. There is conflicting evidence as to what the vial held. Some have said it was poison, others say it was just wine or water. For purposes in this story — and wishing to give Julilla a strong and fitting end — I made it poison.

The prayer whispered at the end is a line from Apuleius: *I approached the confines of death, and having trod on the threshold of Proserpine, I returned therefrom, being borne through all the elements. At midnight I saw the sun shining with its brilliant light; and I approached the presence of the Gods beneath, and the Gods of heaven, and stood near, and worshipped them.*

Within the household was found a statue of Apollo, mythological murals, and a painted *lararium*, which was used to worship the Lares, or domestic divinities. In the painted mural you see the snake *agathodaemon* (protector of the hearth) and the *genius*, protector of the head of the household. A pet turtle's remains were found within the home, and an excavation done on the courtyard showed that the family had figs and other trees/plants growing there.

The way I had our family placed, is the way in which the bodies were found. While doing research for this story, one of the parts I struggled with the most was the placement. Why would three of them be in the other room? Looking at the house, it appears the rooms were connected by a door—why wouldn't they just walk through? Using research and a liberal amount of creative license, I recreated a version of events that took place at the House of Julius Polybius, and I hope that in living through them, we can memorialize their lives and give them the peace their last moments certainly did not contain.

—E. Knight

THE WHORE

UP to this point in my career, I've written about ancient queens. My heroine in *Lily of the Nile* is Cleopatra's daughter, a messianic Egyptian princess who looks to Isis to save her dynasty. So I wasn't surprised when my fellow authors looked to me to provide a spiritual element in this novel. However, I'm sure that I surprised *them* by insisting I was going to do it through the eyes of two lowly prostitutes.

Sex work was entirely normalized and legal in the Roman world, but the people involved in the trade were classified as *infamia* and treated shabbily. However, I was fascinated by a note about Emperor Vespasian's ruling on prostitution in Thomas A. J. McGinn's work on *Prostitution, Sexuality and the Law in Ancient Rome* that formed a bit of a loophole. Allegedly, slaves sold with the express condition that they not be used in prostitution would be *freed* if they were so used.

That knowledge, combined with graffiti in Pompeii describing two tavern whores, inspired the characters of Prima and Capella. It helped to know that such tavern girls might have once belonged to Empress Poppaea Sabina, who is thought to have been born and raised in Pompeii. And though the empress is commonly thought of as a scheming strumpet, the historian Josephus presents a very different picture of her, describing her as deeply religious woman.

That made her an ideal candidate for Capella's former mistress, and, of course, the prominence of the Temple of Isis in the ruins of Pompeii made that the obvious choice for a narrative about salvation in an era before Christian dominance. Though Egyptian in origin, Isis was thoroughly embraced by the Roman world at the time of the disaster in Pompeii. And the henotheistic cult—with its adoption of Egyptian spirit bodies—provided a framework for thinking about the *soul* that has evolved throughout religious history to the modern day.

As for Pansa, he is based on a real figure, and his family history in Pompeii is grounded in fact. What became of him though, we don't know. As for the deaths of the refugees in my story, I based them on the plaster casts found in what is now known as the Garden of the

Fugitives, and I like to think the figure straining to rise on his arms is Sabinus. We're told that after the eruption, the emperor wished two former consuls to coordinate relief for the refugees; it made sense that Kate Quinn's Senator Marcus Norbanus should be one of them.

Pompeii was an embodiment of the Roman dream, a touchstone of human striving, which is part of why we are still haunted by the disaster to this day. So my challenge in this story was to offer a redemptive arc while showing the disaster from both inside the doomed city and from the outside, in the aftermath. That's why I chose two sisters, connected in spirit and heart. And, of course, I gave Capella a present tense, first person narrative so as to leave ambiguity over whether her story was real or simply the way Prima, in her guilt, hoped and imagined it to be.

—Stephanie Dray

ABOUT THE AUTHORS

STEPHANIE DRAY is a multi-published, award-winning author of historical women's fiction and fantasy set in the ancient world. Her critically acclaimed historical Nile series about Cleopatra's daughter has been translated into more than six different languages, was nominated for a RITA Award, and won the Golden Leaf. Her focus on Ptolemaic Egypt and Augustan Age Rome has given her a unique perspective on the consequences of Egypt's ancient clash with Rome, both in terms of the still-extant tensions between East and West as well as the worldwide decline of female-oriented religion. Before she wrote novels, Stephanie was a lawyer, a game designer, and a teacher. Learn more at: StephanieDray.com.

BEN KANE worked as a veterinarian for sixteen years, but his love of ancient history and historical fiction drew him to write fast-paced novels about Roman soldiers, generals, and gladiators. Irish by nationality but UK-based, he is the author of seven books, the last five of which have been Sunday Times top ten bestsellers. Ben's books have been translated into ten languages. In 2013, Ben walked the length of Hadrian's Wall with two other authors, for charity; he did so in full Roman military kit, including hobnailed boots. He repeated the madness in 2014, over 130 miles in Italy. Over $50,000 has been raised with these two efforts. http://www.benkane.net

E. KNIGHT is an award-winning, indie national best-selling author of historical fiction. Under the name Eliza Knight, she writes historical romance and time-travel. Her debut historical fiction novel, *My Lady Viper,* has received critical acclaim and was nominated for the Historical Novel Society 2015 Annual Indie Award. She regularly presents on writing panels and was named Romance Writers of America's 2013 PRO Mentor of the Year. Eliza lives in Maryland atop a small mountain with a knight, three princesses, and a very naughty puppy. For more information, visit Eliza at www.elizaknight.com.

MICHELLE MORAN was born in Southern California. After attending Pomona College, she earned a Master's Degree from the Claremont Graduate University. During her six years as a public high school teacher, Moran used her summers to travel around the world, and it was her experiences as a volunteer on archaeological digs that inspired her to write historical fiction. She is the internationally bestselling author of the novels *Nefertiti, The Heretic Queen, Cleopatra's Daughter, Madame Tussaud,* and *The Second Empress,* which have been translated into more than twenty languages. Visit her online at MichelleMoran.com.

SOPHIE PERINOT is the author of the acclaimed debut, *The Sister Queens,* which weaves the story of medieval sisters Marguerite and Eleanor of Provence who became queens of France and England respectively. Perinot has both a BA in History and a law degree. A long-time member of the Historical Novel Society, she has attended all of the group's North American Conferences, serving as a panelist at the most recent. When she is not visiting corners of the past, Sophie lives in Great Falls, Virginia. Learn more at: www.SophiePerinot.com.

KATE QUINN is the national bestselling author of the Empress of Rome novels, which have been variously translated into thirteen different languages. She first got hooked on Roman history while watching *I, Claudius* at the age of seven, and wrote her first book during her freshman year in college, retreating from a Boston winter into ancient Rome. She and her husband now live in Maryland with an imperious black dog named Caesar. Learn more at http://www.katequinnauthor.com.

VICKY ALVEAR SHECTER is the award-winning author of the young adult novel, *Cleopatra's Moon* (Arthur A. Levine Books/Scholastic, 2011), based on the life of Cleopatra's only daughter. She is also the author of two biographies for kids on Alexander the Great and Cleopatra. The *Los Angeles Times* called *Cleopatra's Moon*—set in Rome and Egypt—"magical" and "impressive." *Publisher's Weekly* said it was "fascinating" and "highly memorable." Her upcoming young adult novel, *Curses and Smoke: A Novel of Pompeii* (Arthur A. Levine/Scholastic), releases June 2014. She has two other upcoming books for younger readers, *Anubis Speaks!* and *Hades Speaks!* Vicky is a docent at the Michael C. Carlos Museum of Antiquities at Emory University in Atlanta.

Find Vicky Alvear Shecter's Books on Amazon

CPSIA information can be obtained at www.ICGtesting.com
Printed in the USA
LVOW01s1548160415

434880LV00022B/1298/P